His eyes held hers, dark and hot.

Nothing for it but to succumb. A lazy, languid feeling stole down her limbs, mixing with anxiety and anticipation.

"Organizing books is a much more perilous diversion than I'd thought," he said in his husky, edged voice, warm and dangerous. "But equally rife with opportunity." He gazed at her lips. "Do you surrender?"

"Surrender to what?" It was as if she couldn't catch her breath.

"To whom."

"To whom?" The words barely formed on her tongue, heavy and low.

He smiled, a long, slow pull of lips, and leaned down. A hint of bergamot combined with the smell of the books surrounding them, spines triangled, pages fanned apart, allowing the scent of fresh bindings and musty parchment to linger.

She licked suddenly dry lips, only an inch from his. "What are you doing, your lordship?"

His gaze traveled her face. "I'm embracing the beauty around me. Or under me, as it is."

By Anne Mallory

SEVEN SECRETS OF SEDUCTION
FOR THE EARL'S PLEASURE
THE BRIDE PRICE
THREE NIGHTS OF SIN
WHAT ISABELLA DESIRES
THE EARL OF HER DREAMS
THE VISCOUNT'S WICKED WAYS
DARING THE DUKE
MASQUERADING THE MARQUESS

Coming Soon

ONE NIGHT IS NEVER ENOUGH

ANNE MALLORY

Seven Secrets of Seduction

AVON

An Imprint of HarperCollinsPublishers

This is a work of fiction. Names, characters, places, and incidents are products of the author's imagination or are used fictitiously and are not to be construed as real. Any resemblance to actual events, locales, organizations, or persons, living or dead, is entirely coincidental.

AVON BOOKS
An Imprint of HarperCollins*Publishers*
10 East 53rd Street
New York, New York 10022-5299

Copyright © 2010 by Anne Hearn
ISBN 978-0-06-157915-8
www.avonromance.com

First Avon Books paperback printing: June 2010

Avon Trademark Reg. U.S. Pat. Off. and in Other Countries, Marca Registrada, Hecho en U.S.A.
HarperCollins® is a registered trademark of HarperCollins Publishers.

Printed in the U.S.A.

10 9 8 7 6 5 4 3 2 1

To Bella Andre,
for the thwhack, the "aha!",
and the many shared doughnuts.
Someday I'll get you to eat
the part not covered with frosting.

Acknowledgments

A thousand thanks, as always, to Mom, May Chen, and Matt—the triple M threat.

A special extra thanks to May for the title of the book (which spurred the story). When it popped up in a title brainstorming session for a previous book, it stuck with me and didn't let go. :)

Thank you to Amanda Bergeron, Karen Davy, and Sara Schwager for production and copyedit mastery.

Also thank you to Bill, Chris, Chris, Ed, Flo, Gabi, Grace, Janet, Josh, Maureen, Matt, Nyree, Robert, Shannon, and Teresa, who all played a part in helping me work, even if it was to simply (and exquisitely) let me sleep in after being up all night. And to S.

Chapter 1

London, 1820

Miranda Chase leaned against the smoothly worn counter and absently curled a finger around a tendril of hair, rubbing her thumbnail along the hump, creating a soft, steady rhythm of sound against her ear as she devoured the words on the page.

"Run faster," she murmured. "No, not to the open gardens—that is exactly where he wants you to go. Run to the tower. Lock the door."

But the heroine darted into the maze of hedges instead. A circuitous route that could offer the freedom she desired or deliver her into his evil clutches for good.

A deep voice came from a hedge in her mind. "Where can I find the section on enlightenment?"

She could feel the warm breath of the villain as he closed in on the heroine's position. Cloven and provocative to match the smoky timbre uttering each syllable.

Without lifting her eyes from the page, Miranda absently pointed a slender finger to a corner of the store. "Third shelf from the right."

Dismissing the customer's interference in the twining hedges and the closing maze, she urged the heroine on. The villain was one thorny wall away. If he turned right at the fork—

"And the section on—"

"Hmmm?" she murmured, her concentration wavering for a moment. If only Peter hadn't taken ill and left her to work the late-afternoon shift in his absence. She had just received the advance book this morning, freshly printed and bound. It hadn't left her side since. And they so rarely received unplanned customers during the social hours that she hadn't argued with her uncle's pleas to man the desk.

"The section on—"

The villain turned right at the fork. Of course. She shook her head. She had told the heroine to stay locked in her tower, that no good ever came of these wanderings. Best to remain where it was safe and comfortable.

"Miss, are you listening?" The deep voice had a husky, scratchy quality, as if the owner had played far too hard the previous night and had just woken to the new day. An appealing voice. Just such as the one possessed by the silver-tongued villain of the tale. The noble hero had a much more direct and transparent manner. If only the heroine hadn't been momentarily seduced by the silver. Miranda had *told* her not to trust him.

"Miss?"

"Mmmhmm." The silvery devil was inching closer.

"Where is the section on—?" Was that amusement in his tone or mockery? Besides their regular customers, when she filled in for an absent worker, patrons rarely interacted with her beyond ordering or collecting their items. Especially voices that clearly indicated Quality. Flat voices and bored tones. Maybe some irritation. They rarely expended effort consulting with the hoi polloi.

But there was a caress beneath the unusually warm tone. The syllables. As if the owner were speaking to her directly, not addressing a nameless clerk. And the voice didn't have the nasal pitch so often found in the lofty gents attempting to mask their inferiorities through the regurgitation of the bookstore's classics. Those types of men liked to practice their arguments and debate on the employees, but so often merely practiced their *noblesse oblige* instead.

She sometimes found it hard to feign ignorance in their presence. Calm, gentle, nonargumentative, dutiful niece . . . that was Miranda Chase, shopgirl. Better to spend any unrestrained energy in letters and correspondence, where she could organize her thoughts and be free with her passion.

But this voice . . . this clipped caress, didn't speak of argument and strife, it spoke of ballrooms and bedrooms.

Her attention half shifted back to the environs of the store. The man had asked for what?

"Sex."

Miranda's eyes crashed away from the page, the heroine frozen with her back to the brambles, as the unseen man answered the question she must have spoken aloud.

Shocked back into reality, her view shot upward

and met coal black and startling white. The strands of hair slipped from her fingers, and the hand holding the book thumped against the counter. It took a moment for her to regain her voice. She cleared her throat, trying to recall her mother's strict lessons in decorum and not succumb to the shock of the man in front of her. "Pardon me?"

"No, I think you're finally paying attention." Amusement, yes. Mocking, definitely. "Though I had to rephrase my question in three different ways. That the last was the one that caught your attention"—one perfectly dark brow rose along with the curve of his mouth—"is intriguing. Your answer?"

"Did you just ask me for sex, sir?"

A strange smile stretched across his face, no less appealing than the previously half-mocking one but more mysterious in nature. "I asked for the section on erotic matters. Though if you feel the desire to pass over the instruction and go right to the participation, I would be delighted."

She stared at him. She couldn't help it. It wasn't every day that a man this well dressed and—*manly*—came into her uncle's shop. And it definitely wasn't every day that a man this . . . she searched for the right word under his heavy eyes and the way he seemed to move even when standing still . . . *virile* . . . made inappropriate remarks to her. To Georgette, who dressed in order to enjoy men's eyes following her on the street, maybe. But not to Miranda Chase.

She looked down at her simple frock. Everything was still in place. Nothing untoward, like a gaping hole or raised hem, that might make a man think something other than mundane thoughts.

His head tilted, an amused smile still firmly in place on a face that seemed to have been carved, then lightly, lovingly smoothed. Sharpness beneath a polished veneer. "Are you attempting to see if you'd be dressed for the occasion?"

Completely nonplussed and disbelieving, she continued to stare at him, probably more than a little stupidly. "Are you—" She paused and examined him, scrunching her brows to peer more clearly into his dark eyes. "Are you *well,* sir?"

"Quite fit, yes."

She carefully examined his tailored clothing and lean, strong frame. Even in the starkness surrounding him, he exuded some predatory quality. A heated focus, the confident way he leaned against the counter, an edge to the lazy way he regarded her. Some unnameable, completely male attribute that would have ingénues running from and mature women running *to.* Georgette would be batting her eyelashes and inching up her hem already, elbowing Miranda to do the same.

The man was a study in black and white, which just seemed to highlight the lack of severity in his amused eyes. The fading sun cast dying rays through the shop's dusty panes, highlighting the startlingly white skin on the left side of his face against the mostly black attire and darkening shadows on the right.

And his hands . . .

"Are *you* well, miss?"

There was that faintly mocking thread again. Woven into the gravelly whiskey of his voice. Her daydreaming came to an abrupt end.

"Quite." She slipped a square of paper into her book and closed it, cover down on the counter. He was just a customer. He'd be gone as soon as his business was finished. Nothing she couldn't handle. She wasn't as tongue-tied as she had once been. She smiled brightly. "Now, how may I assist you?"

But one corner of his mouth curved, and his eyes strayed to her book.

He had lovely lips. Not stark at all.

She nervously ran her thumb along the corner of the cover and tried to stifle such thoughts. "Sir?"

"What are you reading?"

She squared the sale books on the counter near him—all of the most popular titles—in an attempt to shift his attention. "We have some fabulous new works. May I help you locate something?"

"I'd like a copy of whatever you are reading." The other edge of his mouth lifted.

It had been the risk she had assumed by reading the book where others might see. But she had wanted to read it *so* much that she had given in to vice.

She smiled pleasantly, though the edges of her mouth strained. "I'm afraid we don't have copies. Is there something else—"

"No copies? This is a bookstore and printer, is it not?" He cast an eye around the cluttered shelves in a studied gesture. The bare fingers of his right hand caressed the edge of the worn counter.

"It is. And we can order any title for you, of course." She lifted her chin and tucked her hair behind her ear. "But it is not yet in wide print, so you will have to wait a bit, I'm afraid."

"Then how did you obtain a copy?" One long finger snapped out and touched the binding before she could react. "Especially of that?"

Her heart skipped at least two beats as his bare

finger grazed her gloved one. "I, um—" she stuttered, trying to get her breathing under control. "I suppose I was just lucky, sir."

It was a prerelease copy of the latest Gothic romance. All the rage. And he seemed to know what it was if his mocking expression was anything to go by. Most men seemed to run in fear of them. As if the parson's trap was waiting on the last page, or they'd discover the curious secrets of a woman's mind.

"I have little patience for ordering and waiting for something I am eager to read now."

She nodded, trying to still her fingers from touching the spot he had grazed. There was something about the man that set her on edge. A knowing look in his eye that said he could pull forth her deepest secrets. Her fingers touched the spot without her permission and she could feel the warmth sliding up her throat. "I know the feeling. As I said, we can have it delivered as soon as it is printed and released."

The left edges of the man's white shirt dipped into the shadows, causing the whole effect to darken and the remaining white to stand out sharply. Somehow she had the feeling that unrelieved black would also do him justice—and not just in the physical sense.

Some otherworldly figure come to make her think odd thoughts and do embarrassing things. To cause the tremors beneath her skin.

"You can pay a bit extra for express, if you wish."

The man would surely give up his game. He didn't actually want the book.

"I'll give you two pounds for that copy."

Her hand hesitated on the bound leather, and her thoughts froze. "Pardon me?"

"Two pounds. Right now."

Two pounds would buy her a bevy of books. Or a new frock. Or be stashed away in her small cache.

His hand strayed to his pocket. His eyes held some sort of weary cynicism.

Two pounds.

But there was something about the way the man was speaking that put her on her guard.

Everything about the man put her on guard, really. A man who dressed so well, albeit starkly, but without gloves? As if he were hiding some long, delicious, earthy secret beneath the cloaked darkness. He all but screamed danger.

"No thank you, I—"

"Four pounds."

"—would like—"

"Twenty pounds then."

She choked on the rest of her sentence. *Twenty pounds*. She didn't make twenty pounds in a *year*. She could use her every contact and haggle down at Paternoster Row for another early printed copy, surely. For *twenty pounds*.

But this copy was a cherished gift. She had been giddy since its arrival. And she was at the very crux of the story. She wanted to know what happened. She could ask if the man would wait while she obtained another advance copy on the Row—one of their contacts might be able to secure one for five pounds' payment, no less twenty!—but she instinctively knew the man in front of her would not acquiesce to such an arrangement.

It was etched into the lines of his body and the cynical, knowing look in his eyes. This was a game. He would pay the twenty pounds. Oh, he would pay—there was something about the way he held himself, the stark, noble tilt of his head, that assured her of such. It was a game to him.

"A generous offer, but I must decline." Turning down twenty pounds almost physically hurt. Every penny would help her gain ground for her travels, and twenty pounds was more than a few pennies. But she was *enjoying* the book. And the gift of it was unexpected and precious. She'd tour the Continent eventually— go on the Grand Tour that had been planned, then destroyed years before.

She absently rubbed the scar on her thigh. *Enjoy life now.*

She shook away the thoughts. "I'm sorry, but I am enjoying it too much, and I plan to finish the tale." She allowed the mantra to filter through, erasing any uncertainty. She felt her shoulders ease, her smile become more natural.

Something in his eyes deepened, and his lazy stance against the counter tightened.

"Now, you were looking for the sections on . . ." She pulled the memory back and separated it from the book passage she had been actively reading. "Enlightenment. And . . . more intimate pursuits?"

She had thought herself immune to heated cheeks after being friends with Georgette, but there it was, that telltale creeping warmth. Drat. Customers did sometimes request books of that nature, and her uncle kept a supply stocked in the back. And after the recent explosion of books in that vein, it was hardly a *surprise*. No need for blushing. Still, she usually dealt with coy, giggling women or furtive men who had no desire to engage in conversation.

Not men who looked like they excelled at the sport.

He raised a brow, and his posture once more took on an indolent edge, though his eyes were unreadable behind a feigned look of amusement. "You have a section combining them? Be still, my lost heart."

She stared at him. "Do you require sexual enlightenment?"

There were times when her tendency to blurt out whatever was on her mind was useful. Unfortunately, those times were few. That was why it was better just *not to talk*.

His body shifted again, like a predator toying with some small witless animal. The unreadable look turned into one of focused pleasure. He smiled, an even more purely masculine smile that did funny things to her stomach. "I don't believe so. Though it seems a popular pastime these days."

With this man roaming the streets, she had an inkling of how it could be. He looked and moved like no one she had ever seen.

"Oh?"

One long finger pointed toward the small stand at her side.

She stared at the stand. "*The Seven Secrets of Seduction*?" She looked back to his dark eyes. "You require a copy?"

"Not at the moment, no. It's quite a silly thing."

She had thought so too. Initially. And then in the candlelight of her bedchamber she had read it and quite refined her opinion. "I think it's lovely."

"You think a book on seduction is *lovely*?"

"It is a lovely, burgeoning tome that when dissected contains a wealth of personal realization and self-enlightenment." The words, nearly rehearsed at this point from the number of times she had found herself defending them to crotchety men and scandalized matrons, fell from her lips.

The strange smile he had first sported reappeared, as if he found her odd and vastly entertaining. " 'A burgeoning tome'? Is that a kind way to say bloated?"

"Not bloated." Her hip bumped the counter, as her body tried to express its agitation without her consent. "It *burgeons*."

"I didn't realize that burgeoning was something a book did. Do kittens pop from its covers when it gets too full?" He looked at the stand as if a full-grown cat might spring from the pages and catch him unawares.

She drummed her fingers on the freshly printed Gothic. "You are not amusing."

"I daresay you are though." He leaned a little farther over the counter, a long magnetic pull of man and tailored cloth. "What is your name?"

She stared at him, speechless for a moment, her stomach doing an odd little flip. "That hardly signifies in the current discussion, sir."

"Are we still discussing? My apologies." The apology, if one could call it such, was delivered in a tone that indicated that he said the words often but rarely meant them.

"Disingenuous," she blurted.

His smile very nearly became delighted—if a man like that could be delighted and still maintain the absolute aura of control and power. The heady sense of manliness.

She was far, far beyond any comfortable ground. She should bury her nose back in her fiction. But a tiny curiosity bloomed as to what exactly lay over the edge of the cliff.

"Ingenuous." His eyes lazily studied her. "I think I must learn your name now for sure."

"Burgeoning with potential," she said somewhat desperately, trying to return to the previous conversation, willing her tongue to comply for once, to leap away from the cliff. "There is a beautiful layer there waiting to be uncovered."

He tapped a finger in a lazy rhythm on the counter. "I rather agree." The look he cast over her made her heart skip two beats and the edge of the cliff crumble back toward her, enticing a peek.

"Peeking through the soil," she said faintly.

"Wildflowers spring from the cold soil, untamed and free." One finger drew a long curve against the wood, his dark, obsidian eyes were anything but cold. "I do love untamed and freed things."

"You do?" she said faintly.

"And buds that have yet to open. A flower waiting to burgeon, to use your phrase." His hand mimicked a flower blooming, tightened fingers slowly lifting and straightening in an upward and outward dance. "Whether from a tawdry secret or a sure, warm hand."

She could almost feel his warm fingers, still burning hers where they had brushed, even through her glove. She made a last grasp toward her slipping grip on reality. "The secrets, now written, would hardly work in the pure sense."

And it was a shame, really, because the idea of them was quite lovely. To feel such things.

He rested his chin upon the beautiful bare heel of his palm. "So you don't think I could use those tactics on you and succeed?"

The vision of his trying to seduce her sprung fully

formed to her mind. "I don't think one could succeed simply using those tactics, no."

"The author will be crushed." He looked pleased at the thought.

She shook away the lingering spell he had twined around her. "Nonsense. It is obvious there are layers of meanings within the book. One could read it as a book on how to *avoid* being seduced. To recognize the tactics employed by members of both sexes. To bring the innocent to sense."

"You really don't believe that drivel, do you? The author is trying to cause scandal and further his pennies." He gave a cynical tilt of his head toward the prominent stand, his eyes losing their warmth. "And it worked."

"I have encouraged the author not to cover his true vision in his next work."

"You told the author what a bloated tome he created?" He smiled. "I applaud you. The man is probably still sobbing in his frilly pink boudoir."

"Nonsense. Eleutherios is a man of good sense and fine sensibility."

"Pink boudoir included."

"I hardly think his boudoir is pink." Maybe red. And gold. And overwhelming.

"Do you usually contemplate how a man's inner sanctum might look?" He tilted his head, obviously amused.

At the moment, she was simply trying to wave away from her view the haze he had created.

"Veiled beneath the commercial aspects, *The Seven Secrets of Seduction* teaches people to embrace the beauty around them," she said, drumming her fingers militantly once more.

"Sounds a bit complex for a sex manual."

"It's not *only* a sex manual. And I tell you, it could hardly work now as such."

"I don't know." The man looked deliberately doubtful. "I heard a fellow just the other day say that he had seduced three women in three days using the tactics therein. One in the garden, one in the kitchens, and even one in his master's sitting room. However tawdry and irritating the book is, it seems to give results."

Her face flamed. "I don't believe you. It gives the reader the opportunity to seduce the *senses* and open oneself up to nature and life. To take chances."

"Not to engage in and promote titillation then?"

"No." Well, not *only* that.

He raised a brow. "I could have sworn that was the author's exact intent when I read the first page."

"You are quite wrong."

"Mmmmm." His finger caressed a furrow in the counter. "Many people will be vastly disappointed in that."

"They may. People read into things what they desire to read, of course."

He gave her a pointed glance.

"There is a reason the book is such a great seller with women too," she stressed. "And it is not simply to know how to dodge transparent seduction tactics."

He gave the books on the counter a pointed glance. An entire series of imitators had popped up overnight to capitalize—most of them quite earnest in being as explicit as possible in how to best show members of each sex the way to eternal sexual illumination.

"Or maybe they just find it novel and tawdry, as it was meant," he said. "Titillating."

She upped the tempo of her fingers' drumbeat, preparing for war. "It's not titillating."

She'd been only *slightly* titillated.

"Well, then it hardly did its job." The right side of his mouth curved again. "Do you think you are above seduction?" His eyes were heavy and . . . warm.

"Seducing the senses does not necessarily mean—" She waved her hand, trying to dispel both the effect of his expression and his words. "That. I had a lovely sense of seduction just this morning when I watched an orchid germinate."

His smile became more pronounced. "An orchid germinate?"

She lifted her chin.

"You don't even believe the drivel you are spouting."

"It's not drivel. And I love to be seduced by it." One dark brow rose. The back of her neck was becoming hot, and she waved a hand to fan herself. She tried to recover. "My *senses* seduced."

"Don't we all?" He lazily smiled. "I think that is the hook."

Not a second too late, she noticed the direction of his creeping fingers. She scooted her prized book away and under the desk.

"Don't want me to be titillated?"

"Somehow I doubt that would be a problem." She primly folded her hands on the counter. Across from his strong bare fingers, her faded gloves looked even cheaper than if he had worn the finest silk. Mocking almost. That he didn't have to wear them. That he could flout convention.

His fingers were perfectly made and didn't look as if they'd seen a day of work—nor picked up a pen. No ink stains there like the ones that crept beneath the bare threads in her gloves and worked under her nails, the chapped pads, and paper-cut ridges. "Now, if I can be of service?"

"Oh, you have." He ran a finger up the spine of a book on a shelf too high for her to reach without a stool. "I haven't been so amused by a verbal exchange in a long time."

She felt her cheeks warm again as his hand crested over. She couldn't remember the last time she had used a dust cloth in anything other than an absent fashion. His finger curled over the top of the binding and pulled back. The book slipped from its spot, the cover rubbed against those of its siblings, creating a soft swish, loud in the suddenly silent store.

Light swirls of dust rose, then drifted through the fading beams. She should be embarrassed, but what difference did it make? The entire encounter would serve as a fanciful memory later, then fade from view like the falling swirls.

"It doesn't look as if this one has seen the light of day in some time." He nodded at the counter. "It seems as if people are more interested in titillating books than in Shakespeare."

Or perhaps not.

"I'll have you know that Shakespeare is plenty titillating."

He leaned a hip against the counter. "I agree. Tawdry little man, wasn't he?" His fingers veritably *caressed* the book.

She forced her eyes away and met coal black eyes framed by equally dark brows. "You are mocking me."

"Only a little." He smiled. "I find myself fascinated

actually. Who knew that I would find such delight when I set out to purchase a few new books to fill my shelves."

"Shelves waiting to be filled with sexual enlightenment?"

He leaned farther into the counter. "If that's what it takes." His head cocked to the side. "Are you still offering to help me?"

"Only with finding the tomes you seek," she said as lightly as she could manage, completely unused to overt flirtation yet feeling its pull, the curiosity and heat, under his regard. The tilt of his body, the way his hair brushed his collar in a somewhat wild manner. All of the inconsistencies he presented vying to present an incomplete picture. Control and chaos, structure and flouting convention.

And his eyes . . .

She felt like a deer pulled into a wolf's trap. Men like this just didn't *look* that way at women like her. And finding herself being studied by a man who exuded all things masculine and virile was daunting. And magnificent. There was an internal part of her that felt like a star sprung to sudden life.

Dangerous, dangerous man.

"If you like Shakespeare, then perhaps you will enjoy this." She tapped a copy of a book on a stand situated front and center. Right next to *The Seven Secrets of Seduction.*

"*Sonnets for Spring?* Oh, bloody hell. Not you too?"

She looked down her nose at his language. "It's not Shakespeare, but it's not bad."

"Perhaps I need to take a copy to see if I can determine

what you are reading. By chance you might carry a different book altogether than the one I tossed aside after its release."

She pulled a copy from the prominent stand, ready for battle with a charged energy she rarely felt.

"Front and center. Not like poor William," he said, disgust evident.

She put the copy on the counter with a thump. "People have been buying it all week."

"God help us all."

"You know"—she looked down her nose—"if you seek good writing, you should read *Seven Secrets* again. The author writes beautifully beneath the surface."

"*Seven Secrets* is cheap and tawdry and this . . . *thing*"—he pointed at the slim volume—"is full of sappy emotion."

"It is not!"

"It is so. Though I'm sure the man is quite pleased with his profits. Just like Eleu-whatsit, the *Secrets*' author."

"*Eleutherios* isn't that type."

The man laughed and leaned farther against the counter, tapping a finger against the cover of *Hamlet*. "You are entirely delicious. Do you truly think, just like every other lady in town, that this paragon of virtue is real? This Eleutherios?"

She stared down her nose at him, her last bit of reticence evaporating. "I know he is."

The man's smile grew secretive. "Will you be disappointed to find him old, gray, and withered, depending upon the profits of his tawdry tales to support his opiate addiction?"

"Tosh, you are not amusing, sir."

"No?" He set down *Hamlet* and pulled *The Seven*

Secrets of Seduction toward him, opening the cover, the crisp new binding crackling. "And here I had so hoped I would be."

She tapped a finger. "Aren't you missing something? Perhaps an engagement or a meeting at your club?"

"No. Out too late last night. Putting these seduction tactics to use is hard work for the gentleman about town."

"You could put those tactics to work by sitting at the Serpentine and admiring the view right now in the beautiful downward slope of the sun."

"Now I know you are not serious. The Serpentine is a flat expanse of boredom. Duck, duck, swan, boat, floating branch."

She gave him a dark glance. "The Serpentine is lovely. The way the wind glides over the water, ruffling the edges, tickling it." Why did the people who had time to enjoy such things completely lack the notice or care?

"Mmmmm, tickling is always a good tactic." He looked over the page. "Perfectly useful information on that point, though the author seems a bit glib, doesn't he?"

"There is nothing about tickling in there!"

"And I suppose you think that 'baiting your hook'"— he tilted the book upside down toward her and pointed at the words on the page with one perfectly chiseled long finger—"means to find an actual worm and a rod?"

"A baited hook can be the impetus for finding that which will open you to the beauty before you."

He let the cover close with a thump. "Well, I agree that opening a beauty before me is prime impetus."

She tried not to blush further. "And the author is not glib."

"No? He seems awfully suspect to me. Tricking young innocents into thinking that he is talking about the beauty around oneself versus trying to get the beauties around oneself."

She blinked for a second before his meaning hit, and she felt herself go scarlet.

He tapped the cover in disgust. "I just wonder at the gall of what he will write next." There was something dark in the statement that she didn't understand.

"I am sure it will be something of epically good sense."

"Epically." He lifted a brow at her. "And here I had heard it was just another tawdry sequel, *Eight Elements of Enchantment,* or some such absurdity."

She straightened. "I have heard nothing of the sort."

"That alliterations are absurd?"

"That there is a sequel already in the works." She had been hoping that the author might branch out and write something like *Sonnets for Spring.* Except in his own style.

His eyes were heavy lidded as he surveyed her. "Your beloved Eleutherios hasn't mentioned it?" He smiled. "Imagine that."

She narrowed her eyes. If there was one thing her flittering uncle had taught her, it was not to turn away a customer who wore a cut of cloth the way this man did, gloves or no gloves. She had never wanted to eject someone from the shop, not even horrible Mr. Oswald, who had poked fun at her reading material. She had been too flustered then to be angry until after he'd gone.

That didn't seem to be a problem with this man. The horridly delicious man had her wrung in internal knots, but her tongue and emotion seemed quite capable of making themselves known.

"I look forward to anything he writes. I find him enlightening."

He flicked open the cover of *Seven Secrets* again and flipped a few pages.

"'When you find the perfect scene, stand back and absorb the details.'" He met her eyes over the edge of the page. "Enlightening," he said flatly. He looked back down. "'Don't rush. Don't make the mistake of underestimating the beauty before you. Center on the object of your desire and examine the intricacies. Find the hidden treasure. An ill-fitting key scrapes a rusted lock. Requires force to turn. However, find the perfect set of tines, and the door will fall open practically on its own.'"

"Have you never passed by a portrait only to discover later that careful examination shows something much deeper behind the paint?"

"Like another stray hair from my great aunt's natty spaniel?"

She reached for the book, but he easily moved it out of her reach.

"I wasn't done."

"I think you have had your laugh, sir."

"But that was not my intention at all." The sound of his voice changed, and the rich mocha made the hair on her arms stand on end. He flipped another few pages. "'The greatest treasure is that of the everyday variety. One when examined more closely reveals something hitherto unknown. Unseen. Untasted.'"

His eyes lifted from the page and traveled over her slowly, the last syllable of "untasted" hanging on his tongue in a nearly tangible caress.

She swallowed.

"'Let nothing stop you from the experience of tasting the keen pleasure of a new conquest in a mysterious guise. Like the finest wine sipped from the belly of the cask.'"

His eyes raked her slowly, as if she was the receptacle from which he intended to sip.

She swallowed again. When *he* read it, it sounded as if it just might actually *work* as a guide to seduction.

"'Find it. Embrace it. Breathe it. Never let it go.'" His voice, gravelly and smoky, slipped over her like an enchanted breeze, his eyes, dark and mysterious, held her still. She absently wondered if the heroine in her book actually wanted to escape from that maze after all. "You don't think you could be seduced by such? Flinging your morals to the curb and letting go? This paragon of virtue worming his way under your skirts? Or perhaps someone else doing so, someone more . . . real?"

And here she had thought she'd simply be finishing her read and tending an empty counter today.

"Sir—" She forced her eyes to drop from his, equal measures of intense discomfort and tight-wound thrill running through her. "Your library shelves?"

He snapped the book shut. "Do you have a copy of *Candide*?" His voice turned from seductive to firmly businesslike.

"Yes." She paused, a strange impulse gripping her as the thrill still coursed right through her toes. "In the Enlightenment section." She raised a brow.

"I don't know where that is." He lazily leaned back, firm tone suddenly forgotten again, and scratched at the cover of the copy of *The Seven Secrets of Seduc-*

tion. She slid the copy away before he could destroy the edge.

She pointed. "Back and to the left."

He simply smiled.

She withheld a groan. The Quality. Menaces, all of them. This one far worse than most. At least most were unaware of her existence even when they spoke directly to her. She slid from her stool and rounded the counter, stepping around the stack of packages awaiting pickup, trying to keep her feet stepping one in front of the other despite how light-headed he made her feel.

She disappeared into the printed stacks and withdrew the book. He was in the same position, half-lounging against the counter, one bare finger tracing a pattern in the scratched and worn wood when she returned.

"Is there anything else?" she asked as she plopped the book in front of him and withdrew the payment ledger. A man like this would undoubtedly want credit.

"Yes, I believe there is a package for me."

"A package? There is a package for you?" she asked, letting the ledger thump against the counter. "You came here for a package?"

"Yes. Of books." He smiled pleasantly, but the benign curve of his lips did nothing to hide the twinkle in his eye.

She could see that he was enjoying himself far too much for any of it to be anything other than planned torment on his part. All of this time waiting to ask about an already ordered package.

"Fine." All reticence had evaporated long before, and her good humor was starting to follow its path. He unnerved her far too much. "Name?"

He handed her a slip that read *Jeffries* in her uncle's scrawl. She had seen the twined brown package earlier.

"Very well, Mr. Jeffries. We have that ready for you." She waited a beat. "It has been ready for the past ten minutes' of conversation," she said dryly.

She reached over and lifted the first two packages. No Jeffries. She could have sworn it was the third one down. But perhaps it had been moved. She checked the top two. No. She lifted number three to see the package below. No Jeffries.

"Problem?"

Her brow furrowed. "No, no, one moment." She checked the next two. No match. "It was just here." She reread the names on the packages she had lifted. No, they still didn't magically read Jeffries.

"And now?"

Appalling heat started to flame her cheeks. "My apologies, Mr. Jeffries, but it seems as if your package is missing." Had she just cheekily said it had been ready during their ten-minute conversation only to have it *not be there*? She really needed to reinvest in not speaking. "Let me check the back."

A strange smile flitted across his face at her use of his name, then was gone. He waved a hand. "No time. I am late."

She simply stared at him. "Late?" He had claimed nothing but time ten minutes previous.

"Yes, quite late, must go. I'll pick it up tomorrow, then, shall I? With the Voltaire." He lifted a brow. "Won't go missing too, will it?"

She sputtered. "I assure you that it will not."

"Very good. Afternoon, Miss—?"

She stared again, feeling as if the deer had been caught by the wolf after all. "Chase?"

He smiled again—the smile that said he had some amusing secret. "Are you asking me or telling me?"

"I believe you are outrageous, sir."

His forefinger rubbed the edge of the *Seven Secrets,* and his smile grew lazier. "I hope you will discover just how much. Good afternoon, Miss Chase."

And in one smooth motion, he withdrew his hand from the counter, pivoted, and disappeared through the door.

The bell gave a soft twang as the door clicked back into place as if suspended on a breeze for a moment to prevent it from its usual clang. Suspended like her thoughts and breath.

It wasn't until she decided to return the Shakespeare and run the long-unused dust cloth along the shelves that she found the lost package tucked into the spot vacated by *Hamlet.*

She stared at it for a long moment. Then her heart started to race.

Chapter 2

Dear Mr. Pitts,

I find the most vexing rumors to be the ones that show up on my doorstep in unexpected ways . . .

From the pen of Miranda Chase

Miranda touched the freshly wrapped package, one book thicker than the day before.

"Two more to wrap," Peter said, appearing from the rear.

She snapped her fingers back, fiddled with the edge of the ledger, then tucked a wisp of hair behind her ear. "Yes," she said, her laugh a little higher in pitch than usual.

Peter sent her a queer glance, then shrugged. "I'll take care of them. You didn't need to wrap that one."

She laughed again, the sound like the odd clang of the bell above the door when it got stuck. "It was no trouble." She put the parcel on the shelf below the counter and tried to put it from her mind as well. Silly to dwell on such thoughts. He'd probably enter the shop already bored with the odd flirtation of the previous day anyway. Better to move along. "You are well again?"

Peter puffed out his chest. "I'm feeling prime as a pumpkin."

The bell rang, and Miranda's heart jumped. She swung toward the door, unwillingly.

A grand bonnet of peacock feathers brushed the sides of the doorframe, and Miranda's shoulders loosened. The hat's owner laughed lightly—a flirtatious, well-rehearsed sound—and flipped up her head. Auburn locks fell in perfectly curled ribbons around her face. "Miranda dear." She held out a hand to her over the counter and squeezed. "Wonderful to see you this fine morning."

Georgette Monroe didn't wait a beat before executing a perfect quarter turn. "And Mr. Higgins." She toyed with the strings of her hat, twirling one around a finger, her eyes almost perfecting the mysterious edge she had been diligently practicing. "Such a lovely day."

Peter stuttered out a greeting, his puffed chest appearing to vibrate from a suddenly quickened heartbeat.

"Georgette," Miranda warned. It was obvious that her friend was in one of her moods. "I thought you were helping your father this morning?" Georgette often helped to entertain her merchant father's business clients and was quite good at charming them over supper or tea.

Silk-gloved fingers twirled the peacock ribbons. "The investors had coach issues, so we postponed. Daddy told me to go shopping instead. I thought I'd look for new flowers for the trellises. Miranda, wasn't I just commenting the other day that I desperately needed help in the garden? A man with strong arms and strong thighs who knows how to handle both?"

Peter lost his grip on the counter and bumped the edge ungracefully with his forearm.

Miranda sighed as her friend continued to bat her eyes. "Peter, Miss Monroe and I are going to take tea at the table." She lifted the small tea service, happy that she had fixed enough for two, just in case, then muttered so that only Georgette could hear her. "Though I think Miss Monroe needs something to cool her down instead."

Miranda turned back to Peter, raising her voice to a normal level once more. "Will you be able to handle the customers?"

He nodded quickly, and she wondered if she could keep him busy at the counter or in the back while Georgette was in the shop. Her friend's presence directly affected his apoplexy. If he went home sick, she'd have to man the desk again.

She quashed the tempting thought and skirted the counter to steer her friend away. Georgette's fingers wiggled a farewell beneath her nose to the wide-eyed man behind.

Miranda waited until they were in the bowels of the stacks, near the back windows, where a table and chairs were set up, before she furiously whispered, "Georgette, were you . . . were you *ogling Peter*?"

"One should have the freedom to ogle a solid pair of shoulders." She shrugged lightly, smiling.

"You are incorrigible," Miranda chided as she set the service down and pulled out a chair.

A gust of brisk April air curled around the openings in the bookshelf, heralding a new arrival. Miranda's shoulders tensed.

She could hear Peter ask how he could be of assistance. A female voice answered, and Miranda's shoulders loosened. A fraction.

"I am practicing," Georgette answered, patting her hair.

"On Peter?" She sat in the chair, arranging her calico skirts. "The poor dear will expire. And then you'll be onto the next pair of shiny Hessians you see, and he'll pine irrevocably."

"Men live to pine—stalwartly and courageously, of course. And perhaps with a secret longing for the beauty in the curve of my neck."

Miranda gave her a look and poured without splashing a drip.

"You are turning into a grouch, Miranda dear. Your academic repression is starting to crush the spirit I know is there," Georgette said as she patted her freed hair again and set her ornate bonnet on the seat of a spare chair. "Not a fashionable or flirtatious thought in your head for years. I do despair."

A tinkle of bells made Miranda's shoulders tighten again.

"Sorry to be late, Mr. Higgins. Billy and I had to make eight stops first," the regular deliveryman said.

Miranda looked through the side window, foggy around the edges, as Billy, the beleaguered driver of the delivery service, moved the team down the street to wait.

"Lovely shoulders, that Billy, and the way he handles those reins," Georgette said, winking at Miranda behind her cup. "A lovely chance for flirtation there."

Miranda smiled, but it was strained as she listened to the quiet settle around the front of the shop while the two men carted the delivery boxes to the back. She inhaled a deep breath, determined to stop the imaginings Georgette's words stirred of dark shoulders and perfect, bare hands. She shakily sipped her tea and called herself a fool.

The man was hardly likely to appear so early in the day. Secondly, she was foolish to think that he would come again in order to see her. And thirdly, well, all of these jumpy imaginings had her wondering if perhaps she hadn't slightly underestimated what a seductive man could do to one's conduct and nerves.

Thankfully, her friend wasn't paying close attention to her. Georgette was like a beagle on a scent when she smelled secrets. But her head was down as she pulled a folded paper from her bag and lovingly spread it on the table. "Fresh from the presses on Fourth Street."

"I can't believe you didn't devour it on the spot," Miranda teased, trying to relax, as she topped off her cup.

"I waited to open it with you, a laborious five blocks. You'd better be good to me, or one of these days I will stop in the teahouse down the street and sneak a peek."

Georgette reached into her bag again and uncovered a plate, releasing a freshly baked smell of heavenly goodness. The decadent smell mixed with the crisp, newly printed newspaper and the musty books in the back racks. The tightness slowly seeped from Miranda's shoulders.

She relaxed into her chair, turned away from the window, and shut away the sound of the bell above the door. This was normal. Comfortable. And *much too early in the day* to be so nervous. She hadn't realized how greatly unnerved yesterday's visitor had made her until she'd found herself unable to sleep, unable to stop checking the entrance after they'd opened the shop, unable to calm the beat of her heart.

"Mmmm. I swear I've had to let out my corset over a finger's-breadth in the last two weeks," Georgette complained. "And you haven't even budged a seam."

"I don't get heavenly baked goods every morning, noon, and night. Besides, I don't see any of your admirers complaining."

Georgette smiled and winked. "Perhaps I shall eat another one then, shall I?"

Miranda returned her grin and daintily lifted a prized scone. In another life she would have been strictly told to leave it. She paused, the treat halfway to her mouth, then the image of molten dark chocolate eyes and blooming flowers suddenly came to mind, and she completed the motion, taking too large a bite.

They hunched together over the paper's ornate left column—the best gossip section in town.

"Yes! An update on Mr. C. He is returning to the Continent to study." Georgette sighed. "Alas. I was so hoping he would stay in London longer this time."

Miranda shook her head. Mr. C. was a frequent visitor to Georgette's early-morning conversation. "Mr. C. will be studying in Paris. I quite envy him."

"I wish you would just go to Paris yourself. Go to Dover and book a ticket without a word to anyone who might advise you otherwise. Although Paris *would* be wasted on you." Georgette gave her a disparaging look. "Moldering in the museums, you'd be, instead of finding the latest fashions to bring back."

Miranda pinched her and continued consuming the column. A series of the inky letters jarred her. "He said it was so," she murmured, her fingers running over the line. "The gossip must have made the rounds yesterday."

Georgette swatted her hand away to see what held her interest. "A sequel to *The Seven Secrets of Seduction*? Oh, excellent. And you must be thrilled. But why didn't you tell me? I could have been the first one with the news last night at the Mortons'. The author responded to your last letter?"

Miranda felt a blush stealing her cheeks. "He sent a short note yesterday."

Georgette's perfectly arched auburn brows rose. "I suspect an 'and' to that statement."

"And a book."

"A book? Well, that is rather . . . boring." Georgette frowned. "What book?"

Miranda tapped an advertisement for the Gothic's release absently.

"No!" Georgette's eyes widened. "You've looked forward to reading that book for ages. And he found an early copy and sent it to you?"

"I shan't read too much into it." She shifted. "Perhaps it was simply a whim. Everyone desires a copy."

"Exactly. No one sends a present like that on a whim."

"But the note was . . . terse. I imagined he would continue to be, I don't know, more flowery and"—she waved her hand—"wordy. Maybe a bit idealistic."

"I've told you this for weeks. A man who writes the way that author does is not the insipid scholar you seem to find attractive otherwise. He's a rake. An out-and-out rogue."

"He's not." But Miranda looked at the printing on the page, and muttered, "Though I may be in danger of losing the bet now."

"Well, he could be appalling, of course. Hook-nosed and lumpy and humpbacked, just like that Mr. Pitts you converse with. You really have appalling taste in correspondence flirtations, Miranda. Though I'd forgive the hooks, lumps, and humps if your author displays the talent his words promise."

"George!"

"Well! It's true." Georgette flipped her head, curls bouncing. "Besides, what were you doing betting over him? There might be hope for you yet."

"Mr. Pitts dislikes Eleutherios. He encouraged me to write the author, then bet that Eleutherios wouldn't respond. But that if he *did* respond, that his comments would disappoint me. As I said, Mr. Pitts dislikes him. Intensely for some reason."

"Mr. Pitts seems to dislike everything according to you."

"He has good sense," she said loyally. "He's just . . . curmudgeonly at times in expressing it."

"Well stop paying so much attention to your curmudgeons and start ogling a fine pair of . . . shoulders. Real *assets,* if you will."

"George!"

"Do not tell me that you dream of your scholars late at night. I know you do not. You think Thomas Briggs is just as handsome as the rest of us do."

Miranda thought of the man who occasionally kept the books for the businesses on her uncle's block as a way to offset his esquire training expenses. "Thomas Briggs is a goose."

"But a handsome one."

Miranda gave her a look. "He's a prig."

"Fine, then . . ." Georgette put her fingers delicately to her pursed pink lips. "Mr. Chapton. Or Lord

Downing." Georgette shivered. "Delicious. If he does become betrothed to Charlotte Chatsworth, she will be the envy of all of London. Or the pity. One woman will never be able to handle him."

Miranda's curiosity notched a point of interest. Georgette had been chatting about the viscount ad nauseam since she'd spotted him in the park last week. It was a rare appearance for the notorious man, who seemed to spend the majority of his time in hells and brothels and wicked scandals. Full of life and disregard. Sinfully dashing and mysterious. The perfect silver-tongued villain, come to life.

Miranda had actively wished for once that she had attended a park viewing.

"Mr. Chapton is handsome enough," Miranda said in response, having seen the fair-haired man about town a few times. Though Mr. Chapton, better known in the column as Mr. C., didn't fill the faceless void of the man she dreamed about. The shadows clinging and not fully revealing him in her dreams.

That she had glimpsed a bit of the man from yesterday on the normally faceless figure during the night had alarmed her more than a bit.

"You are hopeless, Miranda. You need to get out and about a little more, dear. Put a little swagger in that skirt and find a real man," Georgette said with a relish. "Flesh and blood. Lots of hard, handsome flesh. Spread your wings a little, dear. Start a flirtation." She tapped the paper. "One not on the other end of a quill."

Miranda thought of the previous dusk. Hard, handsome flesh would be quite an adequate description. A man like that would put a true stagger in a woman's step.

Georgette gazed off. "I wish that for you. The adventure you so wish to have but can't seem to embark upon. But when I am unmarried and with child from chasing men like Mr. Chapton, I will force you to live with me, two old women together, and be happy for it." Georgette sighed with a rare bit of self-knowledge and turned back to the column.

Miranda stared at the top of her friend's head, disgruntled.

"Two suitors already for Miss C, in addition to the rumors about Downing. Lucky girl. She will likely not last the season." Georgette's voice was wistful. "She has impeccable fashion sense, Charlotte Chatsworth. None of the frilly pinks that would wash her out. She dresses in royal blue and white almost exclusively when she is in the park."

Georgette had taken ton watching to a higher level, joining those who enjoyed observing the spectacle during the social hours. Miranda loved hearing about the parties and the people, from the fringe routs to the more noteworthy balls, but the echo of her mother's voice telling her to be practical kept her from observing the circuit personally except when she had to make deliveries.

At those times, she couldn't *help* passing by.

The glimpses provided lovely fodder for her daydreams. And the printed tidbits were temptations too rich to resist.

"And Mrs. Q. It says here 'The courtesan of all courtesans dressed in her signature green with a bright red rose shining upon her lapel, her only other accouterments no fewer than ten rakes dripping from her pleats.'"

"You could overshadow her in your undergarments, George. Bring the rakes to their knees."

"Don't tempt me, Miranda." She waggled her perfect brows. "I just might do it. We could do so together. To be Mrs. Q., even for a day, would be grand, don't you think?"

Miranda snorted. She could see it now. The two of them together in their finest, a practical brown wren trailing the bright peacock. She sometimes thought she was Georgette's best asset—a foil to her showy beauty.

Georgette continued, ignoring her. "Some handsome man would come into the store and sweep you off your feet. Abduct you to his lair. Have his wicked way with you while showering you with jewels and other lovely shiny objects."

Miranda wanted to snort again, even if the idea of it held a tiny bit of secret appeal. "And then?"

"And then?" Georgette sputtered. "You have a grand time. Wear those fine jewels. Spend any spare shiny objects."

"And be sent home with paste."

"Paste goes for a pretty penny."

"And so too it seems does the heart."

"Oh, I might as well send you back to the opinion section." Georgette sighed theatrically, holding forth the paper in martyred hands. "See if you can't dig up more correspondents there to salve your cold, shriveled heart."

"I couldn't possibly leave you salivating over the social news by yourself. You might get lost in it and never return," Miranda said lightly, pushing the paper back down. Though she slowly, secretly scooted out the page of the paper that contained the editorials. Mr. Pitts sometimes couldn't help himself and had to post a scathing view of something. Replying was how she had met him.

"I am not the one who needs to worry about becoming lost in pen and ink." Georgette raised her brows and looked down her pert nose. She looked back down at the column and whistled. "Lady W. is to be the subject of another duel."

"Outdoing her husband again today on the gossip scene, is she? You'd think she gifted each new admirer with a sabre just for the task." Miranda shook her head, trying to find the tidbit to read. Georgette had a tendency to sensationalize information that was already quite sensational. And when it came to Lord Downing and his parents, the Marquess and Marchioness of Werston, it often was already shocking.

"Well, when your husband reportedly impregnates an earl's daughter, the scandal needs to be sufficiently large to cover it."

"This is true." Miranda shook her head. It was difficult to believe that people did such things, but society seemed rife with scandal. The stories made for good reading, at the least. "Who is fighting over her hand this time?"

"A Mr. E and Lord D." Georgette tapped her full lower lip. "Rumor has the duel taking place at Vauxhall. I wonder if we can discover where and when, so that we can peek through the bushes. I still can't believe you won't come to the park to see Lord Downing as you are always so interested in his exploits. He passed by yesterday. Only spent a few paltry minutes, but to be seen twice in a week? It's like a bevy of good fortune for the swooner in all of us."

Miranda tried to ignore her. She wasn't going to haunt

the park for a peek at the man. Downing's exploits seemed especially grandiose, that was all. "Fighting for his mother's honor?"

"You always think highly of people. It's sweet." Georgette reached over to pat her shoulder. Miranda glared. "But doubtful. I assume it refers to Lord Dillingham." Georgette pursed her lips in thought. "I will have to check Debrett's to make sure I haven't missed anyone though."

Miranda withheld a roll of her eyes. Georgette was always abreast of who was who. She could likely challenge the ton matchmakers.

"You check then. I am sure that there will be plenty of information over the next week. They always set up scandalous news this way, with just a hook and a lure."

"Well, I will do just that. Look here, there is another column devoted to the sequel gossip around *The Seven Secrets of Seduction*."

Miranda made a noncommittal sound, absorbing the words.

"Since I can't get you away from your ink, I say that you write to the author again. And proposition him."

It took a moment for her friend's words to sink in. "Prop—" she sputtered.

"Any man who writes words like that has to be able to use his hands in other ways too. It would be good for you."

"Georgette!" Miranda clunked her teacup onto her saucer.

"Oh, pish, you could use a little manhandling." Georgette nibbled on a scone. "Write to your Eleutherios or come ogle Lord Downing and try to gain his interest like the rest of us—I daresay you might even be willing to let your bonds free if you had an assignation with one of them. Satisfy your needs."

"Assignation? Satisfy my *needs*?" Miranda gawked, then ground her teeth. "And manhandling? As if you can speak of manhandling. I can't believe you are practicing your wiles on poor Peter."

"If the shoulders and thighs are good . . ." Georgette tapped her lower lip with her pink-gloved finger, smirking.

"Too few of the quality kind around these days under all that padding," a husky, decidedly unfeminine voice said. "How do you ladies ever deduce what is real?"

Miranda's body tensed, and Georgette immediately looked up at the deep drawl.

"Ladies." Crisp black and white once again stood in contrast as the speaker inclined his head.

Georgette uttered a shocked response, but Miranda barely registered it as her body unwillingly turned left toward him.

He raised a brow, and one side of his mouth curved. There was an entirely too-amused light in his eyes. A long finger, enclosed in black today, ran idly along the edge of his crossed arm. "Miss Chase?"

"Yes?" she answered, somewhat stupidly, wondering how long he had been standing in the early shadows listening to their conversation. Mortification, curiosity, anticipation . . . she couldn't discern which emotion was winning. She thought maybe the mortification.

"Perhaps you might satisfy *my* needs instead?"

The mortification. Most definitely.

Georgette said something incomprehensible in a strangled voice.

"What do you need?" Miranda's voice was a bit faint,

her ears slightly buzzing. Her mind was going in four directions simultaneously. A little like the hobbyhorse that she had seen speed down a hill, breaking apart in midstride, and casting the driver one way while the two wheels and wooden body flew elsewhere.

"Oh, I'm sure together we can figure that out." He motioned behind him, smiling. "Shall we?"

She jerkily stood and took two automatic steps toward him before she pulled herself together enough to remember that Peter was manning the counter, that Georgette was gaping like a fish, and that the man in front of her was here to pick up his parcel—which required no help from her in her mortified state. She'd probably do something even more embarrassing at this point. She'd be castigating herself for weeks as it was.

She stopped. "Peter can help you."

"Not in the manner I'd prefer." He smiled lazily, his questing fingers absently caressing the leather bindings on a row of Greek philosophers.

Another choked gurgle issued from the table.

There was that same maddening flash in his eyes, a lone light bobbing in a storm-tossed sea. It made her itchy. She backed up, embarrassment becoming belligerence at the topsy-turvy way he made her feel.

That, and she was pretty sure his presence was starting to make her perspire, and she didn't want to let him see.

"I don't know in what manner you'd prefer, but Peter will be perfectly happy to assist you with your package."

He raised a brow. "I think not."

"Then he can also assist you with anything else you require." Yes, there was definitely an overheated feeling spreading into her hairline. "He is quite familiar with the stacks."

"No."

"No?" She startled. Everything about this man was so beyond her familiarity. She had assumed that without something epically scintillating on her lips, he would withdraw . . . become bored or irritated.

That he had returned today—and so early—made the wheels on her runaway hobbyhorse spin more out of control, but also imbued her with a strange sense of feminine confidence that she usually lacked. The power of it was foreign and heady and clashed against the lingering freeze of embarrassment.

She arranged her skirts and returned to the chair across from Georgette, pulling a sheet of the paper to her blindly. "You are just here to pick up your parcel," she said calmly, pulling forth a breeze to her voice. "I assure you that what you require is behind the desk."

"Is that correct?"

"Yes. And I am busy, as you can see." She pointed to Georgette, who stared blankly back, uncharacteristically speechless.

"Busy discussing the latest rag on dits?"

She colored over being caught with her hand on the gossip sheet, as it was. How long had he been standing there? "I am taking a break at the moment. As I've said several times, Peter will be happy to assist you. I assure you that your parcel is behind the desk."

"But that is what you thought last eve as well. I left quite unassisted. And unsatisfied." He moved along the shelf, drawing his hand along the spines, fully emerging from the shadows, putting himself back in her direct view.

She looked at the black-and-white print, trying

vainly to pretend the page was right side up and that she was highly engrossed in an article. "I placed it behind the counter myself this morning—along with your copy of *Candide*. It seems that the original package was misplaced on a high shelf last night." She peered over the edge of the paper and down her nose. "Mysteriously."

He raised a brow, the flash of light amidst his dark eyes undimmed. "Mysteriously indeed. You should watch where things are moved."

"I will pay careful attention next time. Now, Peter—"

"No. I want you."

She felt the color in her cheeks bloom to life. "I assure you—"

"You have a vested interest in making sure I leave with what I want."

"I assure—"

He tapped a binding and withdrew his hand. "And hopefully what I need as well."

"Uh . . ." With her emergence into womanhood, she had thought she had overcome the inability to complete a sentence. "But I'm busy with—"

"Go." Georgette's voice was strangled. "It will allow me to catch up with you and read the sections about the *Secrets* sequel."

"Dear me, Miss Chase. Speaking of *that* book again?" He cocked that infernal dark brow. "It sounds like this is an obsession. Tsk, tsk. I'll think you truly have a secret desire to be seduced."

Miranda pushed back her chair in a distinctly unladylike manner that would have appalled her mother, and it toppled over behind her with a clatter. She thwacked the paper on the table, crumpling the edges in mortified irritation. "Fine. Let's retrieve your parcel." She started around the stacks, forced to brush by him. "You can view it at the desk."

"And such a fine view it is," he said, as his leg brushed hers, the words low and deep. "Softly bound, the corners curved."

She stopped abruptly, her skirts shifting and coming to rest around her legs in a way that would have been completely normal if all of her raw spots weren't on fire. The feel of the calico might as well have been silk and iron mixed together. She faintly heard Georgette coughing behind them.

"I beg your pardon?"

He looked her over, his eyes still containing the lazy flash. "When one chooses to wrap a prize in such formless paper, it can be hard to tell, but I'm sure I detect some truly decadent curves beneath. Sweeter than words—the ones in your favorite book or otherwise."

A mixture of a cough and chortle issued from the stacks.

"I . . . I beg your pardon? Are you . . . are you *teasing* me?"

"Teasing? Never." He smiled and tapped a finger on his arm again. "My parcel? I'm not sure you truly have it."

She studied him for a moment in heated disbelief before turning and walking again.

"I can't wait to hold it in my hands."

Miranda missed a step as she rounded the last stack.

Peter was fidgeting with two packages at the counter. He completely ignored Miranda and stared at the man behind her as they came into view.

"Peter, could you locate the package labeled—"

"I think Peter was just taking his break," the deep voice behind her said.

Peter's head bobbed, and he disappeared into the back room. Miranda stared after him, nonplussed.

"My parcel, Miss Chase?"

She shivered at the way the words curled around her, the way he seemed to savor her name. "You can't just order people around, Mr. Jeffries."

He leaned against the counter as she rounded it, tapping a finger, smiling. "It's a failing of mine."

"Perhaps you should rectify that." She refused to fall at his feet. She had a feeling women too often did. She leaned down and gripped the coarse-wrapped paper and twine.

"Where is the fun in that?" His voice was slightly less gravelly than the day before, but still laced with the same huskiness.

"It is laudable to correct one's faults."

"Sometimes being naughty is much more fun though, don't you think?"

Miranda stood up and thumped the parcel on the counter next to the two Peter had been wrapping and labeling. Her heart raced even as she tried to think of a suitable response. "Sir, I think you ought to read those manuscripts on seduction again if you think these are good battle tactics."

He slowly smiled. "Ah, at least I know that you aren't completely oblivious. They are superb tactics. You'll never guess my real intent now."

"I assure you, your intent is all too clear. You seek to play now, then have a smile about it later."

"Oh now, Miss Chase, that is entirely untrue." He stroked the edge of the package, the curve of a corner.

"I assure you that I seek to smile now and play with you later."

A spike of desire hit her even as she chided herself the fool. "You are not amusing, sir."

"Isn't it the second secret? Luring your prey or some such rubbish? Shouldn't I be luring you away? Luring you to a deep pool, where you will exclaim over the lovely lily pads gracing the surface, never anticipating my fingers stroking you underneath?"

She folded her hands primly on top of the counter, even as her skin grew hotter, the perspiration retreating deep within, relinquishing the idea that her extremities could be cooled.

He smiled as if he knew what she was thinking, feeling. "Payment?"

She looked down at the ledger, the letters blurring together, causing her to run her fingers down the list twice until she found the right one. "No, my uncle included a note saying your package was paid in full."

Which meant he had no more business in the shop and would walk right through the door, never to be seen again, if she didn't say something to keep him there.

And which she realized, from the conflicting feelings he stirred, she foolishly desired.

When she looked up, he already held the package in his hands, ahead of her and in a hurry to be on his way.

"Well, then." He smiled as if he knew a delicious secret—probably anticipating wherever he was off to next—to violently shake up some other woman's life most likely—far from here. "Until we meet again, Miss Chase."

She nodded tightly, the coil in her belly rock hard.

She tried to open her mouth to say something. Anything. But her training beat down on her, ingrained, her lips stayed firmly shut. Any chance to extend the flirtation with the first man who had made her heart race fragmented as he pushed the door. The bell jingled, and he disappeared from view. The heated coil fated to be extinguished before it fully flared.

And it was a blessing, no matter the crashing disappointment. Men like him flirted, but when it came down to it, they found real prey. She'd likely never see him again, except perhaps on the scandal pages—for surely a man like that would require more than the occasional line.

She headed back around the stacks, feeling more tired than she had before. She sat with a less than graceful thump in her chair, aware that Georgette was staring at her, gaping like a market fish.

"Sorry for the disruption." Miranda wrenched the paper toward her, determined to forget the man. *After* she scoured it for Mr. J's. "Where were we?"

"Do you know who that was? Why didn't you tell me you had met him?" Georgette's tone neared a screech. "When? How?" The devolution into sputters would have been an interesting switch to listen to if Miranda weren't still kicking herself for not saying something, *anything,* before he walked through the door, blessing or not.

She'd *never* castigate Georgette for her instantaneous attraction to rogues again. Being enamored of some rakish beast. Miranda had never had to deal with the direct attention of someone so magnetic before. It was overwhelming.

"I just met him last eve. Completely crazed, is he not?" she muttered as she drew the gossip page closer.

She'd have to quiz her friend on his past. Later. When she had her mind and body under control. "And awfully bossy under all of that false charm. Thinks he rules the roost, I bet. I daresay I shall find him in these pages everywhere now."

When Georgette didn't immediately answer, Miranda looked up to find her friend staring at her blankly. Miranda had the strange sensation that their usual roles were unaccountably swapped at the moment.

"Crazed? Bossy?" Her friend's words were high and slightly strangled.

"A beast. And I can't say that I find him entirely comfortable to speak with. He quite irritates me on purpose, I think."

"Irritates you on purpose?" Despite the lingering, slightly hysterical pitch to her voice, Georgette seemed to be getting ahold of herself again, arranging the stray papers on the table in a fashion that Miranda often used when their roles were reversed, and she was seeking a way to say something other than telling her friend that she was completely insane.

"Yes. And he hates Eleutherios."

"Hates Eleutherios?" Georgette only seemed capable of repeating statements back as questions. "As much as the book thrilled me, Downing probably wrote the book on seduction long before Eleutherios picked up a pen."

Miranda pushed the paper near her away a little roughly. "Well, I doubt Mr. Jeffries even knows how to write."

"What are you on about?"

"He seems much more interested in . . . frolicking. Probably doesn't have the time to pick up a pen."

"Who?" Georgette demanded.

"Mr. Jeffries. The blasted man. You heard him."

Georgette's mouth opened and closed, but no sound emerged for a long moment. Then a delighted peal of laughter rang forth.

A sinking pit gathered in Miranda's gut as Georgette continued to laugh so hard that, in a vain attempt to cease, she took a drink and almost snorted her tea.

"I take it his name is not Mr. Jeffries?" Miranda asked in deepening horror, unsure if her heart could take any more shocks.

"Miranda!"

She turned her head to see her uncle rushing in, the winged fringes of his hair bouncing below his balding pate. He held a package aloft. "Why wasn't the parcel taken? When I just asked, Peter said that you handled it. And Rutherford wants his books, too and they've gone missing."

Her heart joined her gut somewhere near her toes as she looked at the package in her uncle's shaking hand. "The parcel for whom wasn't taken?"

"The books marked Jeffries. For a very important client." He tapped the package, agitated. "Butler was coming to claim them. And Mr. Rutherford's package is gone."

"Oh." Her mind skittered to the less important pieces of new information. It stood to reason he'd have a butler. She looked at the brown wrapping, innocuous and innocent, mocking her. "He must have taken the wrong parcel."

"The wrong one! This is a disaster!"

Three packages sitting side by side. Easy enough to take the wrong one.

Then she pictured his smile, his smirk as he left. The swing of his arm.

He had purposely taken the wrong package.

The pit in her stomach turned into fire and stoked all of the emotions that he had previously spurred. She narrowed her eyes as she remembered his face. His words. The knowing glance as he said they'd meet again. She buried any relief under her increasing ire at his machinations.

"Disaster." Her uncle repeated. "What if he takes back his promises?" He shook his head. "Go now. No, wait, you can't, Parliament will be in session." He muttered something to himself. "You'll go tomorrow. Switch the books. Apologize for whatever you have to. Tomorrow. First thing!" He turned and disappeared back through the stacks, muttering to himself about ink-stained disasters.

Georgette turned in her chair, a satisfied smile on her face. "No, my dear. Not Mr. Jeffries. That was Maximilian Landry, Viscount Downing." She tapped the gossip page. "And it seems that you have an assignation with him after all."

Chapter 3

*Secret #2: Once the book is in
place, the lure must be set.*
The Seven Secrets of Seduction

Miranda stood on the walk and stared up at the
sharp planes of the huge detached home—
separated from the row houses clinging together around
the street. Layer upon layer of white and gray stone
rose to the top of the trees. A window was open at the
top left, and a hand reached out and flapped a foot rug
against the stone sill. Nothing fell from the rug, not
even a whisper of dust. Unlike Miranda's neighborhood,
where rugs were cleaned when they couldn't handle
one more piece of dirt, people too busy making ends
meet, the seldom-beaten rugs dislodging detritus, lost
items, and precious time.

A smartly tailored man passed by, a satchel gripped
tightly in his hand, muttering to himself about ventures
and gains. He never once looked up. When a window
opened in her neighborhood, people ducked.

Here, everything was cleaned in a timely and orderly
fashion. People paid just to make sure that the silver

received a third polish. Everything was expected to be perfect. To be on time. To just *be* without thought.

And yet no one seemed to notice the gorgeous flowers dripping from window boxes or the creepers nestled half-hiding in the nooks and cracks of the stone and wood. The carefully polished brass plates to the sides of the doors. The gleaming knockers. The expensively potted bushes in ornately handcrafted basins. The thousand and one things that took so much time and care to arrange or maintain and were simply taken for granted as another beautiful thing to pass by.

She could have stayed and stared for hours at the way the gardener had arranged the vines to splay like fingers gripping the rails, pulling visitors up in an embrace.

Another man passed, jostling her.

She sighed and took a step down the drive toward the carriage house in the back. The kitchen entrance would be somewhere near. She gripped the paper and twine, a strange feeling thrumming through her. No matter what her lively night imaginings, in the sharp light of day it was baffling to be feeling such anxious anticipation. She'd drop the package off and be on her way. Simple.

It wasn't as if she'd never delivered things to the more expensive addresses in London. She had, a time or two when no one else was available to do so, but there hadn't been any thought to it. A simple drop. Maybe a credit note hinting at payment.

She loved to visit Mayfair. To admire the edifices and squares. But there was a certain sense of self-consciousness that precluded extended stops. That she didn't belong was obvious. And sometimes it felt as if everyone was one moment away from pointing and whispering about it. But those thoughts were com-

pletely irrational and silly. The Quality didn't notice.
Anyone not in their class was completely beneath their
regard.

Unless something was amiss. Then it was better to
move as quickly as possible in the other direction than
to wait for one of them to call the Watch.

Mr. Pitts was always going on about how stupid the
people in power were. The peerage and Parliament.
About the silly games they played.

But she didn't think it stupidity so much as that they
didn't understand that there were other ways to be,
other things to see, other decisions to make.

The gravel drive was well-groomed, and her sturdy
shoes crunched the pebbles beneath. Two liveried
footmen walked by, tipping their heads good day,
their black-and-silver uniforms pressed and gleaming. Miranda returned their greeting and gripped her
package more tightly.

A viscount. Viscount Downing.

She shook her head. It didn't matter. She continued
down the long drive, turning the corner of the house
and stepping to the side as two women lurched down
the steps toward her, nearly buckling under the weight
of a giant wash pot full of used water.

"What yu think it means?"

"Abner says 'tis a sign of the 'pocalypse."

The kitchen maid in front giggled, then nearly tipped
down the steps as she lost her footing. Miranda reached
out and steadied her. "Can I be of assistance?"

"Lord, gal, you just have. Nearly beaned meself."

The other woman snorted. "Be an improvement.
You ding this pot, and Cook'll clip your tail."

The first woman pulled a face. "Well then, I better

be thanking her again, eh?" She craned her neck at Miranda, who held up a hand.

"It was nothing. But might you point me to who handles the deliveries?"

The maid gave a sharp crook of her head toward the door. "Mrs. Humphries will take it, luv. Or someone can call for one of the underbutlers."

Miranda nodded her thanks, and the women continued their haul to the yard.

"Anyways, the lordship's behavior's getting stranger. Rising that early yesterday then du—"

The rest of the woman's sentence was drowned beneath a loud whoosh as the pot was emptied.

"I know. Right mess. Humphries kept muttering about tie-foons, whatever those are. Right strange it all is."

Miranda hesitated, wanting to hear what they were talking about as they began pumping the well for a refill, but good sense told her that it looked entirely too odd for her to linger for no apparent reason.

She entered the open door to the bustling kitchen. Servants crisscrossed and ducked beneath one another's raised arms and stirred spoons, grabbing pots and utensils, yelling orders and responses.

The sheer chaos of the dance was mesmerizing. A bump here and a scrape there, but for the most part it was almost as if the insanity were choreographed—the dancers working together for such a long time that they responded precisely to the way their compatriots would swing and jibe.

Heat from the ovens made the air sweltering, and even the open doors and windows couldn't stop the pressing waves from coiling at the ceiling and flaring downward. The back of Miranda's hair started to pull at her neck, gripping and clinging to the moisture gathering on her skin. She cursed the coiffure she had chosen, keeping her hair tied loosely instead of in the tight upstyle that made everyday tasks around town easier. The strands would be plastered to the back of her neck soon, limp below and frizzing up top.

Why in heavens name had she decided to wear it this way? A sudden decision in the early light of morning, but a style better suited to evening indulgences. She must have taken leave of her senses while tossing and turning during the night.

She caught the eye of a matron who looked as if she ran the kitchen and held the package aloft. The woman nodded sharply and deftly maneuvered through the melee.

"Good day," Miranda said, and held the package out as the woman reached her hand to grasp it. "Book delivery for the viscount through Mr. Jeffries."

The woman's hand snatched back as if burned. Her eyes snapped up and narrowed on her. "Book delivery through Jeffries? From Main Street Books and Printers?"

The sounds in the kitchen suddenly dimmed as if a blanket had been thrown over a ringing bell. All eyes seemed to turn her way.

"Yes?" Icy tingles under her skin made the heat on her neck burn.

"Come with me." The woman turned and headed back through. The servants parted ranks, casting curious glances in Miranda's direction as they continued to work, the sound increasing again, but now with whispered words and glances her way.

"Pardon me," Miranda said, as they exited through

the heavy kitchen door and into a blissfully cooler hall, moving forward into the deeper areas of the house.

Every nerve was on sudden edge with the anticipating thought that she might see him again, vying with utter mortification over the possibility. She had been unknowingly *gossiping* about him, and he had assuredly *heard*. "The parcel has been paid for already and only requires a signature and perhaps another package in return if the viscount has so ordered."

Drop it off. Grab the Rutherford package, if it was available. Her uncle had already half written off Rutherford's books as lost due to the flighty nature of the Quality. She surreptitiously tried to pull her sweat-dampened dress away from her neck as she walked. "If I could just drop it with—"

Not breaking stride, the woman shook her head, as she passed in and out of the partial light filtering through open doorways. "I have instructions to show you to the Red Room." She pointed. "This way."

Miranda followed uncertainly. The woman opened an ornate door and motioned her inside. "It will be just a moment."

Her uncle had told her in no uncertain terms that the package had to be delivered today to their "very important client." Something about a library and books the viscount was shedding that he had hinted *might* be given to the store. Her uncle had devolved into ecstatic mutterings.

Otherwise, she might have been tempted—*just a bit*—to flee.

Miranda stepped inside, and the heavy door clicked behind her. The room was decorated entirely in black, silver, and gold. Even the woods were ebony, with gleaming embellishments. The only testament to color was a lone red vase perched atop a pedestal in the center.

It was obvious someone had a sense of humor.

The room had an unused quality about it. As if it were all for show. Bookshelves lined one side, filled with ledgers and thick, heavy tomes that looked as if they hadn't been moved in years. Someone, some servant probably, had neatly aligned all the books. A bookshelf that was used had at least some titles askew. Put away with a busy hand. Not perfectly positioned next to the others at their sides.

The Quality. Between frolics, they had to pretend to attend to their pursuits and estate business. And Downing seemed to frolic a lot, if the ink on the gossip pages was any indication.

A large desk took up the space in front of a series of heavily draped windows, opened only enough to allow a sliver of light by which to see. As if the room were afraid of being exposed. The desk was trimmed in spiraled carvings of lions and chimeras midroar.

It too had an unused quality. As if someone might sit on the other side only to interrogate anyone who dared enter.

The room was intimidating. For what did one expect from someone unable to be pinpointed as anything other than dark and unexpected?

Only the red vase bent the mood. She walked over to examine it further.

"Do you like it?"

She spun to see the viscount leaning against the wall twirling a pocket watch. A normal man might have blended into the dark decor dressed as he was, but the viscount just made the shadows longer and more pronounced.

She turned back to the vase and tried to stay her breathing. He was the same man who had entered her shop, unknown at the time, she tried to convince herself. Out of her realm of experience even then, but now?

She concentrated on the enameled pottery in front of her. The vase was a lovely piece, actually. Red and gold intertwined with fleur-de-lis scrolls. The one spot of color, and also the one piece that held life. "I do."

"And the room?"

She faced him again, holding the package as calmly as she could against her chest—a shield in front of her even though he was ten paces away. "It is a nice room," she said diplomatically.

"Nice?"

"It is startling," she admitted.

" 'Startling' is quite different from 'nice.' "

"It is."

"But do you like it?"

She inclined her head. "Does it matter?"

He smiled and pushed away from the wall. "At the moment, very much."

"And in the next moment?"

He walked by her slowly, behind her, brushing the edge of her dress bow so that it tugged at her waist in a slight caress.

"We shall see."

He continued to the desk, and she turned to face him. "Is your lordship amused? Playing with the lowly shopgirl?"

"I hardly think you a lowly shopgirl. You have funds of your own, do you not? Perhaps not enough to live on your own, but enough to refuse my offer the other day." He sank into his chair, the action nearly liquid.

"Or am I such a bear that it was a refusal of me?"

He idly twirled a paperweight. The look in his eyes seemed to belie that he thought that possible.

"Have people found you a bear in order to lead you to such a conclusion?"

"I am generally found to be quite pleasurable company." His eyes traveled her. "Or at least I haven't encountered complaints yet."

She clutched the package tighter.

"Or maybe it is because you hold books in such high esteem that you can't bear to part with one before you are done."

"And how will you ever deduce which is the truth?"

"I already know which is true." He smiled. "I asked someone with keen knowledge on the subject."

She wondered whom he had asked—her uncle, Peter, Georgette?—and when he had done so. "I see."

He placed the weight on the desk, arranging it in a sequence with a pen, a piece of paper, and the pocket watch. "Do you?"

No, she didn't. "You are having some amusement. Playing with the not-as-lowly-as-first-supposed-but-still-lowly shopgirl."

The flash from the first night flitted through his eyes again as he looked up. He settled back in his chair, hands clasped together. "I do so hope so."

"Why?" she asked baldly.

"Because you intrigue me."

She watched his eyes, trying not to pay attention to the way her organs seemed to fight to cross an unknown finish line. She had done nothing extraordinary. She had none of the overt flirtatiousness of Georgette. She had no claim to a great beauty or figure that made men claim intrigue.

She hadn't acquitted herself as witty or wise. She was just Miranda. A girl who liked books.

Which made his claim false and raised an unknown alarm.

She shook her head free of any flights of fancy and held out the parcel. "Here you are, my lord. Intact and hand delivered." She walked to the desk and placed it on the surface, the paper on top awaiting his signature slid forward. She pushed it an inch toward him. "I'll be on my way after you sign this."

"Well, I can't have that."

She stared at him. "You do not want the items after all?"

"I do, but they will only be signed as delivered if I take possession."

She nudged the paper forward with raised glimmerings that perhaps she should question his sanity.

His brow cocked, and the flash appeared again—not a benign twinkle, such as one given to mischief or hilarity—but one that a man might wear if he was about to have his wicked way with the woman on the receiving end. "I meant that I am not ready to sign your paper. What if the books are not the items requested? What if we once again have suffered a miscommunication?"

She nudged the package this time. His other brow joined the first.

She raised her own brows, the pepper that seemed to run through her veins when he was near spiced the flow once more, overriding her embarrassment and any feelings of inferiority. "The only miscommunication we have suffered is your purposefully misplacing your package," she said. "Twice, I might add."

"Tut, blaming the customer." He slouched down in the chair, his hands clasped against his chest, even that action unable to mask his leaching virility. "I am completely a victim here."

"Completely." She waited, then tapped her finger. "Are you going to open the package and inspect the books?"

"No."

"Would you like me to open the package?"

"No."

"No? Then how am I to . . ." She took a deep breath, then smiled as calmly as she could manage within the unspecified game he was playing. He smiled back just as pleasantly.

And said not a word. For an entire minute.

He seemed perfectly content to watch her. She held his gaze unflinchingly, though the narrowed glimpse of a question within his eyes unnerved her, as if he couldn't quite discover the answer to a riddle.

Itchy fingers of warmth crawled up her limbs. She absently caressed the package. She had the vague notion that they might continue in this stalemate all day if she remained silent.

"How are you faring this afternoon, my lord?" she asked as gamely as she could manage over the flutters and confusion, the lingering embarrassment and anticipation.

"Better. But those close to me call me by my first name."

She stared at him.

The edges of his mouth lifted farther. "And those acquaintances with whom I plan to become *better* acquainted." He waved a hand to her in some gesture of encouragement.

She stared at him some more.

"We might sit here all day."

She opened and closed her mouth, nothing emerging for a long moment. "Er, how are you this afternoon . . . Maximilian?"

"It's quite a mouthful, unfortunately. Feel free to shorten it at will. And I'm doing quite well, Miranda."

She continued to stare, wondering when she'd wake to find the whole situation a strange imagining.

"I asked." He answered her unspoken question, even white teeth pulling into an appealing curve. "That is your name, correct?"

She looked around her, at the glitter of the gold and silver, the shadows of the dark woods. At the quite fine specimen of masculinity across from her. She nodded to herself. Dreaming.

"Yes. Industrious of you to discover it."

His smile grew. "I think you will find me quite industrious."

Something wild and strange surged within her, making her fingers jitter. She clasped them together and nodded toward the unsigned paper. She needed that paper signed. It was something tangible and concrete. "Is there something I can do to increase your industry even more?"

"I do find myself in dire need of assistance. Would you care to help me with something?"

"What sort of something?" she asked cautiously, fingers twining together, all sorts of mad imaginings springing to mind.

"Nothing too perfidious, I promise." He smiled widely, charmingly, all white teeth showing.

"Will you sign for the package, if I do?"

"You don't want to keep exchanging visits?"

"I expect that you do want your package sometime," she demurred, trying to corral her rampaging thoughts and the way her body responded to his very voice and presence. "You came to the store twice solely to pick it up, so it must be important."

"Did I?"

She narrowed her eyes at him. "I saw you in the store for it just yesterday."

He smiled and leaned back farther in his chair, rocking it back on its heels. "So literal sometimes, and at other times with your head in the clouds."

"I hardly think you aware of the normal sway of my thoughts, your lordship."

"Mmmmm. And it's Maximilian or some such variety, Miranda."

"It is purely Miss Chase, my lord."

"A pity. I had so been hoping to call you Miranda."

"I can't possibly imagine why."

He rose and walked around the desk. She stood still, unwilling to bolt like a scared rabbit as he neared her position. He came within a hairbreadth of touching her before leaning back so he was sitting on the edge of the desk facing her. "It's a lovely name. Quite Shakespearean."

She didn't dare breathe because of the short distance between them. "I think you are a tease, my lord."

"No, a tease is someone who only promises without following through." His fingers interlocked, and one thumb slowly traced a pattern around the edges of the other. "I guarantee you that I am a man who follows through."

She was worried about expiring? About breathing?

She didn't know if she had breath left. She pointed at the package at his side, grasping the last tendrils of sanity. "Then sign for your delivery."

Consternation and a touch of something else passed through his eyes. "Touché, Miss Chase."

He fiddled with the paper for a second, then let it fall back to the desk. She waited for him to pick it up and sign it, but when he failed to do so, she suddenly bent over him, gripped it herself, and held it to him.

She could feel the internal heat coil beneath her cheekbones and flare out, but she held her hand steady.

He slowly took it from her and paused before picking up a pen in his right hand. He dipped the tip and signed with a strange flourish. The signature was a bit sloppy. The g at the end trailed awkwardly as though he didn't write it often. She had merely been grousing the day before when she'd said it, but possibly he rarely *did* pick up a pen.

"And now your task is at an end," he said, his voice holding a note of something she couldn't identify.

Relief vied with something equally unnameable inside of her. "That it is." She carefully folded the slip and placed it in her hanging pocket. "Thank you." Something reached out of the confusion and clawed to the surface, prompting her to say, "And the task you'd like assistance with?"

"Ah, yes. A dire matter of settling an argument as to the placement of a painting."

She blinked, but before she could say anything, he rose to his full height, his presence stretching forward in such a way that she couldn't help but take a step back.

"Come."

She followed him out, touching her pocket again to

reassure herself that he had actually signed the slip and that it was still in her possession and not lifted by some chicanery on his part. "I am hardly a knowledgeable judge of such things."

"Nonsense. You are an opinionated lady. That is all I ask—your opinion."

She followed him through a hall, up one set of stairs, and down another hall. He stopped so abruptly that she almost careened into his solid, too-appealing back.

"Here. What do you think? The Dutch on this side or that?"

A quite attractive Vermeer stood patiently on the floor against a wall. She had seen two other works by the artist, not a favorite of the museums, but she loved his propensity to paint across class. A maid's head bent to her task under the paint, and Miranda could almost feel the mundane aspect of the woman's work, the direction of her thoughts as she daydreamed that she was doing something else. Miranda thought that she could stare at the painting and wonder about it all day if given the chance. A bare spot on the wall was perfectly positioned for the piece.

"This looks like quite an excellent spot."

"But you haven't seen the other location." He pivoted and pointed behind him.

She resolutely turned as well, determined to humor him instead of trying to figure out what he was trying to accomplish.

"My brother Conrad thinks this the best spot, but I think he is mad."

A nice section of wall was cleared here as well, and she opened her mouth to say so, but as her eyes drifted from the empty wall space to his too-attractive features, she caught sight of the most glorious room. She couldn't help but take a step toward it in reaction.

"You can't put a Vermeer in the south side of a corridor, I told him," his rich voice said at her side, the ever-present huskiness underlying the timbre. "Everyone knows this. But—"

The words started to blend together in her mind as she craned her neck just an inch trying to see farther inside.

"Miss Chase?"

"Hmmm?"

"Are you ogling my library?"

She turned back to him, coloring. "Oh. Yes, I suppose I was at that."

"Would you care to take a look inside?"

She nodded, her feet already taking her that way as he beckoned, moving forward. Any reluctance about her strange reaction to his prolonging her visit, or the jumpiness concerning his identity, or the wish to discover more about him, temporarily faded beneath the lure. "Yes, I'd love to."

Entering the grand door was like walking through a portal to another kingdom.

The room was magnificent.

Arching wood and spiraled staircases stretched beseechingly toward the upper stacks. Row upon row of bare shelves calmly sat, patiently waiting. And the stacks of books—they were everywhere. Towering piles. Monoliths of printed words and bound pages. Leather and parchment, ink and glue. The entire room looked as if it had been shaken by a large hand, then haphazardly tidied. But even through the mess, the potential was clear. And the fortune in books. It was absurd. There were more titles here than in all of their store and lending library—front and back.

"I recently redid the room—or my workers did, I should say. And in the interim I was bequeathed another entire manor's worth of titles. So I removed all of them to redistribute and reorder." He idly shifted, his hip sending a towering pile plummeting. "Tatty things really. More trouble than they are worth."

She very nearly dove for the falling stack. "Are you mad? You have a king's ransom here." She grew more appalled as he nudged what looked like an illuminated manuscript with the toe of his boot. She did dive for it, scooping it up and hugging it to her. "What are you doing? That's priceless."

He raised a brow. "If only because the currency used when it was created is long dead. Rubbish, really. Talking about moral superiority and ethics." A hand waved, and he caught another stack with it. She leapt forward and put her free hand out to steady it, afraid that other priceless works might be contained within, only awaiting a careless gesture to send them careening to their deaths.

She could feel him moving around her back. Brushing against the edges of her dress, her left hand frozen on the stack as his low, deep voice continued. "I think one should do as one chooses, don't you, Miranda?"

She clasped the manuscript to her beating chest with her right arm.

"Or else one becomes mired in tomes and mores intent on sealing you into a tomb."

She swallowed around the dryness in her throat.

"There is life here in the chaos, even as order constantly tries to reinstate itself." He motioned toward her hand holding the stack. "If you were simply to let go . . ."

"Something precious could be destroyed."

His eyes were hooded. "There is always that chance. That is why it is called a gamble."

"I—I don't know of what you are speaking."

He suddenly moved away, quixotic and mad. "Of course you don't."

She carefully set the illumination on the navy pad of a chair surrounded by books. She nervously lifted the top few books from the stack she had steadied. There was a lovely French primer on top.

"You have what looks to be a wonderful collection."

"I have made it quite my life's work to collect beautiful things."

She didn't know what to say to that. Nor to the implication behind the words.

"Alas that I often destroy those things in the collecting." He casually ran a finger over the top of a stack.

"Perhaps if you stop tossing them over—"

"And I keep thinking that perhaps it is just the next piece that will complete it. That will satisfy the emptiness." He picked up the volume whose title she couldn't read.

"Perhaps what you are searching for is already in your possession." She gestured around. "Buried beneath the mess?"

The edge of his mouth curved as he studied the cover of whatever book he held. "That is what I'm betting on."

"Very good," she said, on edge with the conversation,

his presence, everything. "With a little direction, your servants can place these volumes back on the shelves with their new counterparts. And you can find what you are looking for."

"I can't trust someone on my staff to do it for me. To find what I seek."

"You can direct them yourself."

"No." He turned the book in his hands. "Besides, I'd rather spend my energy on other pursuits." His eyes were dark and molten, and he tossed the book to the floor, the volumes there swallowing it into their midst, hiding it from view.

She winced at the possible damage that might have been done. "Surely one of your servants can read their letters." What type of other pursuits did one attempt when looking at someone in that way?

"Surely."

She shifted under his penetrating gaze. "Your butler or an underbutler? Your housekeeper? They could arrange them alphabetically. Solve the entire situation. It would be a privilege to be so challenged."

Preserve the precious volumes. Reassemble the glorious room. Shift his energy—so focused upon her, the heft of it pressing into her—to something or someone else so that she could recall how to draw breath . . .

How easy it was to imagine how he had become the apple of the gossips' eyes. It wasn't just his looks or words, his seductive actions. It was an intangible piece of him straining at some bond, making the viewer wonder if perhaps this time the bond would snap. Fascinating and terrifying. For what might he do when it snapped? Might he be captured forever? Or would he destroy everything in his path?

"I do need someone to catalog and organize the

books so that I know what I have." His gaze shifted away from her, the tension easing from her a bit, and he picked up the illumination she had placed on the chair.

"Very good, my lord."

He tossed it on top of a shorter stack and sifted through a taller one until he found whatever it was he was looking for. From the gilt glow, another illumination. He handed it to her, and she automatically took it, relieved that he wasn't tossing it to the floor too.

"Be here tomorrow at nine then?"

"Yes, very . . . pardon me?" She clutched the book against her chest in sudden light-headed alarm.

"You have convinced me. Be here at nine. Wear something comfortable, I'd think. See you then."

He turned and was halfway through the doorway before she caught him.

"I don't think you understood. Or that I understood, perhaps. I was merely suggesting that you find someone to do it for you."

"And I have. Thank you." He smiled, a seductive curve of full lips. He touched his fingers together, and suddenly a severely dressed, very sober man appeared.

"My lord, you are needed in the drawing room."

"Very well, Jeffries. Please fetch Mr. Rutherford's books for Miss Chase before she leaves."

Miranda spared a half-second look at the man with the name she had cursed. He didn't even look her way before nodding and melting back into the shadows. Did everyone in this house live in them?

"Good afternoon, Miss Chase." The viscount began to stride away from her.

"Wait." She hurried after him. "I'm not coming here tomorrow. You have your books from the store. Finally.

I'll be on my way. I'm sure that you have someone quite competent to help you."

"But you are the most competent person I know," he said as he kept walking. "I'm sure it will be a marvelous fit. I will pay well, of course."

"You don't know me. And this isn't about payment."

"No? Twenty pounds a week is not enough? Shall I increase it to fifty?"

"Twenty p— . . . fifty p—" she sputtered. "Are you mad?"

He turned a corner. "My brother delights in telling me so."

"I can't possibly—"

He stopped abruptly, turning, and steadied her as she nearly ran into his chest.

"No?" He touched her gloved hand. His fingers were ungloved again today, not the same class breach of protocol here in his own home. It was a fleeting touch. Almost as if it were accidental.

Her verbal sputtering died abruptly and her blood took up its cause, her skin a thin barrier to the heat suddenly searing beneath.

"Your uncle thought you might enjoy the task. I know I would enjoy it if you'd agree." His fingers brushed hers again as he tapped the book held tightly against her chest, forgotten in her flight after him. "Keep the text regardless. I know you will find my key. I'll see you tomorrow."

Another fleeting touch, then he pulled on leather gloves—produced from a pocket somewhere—turned on his heel, and disappeared into a room. She caught sight of a few faces and heard hazy chatter before a footman closed the door.

She stood mute, her fingers absently tracing the gifted book's carved ivory—embellished with what looked like molten gold casting beacons through the shadows. Closer inspection showed two figures entwined. An early instruction manual for medieval dances?

Or . . . or something else entirely?

Like Pandora's box, rife with seduction, her fingers hovered to turn the page. To open a box that might leave her bereft in the end. With only hope to keep her going.

She traced the gilded lettering and turned the page.

Chapter 4

Secret #3: Pull forth or use the unexpected.
Create havoc and relish in the chaos. Put her off
guard even if she is on guard at the same time.
The Seven Secrets of Seduction

Her cheeks were still blazing hours later, the book tucked under first one dress, then two, then hidden as deep within the bowels of her cracked armoire as it was possible to go.

And still she could hear it softly crooning. Inviting her to uncover it once more and discover what else lay within.

No monk had created *that* illumination. Not something that contained such vivid descriptions and pictures. She hadn't even realized some of those things were *possible*.

Come. Open me.

Perhaps if she were to stand the armoire on *top* of it, it would muffle the call.

Did a woman really . . . really *do* that type of thing to a man? And he in return? Was that what *The Seven*

Secrets of Seduction had truly meant by kneeling to pay one's tribute? She'd always thought it was a veiled reference to worshipping beauty or nature or some such thing.

Not an allusion to how one might *physically* pay tribute. The image of it rose in her mind, the viscount's dark eyes looking down at her in concupiscence. She hadn't even known what the word "concupiscence" *meant*, had never even *seen* the word, until the illumination had *shown* her.

To imagine the ardent desire searing from his eyes. At her.

She shot off her bed, tripping on her flimsy rug and catching the edge of her dented oak dressing table just in time to save herself from a face-first landing on the frigid boards.

She laughed nervously. She'd almost ended up on her knees anyway. But without the flesh-and-blood devil looming above her.

Her bare feet shuffled on the rug bunched beneath and finally found purchase on the cold-split boards, tucking her toes under to grip better. For once the cold did nothing to sap the heat from her skin.

She quickly tucked her feet into her sturdy work slippers and threw on the heavy, unattractive night robe she'd long ago borrowed from her father. She'd never cared before that it was so bulky and, well, ugly. It functioned well, it was warm, and in the dead of a cold London night, that was all that mattered.

Until one saw women in diaphanous gowns, split down the middle, enticing their prey on the other side of the page.

She tied the strap of her robe with suddenly clumsy fingers. The ink-stained, chapped edges of them gripped the heavy layered cotton and pulled. What was wrong with her?

She quickly walked down to the kitchen to pour herself some milk and tea. A nighttime indulgence she was feeling in need of at the moment. A light sifted from underneath the door of the attached work office down the narrow hall. Her uncle was still awake then.

She'd seen payment for "library restructuring" on the ledgers, so the viscount had been serious when he'd said that her uncle had already approved her help, or, well, *someone's* help at least, but she hadn't been able to speak to her uncle yet as he'd been out late at a tradesman's meeting.

His office door was closed. Should she seek him out? There was something about asking him that would make it all the more real instead of a continued illusion. Perhaps he would even stop her from going the next day, having not agreed to the plan after all—a scheme devised by the viscount instead.

Why she was questioning *whether* she should ask her uncle was the real question.

She wandered over slowly and paused outside the door. She could hear the scritch of her uncle's pen. It would take but a knock on the door and a quick word to take care of the entire question. He might say that he planned to send Peter. He might stop her from going. Forbid her from it.

And if he didn't, if he was just the absentminded man she had grown quite fond of in the past two years, then she could tell him that it was highly improper for her to go. Convince him to send one of the others instead.

Her feet didn't move. Her hands stayed at her sides. The light filtered through the bottom of the door, undimmed.

Somewhere inside her she knew that it would have to be her choice. Her uncle had already sent her to return the books without a thought to any proprieties being violated. What difference would her going to work on the viscount's library make in his mind? She would simply be another servant for a time.

She looked at her chapped hands. And why would she think otherwise, anyway? What sort of perverse spell had the viscount cast? Or cruel joke did he play? To make her Malvolio? To seduce her into wearing yellow stockings and cross garters?

But to feel his hands upon her, caressing *her* stockings, those fleeting touches turned into more . . .

She shivered, the chill of the night finally catching up and sifting under the hem of the robe, under her equally unattractive, worn nightgown. Icy tendrils clawing her calves.

She took a step back, then another. She would go. The viscount's words had held the ring of truth. She would worry about any decision she needed to make another day. There was always tomorrow to decide.

She was still chewing her lip the next morning as she approached the kitchen door to the grand house once more.

One of the maids from the day before, the one with the poor balance, was digging in a vegetable garden to the side with another servant. She looked up as Miranda drew closer.

"Cor, you are the girl from the bookshop."

Miranda switched her weight to her other foot as the second servant, a middle-aged woman also looked up. "I am from a bookshop, yes."

"What you doing back here?"

Miranda shifted her weight again, uncomfortable at the echo of the question in her own mind. "I am helping to organize the library."

"Cor, girl, I know why you are here. What you doing *back* here instead of up front?" The maid motioned down the drive.

"This is the entrance," Miranda said, her discomfort rising.

"For us, not you. No need for traipsing the sweaty kitchens."

"I was hired—"

"Girl, don't care what you think your purpose is, your entrance is up front. Cook'll have my tail."

"Again," she thought she heard the other maid mutter.

"I don't think you understand—"

The maid shrugged. "I know you are supposed to go to the front." She pointed. The other woman nodded sharply.

Miranda considered her options but bowed to the command and turned around. She'd likely be sternly put in her place up front, but there was something more unsettling about barreling past the two servants, who were eyeing her so curiously.

She trod back down the long drive and turned the corner to see Jeffries in the doorway, imperiously beckoning her inside as if she were an expected guest instead of a laborer.

She tripped over a stone but righted herself. She turned behind her, sure that there must be someone there to whom he was motioning; but only two gardeners strode the path, neither of whom were looking at the butler. She turned back to the entrance, and once again the butler beckoned her forth.

It was as if the news of her arrival had reached the front of the house before she had.

"Good afternoon, Miss Chase. May I take your coat?" She was a little stunned as she shed the garment, barely remembering her manners.

"Yes, please. Thank you, Mr. Jeffries."

"Shall I show you to the library?"

She stared at him. A head butler didn't "show" servants. At most an underbutler might direct a new hire on where to go, but Miranda had expected to be assigned a random housemaid, or the housekeeper, if the latter felt her authority needed to be established over the new girl.

Then again, a viscount wouldn't pick up a package of books from a store. Who knew what sort of crazed household they ran.

"I— That would be nice, thank you." She remembered the way but knew better than to say so. Her mother had drilled protocol into her, hoping that she might follow in her footsteps one day. The ladies who ran the academy had been disappointed when she had not.

"This way." He bowed, but it was obvious from his tight manner that he did not approve of her. She opened her mouth to say, "I'm only here to organize the library," but that would sound silly beyond measure.

Two maids they passed in the hall stopped what they were doing to watch her—one surreptitiously and the other quite openly. The glances were repeated throughout the house.

If there were ever a day when she felt quite as on display and out of belonging as today, she wasn't sure she had lived it yet. She hadn't realized what a relief it was sometimes to blend into the woodwork.

They reached the library, finally, and she nearly

gave in to the urge to run inside and firmly close the door behind her.

"A lunch tray will be brought for you."

"Oh, no, I can walk to the—"

Jeffries held up his hand. "No need to trouble yourself, Miss Chase. We will be happy to bring a tray to you. Is there anything else you require?"

She shook her head, nothing springing to mind. She couldn't think when she was this on edge.

"Then good day, Miss Chase." He bowed, another tight movement. "Please ring should you require anything."

The movement and the way he said it stated that he very likely expected her to do so. Repeatedly.

It spoke to the types of guests they had entertained in the past. What that said for her she didn't know.

Clipped footfalls faded into the silence of the hallway. Servants were so skilled at moderating their movements to being as quiet as possible in the common areas and halls. Not disturbing their masters. Only the back rooms and kitchens would have a jubilant air. Something that proclaimed them as individual spirits.

Sometimes she wished she could return to the country but not be remembered as the daughter of a strict, well-respected academic, expected to be proper at all times. To go somewhere where all she had to do was enjoy the pleasant diversions of village life. Live in her books and find solace in the forests.

But some forests weren't made of trees. She looked around the large, airy room choked by the stacks of towering books. The room would look beyond marvelous when reassembled. She walked through the plugged space, around the stacks, touching a binding here, picking up a copy there. She couldn't believe that the entire shelf space was bare. Whatever had occurred in the viscount's mind to cause him to remove every copy, then shuffle them all together?

Such random thinking, the Quality possessed. Do what is on the forefront of the mind and leave someone else to clean it up. She supposed that was what came of having manors full of money. Things like time and effort didn't even enter into the equation.

She cursed the crazy temptation that had lodged within her, enticing her here once more.

She stroked a copy of the *Aeneid*. The treat of discovering all of the treasures within was enticing by itself, though the actual task of organizing them might as well have been given to Psyche by Aphrodite herself.

But the other reason for coming . . . a purely flesh-and-blood reason . . . she shook her head and deliberately focused on the Herculean task before her. She lifted the book, sighed, and dropped into a chair located in the middle of the hurricane.

It would take a week just to partially sort through them and discern which categories to use and where, depending on the breadth of the subjects. Of course, she could easily organize the books into alphabetical categories as they did in the store. Though some of the grand houses preferred a straight alphabetical listing. And some went by merit. Or by the sizes of the volumes, as someone had done in the viscount's study below—maybe by the viscount himself.

She snorted at the last.

"If it is too big a task . . ."

She jerked to see the viscount silhouetted in the doorway, hands in his dark pockets, brow raised. An invitation or challenge in the way he stood.

She straightened in her chair, her heart suddenly

lodged and thumping in her throat. "I was just pondering how to begin." She gripped the book in her hand, trying to calm her nerves. She had half expected, *anticipated,* him to appear based on the previous days' conversations, but it was still a shock.

Like something exquisitely formed from the inky letters and drawings of the books and papers she read, the stark black-and-white character stepping forth from the page and onto the Aubusson rug hugging the floor at the room's entrance.

"Did you want them organized in a certain sequence?" she blurted in a rush of words trying to corral her thoughts. "Is there a way you'd prefer?"

He sauntered into the room, one hand caressing the crown of a stack as he read the words written on a spine. "What care have I? Other than for them to be in good order."

She tried to keep the jumpiness in her fingers from showing. "For someone with so many books and such desire to obtain new copies, you seem awfully ambivalent about them."

"I know their power and impact. It is all about perception, is it not, Miss Chase?"

She studied him. "I like to think it is about content, Lord Downing. But perception does lay a gloss on the surface. A finger must but swirl beneath."

He breached the chasm between them and sank onto the arm of the chair next to hers. Far too close. Looming next to her, over her. The only saving grace was that he was perched on the arm farthest from her.

"Then what do you do with it?" His lips moved in a beautiful fashion. Such a contrast to the starkness he at times projected.

She somehow managed to answer him, the automatic

response forming. "I organize it, of course."

A faint smile curled his mouth, and a vague buzzing tickled her senses as she watched his beautiful lips part, then come together. "So literal, yet again."

To adventure into the figurative meanings of his words was where the inherent danger resided. The insidious echo of a *soon* sounded in her mind. To feel those assuredly warm and capable lips upon her.

No. Best to start out as she wished, *needed*, to continue when it came to the viscount.

"I find plain speaking less confusing," she said.

"And yet are you not the one who likes to think that there is underlying meaning to seductive words and silly guides? That is nothing, if not figurative."

She tried to shake off the heavy feeling that had descended. She focused on his eyes instead. Stygian portals and mercurial darkness. "Books allow readers to determine what they wish. People often aren't quite as forgiving if you don't read or see exactly what they wish you to."

He shifted on the chair arm, looking up at the bare shelves. Something shifted in his eyes as they caught the stacks. "So where will we begin?"

"'We'? Begin what?"

"With the books." His dark eyes connected back with hers. "What else could I mean?"

With the way he said it and the look in his eyes, it was obvious that he meant something quite different.

"I am fine on my own."

His eyes traveled her face, studying her, leaning just an extra inch toward her, urging her to pull forward too. "No one is fine on his own. People just say they are."

"I assure you that I am quite content."

He touched the edge of the chair. A studied gesture. "Contentedness is not happiness."

"I like to think that contentedness is synonymous."

The intensity of his gaze increased. "Which is why you beg to be transformed."

Miranda tried to stay her breathing and think of Georgette instead, who thought the same. "Perhaps you would care to meet a friend of mine? She would be quite willing to be transformed."

"No. I am quite satisfied with my choice of you."

She swallowed, searching for anything that might allow her to escape from the intensity of his gaze. "Your lordship, forgive my bluntness, but don't you have other activities requiring your time?"

And where were his servants? Silent or not, servants were always about in grand houses. Even in the presence of their masters, they melted into the shadows, ever ready. But she hadn't seen hide nor hair of one—even in the hall door—since he'd entered.

"I veritably survive on your bluntness, my dear. And I can hardly leave you in here on your own."

She stared at him, uncomprehending. She was quite used to blending into the shadows herself and not being noticed. She was akin to his staff after all, on par with their status. When she was on deliveries—or even when she had helped at the academy—she had learned how to be neither seen nor heard.

"You need my help," he said.

"I do not." She didn't know that she would survive any kind of help he might give.

"I know just the trick too." He slid from the arm into the belly of the chair. Like a country boy on a haystack rather than a lord in his manor. He reached out a hand and pulled hers to him.

She stared at him, caught. Long fingers, ungloved, stroked down her sleeve, to the frill at the edges, then over her lilac glove. Her breath caught as one finger dipped into the bowl of her palm and pulled.

His lips curved as his eyes held hers. He was so close. Uncomfortably close, leaning across the chair next to her, chairs she would have pulled apart if she'd had any thought that someone else might sit there.

He pulled and she leaned forward just a bit, following the pull, unable to stop herself from it as his dark gaze bewitched her. Using some masculine magic—a sailor's call to a siren, instead of the other way around.

He smiled and held the spell a second longer before leaning back just the slightest bit, lifting weight from her palm. Her lips parted on their own. This is what it was like to fall under a spell then, she realized. To even feel the imagining beneath one's skin.

His eyes dropped. "The *Aeneid*. Alphabetizing by title?"

It took her a second to realize that he had just removed a book from her hand. A book she'd forgotten she was holding.

"I— No. Yes. That is—"

He raised a brow.

She snatched the book back. "You are trying to lure me."

"Lure you?"

"Yes." She hugged the book to her chest. "Stop it."

"I don't know of what you speak."

"Sirens."

"I think you have the wrong book." He leaned back and knocked the top portion of a stack down with a flick of his wrist, somehow keeping the bottom half stable. The twenty or so books on top fell in an avalanche, toppling the stack next to it and threatening the one after, crashing to the floor in awkward heaps, set adrift on a sea of pages.

She half rose. "Your lordship!"

He ignored her cry and idly flicked another book off the top of the stack, letting it crash with the others. He picked up the next one, surveyed the cover, then offered it. She took it without thought, glancing down.

"The *Odyssey*?"

He tapped the cover twice, the tremors vibrating up the book and through her fingers.

"Sirens."

She stared at the cover, then up at him. "Do you do it to everyone?"

"Do what? Offer a book?" But his lazy posture belied a coiled thread, like the core of a willow when it was anticipating a wind.

"Try to seduce them?"

He relaxed into his chair, an odd reaction. She would think a person challenged abruptly would tense. "Is that what you think I am doing? Seducing you?"

It was ludicrous, of course. Everything about it ridiculous. A viscount with means and attraction—an overly virile presence. And she a lowly bookworm with little of either. Yet there was something bone deep within her that stated it the truth. Something even beyond the book buried in her room—the licentious text he had given her.

"Yes. I do."

He smiled. A feline smile full of nocturnal secrets. "Why, Miranda. I'm shocked."

"You are hardly shocked, my lord. I think you highly amused."

His smile grew languid. "I am at that."

His amusement vied with some distinctly male satisfaction. And there was almost a *fondness* there that she didn't understand.

"You consider me some sort of challenge?"

"I consider you the answer to a question that resides in my very soul." His eyes held hers, an intensity there that she didn't understand.

A knock sounded at the door. The viscount didn't so much as glance away.

He waved in the direction of the door without looking, but she glanced over to see Jeffries bow and disappear back through. She turned back to see the viscount still watching her.

"I think you are needed," she said. She needed him to leave. Needed him to get out and stop putting strange, illicit thoughts in her head.

"And here I thought it would take far longer for you to admit to it."

"By your *staff*."

"Only?"

"Yes," she said firmly, squishing down any thoughts to the contrary.

"Pity."

He continued to watch her, one finger tapping the arm of the chair in thought.

"Lord Downing? I'll think the saying that madness runs in the wealthy is true if you continue to sit there and stare at me like that."

She half expected him to take offense, but instead he simply smiled. "Shall we initiate a challenge?"

"What? No," she said quickly, automatically sensing danger.

"You don't even know what I was going to suggest."

"I'm sure that it would be to my disadvantage. Knowing what I do of you from the papers."

His eyes tightened momentarily. "Ah, an even greater incentive then. I duly need to be brought to heel, don't you agree?"

She stared at him.

"Ever since I heard you nattering on about looking beneath the surface, I've been slightly adrift." He tilted his head toward her. "You will show me what you mean. *If* you can."

"What I mean?"

"Try to convince me that the Serpentine is not boring. That the theater is not full of the same idiotic play. That the breeze in late spring shows a whisper of the gods."

She stared at him. That last bit was almost . . . poetic. She touched the cover of the *Odyssey*. "I am not the one you should be asking. That is what I said about Eleutherios's work."

"Fine. We'll use that." His lips curved. "Use that rattle-pate guide to show me all of these strange and wonderful new things."

There had to be a catch somewhere. "And?"

"And I'll use it to seduce you."

She continued to stare at him, as if he had rendered her incapable of movement, frozen her with a Medusan strike.

His lips curved fully, and he raised a brow. "You

are the one who initiated the challenge, in truth. In your bookshop."

"I— I did nothing of the kind."

"Oh, you certainly did. Besides, there is much for you to gain by accepting. If you succeed . . ." He drew his finger along the arm of the chair. "I may be able to find a copy of *The Bengal*. And perhaps a cuff designed by Tersine."

She disregarded the outrageous offer of diamonds and focused on the more pertinent piece of the bribe. *The Bengal*? Her uncle would push her into a hack and direct her to show the viscount *whatever* he wanted if she could obtain a copy. He would sit on top of the carriage and call out directions to wherever they needed to go. And her uncle disliked traveling by carriage only slightly less than she did.

She could see by the viscount's face that he was well aware of her uncle's desire. But she could barely breathe seated next to the man now. And she was to offer herself up as a conquest?

"How would you measure my success?" Her mouth moved without the express permission of the rational part of her mind. Something else, her own desire perhaps, curled around, covering her good sense like a tendril of ivy creeping over stone.

"Well, that is dependent on you. Me? I'll be working to have *you* whispering to the gods." He smiled. Slowly. Fully. All lovely lips and chiseled features. "We'll see who *bends* first."

It felt as if her heart would beat clear of her chest at any moment.

"You are going to seduce—" She cleared her throat forcefully. "*Try* to seduce me?"

"I thought I had been quite direct on the point."

"But that is ridiculous."

"You don't care for people saying what they mean?"

"The notion of your *seducing me* is ridiculous."

"I might take that as a blow to my confidence if I had any concept of humility." The look in his eyes, full of the lazy strength he always projected, said that he was deliberately misinterpreting her words. "I might fail." He waved a hand. "Then you will be all the richer."

"I, I can't."

"You don't want the copy of *The Bengal*? I'll tell you what. I will give it to you just for agreeing and seeing the challenge through for a week. And the cuff too. I've heard all the ladies desire one."

Her uncle would kill her for refusing. But everything about the proposal and the silken way he uttered the seemingly casual words screamed, "*Danger! Crumbling cliff ahead!*"

She swallowed. "Where would I wear such a piece?"

"Wherever you wish."

She stared at him. She'd just mosey on down to the market with a fortune in diamonds dripping from her wrist.

"No hidden strings attached as long as you accept the challenge. Just one measly week."

When she continued to stay silent, he leaned toward her with an intensity she couldn't define. "Do it for me," his husky voice wrapped around her. "Try and teach me what you see."

The syllables, the heat, caressed her skin, looking for ways to lock her inside.

"Very well."

Had that been her breathless voice accepting?

He smiled, and her heart thumped in her chest. "Excellent. I can't tell you how pleased that makes me."

He leaned toward her another few inches. She remained frozen in place as his lips grazed her ear. "I promise that I will make the bending very pleasant."

Each word curled inward. Her chest felt unexpectedly heavy—lifting and straining against her dress, which suddenly felt one size too small. His cheek brushed hers as he slid back, the edge of his mouth touched the edge of hers. Her eyes closed of their own will. A corner of her stone rationality crumbled as she wondered what being kissed truly felt like. Would it be like the wonder of finding a new, beloved book? Or the awe of seeing fireworks lighting the sky?

She felt the edge of his mouth curl. "Such temptation that I can't resist," he whispered, the words barely audible above the pounding of her blood, around the dampened perception of everything else in the room that wasn't him.

If he but turned a hair to the left. If she but turned one to the right . . .

He rose suddenly, a swish of warm skin, then cold air. "Shall I send some men to help you?"

She let out her breath, eyes jerking open to blindly stare at the books littering the floor. Had she just accepted a challenge to be seduced by one of the most notorious men in the land? And then almost literally caved within the prologue of the contest?

"I believe I might need to reorganize first," she said as well as she could manage. Reorganize, in both body and mind.

"Ah, I must make up for my carelessness with the stacks. I've caused you extra work." The deliberate misinterpretation of her words struck her again, even through the haze. Signaling the games he might play to win.

Though there was something off in the tones of his voice. As if he hadn't been entirely unaffected by what had just occurred. "I'll return at two."

"What? No," she said quickly, looking up.

"I insist." He dragged a finger across the back of the chair as he walked backward toward the door. "I am responsible for the chaos after all." His lips curved as if there were multiple meanings to his statement. "Until we meet again, Miss Chase."

He turned and sauntered out, and she was left to stare in his wake, feeling more like she had been sucked down and pummeled by Charybdis rather than dashed against a rock.

Had she truly accepted his mad challenge? And what on earth would she do with it?

She took in the greater mess on the floor that he had created. Swirling in the vortex. And she, floundering without a paddle.

She pulled over a chair, stepped on it, reached up, and shakily pulled the first book off a towering stack. Work. She could work. She'd think about what she had done—and what she would do—later. Later, when the essence of the man wasn't still clinging to the air around her.

Thankfully, the stack stayed soundly in place, even with the jumbled spines jutting this way and that and her suddenly clumsy fingers fumbling the leather. She grabbed the next three volumes as well and stepped down, thanking her long practice with library ladders for not making her already shaky limbs pitch her to the floor in a tangle of skirts.

A French tutorial, a domestic household guide, a Greek classic, and a religious tome stared back at her. How in the world had these books been arranged? She looked around the room. She could almost believe that someone had shuffled them up on purpose.

But that would be silly.

She looked back at her unsteady hands.

Silly.

She shook her head, and her eyes unwillingly sought the clock. It was not yet ten. There were at least three hours to go before she needed to recheck.

She lasted three more trips up the chair before she looked again. Ten fifteen. She'd likely expire before the two o'clock hands wound around for the sheer way her heart was beating. She didn't think it was supposed to be pounding so erratically.

She deliberately turned away from the clock and set the book in her hands down with a thump.

It was a tortuous first thirty minutes, but then the rest of the morning picked up pace as she concentrated on her task. Mrs. Humphries, the housekeeper, brought her a tray of food and politely inquired as to whether Miranda needed assistance. She gratefully accepted, and a few men and women rotated in and out, in shifts, doing as she directed. Watching her when they thought she wasn't looking.

The food was perfect. The spread of fruit, cheese, and bread allowed her to graze while she worked. She heard the empty tray being moved near the door. She looked up to see that the two servants who had been standing near, helping her, had slipped away.

She projected around the stack of books in front of her, "Thank you."

"Already thanking me, and I just arrived." The husky voice, once more steady and confident, wrapped around the stack like the fine stockings that clung to the illumination hidden in her armoire. "I could become used to your lips draped around those syllables. Shall we see what else they might beautifully adorn?"

Chapter 5

Dear Mr. Pitts,

*A strange new acquaintance has me asking all
sorts of questions of myself. Perhaps you can
help me straighten my thoughts. Why would a
man pretend interest?*

From the pen of Miranda Chase

Her pulse picked up speed when the viscount appeared, freshly changed but still maintaining the
same style of stark clothing and insouciant regard. He
raised a brow at the books circling her, spread out in all
directions. "Alas, I see you have other tasks at hand."

But all she continued to picture were draping lips
and his fingers buried in her unbound hair. She tried to
curse the illumination, curse her broken armoire, but
the image just overrode everything else in her mind.

She opened her mouth, but nothing emerged for a
second. "It will take me more than a few days, my lord."
She looked down, trying to think instead of allowing
the spreading wings in her stomach to control her
fuzzy thoughts. *Where was everyone?* There had been

people in and out all day. "I hope your pocketbook will survive."

"I will manage somehow."

But would she? "I should hope so. As you said, you have created this mess." She motioned to the books on the floor.

"One of my many talents." He sank into a chair, long legs crossed before him. "I am at your disposal. Feel free to use me well." His mouth quirked.

She swallowed, trying to dispel the image of how he could be used according to the text in her armoire—especially splayed back like that.

With all of these images and thoughts, a challenge was hardly even necessary. She needed to get herself together. To not fail all of womankind by simply succumbing like a hapless dove. "That is unnecessary. Your staff is quite helpful. And surely you have some engagement to attend?"

"My staff is suddenly completely occupied. And I cleared my afternoon." He spread his arms. "Just for you."

She tried to calm the sudden rush of emotions. Exhilaration, fear. *Of herself.* But then all she needed to do was be patient. He would lose interest soon. It didn't matter that he had expressly given her that illumination. She had read all about him. Knew that he was quick to chase and quicker to find new, more lively game.

As long as she stayed smart, she could have a bit of fun—for when he wasn't fuzzing up her head, she had a feeling the viscount would amuse her greatly. And she could seduce him to the writings of Eleutherios.

She just had to prevent the loss of herself in the process.

"I am going to be busy organizing for the rest of

the afternoon. Perhaps you would like to rethink your challenge and come to your senses tomorrow?" she quipped.

"Oh, this is the clearest my senses have been in a long time, Miranda." He smirked and slouched farther into the chair. "And there will be no changing my mind."

"You must be quite bored, your lordship."

He tilted his head. "I don't think you quite comprehend how much so."

Well, at least he was honest.

"But then I met you," he said.

Or not. "I hardly think myself so witty or pretty to have captured the notorious Viscount Downing's attention."

He smiled. "Then I have all of the advantage, do I not?"

She didn't know how to respond to that.

He motioned for her to continue her task. "When you need help, just say the word."

She looked at him doubtfully, then bent and lifted the first five books from one of her piles. She trudged over to the set of shelves on the farthest left and laid them on top.

She returned and grabbed the next five, repeating the action.

"A most unique way to organize a library," he said, lounging back and tapping his chest as he gazed at the haphazard vertical stacking. "Taking the volumes on the floor and putting them in the same position on the shelves. Makes them art then, I suppose."

She spared him a quick glare as she took another five. "You are wickedly droll, Lord Downing. However do you survive with such wit at your disposal?"

He smiled. "It is most troublesome."

She began to stack the next shelf and received a mocking whistle in reply.

"Already beginning anew?" he tsked.

She decided to ignore him and continued her trek. Back and forth. Setting up the shelves so that each category would have a space. Just enough to get the books into the right areas, then she could reorganize each section individually. It required more trips this way, doubly so because she was doing it herself, but her mind was better able to progress by having smaller concrete tasks.

It would also allow her to weed out duplicates. She had already found multiple copies of particular titles spread between piles.

She spared a quick glance to see the viscount still sitting in the chair, one leg hooked over the arm, swinging. He looked as if he would be perfectly happy to observe her all afternoon. She wondered what exactly he *did* during the days usually. She had always thought that in between deciding the fate of peons like her and attending galas, the wealthy had to do *something*. She didn't quite have the gall to ask yet. However, she was rapidly working up to it with each new quip from the bowels of his plush chair.

"How exactly are you organizing?" he asked.

"I am organizing by subject according to the breadth of each, then I will go by alphabet."

"Wise."

Something about the way he said it made her cross her arms. "You don't agree."

"I didn't say that."

"You implied it."

"By saying it was wise? Doesn't that imply that I approved?"

"It was how you said it."

"For someone who says she prefers to read books instead of determine the meaning in someone's spoken words, you seem awfully determined to do the latter."

"For someone who says he has no wish to organize his library, you seem awfully keen to."

"I'm not."

She pointedly stared at him, spread out in the chair, verbally nipping at her. The threads of heightened irritation, amusement, and awareness combined once more.

"I never said I didn't want to watch *you* do it."

"I see." She didn't see in the slightest.

He tapped the cover of a volume on top of a short stack near him. "Where will you bury this?"

She leaned over to check the title. "All things religious, ecclesiastical, or mystical go to the stacks on the right. It is the largest section in our store, most printed books fall into that category, but I have a feeling from these first stacks that it will be dwarfed by your—or your benefactor's—*taste* for other things. So I will keep it to the right for the moment."

He kept swinging his infernal leg, a hook of his brow saying more than any words.

She walked over and took the book from him. "I don't buy your line, by the way. I can see you frown or nod approvingly depending on where I put things."

"Nodding? I haven't moved."

She waved her hand. "It's in the very air around you."

"I'm delighted you are paying attention enough to me to notice."

"Hard not to," she muttered.

"What was that?"

She cleared her throat. "You are paying me to do a good job, I assume. I am only aiming to please."

"I'm happy to hear it." He nearly purred.

She hid behind a nice tall stack until she had reasonable command of her color. She poked her head out.

"You want to be in control of what goes on your shelves, even if you won't admit it. Why bring me inside and let me loose as I please—irritating quips and outrageous challenges from you notwithstanding?"

He cocked his head so it was resting against his shoulder, lazily regarding her. "Because I want to trap you here and it seemed a flawless way to do so."

She stilled, then wiped her free, sweaty palm against her skirt. "I'd say you've succeeded in your trap."

Even her uncle would force her to stay, with the promise of the book. She was truly trapped.

She narrowed her eyes. But that was a weak way of thinking. The voice of Mr. Pitts's pen echoed in her head that she shouldn't need an excuse to stay or feel without recourse. She should make the decision herself to flirt with the trap and say to hell with anyone who disagreed.

The viscount watched her as if trying to discern what she was thinking. "What will you do?"

And hadn't she decided to come anyway without speaking with her uncle? Made the decision herself?

She picked up a few volumes in the conduct, deportment, and etiquette stack and walked to the right, putting them on a shelf that would be easy to reach once everything was cleared away but was harder at the moment, surrounded by all the confusion. "I will continue as I have started," she said without looking at him.

She turned around to see him standing directly

behind her, soundlessly moving, a stack in his hand. "Then so will I." He held them out to her, and she took them wordlessly. She watched him a moment longer, trying to read whatever was written there in his dark, mysterious eyes.

Those eyes haunted her dreams all night long. The shadowy figure of her dreams taking on depth. His motions as he hovered above her, clasped her to him, touched her in all sorts of sinful ways.

And then his lips touched hers with a reverence that caused her to wake. To pant in bed and not return to sleep for a long, long time.

The echo of real lips that promised everything.

The next day she was still wondering what she had gotten into, but in a much more intense way. Her blood thrummed. The dreams bleeding into day.

"Molière is hardly a good fit there," he said, leaning against the wall as she ascended the stepladder. "Closer to Swift."

She put one hand against the shelf wall to steady herself, the book in her other hand pressed against the edge of the shelf. She pursed her lips down at him.

He smiled lazily. "I'm simply availing you of my knowledge. It's extensive."

"It's annoying."

A part of her had long been frozen mute in abject horror that she was speaking to a viscount this way. Her tongue kept forgetting that he was a lord and kept reverting to the ease with which she corresponded. And as he needled her further, something in his eyes seemed all the more satisfied with each exchange.

Georgette would be gleeful.

"I think you just don't like to admit that I am right. It's acceptable to give in to it, Miranda." His voice took on a deeper tone and curled around the space. "I promise to take good care of everything."

She jerked at the echo of her dream. At his lips promising that he would take good care of her wants. Her needs. Her desires.

Her everything.

The images from the illumination rose again, and she could nearly feel his fingers caressing her scalp, his lips on hers.

The book buckled against the shelf, and she pitched forward, then overcorrected and lost her footing. She made a mad grab for a piece of protruding wood, but only caught the edges of the spines already placed there. The books teetered on the ledge, then fell as she slipped. She watched them as if they'd somehow fallen into a vat of half-solid lard, sinking slowly through the air above her.

Stupid books. Stupid dreams. Stupid viscount.

Two warm arms caught her and pressed her back into a solid chest. She could feel the heat of his breath in her hair. Feel the strength of his enveloping arms. Hear the thump of her own heartbeat as it echoed the books falling to the ground.

"Vanilla soap?" The husky edge of his voice was ten times more potent at this close range, whispered right below the lobe of her ear. "It suits you deliciously."

Take a bite. Have a taste. Her neck tilted just an inch in an unconscious invitation.

The heat of him drew closer. His lips brushed the edge of her throat beneath her ear, and she could *feel* his lips curve as a satisfied, husky laugh of a sound tickled and cleared the path.

A connection of lips to skin that would make any imaginings pale. Imaginings that went far deeper than the differences between them socially and financially.

It was hard to think as his mouth stole the very air touching her skin. The difference between a viscount and a girl who worked in a dusty bookshop. Or between a man bent on world domination, one seduction at a time according to the papers, and a woman who couldn't discover the nerve to leave the path of least resistance.

A challenge to see if he could seduce her? It hardly seemed an even minor contest at the moment.

She tried to push away from him, from her own lusty thoughts, and ended up half-turned in his arms. His arms loosened fractionally to let her pull away.

She completed the spin, her breast sliding against the inside of his elbow, crooked perfectly. She panicked again, her jerky motion causing her to slip on one of the fallen volumes. His arms immediately tightened again to save her a second fall.

Unfortunately, he took a step back, and along with her frantic movements, he too slipped on a triangled spine. He swore as he fell back, his arms taking her with him, catching another two stacks with a violent clatter.

She fell atop him with a whoosh of breath, their faces in perfect alignment for a fraction of a second, her legs straddling his, her skirts cloaking the connections beneath from view but not from the skin on the inside of her calves as they hugged his expensive trousers and long, powerful legs. His eyes darkened, his arm tightened.

And he rolled on top of her, the blood pumping in her ears turned into a crashing avalanche of sound.

Something heavy clipped both ankles and her out-stretched wrists, pinning her in place, the weight of him on top of her. Everything seemed to jolt and freeze as she could feel every place on her body where his connected, her entire body spread and chained for him.

His eyes held hers, dark and hot.

Nothing for it but to succumb. A lazy, languid feeling stole down her limbs, mixing with the anxiety and anticipation.

Movement caught her gaze, and she watched a book teetering on his head slip from its perch and fall to the floor, just missing her shoulder.

"Organizing books is a much more perilous diversion than I'd thought," he said in his husky, edged voice, warm and dangerous. He moved slightly, shaking off another volume that had rained down upon his back—a consequence of upsetting the stacks. The movements sent shocks of energy through her as their connections pushed and pulled against each other.

"But equally rife with opportunity." He gazed at her lips. "Do you surrender?"

"Surrender to what?" It was as if she couldn't catch her breath.

"To whom."

"To whom?" The words barely formed on her tongue, heavy and low.

He smiled, a long slow pull of lips, and leaned down. A hint of bergamot combined with the smell of the books surrounding them, spines triangled, pages fanned apart, allowing the scent of fresh bindings and musty parchment to linger.

She licked suddenly dry lips, only an inch from his. "What are you doing, my lord?" A rational question surfacing from somewhere amidst the chaos.

His gaze traveled her face. "I'm embracing the beauty around me. Or under me, as it is. No need to go to the Serpentine if you have that lovely breeze already in your sights."

That he remembered their conversation so well from the first day was almost as alarming as the way her body automatically responded to the meaning of his words.

"I think you are taking me too literally." Was that her voice breaking on a low breath?

He shifted, and she heard another book slide from his hips. "First, I am not enjoying the underlying meaning of things, and now I'm being too literal? I think it a good thing I've challenged you to show me what I should be doing."

His face was so close. His lips mere breaths away. She could see each eyelash like a long spike waiting to spear her.

"I have no expertise to do so." But the temptation curled. Like a living, trapped thing that sought outlet.

And still he didn't move away. "You are one of the most vibrant women I've ever come across. And locked away behind your books—it just makes you that much more of a masterpiece waiting to be unlocked."

She swallowed, but the swelling of her veins would not recede. "You know nothing about me."

"Don't I?" His eyes caressed her face, unreadable, but hot. "I have wanted to know everything about you since the moment I saw you."

The heat rushing around her body filled her face as well. "I don't know why."

And she didn't. What sort of mad dream was this that he had noticed her? Was flirting with her? Ready to *inhale* her. That he had even taken notice of her enough to do so made the rest even more unbelievable. There wasn't a sane connection between it all.

Her thoughts felt as caged as her wrists and ankles beneath their paper and leather bindings. She shifted, trying to unpin her limbs.

"No?" He loosened his position, rising to his hands and knees, still looming over her like a hunter, still holding her in some sort of thrall. "I will work diligently to change that."

"Why?"

"Because I want to." He cocked his head. "And I do as I wish."

She needed to get away, to breathe and think. "So I've read."

His smile became humorless. "So devoted to the written word." He touched a book pinning her wrist. "Foolhardy to put your trust where it is easy to create falsehood. Don't believe all you read."

She smiled back tightly, unable to let the statement go. "I don't. But sometimes it is just the opposite. It can be far easier to spill the truth in an article or letter where you can be free."

"Oh? Those correspondents of yours—they spill their darkest secrets, do they? You believe everything they tell you?"

That partially answered her question as to how long he had been listening to her conversation with Georgette in the shop.

"I have no reason to doubt them yet."

"Lies from those closest to you are often the most numerous and paralyzing."

She narrowed her eyes and stayed silent.

"And your Eleutherios, hanging on word from him, aren't you? The rattle-pate old lecher."

She pushed at his chest suddenly and began extricating her legs from the books pinning them.

"Better to leave dreams behind and go forward with purpose." His voice was strangely intense. He moved to the side, shifting the settled avalanche of paper behind him.

She said nothing, pulling her legs out from under the fallen stacks. She had just gained purchase when her heel slipped on a binding. She again collapsed on her back, legs curled under his, looking up at him, skirts tangled in paper.

Damn books.

"I admire your capitulation." His smile was lazy again, the dark intensity replaced by a languidness that did odd things to her stomach.

"Lord Downing?"

"Yes?"

"Perhaps you might help me stand?"

"My back is quite sore from saving you from all of those heavy tomes. I'm not sure I should be doing hard labor. Maybe you'd better continue lying there, at ease. The view is quite lovely."

Her skin turned unwillingly warm again, her mind actively chalking up the entire situation to a lack of consciousness that must have taken her when they fell. Or perhaps she had fallen days ago, and this was all some strange imagining, an elaborate fantasy.

His eyes turned more amused, and he leaned over her again, his elbow propping him up at her side. "Yes, diligent work ahead indeed. Or perhaps you might just capitulate fully now, and we can move to more comfortable surroundings."

Her mouth opened, but nothing emerged.

The first two fingers of his hand formed an L at his

cheek and chin above his propped elbow as he gazed
upon her. "You have but to say the word. One small
concession to any lingering inhibitions. A simple surrender." His eyes caressed her face.

Men just didn't look at her like that. She didn't
know if her heart could survive if they did.

Or perhaps it was just this man.

"Lord Downing?"

"Yes?"

"Get off me."

"I'm unfortunately not on you." He waved a hand
to her free side. "You can move anytime. I'm merely
serving as an umbrella should more papered bricks
plot to bring about your doom."

"And I am saving you from my coshing you with
one as soon as I am free."

"Very well." He looked falsely beleaguered as he
rose. He held a hand to her, and she warily took it,
popping up and becoming free from the papers as he
pulled her perfectly to her feet.

"Tomorrow then," he said, not releasing her hand.
"Perhaps in the gardens in back of the house? I've
heard they are full of weeds and sprouting things. You
can tell me all about the wonders of them. Perhaps let
me discover for myself the path of a rose whispering
down your bare flesh?"

Flutters, promising and alarming, beat against her
midsection. "That is unnecessary."

He smiled slowly, gazing down at her from his
greater height. "Oh, it is very, very necessary. One
simple concession on your part, and we can even begin
tonight."

She was saved from answering by a cleared throat.
"Lord Downing?"

The viscount's hand tightened around hers, but his eyes didn't stray. Miranda looked over to see the butler in the doorway. She wondered how long he had been standing there, waiting.

Creases appeared around the viscount's eyes for a second before smoothing away. He replied without turning. Without taking his hand away from hers. "Tell them I will be there momentarily."

"Yes, my lord." The butler disappeared.

"Well, Miss Chase." He gave her a lazy smile. "I'll look forward to convincing you to surrender tomorrow then."

His fingers slid from hers, lingering at the tips before breaking free. "And I am quite confident in my ability to succeed."

Miranda chewed on a chapped nail, her gloves hanging on the rack upstairs, somehow the feel of his fingers permanently embedded within them, driving her mad. "Uncle, I can't return."

His head was buried in an open ledger, glasses perched perilously upon the end of his nose. "Return where?"

"To Viscount Downing's library."

He looked over the edge of his glasses. "Oh, right. That's where you were yesterday and today. Forgot you were starting." He looked to the window. "Must have told you about it in a less lucid moment, because I thought I'd gone and forgotten completely."

Miranda waved a hand, happy that she could sidestep entirely how she'd discovered it. "I can't return."

His eyes swung back. "Why not? I thought you'd like it. I'd do the task myself if I had the time."

She continued chewing, unable to stop herself. Her

mother would have been completely appalled. "It's not proper." What had escaped the box first? Greed? Sorrow? Surely it had been pure temptation. How had Pandora even managed to keep it closed as long as she had?

No, the answer was simply to bury the box and never return.

Her uncle blinked. "What's not proper about it? Not getting the promised payment for each week's work—that's not proper. The store coffers will be flush. Not getting the books he chooses to toss—that's not proper. Hinted that I'd get an original copy of *The Bengal*." His eyes glazed and moved to the right. "Not getting that—that would be improper."

Her uncle's coveted book. Within her grasp. All she had to do was put herself in harm's way for a week. A week of long, deliberate caresses and hot, lazy smiles.

"He gave me an illuminated manuscript."

"Eh?"

She froze, her nail tip half-removed between her teeth. "A simple one, far from valuable," she said quickly, removing the nail splinter. Stupid. She couldn't let him become curious enough to look at the actual book.

She laughed nervously as the images from it—not simple in the least—flashed behind her eyes. "But more importantly, I'm there *alone*." Obviously open to rife temptation in the basest of manners too.

He looked away from the spot on his personal book-shelf in the back office room, where he must already be imagining his promised book carefully nestled. His eyes were blank. Zero comprehension in their depths.

"Alone with no supervision," she stressed. Every servant melted into the ether when the viscount came into view, and she had no doubt that it would continue as such. Their disappearances had been entirely too deliberate.

The blank look continued. "You want supervision? He said he wanted just one worker. And I thought you hated Mr. Briggs working with you on the payment books." He pointed down.

"No! Yes! Not that kind of supervision." She spiraled her hands forward, willing him to understand without explicitly stating anything. "Thomas Briggs is . . . we don't work well together. When I say supervision, I mean proper supervision." Blank. "The viscount lives alone." Blank. "A bachelor."

"Well, can't blame the man for that." Her never-married uncle frowned. "I didn't realize you cared about—"

"Uncle! It is not proper. I'm not married." And obviously not as oblivious to temptation as she'd all but crowed about to Mr. Pitts.

"Course you aren't. Hope I'd be invited, if you were."

She stared at him and drummed her fingers again. The bell jingled.

"It's not *the thing*," she tried to reiterate, hoping he would get the message and save her from herself. "It's not proper."

"Proper?" His frown became more pronounced. "This isn't your mother's academy."

No, her mother's academy would have taken a wooden rod to her backside two days ago. And if they knew her thoughts now, they would lock her in a hole for a week.

She sighed. "But it is not quite *the thing* to be alone with a gentleman in his house."

"You are working, not gallivanting. Hardly improper."

"What's improper?" Georgette undid her fashionably large bonnet as she sailed into the back, Peter peeking behind her, around the corner of the entrance from the store proper, where he was manning the counter.

"I am cataloging a library. By myself," Miranda emphasized in her uncle's direction.

Georgette snorted. "Sorting and putting books on a shelf? Really, Miranda, if only it were improper to do such, I'd feel much better about the amount of time you focus on such things."

Miranda drummed her fingers against the table harder. "It is impossible to have a reasonable conversation with him."

And impossible to ignore him.

Georgette coughed delicately and gave her a nudge.

"Not my uncle, Georgette," she said exasperatedly. She turned back to her uncle. "Impossible, uncle, I tell you."

He pushed his completed papers into a messy pile. "What is impossible about it? I don't see the problem. The viscount is a busy man. He is not going to stop by to converse."

And that was just it. Even though they had conversed plenty, conversing did not seem to be particularly high on his list of *preferred* activities. And nor did her mind exactly shy away from thinking about those other activities when he was near. Which was why she needed to cull the temptation and remove the dessert from the feast. She barely knew what *fork* to use at such a table.

And why he would focus those energies on her was completely baffling.

Georgette's eyes widened at the word "viscount," then turned crafty. Miranda looked at her, spirits sinking at the gleam therein.

"You probably won't even see him," her uncle said. "Go, enjoy yourself, and make sure you scoop up every last treasure he lets slip. Like the illumination he gave you, simple as it might be. And you must have wanted it, since you took it."

Miranda blushed, mortification sifting beneath her skin at the mention even if he had no notion of what the pages truly contained.

"And especially watch for *The Bengal*." Her uncle returned to his active ledgers, adding and subtracting numbers, muttering beneath his breath.

"Yes, Miranda," Georgette said sternly, waving her to stand. "An awful shame to let that copy slip from your uncle."

Miranda was reasonably sure that Georgette had never even heard of the rare book. She sighed and resolutely stood.

"I'll just take Miranda up for a chat. I'm positive she will be right as rain to continue," Georgette said, bidding Miranda's uncle a good afternoon. He waved absently, head still buried.

"Well?" Georgette demanded, when they reached Miranda's room.

Miranda touched one glove clinging to the rack where they *should* have been drying. She needed to wash them but had gotten the basin full, then stared at it, gloves raised above the water. The basin still stood full, cold and untouched in the corner.

Like some silly schoolgirl. One in need of a strong rap to the knuckles.

She collapsed onto the top blanket on her bed, faded

roses intertwined with thorns depicted within. "I'm cataloging Lord Downing's library. Alone."

Georgette blinked, as if she hadn't truly believed it, then a slow smile worked along her mouth. "Oh, Miranda."

"Don't start, Georgette. Uncle thinks it is completely reasonable."

"Why shouldn't he? You're in a house full of servants. People just like you. You don't see any of the maids rolling up fierce that they are alone with the master? You don't see their beaus or husbands dueling the lords, do you? That's because there is an order to things, a structure. You are fitting perfectly into that order by helping the viscount with his moldy books."

Miranda wasn't sure that made her feel any better. In fact, she felt a mite more depressed.

"It is up to you to bend this to your will. This is the opportunity of a lifetime." Georgette's eyes turned dreamy. "To be Mrs. Q."

"Georgette—"

"You've always been fascinated by him, do not lie."

"I'm fascinated by a lot of people in the society pages. Like reading about characters in a story. They aren't *real*."

"They are real enough." Georgette's brows rose. "Or else you wouldn't be whining so."

Miranda sighed. "I am whining, aren't I."

Georgette patted her hand. "There, there. I like it when you whine. Makes me feel like the wise one for once."

Miranda smiled at her friend and squeezed her fingers.

"Now tell me what the real trouble is. Not this silly thought of being alone with him."

"It's not silly."

Georgette patted her hand again. "I've already successfully argued on how silly it is. I won."

"Just because it is not *remarkable* does not mean that being alone with him is not a problem." She picked at the coverlet. She couldn't tell Georgette about the challenge. Her friend would clamp onto the information and never let it go. She settled on something simpler, yet still accurate. "He confuses me."

Georgette's wistful smile returned. "How lovely."

Miranda shook her head. "You are more hopeless than I."

"I'm a romantic, dear. You are far too practical. And that this man confuses you is the best thing I've heard in years."

Miranda flopped back on the bed and stared at the ceiling. "Lovely."

The bed depressed as her friend sat. "And if he has gotten to you in this way, it also means that he is interested in you."

There were fourteen bumps on her ceiling. If one connected them, it looked like a box opening and something wicked streaming out. "Interested in driving me batty. That's all."

"I saw you two interact. I saw him nearly *eating* you up. You can't convince me otherwise."

That she was interested in being the meal was part of the problem. And even though she shared most things with Georgette, and her friend would positively love to hear of it, she couldn't admit her thoughts and feelings aloud. It would make them tangible. Force her to act upon them.

Georgette flopped on her side next to her. "What you need is something else to occupy your thoughts before you do something mad and refuse to return to his delicious lair." She tapped her fingers against her upper lip. "Write to one of your correspondents. You always get energized by such, Lord help you. Oh, ask about the sequel to *Seven Secrets* so I can be the first one with the news at the Mortons' this time."

The ceiling bumps also could form a face with a perfect O of embarrassment about the mouth. "Eleutherios hasn't responded to my last letter, and it has been days now."

"So?" Georgette shrugged her left shoulder. "Write him again. If he doesn't respond, what have you lost?"

"But—"

"This is part of your problem, Miranda." Georgette gazed down at her. "You are too caught up in the order of things. You need to do as you please."

Everyone was always trying to convince her to do as she pleased these days. It almost made her want to hunker down further into her studies and cross her arms in defiance.

"I will do so when I get—"

"When you get another few crowns, another few years, another travel book, another excuse."

Miranda crossed her arms and studied the ceiling with more concentration. "There is nothing wrong with being prepared."

"Using preparation as an excuse not to take a leap *is* wrong."

No answers appeared above. "I'm being safe. Secure."

"You are being featherbrained."

She looked over at her friend's frustrated features, a mirror of her own. "It is featherbrained to roam the

Continent alone with naught but my meager clothes and funds."

"Oh, pish. You have enough to hire someone to accompany you. Mrs. Fritz would go."

Miranda thought of the elderly woman who boarded with them. "But . . ."

"Exactly. You will think of some other excuse to resist."

Miranda tightened her arms.

"Ugh." Georgette pushed back up to a sitting position and grabbed for her bonnet. "I can't talk to you right now. I'm emerald with the worst envy and crimson with anger at the opportunity you might let slip. This would be good for you. Downing is notorious."

Miranda shook a finger at her in triumph. "Exactly why I should stay away."

Georgette shook a finger back. "Exactly why you *shouldn't*."

Miranda contemplated Georgette's words later as she looked at her pen and the blank piece of paper in front of her, squared on her scarred little lap desk.

She touched the short note from Eleutherios that had accompanied the book. The spidery letters sloped and narrowly curved. She traced a letter absently with her finger.

Dear Mistress Chase,

Enjoy the enclosed.

Eleutherios

Mr. Pitts would be snorting at the salutation of *Mistress Chase,* his fingers assuredly curled around a hot cup of black coffee. He despised everything about the author's tendency for flowery speech in his text. What was interesting was that the note was almost terse. If not for the expensive and sought-for gift enclosed, she might not have dared reply.

And twice without a response? She chewed her lip. Georgette was right, though—if nothing else, the decision was taking her mind away from the viscount.

She smoothed the paper on her desk, squaring it again, feeling the creases beneath the bare fingers of her left hand. She fiddled with her pen before dipping it.

She curled her letters of salutation, then paused on the downstroke of her comma, lifting her pen before too much ink puddled on the page. She started a new line.

> *I was surprised by the rumors of a sequel to your lovely work, but then this is London, and I should hardly be taken aback by my lack of knowledge in all things social.*
>
> *As to where I first heard the rumors about your new work, a most strange encounter was responsible.*

She looked at the page and fiddled with her pen nib. She could strike it out. Start afresh. She pressed her pen to the start of the sentence, then lifted it. No. It was inconsequential.

So inconsequential that the encounter had only shaken her world and left her reeling since.

She belligerently set her pen down again, determined to wipe away thoughts of the viscount.

A most shameless, confusing man—

No that was unkind. And quite the opposite of not thinking of him. She crossed it out.

> *A patron of the store casually mentioned that he had heard you were writing a sequel, and the next day, it was all over town. I do not know how the patron found out before some of the best gossipers in London, but I suppose the social vine works in mysterious ways. Perhaps he even spread the rumor himself.*

She considered crossing that off as well. It seemed her mind was of one track. She tapped the end of the pen against her lip before deciding to leave it. It *was* a valid explanation. Besides, it served the viscount right for monopolizing her thoughts and dragging her emotions to and fro.

> *In more favorable news, I finished the Gothic and must thank you again.*

Miranda waxed poetic for a few paragraphs, then finished with a note that she did not expect a reply, she simply felt the need to thank him again. She signed with a swirl of letters and sealed the note, carefully placing it near her door to mail.

Next was a return note to Mr. Pitts. She could tell him all about the viscount. He would probably enjoy the man's dislike of Eleutherios. But there was something that told her he would instantly dislike Lord Downing too, so she kept the viscount's title out but filled the page with the encounter.

Mr. Pitts was sometimes a disagreeable sort. He had been from his first note to the *Daily Mill* vilifying Eleutherios. The viscount had merely dismissive words for the author. He had nothing on the vitriol Mr. Pitts could spew. It was as if Mr. Pitts knew the author directly and despised him.

She had written a piece to the paper in response, arguing on the author's behalf. Crotchety, sarcastic man had written to her directly to confront her on her opinion. Few days had gone by where she hadn't exchanged correspondence with him since. And never once had he taken affront to her gender upon discovering it. He could be quite charming when he chose, no matter what Georgette said.

Beneath all of his dark, droll words, she thought he secretly enjoyed their friendly, and at times combative, correspondence just as much as she did.

She fondly signed the note.

He'd probably tell her to throw the scandalous illumination into the sea. He'd been irritated about the Gothic from Eleutherios. Told her in no uncertain terms what he'd thought of the bare note and the gift from the "muttonhead." That he was inconsiderate or had some nefarious ulterior motive and wasn't to be trusted.

But she could no more throw away one temptation over another. Was it more dangerous to take the gift you knew or the gift you didn't?

She touched the cover of the Gothic that she had been given ahead of everyone else in London and tried not to think of temptation, dark men, and charming lords.

Dreams kept one alive. Even the foolish dreams of a working girl. They had kept her going through one devastation after another.

She touched the threadbare palms of her gloves.

Was it naïve to believe a dream wouldn't be punctured? Or did it make one stronger to keep dreaming?

Chapter 6

I most desire in life to have an open eye and an open heart. To dream brings both.

Miranda Chase to Mr. Pitts

He found dreams useless. Maximilian Landry, Viscount Downing, pushed the dips of his specially tailored glove between the fingers on his left hand. Action was undeniably more effective. Naïveté in all forms abhorrent.

Dreams had never gained him a thing. The whims of others were resistant to one's dreams. But action and manipulation were undeniable. Seduction the darkest and lightest tactic.

It was just like him to find someone so opposite to him interesting. And enticing. Miranda Chase was all about reaction and observation. About watching and not participating. About helping instead of grabbing what she desired.

He was going to change all of that.

He had long ago decided he wanted Miranda Chase, no matter what she thought of their having just met. Yes, he wanted Miranda Chase. And he always got what he wanted.

He lifted his finest sword and slowly smiled.

Chapter 7

Dear Chase,

Men don't pretend interest in the way you describe. They are either interested or not. However, that has absolutely nothing to do with whether they can be trusted.

Mr. Pitts to Miranda Chase

Warmth from the sun's rays heated her skin, echoing her increasingly heated thoughts as she walked toward the grand house five days later.

If she had thought the viscount would play fair with their challenge, she had been deluding herself. He took every opportunity to point out the scandalous, to shock her, to touch her.

Innocent touches. Small brushes. Casual meetings of flesh, the heat of his fingers tangible on her skin before the tips brushed, the tingle of cool air on a warmed surface making her shiver as soon as the pad would lift. Drawing her toward him like a hand rippling through water and setting a leaf skimming on a wave. As if his skin had set a hook directly into hers, pulling her ever closer.

On Wednesday, armed with a copy of Eleutherios's opus, she had gamely sought to point out everything in the garden that might open one's eyes in wonder. The butterflies, the ruffled edges of a breeze, the peeking gaze of a rabbit. And then she wasn't sure how it happened, but suddenly she was gazing at each vegetable, each plant, and instead of pointing out their vibrant life and determined roots, she was seeing a ripening female, a developed male. The roundness of the tomatoes, the shape of a cabbage and how the leaves nestled around the center, the hang of a cucumber. The tip of a breast or the curled edge of a snuggled core. And, of course . . .

She had stuttered something in reply to his casually delivered comments. His carefully crafted words and light touches as he outlined each edible object in a very apparent way.

His lips had pulled into the most sensual grin she had ever seen. Enough to set her heart racing and her body firing.

Tomatoes might as well have been rubbed against her cheeks. It would have saved her pumping blood the trouble. She had promised never to allow him the upper hand again.

On Thursday, she had made him sit in a cafe in Piccadilly to observe the crowds. Even dressed less formally, he had stood out in the melee. No one had spared a glance for her, but he could do nothing to mask the inherent power and the blatant masculinity that oozed from him.

But he had ignored the women casting covert or open glances. All of his attention had been on her. Drowning her in his Stygian gaze. His fingers had lightly brushed her elbow, reaching to lift his drink.

She had repeated her promise to herself.

On Friday, she had argued with him about crime and punishment as they walked to Newgate. They had peered at the stark exterior. The way the facade hunched in on itself in some areas and stood proud and tall in others.

And he had simply said, a serious note to his voice, "Never laying eyes upon you again would be the keenest punishment someone could inflict upon me." His eyes had held hers. Unreadable, intriguing, mercurial. And she could almost believe he meant it from the tone of his voice, the intensity of his gaze, the way his body leaned into hers.

The promise became her mantra.

On Saturday, they had strolled to the park and watched the waterfowl. She'd finally shut him up with a hand to his lips. The soft, hot skin beneath her gloved palms. And then she hadn't been able to think of anything but how the moist heat might feel against her bare skin. The soft skin of her wrists rather than the chapped pads of her fingers. She'd dropped her hands abruptly at the thought and swore to lock herself in the library that afternoon and all the afternoons thereafter. Promises and challenges be damned.

He had followed her to the library, steadying her on the ladder, his shoulder brushing her thigh.

Promises? She had found herself later that night touching the door of the armoire in her room, wondering at the pages hidden inside. At the images in her head now overlaid with visions of the viscount above her, touching her, his lips doing the sinful things at which he kept hinting.

Promises of his own.

She felt barely in possession of her own sensibilities.

Her internal voice was growing dimmer and dimmer. The lure of the illicit manuscript and its master growing stronger. Urging her to follow the siren's call. *Come. Open me. Find the answers to what you've always wondered.*

Miranda walked the pavement, the dwindling restraint she claimed sinking into the temptation that seemed ever present in the viscount's vicinity. It was simply amazing that she had refrained from flinging herself in his general direction. She knew she was being seduced. She *knew* it. And yet the call, *come to me, open me up,* was a flame to her moth. And he was Prometheus, keeper of the fire.

Every day she found herself anticipating his appearance in the library doorway even more. And she was ten kinds of fool, for one of these days he wasn't going to show. And one of these days he would have his fill and never appear again.

She shook her head. Stupid moth. Stupid flame.

Two women walking toward her had their heads together, furiously whispering, eyes furtively rising to the left. One blushed violently and ducked her head. Miranda's brows knit, and she turned right onto the walk, then stopped dead.

The gorgeous statue of warmed alabaster clothed in black rose from his seated, lounging position on the stone steps, looking for all that he had been waiting just for her. A cloth bundle was held in his right hand.

"My lord," she somehow managed to stutter.

"Miss Chase."

She clutched her gloved hands to each other, rubbing the cheap shields together. "Hoping to catch a glimpse of the sun?"

"Waiting for her lovely rays to peek through the

clouds," he said agreeably. He didn't glance up toward the sky, he just continued to look at her. Her face heated under his gaze, assuredly rosy red.

His lips curved. "Ah, there it is." He languidly took the last step.

Moth. Flame. Danger.

She attempted to skirt past him and enter the house, trying to disregard what the thump of her heart told her to do instead.

He touched her arm, freezing her in place, her foot upon the first stone step.

"Come." He slid his free hand down her arm and took her fingers in his, lifting them.

Her body froze, any lingering resolve tipped to shatter if it fell. She stared straight ahead. "But I don't want to be late."

Mrs. Humphries would hold it against her, and she'd been trying to worm her way into the woman's good graces when the viscount wasn't present. When she needed to think other thoughts.

"I have already informed the household that you are joining me. They are shelving the piles you sorted earlier and will begin uncrating the volumes that are in the carriage house."

More books? She met his eyes. "But—"

"I pointed to the specific piles. This will save you three days' worth of lugging printed bricks. Besides." He smiled lazily, far too close to her. "I'm the boss."

"But—"

"And I need an escort."

She stared at him. An escort? Her hand shivered in his.

"I'm desirous of your company."

She continued to stare.

His lips pulled into a smile, a teasing lift at the edges. "I need you to purchase some books for me."

A request that was perfectly within the parameters of her hired position. Hard to refuse, as such.

Not that she *would* refuse.

"Very well." She tugged her hand from his and smoothed her two-seasons-out-of-fashion pelisse. "What store are we visiting?"

He motioned for her to walk with him, the parcel still in his hand. "Not a store."

She attempted to keep her gaze on the pedestrians passing by. The curious eyes focused on the man beside her. She was used to being in Georgette's shadow, but this man cast an even wider field. "Oh? Then a warehouse?" His title would likely open quite a few doors on Paternoster Row.

"No, to Lady Banning's."

She stumbled. He put out a hand to steady her. Not in her field of comfort nor expertise—either his action or their destination. She tried to remove her arm before his touch could unhinge her even more—the tingles never truly seeming to dissipate. She didn't bother with a "pardon me" or even an "I must have misunderstood."

"I'm not dressed for such a destination."

"We will stop by the modiste then and acquire something suitable for you." A grand carriage pulled in front of them. The stately matched horses stood at attention, perfectly poised.

The coachman posed on top of the box as a liveried boy smartly opened the door with a flourish. Miranda stared at the boy as he lifted a hand to assist her inside.

She'd woken up this morning. Dressed and chatted

with Mrs. Fritz, who cooked for them in exchange for
her board. Cleaned the downstairs floors. Taken care
of a few things in the store. Walked the few miles to
Mayfair. And somewhere between turning up the walk
to the viscount's manor and approaching the front
door, she'd fallen back to sleep. Again.

Just like every day since she'd met him really.

"Giles," the viscount said toward the coachman.
"We will be making a stop at Madame—"

"No, no," she said hastily.

"Ga—"

"Might I speak with you a moment?" One brow
lifted as she touched his sleeve and tugged him to the
side. "What are you doing?" she whispered harshly.

"Offering to take you to the modiste."

She glared up at him. "Are you serious about going
to Lady Banning's?"

"The last I checked."

"We can walk there."

"How do you know where she lives?"

"Lady Banning lives around the corner."

"Do you follow her, hiding in the bushes?"

Miranda looked down her nose. "Everyone knows
where Lady Banning lives."

"She will be delighted to be so notorious. Please tell
me that I measure up. Did you know where I lived?"

She colored. "Don't be silly."

He smiled slowly. "I'm flattered."

"Don't be. I mistook you for your butler, if you'll
remember."

"I am still smarting from it too." He had obviously
never found anything but amusement in the gaffe.

"It is a game to know the addresses of the Quality.
Not a novelty at all." She had never put much stock in

the games people sometimes played over a pint, but she had witnessed them on more than one occasion.

"Do I get extra sips for being a king among rogues?"

"Sorry, but I had never heard much about you." She clasped her hands together.

"I'm wounded. Mortally." His eyes never left hers as he rubbed a finger across his lower lip.

They both knew that she had. That she possibly was even *intrigued* by him before, not that she'd admit as much now.

"We can walk," she said, trying to get back to the crux of the problem. By design, she had made each of their daily outings within walking distance. Only Newgate had stretched the boundaries, but she'd used the excuse of the walk as part of the "teaching."

"Walk? Never. Not when I can arrive in style."

She stared at him as he motioned to the dark carriage with its drawn shades, urging her forward.

"I'm not riding in that thing."

"I just had it deloused. I promise there are no fleas remaining with a sweet tooth for shopgirls."

She glared at him. "Well, at least you've decided to stop seducing me."

He raised a brow. "Seduce you? What are you thinking, Miss Chase?"

She didn't reply, and he motioned for her to get in the belly of the deadly beast.

She looked at the carriage. Even with the cattle standing perfectly at attention, the entire contraption unnerved her. Horses could be spooked. They could bolt, gallop on a mad spree, destroying everything in their path and everyone within the coffin they were pulling.

No need to get in it if she didn't have to.

"I'll meet you there."

"Can't, I'm afraid. We have to make another stop first."

"Where?"

"You are quite autocratic today. Questioning your employer."

"You aren't my employer. My uncle is. I'm simply doing him a favor by dealing with you." And earning a nice percentage, she internally allowed. But no matter how grand and lovely the carriage probably was on the inside, she wouldn't get in that thing in order to travel a few blocks.

His fingers touched her chin, igniting the heat within her that he seemed to call forth at will. "I promise the ride is smooth. I won't let you fall."

She looked into his eyes. Flame. Moth. Danger.

A simple carriage ride. She nodded tightly, stepping away. The boy near the door offered his hand, and she took a deep breath. She would simply think happy thoughts. She took the boy's hand and ascended.

Her foot was already inside when she heard the viscount's voice.

"To Madame G—"

"I'd rather not," she said as quickly as she could, turning, realizing too late where the other stop would be. Georgette would curse her to the fifth level of hell if she ever found out that she'd turned down a new dress from whatever modiste they might have visited. But dressed as she was, Miranda would never be noticed at the countess's house except as the worker she was. Embarrassment over her clothing was misplaced and, frankly, asinine.

And the thought that he might buy her clothing

made her head spin in mad ways, and she needed to maintain her equilibrium.

She glanced to the side to see the coachman look to the viscount.

"Perhaps later then." The viscount smiled lazily again, then motioned her the rest of the way inside.

Obtaining books. That was all.

The interior looked different than her most radical imaginings. She had craned and peered into more than one grand carriage from afar and had always fancied the insides contained glorious tuffets and yards of gold alchemically turned into silk. But the viscount's was quite plain. The requisite black and grays she already associated with him. Muted silver and gold accents. Hardly a sultan's paradise.

Then again, very little lived up to her imaginings, which was why she tried not to constrain anything to them.

Except Eleutherios. She had a certain image of him. And Mr. Pitts.

She had expected a multitude of shiny objects and expensive contraptions would keep her mind off the fact that they were moving in an enclosed space. She eyed the opposite window. Perhaps she could casually open the shade before he entered without drawing attention to the action.

Her rear touched the seat, and the fabric molded around her, pulling her into a velvety embrace, surrounding her. It gripped and pulled, unaccountably relaxing her, draining the tension from her limbs. She paused a moment, completely sated, then touched the top of the padded bench. The soft, luxurious fabric caressed her hand, inviting her to keep it there, whispering of the glories that would be hers if she did. She didn't know what type of cushion it was, but it was worth a small kingdom.

Probably cost that too.

She looked around the interior with a new, appreciative eye. Not splashy or showy, but sumptuous. Decadent in all the right ways. She had never felt such luxury. Picked out for the way it surrounded and enveloped, made one feel relaxed and open.

She had peered into the interior of an earl's carriage once. It had been gilded and ostentatious from her distance. He and his beautiful countess had looked like the perfect lovely pair except for the stiff way they'd sat. The cold, detached expressions on their faces. She reexamined the memory, slotting this new information into place. Choices based on the external versus the internal.

But the viscount had not made the external choice. In this instance, at least.

The stunning thought must have shown on her face because the viscount raised a brow. "Something amiss?"

He reclined in the seat across from her, one leg extended, almost brushing the outside of hers, the mysterious bundle resting next to him.

"Just surprised. I'd expected something . . . different."

"Fingers swirling beneath the surface. It is what is underneath that matters, no? What the material is made of?"

He looked as if he were having a terrific joke at her expense, and at the same time that intense, too-watchful gaze that occasionally graced his face was in evidence once more.

"I suppose this is where I say, touché." It should

have been a disgruntled statement, but she couldn't work up the feeling over the fast beat of her heart, or through the low whisper of her voice.

"Do not fret, Miss Chase." His knee casually brushed hers as he settled back farther. "I'll not rib you for it . . . much."

She continued to stroke the bench, almost unconsciously. It made her feel like she was in a grand sitting room instead of within a death trap. And all of a sudden there were equally dangerous thoughts running through her mind that she needed to tamp down.

"Why are you taking me to Lady Banning's?" She was glad the question emerged in a more casual tone than she'd thought herself capable. She tried to focus on their destination. The countess was the preeminent member of the literary elite in London. It was said that she had a copy of every book ever printed. Even a secret second copy of *Beowulf*—one in finer condition than the museum's.

And the woman, a countess in her own right, was said to be rigid about who entered her private sanctuary.

If Miranda had been told their destination by anyone else, she'd know they were poking fun. But the viscount seemed to mean more of the things he said than he was likely to admit.

Her hands tightened as the coachman called out, and the vehicle shifted. The viscount casually leaned over and lifted the shades, allowing the bright light to filter in and drown the shadows. She relaxed slightly as the carriage began to move.

"Why am I taking you? To acquire some books, as I said."

The horses pulled into a steadier gait. Worth every penny for the way they seamlessly moved. None of the starting and jerking that she'd expected even in an expensive rig.

She clasped her fingers. "You are as well versed as I about literature, my lord. You have proven that."

"Just because I know Rousseau from Homer does not mean I can adequately make the correct choice of purchase."

But he knew far more than that. She sat back, trying to relax and enjoy the way the carriage rocked like a cradle pushed by a loving hand. Much nicer than the jostling of a rickety hack over cobblestones—which she sometimes had to take, white-knuckled and nauseous.

Still . . . accidents could happen to the wealthy too.

She concentrated on him, and his eyes never left hers as he rubbed a finger across the knee of his trousers in time with the rocking.

She needed to get over her negative associations with traveling if she ever truly wanted to grab her dream and continue her family's aborted goal to tour the Continent. Nice short stops in a comfortable space might just be what she needed. This wasn't so bad, all things considered.

She wondered what renting a rig like this might cost. If the coachman took pennies or pounds. Probably pure silver nuggets.

The carriage slowed, and Miranda's nerves jumped again. They truly were stopping at Lady Banning's then. She touched the soft fabric. "What do I do while you are speaking to the countess or whomever?"

She wasn't his servant. But she certainly wasn't a member of society. She could pretend around the viscount, but stepping a foot into another part of the realm was like waking from a dream to find all one's covers and nightwear on the floor.

She was completely out of her element. Should she act like a lady's maid or a feminine valet? Both images might have caused her to chuckle in another situation, but at the moment she felt a little more like casting up her contents.

" 'Whomever' is quite vague," he said.

And she was a female. The viscount decidedly was not.

"Whomever you speak with in that house will be above my station, so it is not actually vague."

She couldn't contain a relieved breath as the door opened, and she exited the contraption.

"Ah. But station is quite like the fingers in the pool, is it not? A small stirring uncovers far more about one's character."

She glared as he exited behind her. A governess then, with a charge in need of a swat. No. Even the image of the viscount turned over her knee didn't make her laugh. This was going to be terrible.

"What do I do while you are entertaining?"

"Join in the conversation?"

"Are you mad?"

"Not at the moment. I feel quite calm."

"In the mind!"

"That either."

"You are finding amusement then." She touched a patch in her skirt. "You . . . you aren't going to introduce me to anyone, correct?"

"Of course not. A lowly shopgirl like you? Never."

She couldn't discern from his flippant tone as to whether he was joking or not. She found herself unaccountably disgruntled again. Which was absurd. He was making her bold with his flirting.

As they walked through the entrance hall, everything in her imaginings proved true. Lady Banning's house was downright intimidating. Even the servants swaggered. The viscount's servants were upright and efficient, but they seemed a much happier bunch. These servants might as well have had horse dung permanently embedded in the collars of their livery for the way their noses pinched and rose.

There were numerous people loitering in the entrance, more than she'd anticipated. Almost as if it were a coffeehouse, and people congregated there to speak.

The viscount pointed to a blissfully empty corner of the columned room, and she automatically positioned herself behind the farthest column as soon as they reached it. It was a great place to observe first, act second. The viscount's mouth curved as he took in her position and opened to make an assuredly slicing comment.

A woman in bold peacock blue sashayed up and touched the viscount's sleeve, halting his comment. A fleeting butterfly touch that went with her airy plumes and fluttering lashes. "Downing. It has been nearly a sennight since I've seen you."

"Lady Hucknun, a pleasure." He bowed over her hand, and Miranda watched as his fingers slipped over hers. A public display, and nothing beyond the pale. It just seemed that his every action held a certain seductive bent.

Miranda stood still in her partially hidden position. Lady Hucknun's eyes moved over Miranda, dismissing her as quickly as a butterfly touching, then fluttering off.

She tapped the viscount with her fan. "Naughty man, depriving us of your company."

"I endlessly require chastening."

"That you do." Her look was sly.

A man stepped to the viscount's other side, just far

enough so that she had to peek around to see him. "Downing."

"Colin."

Silence descended on the group—awkward to someone as out of her element as Miranda was. She thought maybe she could even slip away in the heavy fog.

The woman looked back and forth between the men with speculative eyes. The gleam that sometimes gathered in Georgette's eyes when a bit of gossip was about to form sprung in hers. The viscount seemed unconcerned. The Colin fellow fidgeted, then stared pointedly at the lady.

Her lips moued. "Later then, my lord."

The viscount tipped his head and looked back at Colin as the woman sashayed away.

Colin's eyes didn't even touch on Miranda, half-hidden behind the column. She supposed even at a glance she looked like one of the dozen other personal servants milling about, waiting for instructions. Colin wasted little time, the other woman barely out of earshot. "The marchioness has been asking for you."

"Has she?" The viscount seemed relaxed, but Miranda saw his fingers tighten around the handle of his walking stick.

"She requires your assistance."

"What a surprise."

"Mother constantly aims to do so," Colin said bitterly.

Miranda's eyes shifted abruptly back to the man. Mother? Colin must be his Christian name. Georgette would know right off where he fell in the order. Miranda took in his appearance. Blue eyes and sandy brown hair.

But then she looked closer. The clothing was similar.

As if the one was trying to imitate the other, however unconsciously. It was obvious who was whom in that matter as the viscount owned the way he stood and the way the fabric draped over him. His clothing was an accent to him versus the way Colin's clothing was almost wearing him.

Colin had the uncomfortable, rough edges of a sculpture being molded and shaped still, showing promise but incomplete. He was perhaps twenty or twenty-one.

"Don't we all?" The viscount's words were careless, but there was a hard edge to the syllables. "There is so little these days to amuse."

"Some of us manage reasonable, scholarly lives and have no need to be splattered all over the gossip pages."

"Ah, the voice of ever-epic reason. Given to you by the inimitable deans in their vast wisdom." The viscount snapped his fingers, swirled them, and continued his studied nonchalance. "I lament what will happen when you matriculate and experience life on your own."

Colin's eyes narrowed. "Drinking already, I see, Downing?"

"What care have you, Colin? Go back to your correspondence and literary pursuits." The last was said in a dark tone.

"Our plight concerns me. The family name."

The viscount watched him without saying a word.

Colin pursed his lips. "My morality and ethics teacher said that we are on a downward spiral."

"He sounds like a boor."

"He's brilliant," Colin said harshly.

"And what do you wish me to do about this sad spiral?"

"It is your responsibility to solve it."

"It is?" The viscount's brow raised.

Colin's hands fisted. "You are the heir."

"And?"

"You need to rein Mother in."

"I am the heir. Which means it *isn't* my job to rein her in. Nor withdraw her funds. It is our father's."

Colin gave an ugly little laugh. "Amusing."

"Is it?" Downing took his drink from a quick servant. "I seem to recall seeing him still breathing just the other week. He could speak to her of it if it bothers him."

"He cares for nothing except his own amusements. We could all perish, and he wouldn't look up from the pair of legs he is currently between."

Miranda tried to keep her color from blazing too warm. The rose would surely show against the stark white Corinthian columns behind her.

The viscount sipped the golden liquid. "Quite possibly."

"And?"

The viscount raised a brow in response.

"What will you do with Mother?" his brother demanded.

"What do you want me to do with her? Beat her?"

Colin's lips pulled together. "Tell her to stop. It is beyond embarrassing. The looks everyone gives me at Oxford."

"Be a man, Colin. Give them right back."

"Have you heard the rumors?" he demanded.

"Gossip groveling, Colin? Tut. I thought such things beneath you." Miranda would have thought the viscount unaffected by the whole conversation if not for the fingers of his hand, hands she always noticed, gripping the glass. "I don't see you getting wroth with Father when he is on the front lines of the scandal sheets."

Colin's fists clenched. "I don't find his actions much more palatable."

" 'Much more.' Exactly."

Colin didn't seem happy with the comment. "It is worse for her."

"Undoubtedly."

Miranda wondered if Colin understood that the viscount's words contained double meanings. She felt oddly pleased with Downing.

"You coddle her," Colin said.

"Do I?"

The man's face grew beet red. "Conrad thinks you will salvage the family name. I don't share his optimism. I want to know what you intend to do."

"I plan to purchase a book, perhaps stop by the club and gamble away a bit of the money left in my pockets, then drunkenly retire with a scantily clad woman."

The last was said with a slight, nearly unnoticeable tilt toward her, and it was as if scalding tea had been poured over her head and left to drip down and coat her limbs.

Colin didn't seem to notice, too coiled to catch any nuances.

"And Mother?"

"Why don't you speak to her if you are so anxious."

Colin's lips tightened in a line so thin all color disappeared. "As if she'd care. You are her firstborn. Her favorite. From her favorite tree."

There was a derisive twist to the words.

"We all have our burdens to bear. Now, if you are through?"

"Why do I even bother speaking to you? You are just as flawed as they are. As tainted."

The viscount smiled pleasantly, saying nothing.

"The family name is being *ruined*."

"You do realize you are discussing this out in the open, don't you? Adding to the family drama? Aren't you concerned with who might overhear? Or are you too *busy* when you come to my house to talk of it then?"

Colin blanched, then scoffed. "There is no one here to overhear."

"Let me introduce you to Miss Chase." The viscount stepped back and waved a hand to her. "New to the house."

Colin seemed beyond embarrassed at finally spying her, but then anger appeared to override the emotion. "Your servants overhear worse every day in your household anyway," he muttered.

"I do hope Miss Chase has formed the correct opinion from what she's overheard me say." Downing's eyes turned languid, and Miranda's face flamed.

His brother's expression grew suddenly dark, and there was a fear there that was strange and unexpected. "You are dallying with your staff now? I thought you had your limits."

The viscount's expression turned deadly. "You overstep yourself."

Colin backed up a pace, face blanching of color. "You can't dally with the staff." The words spilled from his lips. "At least if you were respectable, if you turned the marquess and marchioness respectable, the rest of us could rest upon the goodwill of society should our pockets go to let."

"Do you plan to take up the cloth? Regain our respectability through prayer and sermon? Or to take up trade and refill our rumored empty coffers? Sell your melancholy memoirs?"

Colin's face grew redder still. Huh. She had thought
that awful shade was hers alone. The strange thing was
the sliver of desperation beneath his anger.

"No? Then simply be blind to it like Conrad and the
ladies. Buy your expensive clothing and attend your
favorite events. Go to your balls and think nothing of
where the money is coming from or going to. Think
nothing of the gossip rags." The viscount sipped his
drink. "Woo whom you will and don't take your feelings of shame over it out on the rest of us."

Colin didn't respond. In fact, he looked like he had
been stabbed in the gut.

"You are full of your school's *goodwill*, Colin, and
unable to reconcile your own confusion with that of
the way of the world." The viscount leaned toward his
brother, dark intentions in his posture. "And if you
say aught to Mother in a negative manner because of
it, you will answer to me. Good day."

The viscount strode away, long legs eating up the distance to cross the room, and she hurried to follow.

"The countess should appear soon," he said over his
shoulder, as she tried to keep pace. "We can appreciate
the paintings here in the corner until she does. Better
company that way."

She glanced back to the other man, taking in his
hair, skin tone, and eye color as he stared hollowly
after the viscount. "You are brothers?"

"Strange, is it not?"

"Well, you are both a bit intense," she admitted.

He glanced at her as they walked, slowing his pace a
bit, his expression clearly amused. "Intense, am I?"

"Yes." There was nothing risked by admitting the
obvious.

"Never thought Colin and I had much in common

apart from blood, however much of it he wants to claim." The last was said with a decided snipe.

She dearly wished to ask questions but didn't dare. It was none of her business and beyond good manners. But everyone knew of the marchioness and her exploits. The woman who permanently resided in the scandal sheets as Lady W. Who had a string of liaisons as long as a continuous thread on the largest loom. Only eclipsed by her husband and oldest son.

The father's, the mother's, the son's. The scandals always followed a pattern. If the marchioness performed an outrage, it was almost certain that the viscount would eclipse it in some way.

The pattern was noticeable if one paid attention over time and followed the flow of the gossip surrounding Downing. If one looked between the inked lines to see the strange and complicated picture.

Miranda coughed into her glove. She was sure everyone paid that type of attention, not just her.

The viscount's scandals, while particularly succulent at the outset, eventually turned out *mostly* well. Though there were a few that had been utter disasters. But for the most part, heavy, scandalous bets became new fortunes. Ghastly trade endeavors produced obscene riches. Rakish conquests turned into speedy, happy weddings—other people's weddings. It was almost as if his scandals were designed and planned, when one thought on it.

But the brother's talk about finances . . . perhaps there was something hidden beneath the print.

"Colin is taken with sentiment," the viscount said, examining a magnificent portrait. "Overly reliant on other people's opinions. And on emotion, not unlike our mother, though he'd be horrified to have it pointed out." He tilted his head, a tight smile about his lips. "I will do so the very next time I speak with him."

"Are you . . . are you sure we should be purchasing books?" She said it all in a rush, horrified that the words were spilling from her lips even as they did. Impugning a gentleman's honor . . . questioning the gossip . . . he'd probably turn her right out.

Instead, he looked more amused. "I think I can afford the expense. And you. At least for the moment." He took a drink from his glass. "Besides, you know we live to rack up as much credit as the bankers can extend."

It was a practice that was very common for her to see in the bookstore, but it was completely foreign to her own way of life. "But eventually it catches up."

"Will you take me in if it does?" He leaned toward her, his elbow brushing her arm, hovering just above her breast—one sliver of air away if she as much as breathed. "I could be your kept man. Slave to your desires."

His lips curved as her cheeks heated.

"All it would take is one tiny concession on your part. Give me that concession, Miranda. Surrender to it."

The spell curled around her, demanding an answer.

Demanding capitulation.

The crowd around her melted away as she prepared to give it.

Chapter 8

Dear Chase,

Sometimes the measure of a person can only be gleaned through his interactions with others. But it takes a quick eye to see what he tries to hide behind a disarming grin.

Mr. Pitts to Miranda Chase

A woman with powdered hair ornately and elaborately styled walked through the door, breaking the atmosphere of the room and Miranda's own trance. The answer to the question submerged back into the ever-present tension between them.

The woman was obviously the most important person in the room. In the house. It didn't take the jewels dripping from her neck, strung through her hair, or covering her gloved hands and wrists to determine such. It was the way she walked. The way she stopped, stood, and waited for the perfect moment. Holding herself there a beat too long, making Miranda want to shift. A few of the others in the room gave in and moved in the space of awkward awareness.

Then the woman moved her hand, commanding notice. Successfully gaining the attention of the entire gathering without saying a word. Miranda was impressed. Georgette would likely trade in her interest in Mrs. Q—shove her into the Thames—if she ever met Lady Banning and had a chance to study her.

The woman surveyed the crowd and walked straight toward the viscount. Conversation recommenced, more muted though than before.

"Lord Downing."

"Lady Banning." He bowed over her hand. One white eyebrow rose at how close he came. "Still able to bring everyone to heel. Still as beautiful as the day of your comeout."

"Still the silver tongue, Downing. Your father wouldn't even remember my comeout. And you weren't even a thought in his sapless head when I made mine."

"But I am sure that his thoughts would have been full of me after he saw you."

The countess gave him a frosty glance, but there was amusement at the edges. "Did I call your tongue silver? Do not overstep yourself, viscount."

"I'd never dare, countess. Not unless it was a step toward you."

"Still as knavish as ever."

"Still as sharp as the most razor-edged of blades."

The countess gave her intricately coiffed hair a pat. "Always. Now, what have we here." Sharp icy blue eyes swung Miranda's way, pinning her. Everyone else in the house had glanced right over her, but not this woman. The ruler of them all.

"This is merely Miss Miranda Chase, countess." The edge of his mouth curled, a tendril lifting in the breeze. "A lowly shopgirl."

"Mmmm. As if you would bring someone lowly to me, Downing." The countess walked around her, examining her. "Where are you from, girl?"

"Leicestershire, my lady. Then Main Street Books and Printers on Bond."

The countess tilted her head, just a small movement beneath her mountain of hair and ornament. "A small shop, but with a good reputation."

"Thank you, my lady." Miranda tried not to stumble over her words.

The countess perused her for another second, then turned to the viscount. "Well then, Downing. What do you have for me to sniff my nose at today?"

"A twelfth-century illumination." He untucked an edge of the cloth bundle. The gilt edges caught the light before he pulled the covering back over it.

The countess's face showed nothing, and neither did her posture. "I have many illuminations, Downing."

"But you haven't seen this one, countess."

She examined him, a look that would make most grown men cower. The viscount maintained his indolent pose under her regard. It was just respectful enough not to be insolent. The countess looked at Miranda speculatively. "To the judgment room then in ten minutes, shall we? I have to deal with this rabble first."

Miranda trailed behind as they walked, feeling like a puppy caught in her own leash. The two separated, the countess turning into the middle of the room and its inhabitants. Downing going toward a hall, his steps slowing to a crawl, forcing her to catch up.

She'd rather have stayed behind him, but every time she slowed, he did as well. Soon they'd be inching forward on their toes, odd ducks waddling in a desert. She gave in and increased her pace, pulling alongside him.

They entered a magnificent room full of odd and eclectic items and gadgets. A spinning globe stood in the center, and the viscount spun it as he passed. The glitter of the gold meridians was mesmerizing. She couldn't help stopping and observing it. She touched it with one finger, then withdrew her finger just as quickly. She glanced up to see the viscount watching her.

"I'm sorry, I just—"

"Sorry about what? Touching the countess's cheap globe?"

Her chin dropped an inch, and her finger rose again to touch the wonder. "It isn't cheap."

The viscount's brow rose challengingly, but she could see the satisfied edge to his smile. She narrowed her eyes. "What game do you play?"

"Me? Oh, but to which one do you refer?"

She shook her head and looked at the globe, giving it a gentle spin. "It's lovely." Her finger absently traced the lines of the Continent, touching Italy, pulling back to rest upon France.

"Have you ever visited?"

"What?" She looked up, then down again. She hastily picked up her finger. "Oh, no. When would I?"

"Your uncle doesn't do trade in Paris?"

"Sometimes. But couriers travel between."

"You should go." He leaned against the marble stand of an ancient display, a priceless Greek bust peering down imperiously.

She gave a humorless laugh. "You sound like Georgette."

"Your friend?"

Georgette would be beyond pleased that he knew

her name. Might just push *Miranda* into the Thames and take her place as threatened.

"Yes, she is always telling me to leave my silly thoughts behind and go." She grimaced, thinking about Mr. Pitts. "Everyone is always telling me to leave and see the world."

He pushed away from the stand and took her hand, pulling his fingers along her cut-rate glove. "I'll take you."

She laughed, the pitch a little too high. "I think you might grow bored, my lord, before we even catch sight of the sea."

"You think I can't roam a museum without dissolving into ennui?"

"Not bored by that." Though she couldn't see him studying a piece of art for hours. Not with the way his hands constantly moved or his expression changed with the shadows. Not with how he took every quiet opportunity to further the challenge between them.

"I don't believe you. You think I can't appreciate simple beauty."

She looked around the room, at the expensive décor and intricate pieces. "In my experience, the Quality tend to like more complicated things."

"You've been reading the gossip columns far too long."

"And you've been gracing them for far longer, I think. In increasingly complicated schemes."

"I'm pleased you've been paying attention." He smiled lazily. "But it proves another point—that you read the gossip columns rather than experience such things yourself."

"Living the life written within would hardly suit me."

"Mmmm." His head tilted. "Have dinner with me."

She froze. "Pardon me?"

"Vauxhall."

"Vauxhall."

His mouth quirked. "Gardens."

"Vauxhall Gardens."

"You've heard of them then." The edges of his mouth curved fully as she responded to the teasing with a glare. "Dinner."

"I don't think that wise," she somehow managed to answer, if faintly.

"Who said anything about being wise? Really, Miranda, I thought you knew me better than that by now."

She didn't know which was the more perilous— that she thought she might know something about the enigmatic man in front of her or that she was as much in the dark as the rest of London.

He smiled slowly. "There is a masked party there tonight. Everyone will be costumed. And it just so happens that I have a domino that will perfectly suit you."

"That is absurd."

He lifted a brow. "Many people have extras in case someone should visit."

"Not that. Well, yes, that too. But the other. The reference to suiting me. The offer."

"You want me to rephrase it?"

"I am scarcely your usual company." She tried to tug her hand away. "I'm hardly versed in dinner conversation appropriate to the type of dinner you'd have at Vauxhall."

"I like your conversation the way it is. I choose my own company." His fingers stayed curled around hers, and he tapped her wrist with one long, extended finger. "And I choose you."

"I—"

"Much merrymaking and unwise actions will ensue."

"I—"

"You will be surprised what a little costume can do for overcoming your shyness."

"I'm not shy," she said without thinking.

He lazily smiled, and his smallest finger moved, grazing the edge of her palm. "Excellent then."

"I haven't consented to anything." Her voice went a little high.

"Would you like me to help with that? To choose for you? You just needing to follow and be free?"

There was something very uncomfortable about the sentiment and the way he said it. As if he knew her mind.

Before she could answer, Lady Banning strode back into the room. Miranda tugged her hand free of the viscount's. He seemed willing to keep it indefinitely otherwise. She colored, but Lady Banning gave only the barest hint of a reaction that she had seen any of it.

"Up to your tricks, Downing? Or do you really have something worth viewing?" The countess held out her hand.

The viscount tipped the bundle so the book fell into her palm. Lady Banning showed the first hint of emotion as her fingers hurried to steady the book.

She gave the viscount a frosty glare. He looked innocently back.

"One of these days you are going to test me beyond repair, Downing."

"Never. You find me too amusing."

She gave him another frosty stare, then looked to the book. "It's adequate."

He lazily leaned against the marble stand once more and twirled a hand. "Barely acceptable."

"I highly dislike you, Downing."

"Alas, I live for your favor."

The countess spared a glance for Miranda. "Girl, I hope you know what you are getting yourself into with this one."

Miranda's eyes widened like the rabbit she often felt akin to in the viscount's presence.

The countess's eyes narrowed and turned back to the viscount. "Downing." There was a warning in the word.

For the first time during the conversation, the viscount's posture changed from the lazy regard he had maintained throughout. A minute tightening, but present nevertheless.

Lady Banning stared at him for another second, then looked back to the book. "Tell me of it, then."

The viscount's body returned to its former liquid ease. "It's a book."

"You try my patience, Downing, and I have little of it to spare." Lady Banning turned to her. "Miss Chase. What can you tell me of this tome? I assume Downing has brought you here to verify the provenance in the absence of his good manners."

Miranda gingerly took the illumination in her gloved hands and studied it. "The paper is correct. The writing seems appropriate for the twelfth century."

She delicately turned the pages. "The illustrations

are of the right variety. The condition is excellent."

It was a remarkable thing. Though she felt awkward skimming sections hailing the glory of chastity after devouring the illicit tome hidden in her room.

"It's not a fourteenth-century scandal, but still admirable." The countess pursed her lips.

Miranda tried not to turn bright red. Had the countess read her mind?

"Admirable," the viscount said in the lazy tone he had uttered *acceptable* previously.

The countess gave him a sharp look. "Very well, Downing. The girl has just confirmed what I already knew. As did you. What do you want?"

"You know what I want."

Her lips pinched together, and she stood silent for a second. Then she snapped her fingers, and a servant smoothly dislodged from his position by the door and presented himself in the center of the room.

"Fetch the parcel."

The servant nodded and slipped away, obviously already knowing where to go and what his mistress was referring to.

The servant reappeared with a bundle. The countess snapped her fingers toward the viscount. The servant held the bundle forward with both hands extended.

Downing took it, a faint smile touching his lips before he unwrapped the sturdy cloth binding similar to the one in which his illumination had been stored. John Fennery would be pleased that his newly created preservation cloths were seeing such diligent use by the wealthy of the land.

There was a folio inside, not the book she had expected.

She looked over, her curiosity overcoming her manners. It looked like the quill drippings of a quick hand scribbling a draft. She squinted her eyes and made out a few names and notes. Viola. Sebastian. Orsino.

She blinked and leaned toward him. There were a number of sentences crossed out. Others penned over them, under them, to the side.

"Is that . . . ?" She let her words trail.

"Merely a few scribbles." The viscount tucked the pages back into the folio.

"A good head on her shoulders. And better in all ways than your usual fare." The countess gazed at her, eyes narrowed, then turned her head to stare at the viscount. "How did you find her?"

"I diligently searched beneath a stack of books."

"Mmmmm. And here I thought you barely knew how to read, Downing. Though I suppose you could have just pushed them to the side in your haste to find a new skirt."

"I'm gutted, countess."

She snorted. A very genteel, lofty snort. "How I'd like to see it, Downing. Do leave a card when it occurs."

He bowed. "Of course."

"I've heard rumors that you are looking for more . . . permanence."

"Rumors often reflect the wishes of others."

"And yet once in a while they prove true."

"Respectability has never suited me."

The countess sniffed. "As if you could be respectable. I said 'permanence.' An entirely different meaning."

"And yet they are similar in many minds."

The countess surveyed him. "Are they similar in yours, is the question. I'm inclined to lend the rumors some credence in this instance. There is something different about you, Downing, these last few months."

"I confess to letting my hair grow a mite too long. I shall beat my valet posthaste."

"Hmph." Her eyes narrowed. "And yet . . . yes, I do wonder." She abruptly turned to Miranda. "Good afternoon to you, Miss Chase. It has been a most interesting one so far."

Miranda bowed low. "Good afternoon, my lady. It was a pleasure."

"Oh, I expect our paths will cross again. Do stop by the salon next week, with or without Downing." She said it as if she hadn't just issued one of the most coveted invitations in London. She turned to the viscount. "Downing."

The viscount bowed again, but more stiffly.

Miranda walked from the house in a trance. She didn't remember getting into the carriage. "Actual foul papers. Original writings for *The Twelfth Night* . . ." she murmured as they softly rocked. "How on earth did she obtain them?"

"The countess is quite adept at procuring what she wants."

"I'm surprised she agreed to the trade." She shook her head. To find notes for the plays, or any of Shakespeare's other works, was very rare, almost mythical. The foul papers or notes inevitably slipped into vaults—snapped up before reaching the public.

"There was never a doubt." He lazily tapped a finger on the seat. "The countess is mad for illuminations. I save them especially for her. She'll trade near anything for them. This trade required three of them, this one being the final tome, but it was well worth it."

Miranda's heart stopped beating for a second. The countess had mentioned fourteenth-century scandalous texts—which in retrospect, and without her overriding embarrassment coloring her hearing, pointed to a preference for that fare. And if Miranda weren't mistaken, that was what she had been secretly, *studiously*, paging through again the night before at home. "I . . . I must return your illumination."

He raised a brow. "Why ever would you do that?"

"I should never have taken it anyway." What had she been thinking? She hadn't. Just like she often stopped breathing when he was around. The illumination was doubly valuable if he could use it to trade with the countess. "It is too valuable."

"Nonsense."

"Hardly nonsense," she argued.

"I wouldn't have given it to you if I'd needed to keep it."

"But—"

"You are obviously enjoying it." His eyes sifted over her. "I hope you are enjoying it at least. I want you to have it."

A buzzing began just beneath her thoughts, under her skin.

"Just as I want you to accompany me to the gardens."

"Oh?" *To put into practice the illuminated illustrations, to answer the siren's call, to feel truly alive.*

"A reward to you for returning my books to me last week." His lazy speech was in direct opposition to the increased buzzing, the feelings and desires sifting beneath the surface.

She strove to answer as lightly. "You deliberately avoided taking the books. I could do nothing but return them."

One long finger wove a slow pattern on his knee. "Then for putting together my library."

"You are paying me."

"Then for brightening my day." He smiled. Slowly. Fully. Her heart skipped a beat. Silly, dangerous thoughts and feelings. "Say you will go." His voice was low and whiskey-laced.

She couldn't go. It was madness.

Her mother's ghost would forever haunt her, the academy would bar her from ever entering again. Georgette would kill her for refusing. Her uncle wouldn't notice either way.

Mr. Pitts's scathing voice echoed in her mind—*decide for yourself.*

She was going to say no. Tell him that she wasn't interested. Not in attending a lavish dinner at Vauxhall—as assuredly the viscount would provide. Not in attending a masquerade where she could be anyone she wished amidst the thousands of fairy lamps and the fireworks.

Not in going with the viscount—the most interesting man she'd ever met who didn't reside somewhere behind a pen. A husky siren who promised to teach her things she'd never dreamed.

"Very well," she heard her voice say, far away, almost out of her control.

He leaned back against the seat with a satisfied smile. "Excellent."

They stopped a few seconds later. She was still trying to process that she'd said yes. And meant it.

She realized they should have stopped long before now. That she had been so absorbed with the aftermath of their visit, with the man in front of her, with her thoughts, that she hadn't even paid attention to the ride. To the carriage and death trap. "Where are we?"

"At the dressmaker. You need something to wear tonight."

"I only just agreed to . . ." She let the rest of the sentence trail, the flood of feeling tightening. "I suppose I am as easily predictable as the next woman."

He tilted his head. "Not predictable."

"Well, you certainly guessed correctly that I would agree to attend."

"I was hoping." A sly twist of his lips caused her to bite her own. The carriage door opened.

She stared at him and tried to be light over the conflicting feelings within. She *desired* this. And if she chose this path, she *must* guard her heart. "I thought you said you had a domino?"

"A domino wraps the package. You need a dress beneath."

"I don't require a dress." There was something irreversible about his buying her clothing. She could borrow a gown from Georgette.

"You want to bare all beneath? I find that to be an acceptable plan."

"No! That—I—"

"I don't think it wise to go without the domino as well, Miss Chase," he said, raising a haughty brow. "Really. I thought you a more discreet sort."

She crossed her arms, pinching her lips together. A slight cough on the other side of the door made her realize they had been sitting inside alone for too long an *appropriate* time in an unmoving vehicle. Her eyes went wide wondering what the boy outside the carriage was thinking.

"Miss Chase is trying to decide whether to run about stark naked, Benjamin," the viscount called out. "One more moment."

"Very good, my lord." There wasn't even a pause in the reply.

She popped from the carriage as fast as she could. "I am not. Don't—I—"

"Smart choice, miss," Benjamin said, nodding.

She stared at the boy for a moment, and the light in his eyes made her sigh and respond in kind.

"Incorrigible. Both of you."

"Thank you, miss." The young groom puffed out his chest, pleased to be lumped into a category with the viscount.

She shook her head. The viscount gestured toward the shop, and she automatically ascended the walk. She tried to concentrate on the path and keep her nerve instead of looking at the shop's large windows. A beautifully tailored gown was strategically positioned behind the panes, draped and flowing. Of the highest fashion. Glittering accents sparkled through the tulle of the skirt, wrapping around and out through the train.

"The Countess Drayton wore that gown to the King's ball."

"What are we *doing* here?" She could barely get the words out as her feet automatically took her up the pavers. She was a haze of nerves, and felt adrift on the breeze, floating toward the door. "Unwise," she said beneath her breath.

His walking stick tapped a rhythm on the stones. "You keep saying that. Why don't you let go and embrace doing things that aren't wise?"

"I seem to have a bad case of embracing them around you," she muttered. "The mere definition of the word should be explanation in and of itself."

"I am happy to see you embracing anything of mine." The side of his mouth quirked as he walked. An appealing curve that begged for a finger to trace the lines and share in the humor.

"I'm not going to let you seduce me," she blurted out.

"Not much of a seduction if you simply let me." He opened the door. "I was rather hoping that you would choose to seduce me instead."

She stood on the threshold, one foot half-lifted, as she stared into his eyes, which were more serious than she could credit.

She stepped over the edge.

Chapter 9

Secret #4: Never lose control . . .

. . . He could feel her fingers on his skin, beneath his shirt, as she blushed and touched the fabric Madame Galland draped over her hands, her fingers slipping over it in a caress that he could feel to his toes. He couldn't hear what she said from his comfortable seat in the private waiting area, but he could imagine her soft voice, the way she uttered each descriptive syllable with a reverence that would match the longing in her eyes.

The modiste looked toward him, nonchalantly, and he gestured with two fingers. She nodded, the entire communication taking less than a second and going completely unnoticed as Miranda's eyes were on the fabric, her lower lip curled under her top teeth, an assuredly apologetic negative on her tongue.

Madame Galland simply nodded to her and handed her another sumptuous fabric. The action was repeated until Max tilted his head. The modiste ushered Miranda toward the dressing area, unfortunately outside his viewing radius. He would have loved to see her undressing within his regard. To see the scarlet bloom on her cheeks and the tremors jump beneath her skin.

She emerged reluctantly in a finished piece that would require only slight alterations, the modiste shooing her out before the tall mirrors, which were conveniently in his sight.

The fabric gripped her in all the appropriate places, highlighting her curves and brightening her skin. Revealing a tantalizing hint of undergarments and flesh in the open seams that would cinch and clutch her once sewn but gaped and concealed as she shifted before the looking glass.

It took a few dress changes before she began to relax and enjoy herself, seeming to forget he was there except for the telltale sign of her fingers tucking the hair behind her left ear in lingering shyness and the way her eyes would dart in his direction when she thought he wasn't looking.

He smiled. Things were progressing apace.

He shouldn't be surprised. After all, aside from his family concerns, he always got what he wanted.

But he couldn't even explain it to himself, this need to have her. To break her. To shape her. To remold her.

To keep her exactly as she was and shield her from people just like himself.

It was the knife-edge that had been teetering for weeks. He'd had to take action. Couldn't wait any longer. He'd nearly jumped the starting gun. More than once.

He had to thank her innocence that she hadn't noticed—hadn't seemed one whit suspicious. And why would she be? It was ludicrous. The whole situation was.

And so unlike him. He valued internal control above

all else. The one property that seemed ever elusive in his family. People who gave in to their base feelings were weak. Easily led by their emotions. That someone had tweaked his own was unnerving.

It made him uneasy. And he didn't like that at all.

So here he was, action in motion, sidetracked; watching her wide eyes and shy smile as she nodded tentatively to whatever the modiste was saying. He was determined to get his fill, remake her into the confident, vivacious woman she could be, then resume his normal life, free from her invisible grip.

Easy enough. He had conquered harder challenges. Family financial declines, scandal upon family scandal, turning the family reputation into a legend, cleaning up after his parents.

Not murdering anyone related by blood.

And Miranda Chase provided plenty of material for him to work with. She was a passionate woman beneath her real innocence.

But something about her made him think odd and dangerous thoughts. Thoughts of veering from his path of destruction. Heading off the gossips with firm respectability. Discontinuing the cycle of pain.

Could it be that the destruction of a relationship wasn't the foregone conclusion he'd always thought it to be? That emotions didn't weaken the structure?

Something about her continued to itch under his skin, causing his blood to flow faster. An unidentified element that was just outside of his control.

He shook away the thought. Some lingering piece of the game, assuredly.

But he couldn't shake the fallible feeling.

Chapter 10

Secret #4 (cont.): . . . and never let another pull your strings without your consent. Own your own thoughts, know your confidence, and she will fall at your feet.

Miranda found her way to the library in a haze. The viscount had needed to be dropped at an appointment, but he had kept her in the carriage until he exited. Teasing her in his dark way, making her forget her surroundings, her heart lurching in something far from fear.

He had signaled to the coachman. A twist of his fingers. A casual mention of pulling a cord if she wanted to stop—and how there were plenty of fine stops on the way, and didn't she want to stretch her feet? Then he had exited. And the driver had taken a long, scenic drive of London on the return. A slow ride in the expensive conveyance. Stopping occasionally, never once responding in anything other than a friendly manner when she'd pulled the cord and leapt out.

The viscount could have seen her tightened fingers—
he was remarkably perceptive—and deduced her fear
at the beginning of the ride. But that she wished for a
longer journey? That short jaunts mingled with quick
stops might help her in some way?

Dangerous man.

She heard sounds from down the hall. Curiosity
dispelled some of the haze. She had been working mostly
on her own, for each time the viscount appeared, any
servants assisting her would mysteriously disappear. So
she was expecting to see one or two servants unloading
crates. She stepped into the doorway and froze.

He didn't just have a few servants helping. He had
an army.

She stepped inside to help, but was immediately
surrounded by women. "Oh, Miss Chase, there you are.
This way." One of them pointed back to the door, then
spoke to a woman who had entered behind Miranda.
"Galina, you were supposed to show her to the room
right away."

"She came in the back door." The pretty servant
gave her a formal stare. Cold. "Again."

Miranda had told Benjamin and Giles to take her
right into the carriage house. She had wanted to see
the other coffins—*carriages*—and the horses. She had
even stroked one on the nose. She had felt eminently
better than she had in a long time. A weight lifted
from her shoulders.

"My apologies. I asked Giles if I could see the
horses, and it seemed impractical to walk around to
the front."

Their stares ranged from hostile to surprised at her
usage of the driver's name. Miranda vaguely wondered

again about the other visitors, *other women*, who had visited the house on a rotating basis.

"It is no trouble, Miss Chase," one of the maids reassured her with a kind smile.

"Please call me Miranda."

The woman nodded. "Of course, Miss Chase."

Miranda sighed.

"If you could come with us, we can begin."

Miranda blinked at the women surrounding her. "Begin? But the room is coming along splendidly. You've done a fine job. Thank you so much for your help."

A flash of irritation passed through Galina's eyes before the coldness resumed. "So we can begin preparing you."

"Preparing me? Is there a flood imminent?" Miranda attempted a joke, but when the pretty maid's eyes narrowed, she lost her already wobbly smile. "Preparing for what?"

"For your engagement tonight."

Miranda stared at her. She had just arrived back from the modiste. How would the staff even know? Well, she supposed it had taken over an hour with all of her stops. But still . . . preparing?

"Will it be that dire? Do I need to practice my lines?" The maid didn't seem to appreciate any attempts at humor. Miranda shifted uncomfortably.

"Please, Miss Chase, follow us." The kinder maid once again motioned toward the door.

Miranda followed them down the hall, a short trip, to a large guest room. It was a lovely, styled room, but impersonal. Likely one of a dozen extra rooms. Miranda shook her head. And it would cost more than she had to furnish a corner of the room alone—this indistinct paradise.

"This is to be your room while you are here."

Miranda started. "My room? I am not staying."

"To use as you please. If you require a respite, you may retire here." The maid broadly gestured around the room. There was a large bed with dozens of pillows piled on top. A curling armed bench sat at the foot. A dressing table and chair stood along the wall. A reading chair sat in the far corner beside a personal table and ottoman. Everything was expensive, but uniform. She was reminded a bit of the viscount's Red Room, with its stark, indecipherable style.

And then her attention focused on a small spinning globe next to the window nook. A place to dream and gaze. The globe was smaller than the countess's, which sought to fill the center space of the countess's room, but this one looked equally magnificent. Her hand itched to trace the gilded meridians.

One tiny bit of personality—one just for her—in this otherwise-impersonal room.

How . . . how would he know? They had only just been to Lady Banning's.

"I am here to work," she said in a near whisper, not knowing how to respond.

Galina sent her a disbelieving look, then opened the large wooden armoire. Hanging inside was a diaphanous gown of sea-sprayed white, green, and blue. The white accents were crested waves of a sea that was neither calm nor storm-tossed. Somewhere in flux. In transition from one state to the other.

Miranda reached out a finger to touch the gown, then drew it back.

"Your gown, Miss Chase."

"Mine?" It was hard to vocalize. She was to wear this?

She let her finger complete its journey, touching the fabric, running her finger along the edge of a wave and down to the waterfall beneath. "It's beautiful."

She hadn't tried this dress on. Hadn't seen it in the shop at all.

"Yes, Miss Chase." Galina's response was perfunctory and automatic, but there was a negative thread lacing it. Miranda looked to her but was met with a perfectly blank face. No hint of jealousy or irritation on display. Still . . .

"Thank you, Miss Lence, for helping me. I daresay I am out of my element here."

She thanked her fortune that something had made her ask the full name of this maid in particular when she'd begun her quest to learn them all.

The maid stared at her for a hard second, then something loosened. Something small, but there all the same. She waved a hand toward the chair. "Sit please, and we will begin."

Miranda followed the instruction blindly, her hand dropping from the dress in an almost apologetic manner—the gown seemed almost alive.

Another maid entered, an older woman higher in the chain of command. They undressed her to her undergarments and gloves and began dressing her hair, arguing with each other over the best style. Miranda was trying to wrap her mind around the fact that she was being pawed over—she was used to getting ready as quickly as possible with the help of whoever was on hand, returning the favor just as quickly.

Behind her, the kind, youngest maid picked her hair up on each side, looking at it in the cheval glass of the dressing table. "I saw Lady Jersey wearing it like this in Berkeley Square."

"During the day, girl. We need an evening look," the older woman said.

"But Lady J—"

"Is old," Galina said bitingly. "Now, Caroline Lamb, on the other hand—"

The older maid gasped. "Bite your tongue."

"No." Galina narrowed her eyes. "She was the height of fashion and her hair when arranged just so . . ." A wistful look passed over her more taciturn features. The young maid looked intrigued, but the older woman was having none of it.

"I say we need a classic look."

"And I say that we do something to highlight the gown." The last bit was on the pugilistic side.

The younger maid looked between the two combatants with wide eyes. "Galina, you usually don't care—"

"She can carry off the style. It is a cross between innocence and maturity. She can choose which to display." The maid's eyes met hers in the mirror. "I want to see what she looks like."

"I'm sure Miss Chase will look lovely in any style," the older woman said diplomatically. Miranda shifted nervously. Mrs. Fritz was able to stick a few pins in her hair, when needed. And Georgette had made valiant attempts at styles, though her friend made a much better model than hairdresser. "Lovely" was not usually a description that she would make of any of her previous hairstyles. Adequate usually, perhaps even pretty on occasion if she was feeling especially good.

"You are being difficult, Galina, and as I am the head of this floor—"

"Fine." The maid's face went flat again. "Do as you wish."

The woman nodded firmly, and they began to arrange her hair in a classic upsweep with tendrils hanging down. It was flattering to her face, and Miranda felt a thread of excitement as she gazed at her reflection. She *felt* pretty. And she was going to wear the dress in the armoire? Her excitement increased three notches.

The older maid nodded. Galina's face displayed nothing.

"We are ahead of schedule." The older woman brushed her hands against each other. "But let us get her dressed so we can see if alterations are needed."

Miranda was quite used to clips and pins. The only pieces that needed to fit precisely were her undergarments. The rest were easily taken care of by a quick pin or tuck.

"It won't require alterations." Galina looked as if she very nearly was going to cross her arms.

"Girl, you are becoming a trial."

Galina's lips pinched together, and she said nothing. She picked up the gloves that fell over an accessories hanger to the side. She held her hand out imperiously for Miranda's. Miranda pretended she misunderstood and tried to take the gloves from her.

The maid's eyes tightened, but she released the gloves as if she didn't care. Miranda placed them in her lap and pulled her worn gloves off. Her hands touched the air, and she tried as quickly as she could to pull the left glove on.

She fumbled, and a quick look showed the maid watching her.

Galina examined Miranda's bare hands for a second, then gave her an unreadable look. Miranda tried not to hide her hands, though they twitched toward her lap, the urge great. The maid's hands were probably equally worn beneath her own gloves, but in other ways. Water and soap, scrubbing damage. Sewing pricks or tired, stretched skin.

Or maybe they were buttery soft, the pampered feel of an upstairs servant who had to touch the master or mistress of the house with bare fingers sometimes. The coarse touch of a lowly worker not good enough for the newbornlike skin of the Quality.

She gripped the silk glove in her right hand, her roughened fingers sullying the material.

Why had she ever agreed to go to dinner with the viscount? To go anywhere with him? Ludicrous. The whole idea was like something out of a story, but instead of living in Olympus, she would be turned into a tree or deer in the end. A punishment sent down by a pagan god of old for daring to consort with the king of them all.

The maid's eyes narrowed further, and her lips pursed. She reached forward and tugged the glove from her hand, then pulled it over Miranda's fingers. Not roughly, but not gently either. As if she were fighting her natural inclination one way or the other.

Miranda didn't get a chance to contemplate Galina's behavior further as the other two maids were lifting the gown and urging her into it. Fitting it around her, fastening, and smoothing it.

She could see the middle of the dress in the table looking glass. She wondered what it would look like in a full-length mirror. This dress that she had never tried on. That had somehow been put together in under an hour. She couldn't wrap her mind around it.

And it fit. Amazingly well. As if made just for her. Only two pins were needed, and even those she would have done without if there hadn't been three maids intent on making the dress into a glove.

And the gloves themselves . . . sumptuous. So fine against her skin. Superficially covering up her inadequacies. Making her almost seem like she belonged in the strange other world the viscount inhabited.

The older maid nodded decisively. "Very good. You look beautiful, Miss Chase."

The younger maid enthusiastically agreed. Galina concurred in a less effusive manner with a tilt of her head, but there was still something in her eyes.

The older maid picked up a navy domino, which looked new as well. They tied the wrap in place, the hood hanging down her back, framing her hair and face. Making her into someone completely foreign and new. The last piece was a mask, which they didn't secure, simply handing it to her. Feathered and blue—a royal blue deeper than the shade in her gown and lighter than the domino, a shade that accented both and transformed her into something exotic.

The domino wasn't a piece that had been waiting in the viscount's clutches then. These pieces were a deliberate set. And created uniquely for her, if the fit was anything to go by.

That he had prevaricated was minute compared to the question of why he had done any of these things in the first place. Boredom? The chase? But what chase was there when she folded immediately? Starry-eyed and excited. One hand on the gossip sheet that he always graced.

"Come, Miss Chase, we are to escort you to the Red Room."

She followed, servants in the corridors stopping and staring. Her anxiety increased.

The Red Room was just as she remembered it. Cold and dark. Just that one hint of something more. There were only two lamps lit. A large one by the entrance, standing no more than two feet from her, highlighted the doorway and anyone standing there in white gold. A much smaller, more intimate one perched on the desk. The golden candlelight cast dark and golden shades onto the viscount's stunning face. A sea of black separated the two of them.

He was seated at the desk, leaning back, his left fingers playing with a quill pen, twirling it absently, then switching to his right. He looked up, and the pen whirled off its axis.

She pinched a fold of her gown, the decorum that had been drilled into her doing nothing to prevent the nervous action. His fingers gave a small flick, and a whisper of sound behind her said she was now alone, framed in the door.

"Miss Chase, is that you?" He smiled faintly, but his eyes sharpened and darkened in the shifting shadows as he pulled upright.

"Lord Downing." Something strange rose in her. "I daresay I don't know."

He slid up from his seat and around the desk. "Mmmm . . . then who am I taking to the gardens in her place?"

A mask dangled from his fingers as he approached, and a thrilling boldness rose in her, strange, out of place, heady. Like opening a rare new book and discovering unknown wonders. Or entering a dream and becoming whomever she wished.

She opened her mouth to answer as he came closer, but no words formed.

"Even better. I'll discover it for myself." One hand moved around her elbow, up her forearm, and lifted the gloved hand containing her own mask. The play of his leather pads against her satin ones created an audible friction, a rich, deep sound. Not like the coarse sound to which she was accustomed. "Shall I?"

When she didn't respond—*couldn't* respond—he smiled faintly, his fingers slowly pulling away from hers.

"Perhaps I will call you Estella. The star of the night." The silken cords of her mask sifted through his fingers along with his own. He lifted hers and placed the soft backing cloth against her eyes. She could feel the strong velveteen of his mask as it gently kissed the edge of her ear. Leaning toward her, he stretched the binding around, the material whispering against her cheeks and over the tips of her ears, settling in the soft sensitive area behind the curve.

She could feel his fingers slowly tying the threads, the edges of his stark cuffs making a gentle swoosh on the hair above her ears. He leaned into her a bit more, the spicy masculine scent of him reaching out and wrapping around her as surely as the binding he had just secured.

The smile on his face as he took her in was slow and sure, confident and mysterious. She expected him to make a quip, but his hand traced a path down her arm, wrapping around her hand. Everything stilled in the room. Anything not directly connected to the viscount became hazy and unfocused. The only sound she could hear was the steady thump of her heart in her ears.

"Or Artemis, innocent goddess of the hunt, bathing on the mount. And I poor Actaeon, unable to help myself."

He led her like the hunter he claimed to be from the house to the darkened carriage outside.

The walls of the carriage were still close, a little too

close, but the viscount maintained a steady stream of chatter, picking arguments precisely when tendrils of fear lifted from her deep well.

She touched the mask on her face. She could be anyone. Someone unafraid of, well, anything. A magical girl upon a quest.

The carriage pulled to a stop, the butterflies rising and swirling within her.

He lifted her hand and helped her descend the steps of the carriage, his mouth curving as she uttered a soft thanks. She concentrated on the last step, the merriment she had heard from the interior of the carriage turning into a dull roar in her ears. She took a moment to gather herself before looking up. She withheld a soft gasp. The entrance to the gardens gleamed as if sprinkled by fairy dust. Thousands of lamps were lit as if millions of stars had been plucked just for the purpose of lighting their way.

She had never entered from this avenue where the Quality entered in their pomp and circumstance. Where the gorgeous chandeliers began, framing the main walk, giving way to the fountains, the pavilions, the arches and temples. Where thousands of people stood, watched, and promenaded, eyeing each new visitor and gathering gossip for the pages and tomorrow's rounds.

Georgette enjoyed watching the ton and connecting faces to the names, but Miranda had always been uncomfortable overtly doing so. Carrying the guilt from her mother's early teachings.

She had always kept her eyes from drifting too often. It wasn't the thing a lady did. And though she could snort at being called a lady when she was far beneath the social structure of one, it was how she had been reared.

But she should have disregarded her training earlier and let Georgette drag her off the side paths. The carriage entrance to the gardens at night was breathtaking.

Vauxhall itself was a bright, shining gem. And as she automatically touched the viscount's sleeve, she felt for a moment that she was shining herself. They walked through an arch and into the merriment. People twirled and chased, danced wildly and softly courted.

Here the noble and common alike graced the same space, though on a night when the Quality were out in full force, there was a distinct separation between them, personal servants keeping a fine line between the masses and their masters. A distinctly hazy line that one didn't cross if one didn't want a swift kick in the shins or a mysteriously called watchman asking questions.

But tonight was filled with the more notorious of the set. The debutantes, matrons, and marriage-minded gentlemen were away at Almack's or some other hallowed haunt. So the crowd was intermixed and raucous. Gentlemen accompanied by mistresses, women of questionable virtue holding court, the young and wild sowing their oats and daring each other into increasingly crazy stunts.

A number of women—the ones who desperately wanted to be part of the inner sanctum of the scene—paraded the edges, showing off a bit of ankle here or a fallen shoulder of a gown there. Occasionally one would be called over to a box filled with rowdy men fresh from school, urging one another on, slapping each other's shoulders, exchanging money and bets. The women jockeyed for key positions in their eyesight.

The viscount steered her past the crowds, some of the people called out greetings in the exuberant air, others restrained themselves to simple nods. Miranda caught more than one curious look tossed her way, but the viscount whisked her into a dining box before she could grow more nervous or feel increasingly out of place.

A lavish table was set. Baskets of fresh fruits and thinly sliced ham, biscuits, and cheese cakes, were placed on top with a quart of the heady punch the gardens were known for. The servers disappeared into the shadows as soon as each was placed.

Miranda watched one of the men take his position in a dark hollow, leaning slightly forward on the balls of his feet, ready to move in an instant. His eyes caught hers for a second before he looked away, examining the area for anything amiss. When she continued to stare, he looked her way again and stepped in her direction before she remembered herself and shook her head quickly, indicating that she didn't require anything. He stepped back, at the ready again.

Miranda swallowed. What was she doing here? She should be out in the fray with the riffraff or at home holed up in her cold room snuggled in the seven layered blankets she kept upon her bed, more than one with frayed edges and tattered or patched holes.

She looked at her gloves. Her perfect, new gloves.

"I'll think you like your gloves more than the gown or the setting."

She tried not to shiver as his husky tone washed over her in a pleasant wave. Her new gloves represented far more than new finery in the scene around them. She hadn't had new gloves in so long. And never anything like these.

"I can appreciate the beauty of them as I can see them in their entirety at the moment."

"Well, then take it from me, the gown you wear is even more exquisite. On you or discarded to the floor."

His eyelids were heavy as he leaned back in his chair, examining her, a slow smile stretching across his cheeks, raising the skin above his cheekbones and making him even more appealing.

Good Lord.

Her eyelashes brushed the bottom edge of the mask holes, and something lit inside her. A decided spark that shifted the uneasy thoughts to a back corner of her mind, hidden but not forgotten. "It seems a shame to discard a gown so fine to the floor."

The challenge was pulling to a close. She could feel it. She knew the viscount could feel it too. It was pulling at them like a marionette on strings.

"It seems a shame not to."

What was it about this man, so far above her socially that he wasn't even in the realm of dreams, that spoke to her? Was it simply timing? Loneliness or the beginnings of apathy that she was trying to shake? A desire to stop being an observer and to become a participant?

Lord knew that Georgette was constantly after her about taking more chances. Always encouraging her to spread her wings and develop some gumption. And Mr. Pitts too. Though he tended to phrase it a bit more bluntly and in less flattering terms.

The viscount reached forward and ran a finger along the soft fuzz of a ripe peach. "It would crumple so charmingly beneath your arched bare back."

And there had been something growing in her, ready to fan that spark into a full flame. It had been two long, sad years since the deaths of her parents and brother.

And she hadn't taken one step toward the things she'd always talked about doing.

Her erstwhile correspondent would be quite cutting about the finality of that revelation.

"Is that why you purchased it?" she asked as lightly as she could, staring down the shadowed path that the flirtation spread wide open. One toe rose in anticipation. Two froze in the same.

His lips curved at her direct question. "Whatever the state of your gown at the end of the night, the style is quite flattering on you."

"And here I thought you uninterested in the vagaries of fashion." She sought to follow his direction back to the lightness of their library conversations. Just when he might send her skittering off, he always said or did something to keep her firmly planted next to him, continuously on edge.

Thoughts of sirens emerged once again.

She switched her gaze to the boxes across from them, where a number of women held court in separate spaces, vying with each other. One was clearly winning. Her green gown was at the height of fashion. Everything about it accented her features and carriage.

And yet she wasn't beautiful. Not conventionally, at least. There was something about her though as she surveyed her court. A quickness to her eyes, a clever turn of her mouth. She laughed and said something in a saucy manner to a man at her right, who laughed in delight. There was definitely something about the woman.

And her identity was clear. The rose pinned to her lapel proclaiming her to all. The notorious Mrs. Q. Georgette would be in heaven with the clear window through which to watch.

"Intrigued by our dear Mrs. Quembley?" the viscount said, lounging in his seat, languidly rolling a grape between his thumb and forefinger.

"Yes," she admitted. He had caught her hunched over the gossip columns, it would be silly to deny any knowledge of the woman. She had never followed her exploits in the papers as Georgette had, but she did read the papers daily.

"She is on the hunt, I see. She will find someone quickly enough. She always does."

"Yes," she said absently, still watching the woman; the freedom of her disguise seemed to have switched off her normal inhibition to do so. "I remember she was connected to you."

Her mortification was instantaneous. She tried vainly to hope that she had only thought the thought and not actually said it.

"I think Mrs. Q. has been connected to nearly everyone."

Well, that took care of the hope.

She touched her expensive glove to her forehead, hoping that she would somehow come up with the perfect rejoinder to minimize her embarrassment.

His statement was only partially true—Mrs. Q had indeed been connected to a number of men, but only to the more coveted members of the ton, of which the viscount was a decided part.

"Are you jealous?"

She looked at him strangely, the vain search for a response rendering her dumb. "Of being connected to everyone?"

He smiled, and the usual mysterious nature of it stretched into something far more genuine, and even more appealing for it. "I think I should feel deeply wounded, but instead just find myself highly amused." He rolled the grape down all of his fingers and back up again, then tossed the fruit into the air and caught it on the back of his hand in the valley between two fingers.

Her brain caught back up to a somewhat normal flow. Jealous? The possibility of some sort of unique relationship with the man next to her was so far from her realm of reality that with her mind in pure social survival mode she hadn't even realized what he was referencing at first.

Jealousy? Perhaps a bit of longing.

Longing?

She swallowed quickly and tried to tamp down the nervousness at the thought, mingled with the strands of adventure and want that crept forth on mischievous tendrils. That reached across the space from the magnetic man across from her.

She concentrated on Mrs. Q. "It's interesting really. She isn't as beautiful as the woman on her right."

The other woman, perfectly blond and haughty, didn't command half of her court, and if anyone was envious, her cheeks were veritably green whenever her eyes connected left.

"Beauty is something that is hard to debate. Every man thinks his ideal the best." His eyes raked her hotly, and she felt her internal temperature increase like a kitchen stove overly stocked before being lit. "But the wittiest women rise to the top of this structure, conventional beauty often taking a backseat to a woman possessed of a clever tongue."

"Why?" she asked, truly curious.

"Iced beauty can be had in marriage, in the pressed palm of a switched partner in a dance. Heat though . . . passion and earth, stimulating all of the senses . . . that is what is desired in a companion."

"And a wife isn't a companion."

He raised his brows, visible above his mask. "Are you asking me or verifying the sentiment?"

"Asking you."

"I've only seen it happen in a handful of cases, and those too unique to replicate." He looked away, too casually. "Most *love matches* are actually untamed desire not allowed to run its course."

"That is cynical of you." And yet, with parents such as his . . .

"Realistic."

She watched him. The too-casual set of his shoulders. The way he moved the grape between his fingers in a decidedly idle motion. "You say it as if it irritates you that it is so."

"Irritates me?" He raised his infernal brow again. "I hardly think you aware of the normal sway of my thoughts, Miranda." He echoed her previous words to him.

She colored. "Perhaps not. But for all of your apparent cynicism, you at times have a most gilded tongue. Even Lady Banning remarked upon it."

She tried to back away from the edge of the knife that was the topic of his parentage.

"A gilded tongue can be had on the most crafty of serpents."

"I meant it in the lyrical sense."

A number of emotions crossed his face in quick succession. Such a change from his normally sultry or indecipherable features that she nearly missed them in her surprise.

Irritation, amusement, desire. Desire? But then he always had that in his arsenal.

His lips tightened, then parted, and she tensed. Would he agree or draw sword?

"Downing. What a surprise." A man entered their box on slightly tipsy feet, a mask dangling perilously on his nose, the curve of a loosened knot making a noose on the side of his head.

"Messerden. What a lack thereof." The viscount's eyes grew icy.

Messerden clapped a hand against his thigh and rubbed the edge of his forefinger against the tip of his drink-reddened nose. "Thought you could hide?"

"If I did, it would be in vain now, wouldn't it?"

The man turned to her, frankly appraising her. "Mrs. Collins? Lady Tenwitty? Is that you, Marie?"

She opened her mouth to respond, but the viscount tossed the fruit toward an empty bowl with a small ping. "What do you want, Messerden?"

The man cheerfully accepted the snub to his question, as if it were not unusual. "Wondering where you've been the past week. Betting has been hot at the club."

"Has it?" the viscount said coolly. "I don't recall hiding. I saw you stumbling your way through a waltz at the Pemberleys' two nights ago."

The man waved his hand and sat in a chair that magically appeared. "Everyone was there. I meant at White's or Newmarket. Or the Merrick brothers' new little hell down east. Can't believe you haven't been yet. And then for you to show up here with the gossip churning over the possibility of a duel on top of the other bits. Well, you do know how to make an entrance."

Miranda grew increasingly uncomfortable. She wondered if there was something in Messerden's personality or in the amount of drink he had consumed that made him unaware of the forbidding look and tenor of the conversation with the man he was trying to verbally engage.

"I was unaware that my presence necessitated such discourse."

"Gads, man. She's got both of them in a box on the other side." Messerden motioned right, swaying as he went off-balance. "Can't tell if they are going to take a turn with her in the bushes or kill each other first."

"Sometimes the world is better off if one always defaults to option number two." The viscount picked up another grape, his posture too idle once more.

"Is Werston making nice with Tarking?" Messerden said in reference to the viscount's father and his latest scandal. "Been missing for a month. Both of them."

"Is that so?"

"Rumor floating that you were going to marry Tarking's chit. Make the sprog legitimate to the line. Keep it in the family even if it's the marquess's."

The viscount raised a brow and said nothing.

Messerden stared over his red nose and through bleary eyes as if the viscount would reveal the information if he but concentrated hard enough. The silence stretched. Miranda wished she were somewhere else. Reading about gossip was much easier on the nerves than watching it take place.

Messerden cracked first. "Everyone has been wondering what you'd do this time in response, and you go and do nothing."

"I will have to extend my apologies for damming the entertainment."

Ah. The root of his disingenuous apologies was starting to take shape. She tilted her head.

The motion must have been just enough to call attention, because suddenly Messerden blinked at her and leaned forward. "I say. I don't recognize you at all now that I think on it. A good disguise? Or maybe not. You been hot for something new, Downing? Who is this?"

"A Russian princess," he said smoothly and without a pause, as if he were speaking the truth. "Here for the festivities. Do keep it to yourself, Messerden."

"Of course I will." The man looked affronted. He leaned a bit more forward toward Miranda. "Are you really?"

She looked to the viscount in a panic.

"Doesn't speak a lick of English. Alas." The viscount popped a grape into his mouth.

"Don't need to do much speaking though, do you, Downing?" The man obviously thought himself highly amusing. He chortled at his own joke. He turned back to her. "What is your name?"

Miranda stared at him.

"I"—he pointed to himself—"am Messerden. You?" He reached out to touch her.

The viscount made a motion, too small for the other man to catch, especially in his inebriated state. Two attendants immediately stepped forward, and one placed himself in the man's path, Messerden's finger hitting the button on his shirt instead of touching Miranda.

"Sir, let us escort you back to your box. There is an excellent bottle waiting for you there. On the house."

Messerden shook their hands away, needing to stand in the process. "Gads, keep your dirty paws away. Do you know who I am?" He straightened his jacket. "Service here is going straight to the dogs, I tell you."

The viscount shrugged lightly, almost apologetically. "The Russians are very protective of their princesses."

Miranda stared at him. His mouth didn't even curve in shared amusement.

"Well, I suppose that could be." Messerden brushed a hand down his trouser leg. "But they should know who they are handling first. Gads, I'm the grandson of a duke." He gave the men in the shadows a glare, then turned back to the viscount. "Downing, stop in and have a chat later. Need to know where to place my bets."

"Place them where you please, Messerden. I can't help you there."

"Don't be coy, Downing. Of course you can. Bring the princess too. I won't tell a soul." He crossed his chest and staggered away.

Miranda watched him go, remembering just a moment too late to close her mouth. He stumbled into a couple and gestured animatedly, pointing back at them. The couple craned their necks. Miranda shrunk back into the shadows. The couple simply craned farther.

"It will be all over the grounds within ten minutes," the viscount said idly, fingering another grape.

"I can't believe you told him that."

"Why?" He smiled slowly. "You are my princess."

"Do you have no shame?"

"Me?" He raised a brow, settling back into his chair. "Not a lick last I checked."

More of the attendees craned their heads for a better view. She tried not to return their frank stares. *This* was why she didn't opt to come and stare. And she promised herself from here on out that nothing Georgette said would make her change her mind to do so.

"Don't pay them any heed, it just makes them more rabid." There was a bite to his words.

She didn't think it possible not to pay attention though. It was a little like watching the black-and-white pages suddenly turn to color, active and alive. And she in the middle of the print. Twisted in a sinking splotch of ink.

She watched a pair of tightrope walkers tossing pins and a number of acrobats flipping and flying through the air. One pin landed atop a man's head in a balance-defying manner.

"Are you enjoying them?"

The colorful men were mesmerizing with their tricks and served as a distraction. "Yes, they are wonderful."

He waved the performers on the floor toward their area, signaling a man in the shadows. To pay a tuppence, probably, for the show.

"Straight from Paris. The latest rage. Though much more spectacular when seen in the proper setting."

They must be part of the Cirque Diamant then. She smiled wistfully. "Someday I shall see them in full then."

"Someday? Why not tomorrow? They are in town for a few weeks at the Claremont."

"The papers said the show is sold out through its entire run."

"Tickets can always be found if one searches the right places."

"I have to catalog your library tomorrow."

"And the next day as well. I will hardly let you leave. But at night you are free." One side of his mouth crooked deliciously. "At least for now."

She tucked hair behind her ears, coloring. "Perhaps."

But there was working for her uncle and saving for her grand visit. Something always came up.

"Mmmm. That hardly sounds convincing." He tapped two fingers together. "I will have to take you to a royal court performance sometime then."

She stared at him, mind frozen. "Why?"

"Because I wish to." He smiled lazily. "And as I've said, I do as I wish."

The players were even more marvelous at closer range. The supporting musicians beat a rhythm as they threw batons and pins, performed flips and death-defying leaps onto one another's shoulders.

She leaned forward, her body feeling the euphony.

"You enjoy the rhythm of the music," he said.

"I do. And the spectacle. The freedom."

"You do not feel that freedom yourself?"

"Oh, I have more freedom than most. I do not live in ignorance of such. But still, to do as one pleases." She waved a hand at him absently. "It must be glorious."

"Sometimes one appears to have more freedom than one actually possesses. It is easy to see what one wishes to see."

She opened her mouth to respond, but a sudden clamor of voices had her looking to the side.

The pervasive feeling of not belonging grew stronger as an unmasked woman who could only be the Marchioness of Werston, with features so reminiscent of her son's, stepped gracefully into their box with a man at her arm.

"Dear! They said that you had arrived and were dining."

"Mother."

"And who is this?" She looked Miranda over in a full, curious glance.

He waved a dismissive hand. "What do you need, Mother? Dillingham." His voice, while warmer when speaking directly to his mother, was veritably chilly when uttering the man's name.

The marchioness leaned against her partner. "Mr. Easton has taken an unfortunate tumble in our dinner box. A bit more than was bargained for. Do fix it for me, Maxim, dear." She reached over and touched her son's cheek, an emotion showing in the marchioness's eyes that Miranda was surprised to identify.

Everything about his posture tightened, all the way from his thighs lounging out in front of him to the tendons of his neck above his simple, tastefully tied cravat to the suddenly pinched lines around his eyes. He touched his mother's hand against his cheek and pulled it down, his face smoothing back into unreadable, chiseled lines.

"Very well." He looked off into the distance—and was that self-loathing she saw in his gaze? It was gone quicker than she could confirm. He gave the marchioness's hand a soft pat. "Why don't you return home."

She sighed. "Put the fun at an end? Very well," she echoed. "Come, Dilly, onward to other pursuits. You did win this round after all."

"And I intend to win again, my dear."

"Directly home, Dillingham." The viscount's syllables were clipped.

The earl shifted on suddenly uncomfortable feet, his smile slipping. "Right. Evening, Downing."

His mother stepped from the box, Dillingham hurrying after her.

Silence descended upon the space.

"Your mother is quite . . ." She searched for the word.

"Frivolous?" His voice was remote.

"I was going to say carefree."

"A much nicer term."

"She seems sad."

His eyes narrowed on her. "What makes you say that?"

She shrugged, uncomfortable. Uncomfortable with all of it. "Something in her eyes. The way she looked at you."

"Most people find her overly exuberant."

Miranda said nothing. For what was there to say? *Your mother wears a mask. You obviously know it too judging by your reaction and expression. She appears so often in the scandal sheets, that it is nearly a cry for help.*

"Or tawdry." He smiled without humor. "Irresponsible, scandalous, loose. Many descriptive words. But not sad."

"I'm sorry."

He looked away for a second, and she could have sworn that split second of self-loathing was evident once more. "You have nothing to be sorry for."

She started to respond to the strange implication that *he* might, but he glanced back at her, face cleared as though it had never changed. "What other events or things do you wish you could attend or see, but haven't yet grabbed?"

She startled at the abrupt change of topic, but understood. "You say it as if I have no courage to press forward."

"Not a lack of courage. Not reaching out and grabbing the things you want is not necessarily indicative of a lack of courage. More perhaps a lack of initiative and impulse."

"Or a lack of courage."

"Fine. Or a lack of courage."

"You are suddenly trying to be conciliatory to me."

He laughed without humor. "It doesn't quite flow off my tongue, does it?"

"Everything flows off a tongue lined in silver or gold. It is just not your usual gambit."

He smiled slowly. "Do you know my usual gambit? What if I'm doing the exact opposite in order to ensnare you?"

"I suppose I will have to take my chances."

He reached over and idly touched a lock of hair outside of her mask and domino. "'*I must be here confined by you.*' I want nothing more but for you to take chances with me."

Her heart picked up speed. "Why?"

"Because you intrigue me." He tilted his head. "And because I wish it."

He looked off into the distance a second more, then pushed back his chair and rose. "Come. Let us leave the scrutiny for a time."

She took his hand, the silk fingers of her glove curling into his leather ones. Both exquisitely fine. Opposite and complementary.

They walked along the main garden corridor, the

revelers parting around them. Miranda ignored the whispers and stares, feeling instead the draw of the dark man next to her.

The dark walks beckoned ahead. The hedges curling in invitation or warning.

He turned, his back to the path, and lifted her hand in his. "Come with me, Miranda." His voice was coaxing, the call coiling around her.

Come. Open me. Find the answers to what you've always wondered about.

He stepped back onto the dark path. And she followed.

Chapter 11

Element #1: It isn't just essential to entice your prey, but you must make absolutely certain that you are the only thing on her mind morning, noon, and night.

The Eight Elements of Enchantment
(work in progress)

He smiled at her, confidently walking backward without a thought as to where he would place his feet, already seeming to know the route. It should have been a disquieting thought that he had been here before and knew the area so well that he had it memorized, but she simply followed the spell and let him pull her into the darkened corridors. The twining hedges and sleeping flowers.

The lamps were sparse at the beginning of the path, only serving to cast enough light to increase the shadows and make the scene more intimate. The moon was a chipped disk, three-quarters full, increasing the feel.

She was tired of fighting it, fighting the urge to *see, explore, feel.*

A small area opened around the path. A place made

just for a couple who wished to stop and enjoy themselves in one way or another. A brass sculpture of a cupid in flight nestled in the green stalks.

His fingers caressed hers. "What would your expert on seduction say about this scene?"

She looked around her, at the way the moonlight caught the closed edges of a flower, like a lover in wait. "You haven't seemed very receptive to my attempts to translate previously. You are either a glutton for punishment, or it is I."

"Or perhaps I just desire to hear you speak in your enraptured tones. To feel your voice wrap around and squeeze me." He followed her eyes and touched the edges of the closed petals. "Come, what secret describes this scene?"

"Enjoy everything around you, even if you've seen it a thousand times before?" She said it as lightly as she could, as was often the case around him. She never knew whether to treat his attention as lingering amusement or seriousness.

His fingers touched her chin, lifting it softly. "Even should I see you a thousand times. Each time would be a new lure."

She swallowed around the tightness in her throat. "You must be lured frequently."

"Not often enough." There was a ring of truth to the words that made her heart pick up more speed. Rationally, she knew that she was merely Miranda Chase, commoner, but he always made her feel as if she were something much more.

"You should write your own book, your lordship. Bottle your secrets."

One brow rose, and his fingers moved along the edge of her chin and brushed the hair behind her ear, lingering there, the lightest touch of pressure urging her forward.

"I'd rather discover yours." His fingers slipped down the side of her throat and over her shoulder.

"Oh?" she said faintly.

"Oh, yes." The words tickled the heated flesh of her cheek. "I want to taste your secrets." His lips grazed her earlobe and whispered into her core. "Will you let me, Miranda?"

Her fingers rose without conscious thought, up to his shoulders, and curled around, gripping the strength beneath with finality. She could feel his smile as he pulled her against him, his lips touching the skin behind her ear, igniting heat and flame. His hands moved down her back and over her backside, pulling her against him completely below.

Her head tilted back, almost unable to support itself under the onslaught. He bent forward, his lips sucking at the point where the beat of her heart threatened to explode. Luring, hooking, baiting . . . all secrets to seduction were laid waste by the pure heat of actual desire. The aroma of jasmine and lilies surrounded her. The tendrils of scent slipping over her skin, the viscount's own heady cologne making her feel drunk and branded.

Her skin would undoubtedly smell of the spice forever as his lips trailed across her neck, infusing the scent, and his fingers quested downward, awakening every pore to absorb more.

"I've wanted to see you fully exposed by the moonlight since the first time I saw you."

"In the shadows of a dusty bookshop," she said as lightly as she could, gasping as teeth nipped and grazed a sensitive spot behind her ear.

He paused for a moment, but then it was as if the pause had never been, and his hands reached into the soft edges of her hair and tilted her head back farther. "Never in the shadows."

His lips touched hers, and it was like the moon had shaken off the lingering collar of darkness and turned on its full light. A first kiss, then a second, and soon a tenth, and the count was lost as his fingers stroked down her neck, pulling around to caress her cheeks. Thumbs grazed her throat and curved over her shoulders.

Igniting feelings that could not be captured on the page, nor in an illustration.

"'Release me from my bands with the help of your good hands.'"

Her heart picked up speed as he divested her of her domino with a quick flip of his fingers. As he continued to devour her, leaning into her, backing her up a step, leaning her back over something curved and marble, cold against the hot flesh of her elbow. Her own hand curling around his neck and touching the dark hair there, silky and coarse, at odds with itself.

She had never felt anything like the burst of feeling inside of her. The pulses of heat that followed everywhere he touched.

Her head tipped back as his lips traveled down and over her throat. "I believe this means you have won, your lordship."

"Oh, I like to think of it as *we*." He placed a kiss over the beat of her pulse, his lips lingering. "We have won, Miranda."

His hand wrapped around the back of her nape, lowering her gently so she was lying on the bench, he seated himself next to her, her neck carefully nestled in his hand as he laid her head carefully on the stone.

One hand caressed down the hollow of her throat and over her exposed flesh, down the middle of her chest, her back arching up as if her body was attached to his fingers by strings. Flowing tendrils of flowers swam in her vision, then he was pulling a line down her midsection. Her head tipped back, and she gazed, barely seeing, up at the heavy cracked moon above her as his fingers coasted over the juncture of her legs below.

Her breath caught, and he leaned over her, smiling down at her. "And I assure you that this is only part of the overall seduction. A bite." His lips grazed her throat. "A promise." Her chin. "A hope."

His lips claimed hers once more. His leg was between hers, pressed against her. Where the illicit pictures usually concentrated.

Something built within her at every touch. Something that he had ignited at their first meeting and steadily stoked each day thereafter. Small gasps of sound escaped from her lips.

His eyes connected with hers as he pulled back an inch to look down at her. "Oh, my lost heart." His lips pulled into the most sensual smile she had ever witnessed. "Such passion under that delicate skin. Barely touched and already reaching for completion."

His fingers grazed her breasts, over the fabric, her skin scorching beneath the touch. The stars overhead in the dark night sky burned brighter, hotter.

"I think I could go mad touching you. Watching you burn."

His lips were sweet and hot. Like a dessert she could consume forever. But the heat was hottest below. Against him. He seemed so far away all of a sudden. She pushed against his thigh, and the burn between her legs became a feverish need. Too hot, the flame of it too close.

The stars grew bigger as if they were expanding just so she could reach them.

Never had she thought such a thing could be possible. To touch the stars. To absorb their brilliance and hold it in the palm of her hand. To feel the light flow over her fingers and through her palms, wrists, the curve of her elbow, down to her core. Curling there, pulsing, before bursting out. The waves of it gentle and fierce, the peaks high, but softly arced.

He drew back and she looked into his eyes, the intense darkness pinning her. "Barely touched. I knew the potential lay there. Ever since . . ."

His lips stayed parted on the syllable. There was something in his eyes, some emotion that caused a wave to spike within her.

"Since—" Thundering noise rang in her ears, drowning out the sound as his lips moved. The words lost in the ring.

She drunkenly wondered if the earth would continue to shake beneath her body. If the ringing would forever exist.

"Downing!" His fingers tightened against her hip at the outside voice. "I'd know that black head of hair anywhere and that dark back stretched over a woman." A low, drunken whistle accompanied the salutation of another male voice, as the tremors in the earth became heavy footsteps. The viscount might as well have turned to stone for the lack of movement he suddenly possessed.

"Look at the legs on her. Lucky devil. Good gods, man, where do you dig them up?"

His back was to the men, and his face drew to

shadow as the moonlight melted around him, hiding his expression from her. "I picked this one up in the back of a dusty shop," he said, coolly, frostbite in the clip of each syllable.

Miranda's heart stopped beating.

The man laughed. "Good one. Where did you really find her?"

"Perhaps you aren't looking in the right places then, if you have to ask." The viscount's fingers curved into a fist at her hip, his clipped tones harsh, as if he was about to do someone irreparable harm.

Or maybe just simply to crush her with a careless motion of his perfect fingers.

Another man joined the chortle. "I have something for her to sweep when she's through with your heavy load."

Mortification joined the crushing feeling, and she hid her face in the heavy shadows.

"She's a princess," one of the men whispered, somewhat drunkenly.

"I know that," the vocal man snapped. "And I have something for her to wear on her crown when Downing's done with her." The man guffawed. "Whoo. Always look for Downing's scraps, I say."

The viscount abruptly stood and turned. She immediately swept her legs to the other side of the bench, away from the men, and set about putting her clothing to rights, head tucked down.

Another sudden shaking of the earth had her looking up and behind her. Only the viscount's tight back remained in view, the other men gone in a rush of feet. He turned, a distant and cold expression on his face. Forbidding and fierce. The fleeting glimpse of the same dark emotion that had crossed his face during his mother's visit flitted through his eyes again.

He held out a hand. "Come."

She stared at it for a moment, the remaining warm feelings receding in the cool night.

His hand moved slightly, still outstretched. "It was the fastest way to do it. I apologize." His tone was cool, formal, his eyes stormy, but distant.

The fastest way to do what? Get rid of them? She studied his hand a moment more, then met his eyes. "But are you being disingenuous in your apology this time as well?"

His hand dropped. He stayed silent for a second, then raised his hand back to her.

"I've never meant it more."

He looked as if he were at war with himself. As if his words had multiple meanings. She watched him another moment, nodded, and took his hand. His fingers wrapped around hers, firmly, a caress of his thumb to the back of her hand, then tugged her forward.

They strode back along the path of the walk. Two steps from stepping out of the moonlight and back into the lamplight, he turned to her. He secured her mask once more, his fingers lingering on a lock of hair, his knuckles brushing her cheek. She unconsciously leaned into the touch. The tips of his fingers stroked lightly, gently, then curled into a fist as he looked away.

He took her hand and strode into the merriment once more. But the languid pace of earlier was gone, an urgency to be gone and on to other things in its place.

Faces and colors blended together as they strode through the crowd. Miranda barely processed any of it through the aftermath of confusion and embarrassment. The vestiges of tightly-wound thrill.

Benjamin jumped down and opened the carriage door immediately upon seeing them, and she stumbled inside.

A strange silence pervaded the interior. The viscount's words as she'd drawn shaky breaths in the garden at complete odds with his demeanor at present.

"An odd night for this much moonlight," the viscount said, almost contemplatively, his face still closed in the flickering low lamplight and shadows as they began to move.

"Yes. And as it is, the moonlight hides as much as it reveals," she said in a near whisper, the conflicting, heavy feeling draped over the air.

He reached forward and touched the curl at her temple, pulling it around the mask, brushing her cheek. "Each time a new lure."

She wished she could see his eyes, so dark in the shadows of the closed carriage.

"*In this bare island by your spell.*" His fingers slipped from her cheek and fell to the padded bench, the Shakespearean spell formed by his third such quote lingered behind. She clasped her hands tightly together, uncertainty and longing running through her in equal measures.

It didn't take long for the carriage to reach her uncle's store. The early-evening and late-night traffic had cleared and the late, late-night traffic had not yet started.

The viscount's hand reached out again, then drew back. "Good evening, Miss Chase."

She felt a divide open and stretch between them, though she didn't understand it, as she stepped through the portal and onto the common pavement below.

Chapter 12

Dear Mistress Chase,

Never let anyone tell you how to feel. And never let seduction threaten your good sense.

Eleutherios

Miranda walked blearily into the front of the shop the next morning to see Georgette sporting a new bonnet and pelisse, bag clutched in her hand, badgering Miranda's uncle as he was leaning over his ledgers, and teasing Peter standing wide-eyed to the side.

Georgette smiled like a cat cornering a bird as soon as she spotted her. "Miranda!"

Miranda murmured greetings to everyone. She had gotten in well past her usual bedtime, then tossed and turned all night. Thoughts of the night had run through her head over and over again. What she could have done differently, what she might have said at the end, what had happened in the garden under the moonlight. Both wonderful physical memories and uneasy sifting thoughts.

"Come." Georgette took Miranda's arm. "Let's

leave your uncle to his figures and dear Mr. Higgins to his manly handling of the counter." She steered her toward the back table behind the stacks. The paper was tucked beneath her arm. Miranda stared at it in sudden dread, all of her uneasy thoughts overriding every single dreamy one.

Her friend waited until they were out of earshot before pouncing. "So? Last night? I stopped by to see you, and it seems that you hadn't yet returned home. And it was going on *ten* in the evening."

She pulled out a chair and gave Miranda a push, seating herself on the other side and leaning across the table without even removing her coat, the paper sliding onto the top of the wood. "And you look like the cat dragged you in screaming this morning."

"I just woke," she admitted.

Georgette stared. "Just woke? It's a good thing your uncle barely has a thought about stricture. He just waved last night away and said you were a good girl and likely around somewhere. He must have had no notion when you returned, especially with you looking as you do this morning. Even *my* father would have been pacing, and I get away with everything. Where were you? What did you do? Tell me everything."

Miranda rubbed the back of her neck and laughed uncomfortably at the dichotomy between her uncle's words and her actions the previous night. "Your timing is always impeccable."

"I know." Georgette gave a wave of her hand. "Now speak."

"I was out."

Georgette stared, then waved her to speak again.

"I went to Vauxhall."

"On a masquerade night? You?" Her friend's brows

rose like feathers caught on a stiff wind. "Oh, there is a story here." She quickly divested herself of her fashionable coat, her new bonnet covering the paper. Her merchant father always made sure she had the best.

Though even Georgette would have been dumbfounded by the gown hanging upstairs.

"Now what were you doing at the gardens on a night when the naughty come out to play?"

"Dining?"

Georgette's mouth turned up. "This is delicious. Downing took you to dinner at the gardens. Then into the dark walks, mmm?"

"I didn't say that," she said in a weak voice.

Georgette's mouth dropped for a second before she regained herself. "He *did* take you there? Good Lord."

Miranda's brows drew together, and she cast a look around the corner to make sure they were still out of earshot. "Well, first you assume it so, then you say it as if you'd never believe it possible."

"You have to admit, darling, surprise over that response is warranted under the circumstances. You are hardly one to walk the dark path with a gentleman." She whistled. "But what a one to begin with."

"I hardly stepped onto the path." He had lifted her above the path and laid her out over it. "Merely to observe a flowering bush." At very, very close range. Upside down.

"You went *onto the dark paths*?" Georgette leaned forward, mouth gaping.

"You just said—"

Georgette wildly waved her words away. "Tell me everything. Leave nothing out."

"He was a perfect gentleman." A perfectly naughty

gentleman. "There was nothing unseemly about it." One of the seams of her gown had been ensnared by a bramble when his leg had gone between hers, lifting against her. "The moonlight was exceptionally bright." Bright against bared skin and naked desire.

Georgette looked disappointed, and to Miranda's relief and chagrin looked as if she believed her. "Why did he invite you then?"

"I don't know." Miranda shifted nervously. "What did you do last night?"

"I went to the Mortons' revel. It was a bit of a bore though. Dinner next week should prove far more exciting. There are some new men in town." She shifted her bonnet, the paper shifting into view. "I am sure there is something about Vauxhall in the paper. Anything exciting happen other than you stepping a toe onto an illicit chip?" She pulled the paper fully into eyeshot.

Miranda watched the paper with a sudden panic she had never quite experienced upon looking at a printed piece. "But I want to hear more of your night."

"I'm sparing you the rehashing of an uneventful time. I'd rather hear about your time with the delicious viscount. I'm sure that I can get at least a modicum of naughtiness from your mind in regards to him." Georgette gave her a wink and opened the paper perfectly to the gossip section.

Miranda watched in terror as Georgette scoured the page. "Oh, the Cirque Diamant players were there? Drat. I can't believe I went to the Mortons' revel instead. I've been wanting to see them. Sold out for their entire run. How were they?"

"Um . . ."

"Um?" Georgette raised a brow. "I think your late night has hampered your ability to utter a coherent sentence."

"They were very good."

"They were very good. That's it?"

Miranda saw the shining window of opportunity. "Oh, they were beyond good. Jugglers and acrobats. And the stunts. Why, they were beyond marvelous. Let me tell you all about it."

"You wretched friend, seeing them and *nearly* taking dark walks, and here I have to pull it from you."

"Oh, I'm just tired. Exhausted from watching them. Let me tell you all about it." Miranda warmed to the topic. "There was a man who could do two flips and land on another's shoulders."

Georgette looked impressed. Then her finger started to move down the column.

Miranda leaned forward, attempting to block her view. "Don't you want to hear more?"

"I can listen and read at the same time. Keep talking." She looked back to the page.

Miranda leaned in more and put a hand on the paper. "And there was a fire-breather who could—"

"Hold on." Georgette shooed her hands away. "I saw something about a princess. Hold your thought."

The panic became a very real itch under her flesh, clawing at her like a dozen spider bites all in the same region of skin.

"But it's quite an important tale!"

However, Georgette was no longer listening. She peeled Miranda's fingers away. "Look here. A Russian princess? Oh!" She pointed at the evil text. "Did you see her?"

Her friend didn't wait for the answer. "Dressed in

the finest silk. Oh, the description is divine. A masked princess. How wonderful. They go on and on about her for an entire two paragraphs." She tapped the page, lifting it slightly. Miranda had never wanted to read a paragraph more, nor less. "I do so hope I will catch a glimpse of her."

"Oh," Miranda said faintly. "I'm sure you will."

"Really? Why?" But before Miranda could respond, Georgette's finger stopped. "Sitting with Lord D.?" She blinked. "Engaging with him in the *bushes, legs in the air*?"

"Really?" Miranda said, even more faintly. "Not very princesslike. And all of these Lord D.'s lately in the papers."

Georgette slowly looked up at her. "All three of them that would qualify for such a thing."

"Three? Surely there are more than three who would qualify."

"There are three. I looked it up last week, remember?" She kept her eyes pinned to Miranda. "It says briefly too that Lord Dillingham was seen with the marchioness. And I know Lord Dustin is in Yorkshire at the moment."

"Oh?"

Georgette drummed her fingers against the page, then calmly folded her hands together.

"Georgette?" Miranda asked tentatively.

"Shh, don't interrupt my thought process. I am contemplating precisely how I'm going to murder you for your silence."

Miranda sighed.

Her friend stuck one forefinger out and touched her other to it in a ticking fashion. "Firstly, I want to see the dress."

"Dress?" Miranda asked in some last feeble attempt at ignorance.

Georgette gave her a look that would freeze the Thames, her second finger already out to tap whatever was next on her list.

Miranda sighed again, her shoulders drooping. "It's upstairs."

The frozen look turned to unmitigated excitement. Georgette tried to temper the excitement but was doing a poor job. She folded her hands once more, ticking fingers forgotten. "Very well." Her fingers threading together. "Very well."

"Georgette?"

"Oh, Miranda!" she very nearly squealed, her hands parting and pressing against her chest. "I will kill you *later* for not telling me. *In the bushes, legs in the air?*"

"Shhh!" Miranda leaned back frantically to gaze around the corner. "It wasn't like that." Her legs hadn't been *in* the air.

But Georgette was hardly listening. "Learn *everything* you can from him. Take notes if you must. And make sure you share it all with me." She propped her chin on her hand, avidly watching her as if she would start spilling secrets right then.

Miranda stared at her, nearly speechless. "Learn from him? Take notes?"

"Yes. Everything you can. Then use those tactics on the man you mean to marry."

Miranda just stared at her. She felt like her uncle for a second—not comprehending anything outside the sphere he had set for himself. "Use them on . . . Georgette, have you gone mad?"

"I admit to a *slight* madness of envy." Georgette pinched her fingers together to demonstrate, seemed to reconsider, then expanded the space between her thumb and forefinger.

"Use them on the man I mean to marry?"

"You will own that man, if you do." Georgette twirled a lock of hair dreamily. "Oh, I do intend to pry all of the details out of you, I hope you know."

"I have no details to give." Nothing willingly, at least. "It was a misunderstanding. I shan't repeat it." Not if the strange atmosphere of the carriage was anything to go by. The sudden separation between them.

"Of *course* you must repeat it!"

"I'm in the *paper*."

"I know, I'm absolutely *green*. As green as a dress of *Mrs. Q.*"

Miranda sat in stunned silence for a second, then folded her arms and dropped her head on top. "Oh, Lord. I can't return to the house."

"Not return? I thought we had already discussed this before. I won the argument, I do recall."

"They will all know."

"Who?"

"The servants! They dressed me last night!"

"Oh! They did?" Georgette gave a dreamy sigh. "I bet you were lovely. What coiffure did they use? I *must* see the dress."

Miranda put a hand out to stop Georgette's rise. "I'm in the paper. Surely they read the paper. They'll know." She laughed a little hysterically. "What am I worried about, I have a room! They made me a room!"

"Dear," Georgette said soothingly, as if petting a crazed beast. "You are talking like a madwoman."

"I *am* a madwoman."

"Really, Miranda," Georgette chastised. "I am the one who reserves the right to be dramatic."

Miranda put a hand to her head. "Everyone will think I'm doing something else with him besides organizing his library. Even the papers." And really, they wouldn't be wrong based on the previous night's events.

Miranda opened her mouth to verbally kick herself some more, and Georgette held up a hand. "Wait. *Who* is going to think a thing?"

Miranda pushed her hair, which had fallen in a nicely dramatic manner into her face, behind her free ear. "His servants. And anyone who found out that he'd escorted me there."

"You mean the aristocrats that pass you and greet you on the street? All of the society matrons who might bar you from your grand debut at Almack's?" Georgette said, an overly serious expression upon her face.

Miranda flushed beneath the overt sarcasm. "Well, no, of course not."

"Oh, you mean all of the people who know you are a Russian princess?"

"Um . . ."

"That bit of news—a scandalous foreign princess in our midst—eclipsed even the scuttlebutt of Lady Werston and her erstwhile suitors. The promised duel." She pointed at the page. "There is a tiny footnote about someone hitting someone else. Barely a word. All of it is taken up by you. Believe me, if they knew who you were, it would be here on the page."

"Well, that . . ." Her voice trailed off. That was . . . interesting information.

A curl of unease threaded through her.

She grabbed for the paper. "Let me see that."

"Miranda!" Georgette huffed.

But Miranda was too busy scouring the section.

It was hardly an occasion that Mr. E. was found knocked
cold in Lady W.'s box. We, dear readers, are much more
interested in what her son was up to . . .

She stared at the page. "He did it on purpose."

"What? Who?"

"The viscount."

"What? What did he do?"

"He used me to cover up the news of his mother."

Georgette blinked at her, her expression completely
blank.

Miranda narrowed her eyes. "He used me."

"Oh, well, use him back, dear. And tell me exactly
what works and *how*."

Miranda drummed her fingers militantly. "Oh, he
had his amusement already."

"So the papers were not making it up about the
bushes? The legs?" Georgette leaned forward. "What
was it like? Did he make you mad with desire? Did
you feel all those things everyone goes on about? Tell
me everything. Leave nothing out."

Miranda ignored her. "It is probably better this
way anyway."

"Better what way? You are torturing me." Georgette's
hand went to her forehead.

"Because frankly, temptation that he is—was—or
not, there was something, well, rather alarming about
the whole matter. And about the viscount."

"He's not a fluffed cake. I keep telling you that you

don't want one, but do you listen?" Her friend shook her fist at her.

Miranda drummed her fingers, thoughts colliding. "He purposefully baited me to help him with his library even after speaking of it with uncle."

"So?"

"Like some nefarious scheme."

Georgette's eyebrows lifted. "Really, Miranda. A nefarious scheme?"

"I tell you, he purposely baited me."

"And?"

"And . . ." Miranda drummed her fingers harder. "There is—was—something quite off with the whole matter." She pressed her lips together. "Very off. Why me?"

Georgette's eyes softened. "Darling, why not you?"

Miranda shook her head, lips unable to move for a moment, lest some other emotion peep through. "And now this? What is his game?"

Georgette sighed. "You are in a mood, and I know better than to argue with you though I'd like to murder you right now in my complete madness to question you on everything. You are being unconscionably tight-lipped, and really, it is beyond poor of you to keep your best friend on edge like this."

Miranda swallowed, unable to say anything else.

Georgette's eyes turned concerned for a second, then she strove for lightness. "I'll forgive you, dear. Just this once."

Miranda cracked a smile under slightly blurry eyes.

"I don't know what happened, but don't hide away," Georgette said softly. "I can see on your face that you want to. Catalog his books. Leave if you become uncomfortable. Visit his bedroom if you don't. Just don't dream about villainous plots and white knights while the perfectly delectable real man escapes from your grasp."

"He's not in my grasp."

"Well, then use those seduction secrets you are always nattering on about and get him there."

"I don't want him in my grasp. He is uncomfortable."

"Of course he is," her friend said in an overly patient manner. "He's a man. A real one, not one of those fluffed cakes you pretend to want."

"I don't pretend. A good man of sense—"

"Is boring. You need this, Miranda. You truly do. Just guard your heart, and the rest will be fine."

Returning to the house took all of her courage. She could feel the stares of the servants. But honestly, she was being a ninny. What had she expected them to think? They had probably even heard the viscount challenging her to a test of seduction. They probably knew everything.

Well, maybe not all of the princess bits and the actuality that she had been used in some cold way—but the seduction, the dress, the room, his attendance each day to her. Where that all might lead . . .

Had he really trapped her here in some piece of master villainy? And if so, what was it? And why? To be his mistress? But Downing never kept a mistress. He always had *liaisons*. Short-term affairs. Mistresses were too permanent for the man according to the papers.

The room she had been given was probably turned

over on a regular basis. Miranda frowned in sudden distaste.

And if not that, then what? To make her into a princess and cover his mother's scandals? To cover the duel that had been threatened in the papers, should it occur? But he could have persuaded anyone to play that role—better suited to an actress who could tread the boards and pull off the part.

Why her?

Had it simply been a convenience because she had been in the position when he'd needed her to be? That made the most rational sense. That she could think rationally about it at all made her feel a bit better.

Miranda tapped her pen on the library desk while she ate the slices of apple that a quiet, watchful servant had kindly brought. She needed to organize her thoughts before she saw him. Perhaps shoot off a note at the same time.

Dear Mr. Pitts,

I confess that I've met someone who turns me inside out. Is respectability something that one should seek? Or is it so constrained by the norms to which everyone else conforms that I should strike out on my own path?

I know you always tell me to follow my good sense, but I feel as if my senses are pulling me in opposite directions. One toward the passion of adventure and the other toward the respectability that I have always been taught to crave.

When reading a tale, confusion and dangerous desires are always so captivating. But in reality, it causes my stomach to knot, my pulse to race,

*my feelings to soar up and down like a butterfly
caught in a gale.*

*What to do then . . . grab the adventure or feel
contentment with the reputable choice?*

Mr. Pitts always had an answer, whether she chose
to follow it or not, he always made his opinion clear.
She gave the note and a penny to a waiting servant to
put into the posting box.

What would he think of her liaison with Lord Downing? How would he view her splashed across the scandal
pages, however hidden her identity was?

She thwacked a book on a stack. She was going to
murder Lord Downing when she saw him. For making
her have these confusing, conflicting thoughts.

But he never appeared.

Not once through the long morning or afternoon.
Lunch was brought, and she ate it alone. Snacks and
tea, quiet offers to assist, a question of whether she
would like to retire to her "room" for a bit . . . all done
without a single glimpse of the man himself.

She walked down the steps toward the front entrance
as the shadows grew long. Jeffries emerged from their
depths.

"Miss Chase, the driver will see you home."

"Oh. Thank you, but that is unnecessary."

The butler reached out a hand and opened the door.
"The carriage is waiting at the end of the drive. Lord
Downing insisted." He held something out to her. "Also,
this is for you. Good day, Miss."

Miranda took the offered folio. *The Bengal.* She'd bet
her week's salary that the parcel contained the book.
She numbly walked down the stone steps, feeling even

more confused. Really, confusion didn't even begin to put a name to it, especially after Giles and Benjamin jauntily greeted her at the carriage as if she were still an honored guest.

The viscount didn't appear the next day either.

Jeffries apologetically stated that the viscount was away on suddenly urgent business and that he sent his regards.

Regards? Not even a personal note in his illegible chicken scrawl to the woman he had seduced?

All of the camaraderie and the flirtation disappeared in the dark thorny gardens and waning moonlight. Underneath the chortles of raucous men and odd secrets in the night.

Another box was wordlessly handed to her. A beautiful diamond cuff nestled inside. She stared at it and tucked it into her armoire that night, along with the other temptation he had offered.

And Mr. Pitts still did not reply.

Miranda thought about Georgette's words as she collected the post. Her heart gave a tentative lurch at seeing the looping scrawl of Eleutherios upon a package. He wasn't a fluffed cake. Well, all right, if he looked as she pictured him, perhaps he would fall under the category of a fluffed cake. Mr. Pitts would definitely concur. But Georgette had agreed that Eleutherios was likely a man who knew how to use his hands.

Miranda sniffed at the idea of fluffed-cake men. Just because she liked to picture her heroes with flowing brown hair and soft, kind brown eyes, didn't mean anything. The image of black eyes and blacker hair overrode the image. She firmly shoved it aside. And just because she didn't prefer sarcastic words and sharp features, and instead dreamed of vacant—no, *dreamy*—expressions, didn't mean a thing.

She frowned and broke the seal on the note attached.

Dear Mistress Chase,

My heart beats in utter pleasure that you enjoyed the book. Please enjoy the enclosed as well.
                                    Eleutherios

She couldn't believe her eyes as the wrapping opened beneath her fingers. Another novel she had highly anticipated, and which had not yet been released to the public.

She immediately opened it and began devouring it, happy to have something to take her mind off the viscount. But every time the man who appeared to be the hero of the tale, a slightly fluffed cake, showed on the page, she compared him to the dark man antagonizing the heroine from the shadows.

The stump of her candle flickered the last of the flame as she was halfway through. Normally she might be tempted to use another of the precious sticks, but she needed to help her uncle in the morning before returning to the viscount's library.

And she could barely concentrate on the tale. Her mind refused to stop conjuring images of dark men who weren't as faceless as they'd once been.

She sent an irritated thought the viscount's way. And to Mr. Pitts as well. Why hadn't he responded? The one time she needed to see his scathing opinion, and he chose to stay silent.

* * *

The viscount didn't appear the next day either.

Not even a glimpse of him in a hall or outside the door. Another adequate apology for his absence was delivered by his taciturn butler, along with a box of something that she firmly set on the library table without opening.

The house was quiet. Watchful. The servants who rotated through the library to help her were warming up a fraction with each passing day sans their master. She was actually amazed at the number of servants he had who were able to help with the titles. She mentioned it to Lottie, the woman she had met outside in the yard during her first two visits.

"Naw, I can't read. But can recognize the same pattern. This one and this one." Lottie pointed. "They are the same author, yes?"

Miranda looked at the spines, which both read Locke. "They are." She surveyed the maid. "If you can see that, it is only a short step to reading. Would you like to learn how to read?"

"Cor, girl. What need of it have I? Chester'll read for me. God granted me with this giant maw and large ears just so I'd be able to find my way around by asking."

Lottie turned and continued her task. Galina though stared hard at Miranda. Miranda opened her mouth, but the pretty girl quickly turned and went back to her task, a deliberate dismissal of conversation. She was a bit more strident than the others but still inclined to show that extra bit of respect and reserve that Miranda's position, whatever it was, demanded.

Frankly, Miranda couldn't stand the odd limbo any longer.

She determinedly walked down the hallway to the

back stairs of the grand house later that day. More servants watched curiously as she moved farther into the bowels of their domain. But she could hear the noise and camaraderie, and she resolutely walked toward it, determined to join in.

She came within ten paces of the kitchen before the cook intercepted her.

"Miss Chase. May I be of assistance?"

"Good day, Mrs. Harper." The woman's eyes changed from how one might view a bug to a more passive form of militancy. Even though they hadn't immediately come into contact, Miranda had deliberately learned her name along with those of the other upper-tier servants on the first day. She'd concentrated on learning the names of the lower ones next, and could almost pick each one out by name now—quite a feat with as many as worked here.

Always good to know one's environment and to gather allies. Or at least not enemies. "I was just thinking of picking up an apple or some bread and cheese."

"I will send up a tray, Miss Chase. As usual." She motioned back to the stairs. "Please."

"Oh, I don't mind grabbing something and saving someone the trip." She tried to skirt the woman.

Mrs. Humphries, the housekeeper, appeared and smoothly stepped in front of her too, the two rulers providing a united front. "Don't be silly, Miss Chase. Please." She motioned as well.

Miranda sighed and took the "suggestion," returning above stairs to the cool, uninhabited library. It was a curse really. If the viscount hadn't paid her attention, especially the inordinate amount of attention he had shown, she could have been on friendly terms with the staff. They seemed a mostly jolly bunch aside from the upper-tier detachment. Now that he had played with and abandoned her, she was on her own.

Sometimes it seemed her lot in life to be left behind. She shook off the maudlin thought and squared her shoulders, grabbing the next stack of books.

She had worked up the gumption that morning to inquire about the viscount's whereabouts and whether he remembered how to hold a pen, but after the butler's stony reply, had determined to hold her tongue.

Besides, it wasn't any of her business. Truly. She had been hired to catalog and sort his library, and that was what she was doing. She had had a lovely moment of pretending to be someone she was not. A singular memory, nothing more.

Hot hands and whispered words.

She chose to remember the fantasy and forget the awkwardness at the end and after. It served no good to spend time dwelling on the negative thoughts. *Enjoy life now.* She refused to part with the mantra that had seen her through the second year without her family. The first year had been horrific. For how did one enjoy anything when loved ones were forever lost?

She buried herself in her correspondence instead, and slowly but surely the notes from Eleutherios lengthened and started to come every day—one day even three appeared. Some hired courier was wearing down the soles of his boots running all about London.

Dear Mistress Chase,

I apologize for my lapse in responding to your delightful notes with naught but a few words.

Dear Mistress Chase,

I am working on a project where the fruit is just starting to bloom. Too tender yet to say when I will be able to have anything to show or in what manner it might be plucked. As to the type of project you reference, rumors often swirl in smoke.

Dear Mistress Chase,

It is with great reverence and respect that I received your latest correspondence.

Dear Mistress Chase,

Your notes make me feel alive.

That last missive had made her heart beat a little too quickly. Made her think of the viscount, the scent of jasmine and lilies drifting through her thoughts.

Interspersed were also notes from Mr. Pitts, finally, who had been oddly reticent in his responses at first, but had once more picked up steam, especially once she had begun to wax poetic about Eleutherios again.

But still the viscount didn't return. The only evidence of his acknowledgment came in the unopened boxes she began to stack in the corner of the library. She had opened her box of secrets already. She'd decide whether to open another when next she saw him.

*   *   *

The following day she tried to gain entrance to the kitchens again and was turned away.

The next day she tried again.

On the third day, they grudgingly let her in.

She sat at the back table of the bookshop, fingering the cuff of an older calico. It had been a week. She was starting to feel more than a little odd about the whole matter. Had she done something so wrong? Or was this just the life of the Quality and their whims?

Georgette reached into her bag. "Come, I saved the paper. No stop at the teashop today."

The daily scandal sheets had been full of speculation. It had been an odd week of gossip and news. A waiting period, some grand lull. The viscount's family had been unusually silent and well behaved. The gossips were starting to show signs of clawed-finger starvation.

She kept her own itchy fingers still.

Georgette withdrew her hand and smoothed the paper upon the table. "Let's see what the bard has for us today." She skimmed the column. "Talk, talk, talk, of the Hannings' masked ball tomorrow. Can you imagine?" Georgette gave a dreamy sigh. "You could show up as the princess. It would be grand."

Miranda had to agree that the ball sounded magnificent, even apart from Georgette's mad imaginings about her attendance. The Hannings held the best-reviewed masked ball each year. And each year it seemed to become slightly more salacious. But even the starchiest of matrons still attended because everyone who was anyone did. It was a night when odd things could sometimes happen—or at least that was what the gossip columns always claimed.

"And what is this? A shadowy agreement again took place with Lady W.'s suitors and both have mysteriously taken leave. *Is there something new in the air? When will the marquess and marchioness return to our stage?*" Georgette raised her brow. "Did you see or hear anything at Vauxhall? Other than your discovery of just how delicious the viscount is in truth?"

Miranda shook her head, a lingering loyalty toward the man staying her tongue with regard to what she had overheard—a kernel of something that would be gossipworthy. "He would hardly confide in me," she said with all honesty. He hadn't confided in her, after all.

Georgette looked disappointed.

Miranda saw the line before her friend and tried to hide it. Georgette pushed her finger to the side.

"Oh!" She crowed. "*The lovely princess hasn't been seen since that moonlit night in the gardens. A figment in the minds of the attendees? One hopes she will return for all of us who lie in wait for a glimpse.*"

Miranda's face flamed.

Georgette looked satisfied. "And that expression right there, that heat, is exactly why you should come with me to the Mortons' tomorrow. Goodness, it is why you should keep returning to the viscount's dreary library, no matter how many times he doesn't appear."

Miranda snorted.

"You know, dear, one absent day—or five—does not make everything else in the past go up in smoke." Georgette tapped a digit.

On any other topic, Miranda might agree. But when it came to the emotional weight of a viscount, especially of this man, she just couldn't grasp it.

She was glad that she hadn't told Georgette about the boxes. Georgette would have had them opened and the contents released into the world faster than she could have uttered the name "Pandora."

Georgette shook her finger. "He's gorgeous. And wealthy. And those eyes. Seek him out and capitalize. Go to his country estate, if you have to."

"Are you listening to yourself? You want me to stalk a viscount? You will be bringing the paper to me in Newgate."

"Not if you use whatever wiles on him you have been employing." She waved her hands around in a blustery manner. "Mrs. Q., Miranda, *Mrs. Q.*"

But that was Georgette's desire, not hers. And she wasn't going to chase the man around England. She had had a lovely time at Vauxhall—at least right up there until the end—and that was that. She had a splendid memory and couldn't really ask for more. But that didn't mean there wasn't a part of her that didn't wish to repeat the experience in the darkness of night.

She'd never felt so alive. How terrible was that?

Georgette frowned at her. "You are *pining*. I can't believe it. Why you couldn't have started with a smaller version of a rake—a Mr. Hanning or Thomas Briggs—and left the prime cut to me to carve is appalling; nevertheless, there it is, and now you are pining."

"I'm not pining."

"You are pining. It is quite sad."

Miranda shook a finger at her. "I'm making a stalwart attempt at thinking positive thoughts, and you are ruining it."

"I would take those thoughts and carve him into tea cakes."

"Would you like me to introduce you fully should

he ever return?" A violent itch made her scratch the underside of her arm at the thought.

"Kind of you. But for all my talk, your Lord Downing wouldn't look twice at me even if I were lying naked across the works of Shakespeare, handwritten by the bard himself."

"He has those," Miranda muttered, rubbing her arm.

"What?"

"Nothing. Besides, I doubt that is true." Men didn't spare a second look at Miranda when Georgette was in a room.

"Like when he came into this shop expressly to see you and spared not a glance for me? Mmmhmm."

"He was busy at the time. Getting his books."

"No. Uninterested. Believe me, I know the difference." Georgette looked down her nose.

"He was simply a trifle bored, I think. And perhaps a bit mad."

"And he's a wretched rake, and you are far too good for the likes of him." Georgette nodded decisively, her attitude switching as it did when someone she loved was threatened. "So forget him, grab your skirts, and use these fabulous new lusty thoughts I see brimming in your eyes and start attending functions with me. Dust off those flirtatious quips that I know you have roaming your dusty skull."

Miranda didn't immediately say no, which seemed to appease Georgette. "Good. We will go to the Mortons' dinner party tomorrow and find some manly treats."

Miranda picked up a copy of *The Tempest* from the floor of the library the next day. Adequate imagery for the mess around her, which seemed to grow each night after she left. The servants always brought in new crates that made her nearly have to start anew. If she still had thoughts that the viscount was trying to keep her there for some nefarious purpose, then she'd have mounting evidence.

But a nefarious purpose required his presence.

She tapped the book against her leg, then settled on starting a new section for Shakespeare. The viscount was obsessed with the bard. There were three and four versions for each title—some even had five with the translations or various printings—and she hadn't made but a scratch in the surface of the library, so she could only assume she'd double or triple their number. He seemed to especially love the darkest tragedies and the lightest comedies—the ones where the hero went to ruin or everything revolved around farcical situations with ever-changing identities.

He would get along well with Mr. Pitts. The man seemed to find dark humor in most things. She imagined him as a crotchety older gentleman with little tolerance and a rapier wit. Much different from Eleutherios, who had an almost Byronic bent and whom she pictured with wavy brown hair and emotive eyes. They tested her differently in their correspondence. And though Mr. Pitts drove her to distraction, she was willing to admit that she enjoyed writing to him more than she'd enjoyed corresponding with any other.

She'd never be able to live with the man, however.

She had sent him a quick note the day before telling him of the most recent gift from Eleutherios—eternally trying to prove to the man that his enemy was not evil—and that she was planning to accompany Georgette to the Mortons' for a dinner party and some lively company. Let him read into it as he would. She had never told him exactly whose library she was cataloging, but she had mentioned the owner a few too many times for it to have gone unnoticed that he had interested her. She was looking forward to whatever crusty piece of advice or warning she received.

He had been increasingly nasty about Eleutherios.

And Eleutherios . . . he was almost *too* good to be. Everything that she had hoped for and read in his writings. Words penned like those of the finest sonnets. He was frankly intimidating in a way that she hadn't realized when she'd simply thought of him in the abstract.

She picked up the stack she had sorted earlier, a number of more licentious tomes ready for preliminary placement on the correct shelf. A brittle copy of an explicit, licentious manual sat on top. She sent a furtive glance around the blissfully empty room, relieved to be alone for once. The servants had been increasingly friendly. She'd even received an invitation to attend one of their social gatherings.

It spoke to the relationship—or lack thereof—with the viscount. The only remaining ties were the presents (sans notes—she had checked the tops of the first few, then realized she could simply shake the parcels to determine whether the contents contained an envelope) and the continuing use of his carriage for her ride home—something Jeffries said the viscount insisted upon.

The daily ride made her increasingly comfortable in a conveyance. The only barrier to leaving the country that would soon remain would be her own reluctance to grab what she wanted and not torment herself about the consequences.

She carefully opened the cover of the book, taking

care not to damage the binding or pages in any way. She randomly turned a number of pages. An illustration of two figures joined in a logic-defying way cavorted on the page, indecipherable text beneath. There was a more *descriptive* edge to the pictures here versus in the medieval illumination buried in her unmentionables.

But the expression on the face of the woman was perfunctory. As if she were demonstrating the movement and not reveling in it. No feelings emanated from the page like the ones she had felt at Vauxhall. The pure, exhilarated fear of a carriage careening out of control. The beauty of a thousand lamps lit at the same time. The explosion of the fireworks echoing the trembling in her limbs.

Georgette was right. And even surly Mr. Pitts, who had been more vocal, if less kind, about it. She needed to experience more of the wilder side of life and not let it pass her by, secure in her carved-out corner of the world.

She nodded. She would go on more outings to the park and to more dinners with merchants' sons. To the Mortons'. Use her fledgling ability to flirt. Harmless flirting—she wasn't quite ready for anything more.

Unless it was with the man who had been missing for the past week . . . She shoved the thought from her head.

Light flirting. She nodded. A time-honored, precourt-ship tradition. She did have a reputation to maintain after all. Though she could hear Georgette's voice in her head.

"*Pish. Those starchy bourgeois women who think they run the middle class . . . Think of Mrs. Penny-weather. Once a mistress to three earls simultaneously and invited everywhere. And right now, the papers think you are a princess. If it comes out, you will be notorious, your name on everyone's lips, the good and the bad, but on their lips all the same. You will be in demand, darling."*

She shook her head. That was Georgette's dream, not hers. But she could put herself about a bit more. Feel that spark renewed.

It had been glorious.

It had also never occurred with anyone else. But maybe that was because she'd just needed the spark lit. She turned the page, another illustration illuminating the next side, the couple demonstrating yet another pose. The woman's head was flung back, but fixed.

She wanted to experience it again. The wild cavorting that couldn't be captured on paper. His breath shivering over her skin. His hands pulling the ice from her bones, filling her with fire instead. His eyes dark and shining in the moonlight, something written there that she couldn't yet translate. The sound of her name falling huskily from perfect lips.

"I would dearly love to see which page has you so engrossed, Miranda."

The warm, whispered words hit the back of her neck and she jolted. The book dropped from her fingers. She scrambled to catch it, dark hair and onyx eyes swimming in her vision as he reached around her and captured it. Her fingers hit a solid, warm hand—perfectly bare once again. She wrenched away, knocking the book from his hand, and lost her balance.

Solid, warm arms encircled her. The thrill ignited as if it had never dimmed.

Chapter 13

Dear Mr. Pitts,

It is difficult to choose between the thrill in one's beating heart and the caution born of sound mind. How does one determine a path between?

From the pen of Miranda Chase

His hands clasped around her waist, feeling as if they belonged there the same way they had at Vauxhall.

The last week had been dreadful. Becoming involved in family drama long wished forgotten, pushing against Miranda's pull, drowning in the madness of the entire scheme. Hating himself for what he had done. What he would do.

And then he'd been unable to ignore it any longer. The pull toward her.

He felt her slight shiver and smiled into her hair, the fresh vanilla scent washing over him. Real and solid. Someone he could return to at the end of a trying day. A trying week.

His hands clutched more fiercely against her waist, and then skimmed down. He toed the book, flipping it open in front of her on the floor, a rather detailed depiction of a man taking a woman from behind visible on the page. He could *feel* the color rise to her cheeks.

"Interesting. Miss Chase, what *have* you been up to in my absence?"

"Nothing," she squeaked.

"Nothing?"

"Just organizing," she said quickly, trying to escape. But not forcefully enough for him to release her. He smiled against the soft strands at the top of her hair.

"I regret that I haven't been around for your *organizing* sooner." He toed the book again, putting it prominently in her view, and moved his hands to her hips in the exact position that the man on the page held.

"Your lordship," she whispered on a breath. "What are you doing?"

"You have cleared quite a path through this room. If only to get to the tomes you are more interested in, hmmm?"

He'd argued with himself, hunched over his desk days after Vauxhall. Then he'd thrown in his cards and decided if he was going to do the thing, he might as well do it with all of his chips in the pot. It was all written there in front of him that as long as he continued his path, he would get what he desired.

And his desire was not going to change, no matter what the suppressed voice at the back of his mind whispered.

Of a much higher price he'd have to pay.

He let her wiggle free.

She smoothed her dress along her hips. "You have many interesting books."

"Some more than others." He smiled lazily and was pleased with the reaction on her face.

She bent and scooped the fallen book, cheeks rosy as she quickly closed the cover and set it upon the shelf nearest her. She paused a moment, then her chin came up, and her expression smoothed into pleasant lines, the heat hidden beneath a carefully constructed barrier. "I trust that you have had a pleasant week?"

She moved away from him and over to the stack she must have been sorting before he'd entered. He had entered to see her flipping through the book, brows furrowed, lower lip drawn between her teeth, engrossed. He'd simply stood and watched her for a long moment, breathing the scene in before he had become too curious over what she was reading.

Too curious period, he had held himself away too long.

"The week has been . . . interminable." Endless, really.

"Oh?" She lifted one book, then another, the hair nearest her face falling against her cheeks, hiding her expression. "That is a shame." Her voice was pleasant, cool.

She took the books to the shelves and placed them in different spots, then returned to the stack.

The side of his mouth curled in amusement. "Are you trying to ignore me?"

"I am merely performing the task you set for me, your lordship."

A week of dealing with Colin, their mother, his other siblings, Charlotte Chatsworth and her father, Dillingham and Easton. His father.

That had been the most trying. Always was. For all her obvious faults and flakiness, his mother was easy

SEVEN SECRETS OF SEDUCTION   231

to anticipate. Her motives transparent. His father's never had been.

"And also trying to ignore me, I think." He took her hand in his, slowly pulling the book from her fingers. A week of hating himself for how he had left her. For what he had done. "Are you wroth with me?"

"Why would I be?"

"For not reappearing after a lovely night in the gardens?"

For ignoring her for reasons he dared not name. Decisions made in the dark of night to perhaps change his course and embark on a new tack. Fear, an emotion he didn't often deal with, lacing his thoughts. That he might make an irreparable mess of the whole thing and lose her completely.

"I have no reason to be angry with you. You are free to do as you please." She looked away from him. "There is no commitment between us, other than for my work here." She looked back to him, actual sincerity beneath the lingering irritation. "It was a nice dinner, and I thank you for taking me."

That she was thanking him made him feel like the lowest cad. He *was* the lowest cad.

"You make it sound as if I simply sold you some shoes."

"I am expressing my gratitude." Fire lit in her eyes. "I am not the disingenuous one."

"You *are* wroth with me." He was pleased at the decided snipe in her voice. Fire he could work with. If she broke into tears, he just might offer to stick a sword in his own gut.

She pursed her lips and gathered another stack. "Why ever would I be angry with you?"

"Why don't you tell me."

She tilted her head for a second as if thinking, then said, "No," and continued her trek.

"No?"

"No."

"Well, that hardly seems fair."

"Are you speaking to me of fairness, your lordship?"

He raised a brow. "Is it a subject that is disallowed?"

"You deliberately seduced me in the garden."

He smiled. "That is hardly newsworthy or aggravating. I have been trying to seduce you for weeks now."

Months.

"No, not that. You *nefariously* seduced me."

"Nefariously seduced you?" His lips quirked automatically.

"You did it to create an overriding scandal."

Ice crept into his bones. He knew he shouldn't have left her to her own devices for so long. She was far too perceptive. It was part of what had drawn him to her in the first place.

That and the keen desire to be someone better. To be the apple of her eye, not to let the pleasure of that go to some anonymous source.

"You think that I feel the need to grace the gossip pages?"

She tapped her finger against the book in her hand. "I don't know. Do you?"

"No. In fact, I'll retire to the country. Live a pleasant bare existence." He tilted his head at her snort. "If only you'll but come with me."

Ah. There was the color he loved, blooming under her skin. The jump in her pulse. The lovely awareness in her eyes.

"You are not amusing."

"No?"

"No. Is this part of your plan to stave off boredom? To tug me to and fro? To use me in order to divert the gossip?"

"May I use you in such a manner? Spread you fully over the paper, crinkling the pages beneath you?"

She colored more deeply and lifted her chin. "You probably could, should you set your mind to it. I am hardly much of a challenge to the likes of you."

She discounted herself far too often. He wanted to dress her in silks and satins, dress her in nothing at all. Teach her all of the ways that she was intoxicating.

There was too much passion there waiting to be released. And perhaps if he were just seeking a physical game—like he had planned at first—then she wouldn't pose much of a challenge. He could have methodically continued to seduce her. Turned the entire scene at Vauxhall to furthering his cause. The masked, illicit encounter. Freedom for her to be scandalous.

He could have approached her again the next day. Probably had his way with her right here on the library floor, or in the chair, or up against the wall. Thrusting into her, sating his physical thirst for her, swallowing every lovely cry she was sure to utter, watching her eyes drunk with passion.

But he hadn't been able to do it. The path of seduction had grown murky and deadly. He no longer wanted a simple physical response from her. He had been deluding himself into thinking that he ever did.

And he didn't want his own response to be simply physical. Therein lay the true danger now.

So he had banned himself from the house and given his parents their ultimatums. Then he'd gone to plant the seeds for a mad alternative quest. The start of his own destruction, surely. For any sort of permanence never ended well.

He smiled without humor, and her brows drew together at the expression. He smoothed out the lines of his face intentionally.

"There is still our challenge."

"Did you seduce your governess before she finished your lessons on mathematics?" She plopped a stack of books onto a shelf. "The week has long since passed. And you won."

"Not in my heart, I didn't." Not in the seeds of his demise.

"If I believed in its existence, perhaps I could concur."

"Oh, it is there. Shriveled and bound. Just waiting for you to set it free."

"You are an unrepentant tease, your lordship."

"As I said previously, a tease doesn't follow through." He stretched a finger along a strip of softly bound leather.

"An *emotional* tease. You are physically quite happy to follow through, but you make far too many empty promises concerning your feelings."

It took effort to call forth a sunny smile, a breezy, languid look. He nodded to the stacks of unopened gift boxes in the corner. "Did you not enjoy my presents?"

She gave him a dark look. "I question their existence."

"A token of my affection. A nod to your acceptance of the challenge."

"A handwritten note would have sufficed."

Of course it would have. For above all else, he knew

she treasured such. But it was the one thing that was out of the question.

"Not a declaration of my affections?" he said lightly.

Her eyes narrowed.

He walked toward her. Her back and shoulders tightened as he neared. "Come with me."

"No." But he saw the shiver there at her nape.

"You do not even know where I wish to take you."

"I am sure that I will be at a disadvantage no matter where it is."

"If so, it would be a change. You more frequently have the advantage over me."

Honest and irritated disbelief darkened her features as she crossed her arms. In truth, *his* advantage was only maintained by her not knowing how accurate his statement was.

He kept his voice light. "Then come with me because I promise you will find it a treat."

"I'm busy." She pointed at the stacks around her.

He smiled lazily. "And I'm the boss."

Her shoulders tightened further and she turned. He wished he could see her face. She thumped the books down, obviously irritated if the less-than-gentle way they hit the others below them was any indication. Her face was unreadable when she faced him once more. Her expression clear.

It unnerved him. Was he corrupting her already then? Dragging her into his hell?

"Very well."

Miranda didn't trust the slow smile that spread across his face, not for a second. Not with the darkness reflected in his eyes, beneath the temptation. As

if he was mortally wounded and needed her to find
the injury, to heal the harm.

He turned, and she followed him from the room.
Down the hall. Her ire thumped along with the beat
of her too-fast heart, and her brows drew together
as he entered the room that had been designated as
hers.

If he thought he was going to finish what he had
started in the gardens of Vauxhall right now, then she
would quickly disabuse him of the notion.

She hadn't been in the room since that night. There
had hardly been any reason to visit after all. And she
had felt distinctly as if she didn't belong.

He touched the armoire at the side, sliding his fingers
along the wood, crooking them into the notch and opening it. A selection of beautiful gowns hung inside.

They all looked to be her size. As if they had been
continuously delivered throughout the week, populat-
ing the belly of the wooden chamber as soon as they
were sewn.

Some seamstress at Madame Galland's assuredly
had pricked and sore fingers. And a fatter purse.

She swallowed, touching her own fingers together
through her gloves. Feeling the urge to touch the gowns
even as she pushed against the idea of it all.

"This one." His thumbs smoothed a path down the
fine green muslin of the gown on the left. He rubbed
the edge between the pads of his fingers, then lifted
and draped it against her like a lady's maid might.
Except the sweep of the dress rested across the bared
upper skin of her throat, the hanger dangling over
her shoulder, sliding down a fraction, the back of his
knuckles caressing her . . . all of it in a way that no
servant would dare. "Yes, perfect."

She cleared her suddenly dry throat. "Perfect for what, your lordship?"

"I really think you should call me Maximilian. Or Max. Or Maxim, if you like."

He said it lightly, the offering of the name only his family dared call him, but there was something there under the words. A thread that caused her ire a momentary pause.

"Given names are used only by those quite familiar to each other." Her ire crept back in. "Such as those who might speak every day."

The edges of his lips curved invitingly. "I really must make you wroth with me more often." He let the dress slip farther down, the edge of the hanger lightly tickling the sensitive pulse of her throat. "And I must rectify your notion that we aren't yet familiar with each other. I plan to be quite familiar with you, Miranda."

The way he said it made her swallow again. As if he didn't plan to sample her but to make her his entire meal.

"Wear this."

"Why?" Her voice was a little too high. "Where are we going?"

"It hardly matters, does it?" He tipped his head. "You don't plan to fall to my nefarious tactics." He leaned toward her. "Consider it an apology, our destination. I promise that I will be a good boy."

He casually dropped a slim book onto the table. "I lifted this from Colin when he wasn't looking. Perhaps you might enjoy it."

She stared at the slim book, a compilation of Shakespearean sonnets in lovely, expensively bound leather. "Won't your brother miss it?"

"It was undoubtedly for an assignment. He wouldn't be caught holding a book of sonnets he hadn't written himself." His lips pulled into a sharp smile. "I'll buy him another should he grouse." He pulled a finger along the leather. "Come with me, Miranda. Willingly. On your own."

She pushed at the siren call. Pulled forth every rational thought to which she could lay claim. "I will hardly finish cataloging your library if we go out."

"Then I suppose I will be able to keep you indefinitely after all." There was something to his words . . . she could almost believe him. He walked backward from the room, a lazy regard underpinned by an intensity that stole her breath. "Soon perhaps I will, Miranda."

Miranda stared after him. Everything in her tangled and confused. She looked down at the gown.

She shouldn't let him toss her to and fro. She should set the gown back in the armoire and calmly walk from the room.

"His lordship has excellent timing. The old bat is busy. I can do you up as I wish."

Galina must have been waiting on the other side of the door to have appeared so quickly. Waiting, listening for her cue.

Miranda was nonplussed for a second as she again realized that people in the house were likely listening to all of their conversations.

Galina had thawed a bit toward her in the days since Miranda had forced herself upon the staff in the kitchens. But she was still cool, her nature seemingly that way in general.

The maid gestured her to a chair. "Knew that his lordship would return to you. I've been eyeing a few styles just for when he'd do so."

Miranda blinked, then swallowed. "Oh?"

The maid said nothing, simply pointed to the chair again.

"You listen," Miranda said softly. "In the halls."

The maid watched her for a moment. "Yes." She seemed to consider her words. "Which is why I knew he'd be back for you, unlike any of the others we've had."

Miranda went scarlet.

The maid's eyes narrowed. "You aren't like any of the others. And they—" She tilted her head. "They were for show."

She gestured to the chair again, more imperiously. Miranda sat bemusedly, but her attention remained focused on the maid.

"For show?"

"Do not fear that we listen to each licentious gasp to determine such." There was a hint of a smile about her mouth.

Miranda colored again, still unbelieving that she could do so. But there it was in the cheval glass, rosy splotches on her cheeks.

The maid leaned forward and lifted a brush. "But it is obvious that he's never cared for any of the others. That there is something about you."

Miranda stared into the mirror without focus. "I am a simple shopgirl."

"Not so simple now, no?"

"I suppose not," she said softly, as the maid lifted her hair, examining how it fell.

The path of least resistance in the short term was to remain in the chair, to let the maid dress her and go willingly with the viscount. But it was also fraught with the most long-term risk. For she could simply return to the library, demand that he leave her alone, and go on her way, mostly unchanged.

Never knowing what lay at the end of the adventure. In his arms. The challenge changing from one of physically or intellectually seducing the other party to becoming part of the fabric of his life—at least for a short time.

Galina smoothly pinned a section of hair. "One becomes used to listening when one is a servant. There is a rhythm to things here. But there has been a different rhythm for the past few weeks. Pauses and footsteps. Boards creaking. Even the muffled sound of shoes on a rug. On edge." Her smile was darkly self-deprecating. "One becomes used to listening when one is a servant."

"One becomes used to living in the pages of a book when one is a shopgirl in a bookstore," Miranda answered lightly.

She could see the maid's pursed lips through the reflection of the mirror. She thought for a moment that the woman wouldn't answer. "You read a lot?" Galina finally asked.

"Yes. It's an escape into another world." She tried to keep her words light instead of sad, thoughts of her family in her head. "Sometimes that is the best part of a hard day."

"Not much time to escape when you are a servant."

"But reason to escape, no?"

The maid tugged her hair a little roughly, then gave a muffled apology, her fingers gentling. "Perhaps."

She finished dressing Miranda's hair and helped her into the day dress. It was a simple style, but lovely. Lovelier than anything she had worn other than the Vauxhall dress. The maid put on the finishing touches, pinching here and there, making everything just right. She reminded Miranda of the seamstress, Madame Galland.

"Thank you, Miss Lence."

The maid said nothing, tying the last bow. She nodded and stepped away to let Miranda pass, then tapped the brush suddenly, examining it, not looking up. "Of course, we do overhear things beyond what our masters might like us to hear. Things that might cause us to extend a wary warning, even in the face of it all."

Miranda paused and tilted her head in acknowledgment. She knew that any endeavor she undertook with the viscount was fraught with peril of all sorts. The last week had shown her that if nothing else.

She touched the maid's hand. "Thank you."

The maid looked back, her face carefully blank. "It is silly to extend one's view so high. But . . ." The woman looked to the side. At the book the viscount had left. His brother's book. "But perhaps we are all hoping that it is not without hope to do so."

Miranda opened her mouth in surprise, but the maid excused herself and strode from the room, leaving her standing next to the table, dressed in her strange new finery. More conflicted than before.

She lifted the book and was directed by a hall servant back to the library. The viscount was inside, paging through a slim volume. He snapped it shut and stood when she entered. He sauntered toward her, lifting her free hand.

"A rose in winter."

"It is spring."

"But it is the winter of my heart." His lips grazed her wrist.

She removed her hand and smoothed it along the bow of her dress, feeling the beautiful silk of the glove rubbing against the fabric, concentrating on something other than his heated eyes.

She held up the book in her hand. "Does your brother often visit?"

"All of my siblings do. They like to pretend they are checking in on me. But they do so to avoid our parents. Colin likes to come and make life miserable. To visit the staff in the kitchens. I think he is attempting to stage a revolt. Or to conquer his hypocrisy." The last was said too lightly.

"Oh."

Perhaps we are all hoping that it is not without hope to do so. To extend one's view so high.

She swallowed and squared her shoulders. "I'd like to organize an outing for your servants."

He raised a brow at the abrupt change of subject, his narrowed eyes obviously trying to figure out how the topics were related. "An outing?"

"Yes, for your staff. I've heard that the Duke of Brexley holds fantastic parties at Hyde for his town household." She tried to pretend interest in examining the book. "Lunch perhaps. You could even invite your siblings. Colin. Stave off the revolt."

"I'm not sure *I'd* want to attend, in that case."

She lifted her head and met his eyes. "I'd attend." Her response was twofold.

He didn't speak for a long moment. "Fine. Speak with Mrs. Humphries. Don't be surprised if she thinks you are trying to take her job though."

"Mrs. Humphries and I have come to an accord."

His brows rose again. "Do I need to build an ark?"

"You say it as if I am hard to get along with."

"My housekeeper is unused to . . . guests like you."

"Guests that you dress and escort to outrageous places?"

"No. That isn't quite as unusual."

She felt a little pang of jealousy but stuffed it down. No, this was her adventure, and that was the way she'd treat it. Adventures took place in the here and now. The present. The near future.

"But my guests are usually quite aware of the way things work with me, or with the family member they are associating with, and are not interested in taking up with my staff."

"You are far above my station. I assume the women you consort with are as well."

One finger curled under her chin. "Ah, but the reality of that statement is far from true. I sometimes feel you are completely out of my reach."

She blinked.

His hand slid down her back and urged her toward the door. "I've never been good at knowing my place, however."

The grand carriage was waiting for them outside. She took a breath and stepped inside. It was easier every time she did. Thoughts of other things collected in her mind.

Someday—someday when she was irritated with him no longer—she would have to thank the viscount for that.

"Where are we going, oh shriveled and wintry one?" she asked as she settled into the plush seat, determined to think of it all as the adventure she had deemed it. To guard herself against what she had been emotionally slipping toward at Vauxhall.

"To see the Cirque Diamant perform. An apology, as I said."

She stared at him. She had thought about going to a performance after their conversation at Vauxhall. About how she wouldn't step out of her comfort and grasp the ring. But the paper had reported the run as being sold out yet again, so she hadn't even tried to secure a ticket to the pit, where room might be found to squeeze.

"It is the middle of the day."

"Well spotted."

She let her slipper hit him in the shin with the rhythm of the carriage. Twice. He grabbed her heel in his hand the third time, his fingers slipping down her ankle.

"What—" She swallowed. "What are you doing?"

"Your leg seems to have a twitch. Let me help you."

"That's unnecessary," she said, her voice a little high.

"No? But you are so helpful to me. With my staff. With escorting me to the gardens. Dressing up in this gown that makes you shine in the darkness of the carriage. Brightening up the day like a jewel sparkling in the sun."

His fingers curved over her heel, the slipper falling from her foot. The feel of his fingers running over her fine stockings was erotic. Like an echo of the crescendo from the gardens.

Her lips parted on a reply, his eyes locked with hers. Trapped. Seeking something as his hands traveled her silk-clad skin.

The carriage stopped, and he slowly reached down and slid her slipper back on her foot. Fitting it over the curves. Perfectly made. Just for her.

"Shining as if a star just for my eyes."

A knock sounded on the door, but his hand lingered, his posture that of a knight reverently touching his chosen lady, his eyes never leaving hers. He answered the knock and she shakily accepted Benjamin's hand.

The viscount offered his arm and they strode up the walk with purpose, as if they were a respectable couple attending an event. As if he hadn't just turned her world on end again.

Without the lights and orchestra blaring, the theater looked like just another storefront on the street. Bereft of the crowds of people moving and chatting, streaming inside, eager to see a new production or a beloved classic. The riffraff moving downward and the wealthy moving up. The separation like the ancient divide. The common people staring up and watching their betters, the gods and goddesses of old. People who had been born to privilege, mostly, and those few who had worked tooth and nail to get there.

Miranda stared at the empty boxes, the empty orchestra and pit, her feet carrying her into the belly of the theater alongside the viscount.

"Welcome!" A man with colorfully patched trousers strode up the corridor toward them. "Your lordship." He bowed to the viscount. "And beautiful lady." He bowed low to her. "Welcome to the show." He smiled broadly. "Or at least the death-defying acts of practice."

The man gestured to the orchestra and the boxes above. "Anywhere you'd like to sit, your lordship. We have the King's box spruced and ready. Or the critics' seats in the back."

A sudden commotion onstage claimed his attention. He clapped his hands together, then cupped them around his mouth. "First stretch is complete. Places for second rehearsal. Tell Eleanora and Leonardo they are up."

He turned back to them, his feet already taking him backward down the corridor. "Anywhere you'd like." He extended his hand. "Please, enjoy."

He turned and walked briskly to the stage; some of the performers cast curious glances at the two of them, but most of the men and women ignored them and walked to their blocked spots.

"Rehearsal?"

The viscount's eyes glimmered mischievously. "I'm told that rehearsal is even superior to the actual show." His eyes took her in. "Sometimes practice can be more enjoyable than the main event in that you have to rehearse over and over again until everything is in its perfect slot, its perfect place."

Her heart picked up unwilling speed.

"Mmmm. Where would you like to sit, my lady?" the viscount asked, gesturing around the empty theater.

"Well, one can hardly resist the King's box, can one?" she said, unwillingly looking forward to the spectacle. And to being with him.

It seemed the moth never learned.

He smiled and held out his arm.

The King's box was in the prime viewing spot at stage left. Perfect for overlooking the melee on the boards. And with the acrobatics, quite close while at the same time maintaining an illusion of privacy.

She touched the fabric on the chairs. Such an odd thing. To be sitting here like a true princess.

She couldn't let his spell overwhelm her. She shook her head and turned her attention to the stage.

Women and men in different costumes—some in full dress, and others in undershirts and hose, just enough to cover them—strode in from all sides, assembling in place. The jovial man who had met them stood below, raising his hand to initiate the spectacle.

The cues took shape as the curtain was pulled to the side, nothing hidden from view like it might have been during the main performance. A beat of a drum rolled, and a wave of the orchestra crested with the man's hands. Then stopped. He yelled at someone in the back, then began again. They restarted three times, and the man sent a nervous look up toward the box.

And then the performance began in earnest, nothing hidden as the production took shape.

The men pulling the ropes stood in plain sight, taking away some of the mystery, but replacing it with curiosity and interest. How they pulled and caught, their muscles straining under their rolled-up shirtsleeves. The black garb they normally wore hid them mostly from view during performances—and some theaters' hands were better at it than others. She should probably be scandalized by the show of skin, but then she wasn't a courtier or a lady. And she didn't have to pretend to be the dour daughter of a schoolmistress here. No one knew her or cared.

The performers were incredible yet again. Here in this temporary home, they had all of the sets and tricks ready and waiting. None of the freedom was lost, it was simply changed. The wonder at what might happen if an acrobat slipped on a wet patch of grass or how they navigated the crowd, blending in, threading through, was absent, but their performance was more daring because of the risky new twists and flips they attempted.

Players flinched when an occasional compatriot landed with a thwack on the floor. Yells accompanied successfully completed starring moves. The well-rehearsed acrobatics and air of joy were intoxicating. They obviously loved what they did. And had no problem showing it. Grabbing the bar and swinging. Jumping into the air without long, drawn-out thought. Letting out a shout when a new trick was properly executed.

It was lovely, she thought a bit wistfully.

"You like it," his voice said at her ear.

"I do."

"What do you love?"

"The freedom. The joy."

"You do not seek such for yourself often, do you, Miranda?"

"I have a nice life. There is happiness."

"Contentedness. The joy and freedom you wish for is there for you to grasp."

She turned toward him, his lips so close to hers. "I think you call me a coward, your lordship," she murmured, eyes on his mouth.

"Do I? About some things, perhaps." His thumb stroked her lower lip. "But about others, no. You have so much passion and life brimming in you. You just have to be freed to show it."

"Are you volunteering for the task?" she asked as lightly as she could over the heavy beat of her heart.

"Volunteering? Never. I am simply appointing myself to the role."

"Quite high-handed of you."

"As I've already confessed, it's a failing of mine." He smiled lazily, his fingers curling into her nape. "Do you forgive me?"

"Do you ask forgiveness? I can't credit that you do." Her lips curled beneath his thumb, her heart beating more wildly, but she was determined to duplicate his expression of lazy regard and ease. "I think you rarely ask for it, in truth."

"Ah, that too, I confess, is a failing as well."

"You have many."

His fingers stroked her nape. "But you so few. A good prospect for us to balance each other, don't you think? You will be my conscience, and I will be your shame."

"I do not find happiness shameful," she said quietly. "It is simply fear that I fear."

His fingers paused, then he drew her forward. "And that is why you are a lure I can't resist."

Her eyes closed unwillingly, feeling the draw. "Because of the fear?"

"No, because you are emotionally willing to experience the thrill yet so physically reluctant to grasp it. So often it is the opposite. Hence, I find it intoxicating."

And yet, she couldn't keep the thought to herself. "You hardly seemed intoxicated with your absence after the gardens." Her eyes opened.

There was a moment's pause. "You do not know the pain it caused for me to stay away."

"I do not."

A low laugh vibrated from his chest. "Someday perhaps I will explain it if I can explain it to myself."

And there it was again. A pointer that there was some future between them. Confusing and provocative.

The red flash of an acrobat flipping through the air showed in her periphery. A shout of accomplishment.

"Someday perhaps I will demand it from you." His eyes darkened at her words. Desire turning them black.

The wonderful and heady feeling of feminine power beat in her. She wondered if she could bottle the feeling and clutch it to her in the darkness of the night. Under her frayed bedcovers and simple nightgowns.

His thumb traced her lips. "And someday perhaps I will beg your forgiveness in earnest." He leaned into her, his lips a hairbreadth from hers. "But not today. Today I still seek to take." And his lips claimed hers, dominant and overwhelming.

The colors and shouts, the flips and twirls were sucked from the outside of her world and sent swirling beneath her skin. Bursting from within.

"Will you let me take you, Miranda?" he whispered against her lips.

She nearly replied that he could take her anywhere as long as his lips continued to do those lovely things to her, to produce those overpowering sensations within. A taste of the finest liquor. Of something that could cause one to be drunk with one sip.

"Yes," she whispered.

"Excellent. Tonight?"

Tonight. The Mortons'. With Georgette. "I am to attend a dinner party tonight."

"A dinner party?"

"Yes. With a friend."

"Cancel it," he whispered, eyes hidden from her as he traced the curve of her tilted jaw with his mouth.

"But—"

He drew back so he was looking into her eyes, his voice even more like the smooth-edged aftertaste of whiskey. "I promise I will make it well worth your sacrifice."

Considering the invitation, Georgette would hardly mind if she canceled. Putting herself forward at the

Mortons' suddenly seemed like extending a formal handshake rather than opening herself to light flirtation. The viscount's fingers played at the ties of her dress, making her skin burn beneath. It seemed obvious that *opening up* was something the man at her side was very keen to do to her.

She looked toward the stage. An acrobat flipped through the air and landed precariously on the shoulders of another. He tottered for a moment before gaining his balance and raising his arms in triumph.

"Very well," she whispered, hoping her own actions wouldn't cause her to crash instead.

"Excellent. We will stop by Madame Galland's on the way back."

"I have a number of dresses already." They had all been hanging there, waiting for her to run her fingers wistfully down their silk. Some of them doomed never to be worn. At least by her.

Because while this thing with the viscount was exciting and exhilarating, it would soon ebb—again—and she would go on to other pursuits, hopefully with her heart intact.

She couldn't see herself in the role of a mistress, discovering more about a man as mysterious as the viscount, falling in love with someone she could never claim. Always guarding her heart, waiting for him, or some other paramour, to lose interest.

It was also why she never wanted to meet Mr. Pitts. The man completed a part of her that she'd never known was missing. Invigorated her in a way no one else had. She knew nothing about him physically, but oh so much about the deeper self he held within.

But she would never meet him. Never need to reconcile any wish that the crotchety man on the other side of the page could be someone who could spark her in other ways. In the same way she didn't need to discover if the viscount was someone who would touch her more deeply and make her lose herself in the end.

"You do not desire another?"

"No," she said calmly, as he tucked her loosened hair behind her ear.

"There is nothing that could entice you?"

"Were you planning to take me to the Hannings' masked ball?" she joked. The invitations and responses had all been generated long before. The coveted vellum secured in hands across London. In fact, why wouldn't the viscount be going? She would have assumed he would be.

"As a matter of fact," he said lazily, twirling her hair. "Yes, I am."

He watched her face, full of color as she pressed her hands to her waist and examined the dress from the side. Not as animated as when she was arguing over books—when her face was overflowing with passion— or on paper—her pen creasing the page just an extra touch when she was debating—but in a purely female, satisfied way.

It made the purely male side of him purr.

She'd make the perfect mistress. She really would.

The curving lines on the paper in his pocket were etched in his mind. He touched the correspondence and removed it. Looking at the soft slopes, he smiled and looked back up as she gave a small twirl, the dress curling around her just as the end of her salutation curled on the page.

If control were something that he always sought, then tempting fate had always been his fatal flaw. A piece of his father that he had never stamped out of his own personality.

He fingered the expensive necklace in his right-hand pocket, caressing the lovely stones and simple setting.

She ducked back into the dressing room. He reached with his left hand and lifted Madame Galland's pen from its pot. He tapped it against the side and set it to a loose piece of paper, his natural sloping scrawl allowed to scritch without outside regard.

Dear Chase,

I can only offer the loosest of advice when dealing with a rogue . . .

She emerged in a peacock blue that would set off her eyes, making them blazing sapphires. The swan who had never imagined herself as such.

The perfect mistress. One he could keep, well, forever, quite possibly.

But I can tell you—never trust one. A rogue always has ulterior motives.

Chapter 14

Secret #5: Some are more ripe for seduction than others. But the sweetest fruit is the woman who doesn't realize she is plump on the vine. The one who bursts upon your tongue as soon as you set lips to her.

The Seven Secrets of Seduction

The equally grand but rented carriage rolled to a stop. Miranda touched the drawn shade. She'd drawn it upon entering and felt no urge to panic—at least not about being inside the carriage. She had plenty of unrelieved tension about her destination. But surely they weren't yet at the Hannings'? The viscount was meeting her at the ball. He'd sent his primary carriage team with the rented carriage though, so she wasn't alarmed at the sudden stop, just curious.

The viscount had said he would find her at the ball. That it would be part of the fun.

She was a little surprised, truth be told, that he wanted to meet her there. As if he was courting her. The first day she had met him, she would have said that he was the type to flout convention and enter a society ball, scarlet woman on his arm. And after she'd discovered he was Viscount Downing, she would have expected it.

But he'd been adamant about meeting her there.

The door opened, and an excited voice met her ears. "Thank you, kind sir. What strong shoulders you have."

Miranda's eyes widened, and she leaned forward to see the crown of a perfectly coiffed head duck into the interior. Benjamin's goofy grin disappeared behind the door as it closed, and the entering figure of Good Queen Bess thumped onto the seat.

"Ooh, cushion comfort."

"Georgette!"

"Miranda! Imagine seeing you here." Her eyes sparkled as she put a hand to her bosom. "You are a vision of Artemis. Oh! Look at your arrows." She touched the gilded set on the seat.

"What—I thought—you were—"

"Going to the Mortons'? With you? I was." She patted her hair, her smile undimmed.

"I apologize again for canceling—"

"Good gads, Miranda. *Whatever for?* I was excited for you when I read your note. I was thrilled for you when I thought of your fate. Exhilarated for the adventure you'd experience, and that was all *before* I saw the very nice carriage that was waiting to take me shopping. And the stupefying explanation as to why it was taking me." She happily looked around the interior. "And now, well, I think I might just love you forever."

"You are coming then? To the Hannings'?" She wouldn't have to arrive alone. Nor brave the lofty crowd of the event with only the viscount for comfort.

The viscount not a very *comfortable* man. Exciting, thrilling, exhilarating—all of the words Georgette had used—but not comfortable.

"I am." Georgette's smile threatened to split her face as she held up a gilded invitation. "I've been practicing my Russian all day in case you cause too big a stir. *Nyet!* No dance!"

Miranda stared at her for a moment, then couldn't contain the grin that spilled into laughter.

She touched her friend's hand when her laughter finally subsided. "I'm so glad you are coming."

Georgette squeezed her fingers back. "Me too. You can't imagine how hard it was to keep it to myself and not fawn all over a reply to you. And that charming viscount of yours . . ." She waggled her brows, obviously forgiving him all of his sins. "Well, if I don't see you for a time at the party, I assure you that I will be *fine*."

Miranda colored. "I—"

Georgette smirked. "I love that you can still blush."

They exchanged excited chatter for the rest of the long ride, the Hannings living on the outskirts of London proper.

As they drew closer, they both craned to peer through the window as surreptitiously as they could because there was a small crowd of people moving slowly along the curbside. Trying to catch a peek as the grand carriages moved slowly up the drive.

The house sparkled at the top of the curved drive. Lit by what looked like more lights than all of Vauxhall contained.

"Oh, Miranda." Georgette's face shone.

Miranda looked at her, shining in the interior. Staring out at the lit facade, face nearly pressed to the glass.

The viscount had done this. Maximilian. Had probably deduced it from their earlier conversations that not only would Miranda love to attend, but that it would absolutely be her friend's dream.

"I think I love your viscount," Georgette whispered. "I hope you don't mind."

Despite her best reservations, at the moment Miranda had to admit to feeling just a tad in love with the man herself.

Lights brimmed from the entryway. The viscount's house was grand, but the Hannings' house, lit the way it was, was magnificent. The entire scene was something out of a fairy tale.

As they entered the house, only Georgette's excited hand upon her arm persuaded her that this was real. People were milling everywhere, though the overwhelming crush that was likely to attend had not yet arrived. They were early, and many would come fashionably late.

Those that wanted to set up their stations early were already doing so. Some wanted prime viewing spots while others preferred to be the ones in prime view. The mixture of attendees was part of what made the spectacle intriguing. One didn't know if one was stepping onto the floor with a duchess or an actress, a prince or a dancing master.

Tales would run for weeks in the papers of simple folk who had brushed elbows with royalty. Or a countess seduced by her own husband, unknowingly. It made the whole spectacle possible for them to attend without too much of a concern.

They walked into the main ballroom and immediately everyone seemed to look their way. Georgette looked lovely, her figure on fine display in the queenly gown draped about her. And Miranda had to admit that she was quite pleased with her own appearance. Galina had been given free rein and done a wonderful job.

There were enough people entering with and around them that it made their own entrance mostly unremarkable. Too many people were trying to establish themselves in the crowd, though a few glances were sent their way. Groups established their spaces, then turned to watch the throng. To attempt to determine who was who by the way they held themselves or by what they were wearing.

Next to her, Georgette was nearly vibrating in excitement. She kept a running, whispered commentary every time a new couple, group, or person entered the main corridor through the throng. Some attendees were easily identifiable. Others were masked quite well. Goddesses, jesters, kings, puckish spirits, fictional characters, and darkly masked villains roamed the parquet floor as the space filled.

But where was the viscount?

The murmurs of the crowd suddenly rose. A woman walked into the thick of the room on the arm of a dark man. Georgette was avoiding the temptation to crane her neck, though she looked as if she wanted to do nothing short of standing on her tiptoes to see. "Who is it?" she whispered.

Currently in a better vantage spot due to the movements of the crowd, Miranda watched the woman, half of the pair of Romeo and Juliet, and the way she tried to smile gaily at those around her. The way the lines of her body were just a little too tight. "The Marchioness of Werston."

Georgette's neck craned slightly. "Really? Who is Romeo?"

Miranda shook her head, observing the rakish way the man sauntered. A decidedly scandalous sort as he began undoing his mask. "You would know better than I."

She wondered what the viscount would have to do tonight to cover this one up, she thought somewhat cynically, then shut down the thought, determined to enjoy herself without restraint.

"Werston has nerve," a woman muttered near them.

Miranda blinked and watched the man with greater interest as he sauntered forward, the mask dangling from his fingertips. So this was the viscount's father. He was quite dashing.

And he was with his wife. As doomed star-crossed lovers.

At the moment they were creating more of a scandal together than apart.

Voices grew in volume. Miranda watched as a very familiar figure stepped into the room behind the couple wearing a simple masked outfit. He was dressed entirely in black, and though he was surrounded by outrageous costumes, he somehow commanded all attention. One hand was at his pocket, another held a glass. He looked bored as he gazed absently around the room, but then his eyes stopped on her, and a slow smile curved his lips.

"Oh, dear. I must harness my jealousy. That look." Georgette fanned herself. "And he is heading this way." Her friend lifted her skirts for flight.

"Georgette," she hissed. "What are you doing?"

Her friend smiled mischievously. "Leaving you to your villain, dear. I am off to find a white knight. Ta!"

And her friend—well, she'd considered her a friend

two minutes ago, but perhaps she ought to rethink it—took off, leaving her in the middle of the floor as a dark overpowering presence stepped beside her.

"That didn't take very long," she said as lightly as she could about his quick progress through the crowd, then turned to look up at him. His eyes caressed her face, lighting her on fire all the way down to her toes. Lord, he looked marvelous. "Good evening, your lordship," she breathed.

He smiled—the smile that always did strange things to her insides. That mysterious, lovely pull of lips. He bowed over her hand, his eyes never leaving hers as the first notes of a waltz lifted into the air from the orchestral floor. "May I have this first dance, dear lady?"

And every dance thereafter, her heart nearly answered. "Yes."

He spun her onto the floor, the lights a glowing halo above them as they moved. The faces in the crowd melted together. The onlookers became a simple backdrop in the pages of a storybook.

He was a wonderful dancer and made it easy to follow. She had taken many dancing lessons, but dancing with the viscount was a completely different experience. She had been taught the correct steps in order to be able to teach them in turn. But she had never danced with someone like the viscount. Someone who affected her in such a sensual way.

The waltz ended, and a new one began.

Her breath caught as his eyes met hers over touched fingertips. "I thought it improper to dance together again so soon."

"At this ball, nothing is improper as long as one remains anonymous."

"I don't think you can be anonymous."

His lips curved. "Anyone can be anonymous should it suit him."

She shook her head. "No, I don't think you could ever be."

He looked away. "Then you might be surprised. I hope that should it happen, you will not be too displeased."

She raised her brows.

He twirled and twirled her, taking her breath away, making her forget anything but the way they moved together. The music came to a close, and he opened his lips to say something, but they tightened as he looked at something over her shoulder.

His eyes met hers, darker and more focused. "I had meant to wait to greet you, to perhaps do so in some darkened hallway or behind a closed door, but I just couldn't help myself." He looked back into the crowd. "As always, when it comes to you."

She tried to read his expression, but he quickly wiped it free.

"Don't take off your mask, now that I've paid you attention," the viscount said casually. Too casually. "Lest you be mobbed. The ton likes nothing better than a mystery. They'll avidly try to discern your identity from afar until you slip and make it known. Messerden will want to speak nonsense for a few minutes without pause, trapping you here. Walk around the room, if you need to escape. I charged your friend with watching out for you."

She startled at that piece of information but followed his eyes to a man in a dark cape drawing closer, another man in his wake. Onlookers gazed between them and the oncoming men, fascinated. Hoping for a bit of gossip.

"Leave if I can no longer stand the considering stares?" she asked.

The lines about the viscount's mouth tightened farther. "I apologize."

"Why?" she tried to say lightly. "It is a grand adventure, isn't it? To be mistaken for a princess?"

His shoulders loosened minutely. "As long as you let me save you later from the wicked king."

"I may, should I require aid." She squared her shoulders as Messerden and the slighter man reached them. Both men eyed her but greeted the viscount first, as propriety dictated. Messerden turned to her, and she braced herself for the conversation.

Suddenly, the flowing silks of Juliet materialized in her view, at her side, stepping just a hair in front of her. Greeting Messerden in a twinkling voice.

Then she felt a presence near her back and turned to see a rakish, dark man bowing to her, lifting her hand with so much practiced ease.

Dressed as Romeo.

The viscount's posture tightened, but he was busy answering his mother and the other two men. From his actions at Vauxhall, she had the feeling that he would easily ignore the two men to retrieve her, but the same couldn't be said of ignoring his mother.

And his father had neatly and precisely cut her from their circle. She was somewhat relieved, truth be told. There was just something about Messerden and his continued appearances that put her on edge.

That didn't mean that facing a marquess, even a decidedly scandalous one, was somehow an easy task. A marquess. Might as well be the King for all of the space between them socially.

"Good evening, dear lady."

"Good evening," she replied softly, unsure of a proper response in such a situation.

He smiled charmingly at a couple walking toward the dance floor and stepped backward and to the right, causing her to mirror the action as he hadn't yet let go of her hand, allowing the couple to pass between their two groups, drawing her a little farther from the foursome now a few paces behind her back.

She narrowed her eyes a bit at the deliberate manipulation yet again. "How may I assist you, your lordship?"

The marquess looked at her, a steady long look, the edges of his eyes crinkled permanently in a charming, rather puckish way. "I know who you are."

She swallowed. She wasn't quite sure what she had expected him to say, but it had definitely not been that. "Oh?"

His lips briefly lifted. "I was a fourth son, never expecting to inherit. I'd rather have joined the navy. Set to sea." His puckish smile grew. "Used to spend nights down by the docks. Lovely women there with a keen eye to teaching a man new tricks."

She blinked.

His eyes sought the entrance again, as if he were waiting for someone. "Good place to pick up contacts. Ones that serve a man well in the future, no matter his status. Or perhaps better for his status." His eyes slid back to her and held. "Of course, a few loyal servants also help. I make sure to keep an eye on the children. And their . . . interests. Sometimes their interests surprise even me."

She smiled tightly. She hadn't sought this man's approval in any way, no matter his power, and didn't feel a need to seek it now.

"Oh, you mistake me. I see it in your expression." He leaned in. "I make it my concern to read women's expressions too. Only my wife's have ever fooled me. And yours says that you think I view you as a base servant." He shrugged. "I have never been one to care much for such things. Figured I would marry a girl in some port. Perhaps two or three, one for each frequently scheduled destination." His eyes almost looked dreamy for a second. "Love lasts so much better with plenty of space and bursts of passion, don't you think? Alas, inheriting put quite a damper on such perfect plans."

"That is outrageous," she sputtered.

He smiled, his mercurial eyes changing once more. "Ah, a point in favor of your disguise, should anyone overhear. Mistresses routinely keep a bevy of admirers warming their sheets and accounts. A fallen woman would not be outraged by such. A princess, on the other hand . . ."

She got her sputtering under control. "Perhaps I'm a fallen princess."

He just smiled as he examined her. "Perhaps you are falling. Maxim always did have a keen eye."

She tried not to let the reminder that she was another conquest dampen her mood. Too much.

"Ah, again I see your face. My son is far more constant than I. I do my duty. But Maxim always takes care of things I let wallow. You are hardly something he is picking up to spare a wallow."

"I see."

Once again, she decidedly did not.

"Everyone is so concerned with the state of our affairs. Tiresome. I don't know why Maxim would even listen to some of his siblings' natterings. Being proper is boring."

Miranda thought of the tight, sad expressions on the face of his wife. Perhaps he couldn't read her right because he didn't wish to see the truth. To see how he truly affected her.

A wave of gossip pierced their space.

"Eleutherios, here?"

The edges of the marquess's lips turned up. Much like his son's. He looked to the entrance, to a brown-haired man there. Miranda couldn't see much more of the man through the crowd. Though she craned her neck in curiosity. She had repeatedly restrained herself from doing so since she'd entered, now all restraint caved at the mention of the author's name.

"Do you fancy the man's writings?" the marquess asked.

Miranda blinked, trying to discern more of the man everyone was trying to see. He suddenly slipped away, into some room off to the right, and the voices dropped to whispers. "I do."

"Thought the idea of a primer on seduction was silly myself at first. It's more of an innate thing, a gift." The right side of the marquess's lip curved. "But I've quite changed my mind recently."

"And?"

"And I thought of coming as the author myself tonight."

She stared at him, and he laughed.

"Maxim would have sliced me to ribbons though. Probably socially disowned me once and for all."

She looked at him closely. "Why would you dress as the author?" She tried to wrap her thinking around the idea that the marquess could *be* Eleutherios and failed.

"Merely as a lark. I have little talent with the pen, I assure you." He gazed at his son, then back to where the man at the entrance had stood. "But I admire those who do."

He smiled again. "And I can't help but be enraptured by story. And desirous to stick my untalented pen in places where it doesn't belong to make a tale dance to my bidding."

She wondered if perhaps madness did run in the family.

The marquess laughed suddenly, a warm sound. "Oh, yes. Stirring the pot is necessary now that I've been reined in for a time." His eyes danced as he looked at her. "To his benefit, anyway."

She nodded, agreeing with whatever the madman was saying.

"Giving me an ultimatum. Taking away my search for true love. All of my searches. I think it my duty to point him toward his."

He looked into the crowd and suddenly cocked his head, a mischievous light brightening his eyes again. "Ah, my Juliet awaits."

Miranda looked over to see the marchioness separating from the men and staring coldly their way.

The marquess winked at Miranda and lifted her hand. "To the dagger or poison, I go. A pleasure, princess. Until we meet again."

He deftly stepped toward Miranda, still holding her hand, and she stepped back into the hole he had once more created in the crowd. She felt the familiar presence of a warm back at hers.

The marquess winked again and slipped into the crowd.

The viscount's warm hand steadied her as she turned again into their circle. Two more men had joined the group, arguing about politics, ignoring her for the moment.

The whispers were loud in her ears now that the marquess wasn't distracting her. Her mind had nothing to focus upon other than the frothy words in the crowd's surf.

"The Russian princess."

"I heard she was the illegitimate daughter of the czar."

"No, the next in line to the throne."

"Heard she doesn't speak English."

"I heard she does but feels we are all beneath her."

"Look how she stands. Apart from everyone. Even Downing."

"Holds herself like a queen."

Miranda tried not to stay as rigid as her body wanted to remain. She was frozen. Her immobility taken as snobbery. Her posture taken as arrogance.

Suddenly the gossip shifted. Looks still sent her way, but also toward the other side of the room. The waves of chin-wagging parting in two directions as if the keel of a heavy boat had sliced through the waters.

Flowing brown hair, ruffled and wavy, bobbed through the crowd. Murmurs seeped through the guests, and more than one woman openly watched the masked man.

"*Eleutherios*," one woman squealed.

The viscount's hand surreptitiously moved down her spine, and she shivered. She looked up, seeing his black hair above his black mask. Severe and captivating. He continued to speak with the men, his fingers tickling her back almost absently.

She looked back to the man the whispers were proclaiming as Eleutherios. A woman stepped in his path, the blond ice princess from Vauxhall. She said something, and he smiled, bowing low in a Byronic bend, light tendrils of hair brushing his forehead as he straightened. A hundred sighs echoed through the crowd.

The viscount's fingers caressed her flesh.

The subject matter of their group abruptly changed to mistresses as one of the men said something about the ice blonde. Miranda shifted as more than one eye looked speculatively upon her at the introduction of the topic. The viscount's eyes tightened.

She was having trouble catching her breath all of a sudden. She caught sight of Georgette in the crowd. She needed to escape. Just for a moment. She touched the viscount's hand. "Please pardon me," she murmured, trying to inject some sort of shadowy accent to the words, dark humor the only thing saving her from uttering a slightly hysterical laugh.

The men nodded, the viscount watching her with his dark eyes, seeing her gaze go to her friend and tipping his head.

She tried not to hurry as she walked to Georgette.

"Mir-Artemis!" Georgette exclaimed, and hooked her arm through hers, starting to steer her back into the fray. "I just met the most fabulous women. Shall I introduce you? I have figured out the best way of pretending to speak Russian. All you have to do is take the first—"

"Perhaps later." Miranda stopped their forward progress. "I thought I might head for the retiring room."

Georgette's brows rose. "Very well. I'll go with you."

But halfway to the room, Georgette stopped in her tracks and pointed a shaky finger. "Miranda! *Mrs. Q.*"

Miranda kept the sigh to herself as her friend stood transfixed by the woman in green descending the stairs, all eyes glued to her. "Go."

Georgette looked torn, her eyes still on her idol. "But I don't want to leave you."

"Go. I'll be fine. I'm just going to retire for a few minutes. I'll look for you when I return."

"Are you sure?"

"Yes." She gave her a push. "Go."

Georgette blew her an air kiss. "You are a peach. Ta!"

Miranda shook her head and kept her eyes straight ahead until she entered the blissfully empty room. She leaned against the door and closed her eyes.

She opened them slowly, gazing at her reflection in the wall of mirrors across from her. A woman in a flowing white gown and gilded combs stared back. The silk pooled around her. The gold beads and stitched diamond chips made the woman sparkle.

She allowed a small smile to curve her lips. She *was* sparkling. Galina had ruthlessly made it so. She stepped away from the door and walked to the oval looking glass in front of her. Yes, that was Miranda Chase there behind the mask. But it was the siren touch of Maximilian, Lord Downing, that had lit the spark.

Voices clamored, and the door to the hall opened. Miranda quickly ducked behind a screen, peering through the small crack. Five young women entered the room.

"I heard him say it himself. He is Eleutherios. Imagine

what he looks like beneath the mask. Who do you think he could be?" one woman said to the other as she patted a puff of powder on her forehead.

"Could be almost anyone. Though I'm betting on the third son of the Hannings, since he chose their rout to reveal himself. Been gone to the Continent all this time, didn't you know? Availing himself of all the lucky women in Paris. I do wish he'd visit me and unveil himself fully," the woman twittered. "I'd let him seduce me right out."

The woman pulled her dress down while gazing into the mirror, pushing her bosom into better view. Twisting this way and that, trying to make the visible crease more enticing.

Miranda watched and listened as they gossiped about all manner of things. Eleutherios, Downing, the Werstons, even the "Russian princess." It was beyond exhausting to listen to, until finally they left.

She stepped into the hall before she could become trapped once more, but she wasn't ready to return to the throng. In the retiring room, women might work up the courage to ask her direct questions. Questions that she didn't yet have answers—or a true accent—for.

She decided to admire the magnificent paintings along the wall, closing herself off from anyone traversing the hall. A group of men walked behind her, slowing as they neared. She nervously held herself still and pretended to be absorbed. Let them pass, then she'd find Georgette.

They passed. She shook her head and squared her shoulders, then turned. Only to be greeted by a head of ruffled brown hair mussed by a careless hand.

"You," she uttered in crisp English, tones taught to her by an exacting teacher since birth. With nary a Russian syllable in existence. Too shocked to find the man people were claiming as her correspondent suddenly next to her.

He looked her over frankly. "Me. And you? A princess, or so I hear?" There was a mischievous gleam in his eye as he lifted her hand, bringing it to his lips. "Enchanted."

The man smiled with secret humor. He was almost too young to be called a man, now that she was scrutinizing him closely. More of a mischievous boy on the verge of manhood. A very handsome verge though from the parts she could see.

She tugged her hand back and rocked a bit on her heels. "You find my tongue at a loss, I'm afraid."

"That will never do. I confess that I didn't know what to expect from the Russian princess that Downing has been squiring around."

"Oh?" It would be obvious to anyone hearing her that she wasn't Russian. Then again, the viscount had claimed her a Russian princess merely to muck up gossip. Stir up the nest and then, likely if needed, have the revelation that she *wasn't* Russian stir things up even more.

"Yes. I've heard all about you. And I've looked forward to meeting you." He smiled in a slow, seductive manner, but it had none of the implicit overt force that the viscount projected. For some reason, a picture of an actor treading the stage came to mind. Or of Georgette practicing her wiles in front of a mirror. Or Peter trying to return Georgette's coquettish quips.

Her eyes narrowed, then she smiled brightly, touching his sleeve. "I have looked forward to meeting you too. I frankly never anticipated that I would."

She had said in her letters to both of her correspondents that she was to attend. She'd had no notion that she might finally meet one of them though.

That notion hadn't changed. The man in front of her wasn't the author. She'd believe the viscount was the author, that *Mr. Pitts* was the author, before she'd believe this man was.

He returned her bright smile, and she retrieved a metaphorical hook from her arsenal. "I must thank you again for the books," she said. "Both of them."

His smile slipped for a second, but then came back in full force. "You are welcome, dear lady. I'm glad you enjoyed them."

"I didn't ask you on paper . . . but, but how did you know to send them?"

He coughed and examined her more fully. "Discerning man, aren't I?"

"Yes, you have true talent."

Eleutherios did. Only Mr. Pitts might be able to challenge him with a pen—both brilliant in different ways.

"I am grateful to hear 'tis so. I try to be the best at everything." He put a hand against the wall, leaning toward it in what could only be deemed a seductive manner.

It was difficult to hide her grin. The man in front of her seemed like a good sort. A puppy wanting to practice his wiles on the debutantes. She wondered if he had concocted this scheme just so he could do so.

She actually thought it quite industrious that someone had taken on the secretive author's identity. Would the real author finally reveal himself?

"I would be delighted to show you how much," he said.

"Oh, fabulous. Perhaps now is a good time?"

He blinked at her unexpected response, one hand on the wall, the other at his pocket. "I'll—I'll have to fit you in, of course. Many demands on my time. Especially tonight." His hand snuck into the fabric pocket.

"Of course."

There was something about the man in front of her. Something close to what she had expected. His looks fit—the flowing brown locks and kind eyes. She hadn't expected quite that much mischievousness though. There was something sober about Eleutherios beneath the flowery words.

The thoughtful, keenly sensitive notes contained just a hint of darkness.

"Right." She smiled. "Well, your last note was truly lovely. The way you spoke of the wind on a crisp autumn's day."

He smiled back charmingly. "Thank you, dear lady."

"I was serious when I said that you should write a book of sonnets. You might rival the bard himself."

He tipped his head. "I do have a talent for the pen."

Eleutherios was practically humble in his letters. As if he were unused to sharing himself. She might have expected him to be exactly as the man standing in front of her based on the superficial aspects of his book, but his correspondence had shown someone entirely different and deeper.

"You do. I hope that you will continue with your new works."

"Oh, working on a sequel, didn't you know?" He lifted her hand again. "The sixth secret is to keep one's eyes focused. And I'm a master at that."

Her mouth quirked, and it took all of her effort to keep the edges down. Truly she was glad that Eleutherios wasn't in front of her. Nor Mr. Pitts. This was far more fun, and she had entirely unrealistic expectations of the other men. Frankly, her expectations were unfair. But she never needed to reconcile them because she could continue to live the fantasy.

"Yes, you are. Perhaps—"

A cool, firm hand wrapped around their attached hands and all of a sudden her gloves were touching nothing but air and the fake Eleutherios was stretching his at his side, as if stung.

"I don't believe we've yet *met*." The viscount's eyes were cold as he surveyed the boyish man who suddenly looked much more foppish in the presence of Downing's stark, perfectly worn attire and complete aura of hard power.

The boy shifted on his feet, something close to terror in his eyes.

Miranda stepped into the fray, something about the boy calling forth her protective instincts. "Viscount Downing, this is Eleutherios. The author. A charming lad."

The other man regained himself quickly, the rakish gleam back in place—quite like the marquess's puckishness actually. "At your service, my lord." He extended his hand.

Downing didn't even look at the digits, his gloved hand played with a watch at his pocket. "The author of *The Seven Secrets of Seduction*?" Feigned interest wasn't enough to fool either of them. "In our humble presence?"

"I would never presume to humble anyone," the boy said in the most humble way she'd been privy to since their conversation had begun. He shifted on his feet. "The lady was merely interested in . . . my works and writings."

The viscount's eyes pinched and he looked almost violent for a second before he turned coolly dismissive once more, much as he had at Vauxhall or Lady Banning's when confronted by something irritating.

"Is that so?"

"Yes. But do excuse me for a moment. I seem to recall an urgent appointment." The fake Eleutherios moved quickly down the hall. Faster than she'd seen a man with that high a cravat travel before.

"I think you frightened him away," she mused, conflicted. She had enjoyed the boy. And she'd barely set her hook to have some benign fun. And even though he looked only a few years younger than she, he also looked like he could use a motherly hug.

The viscount shrugged, eyes dark. He smiled, every fiber of it more seductive than anything the boy could have claimed. There was an edge to the smile though.

"Did you want him to stay? Doesn't even have the sense to play the muttonhead of *his* writings. Rattle-pate glory hound."

Something twinged in her mind, but the look in his eyes distracted her. "I did wish to speak with him. Though he isn't—"

She suddenly found herself tugged forcefully forward. The viscount spun her, and she heard the clack of a door engaging its lock.

"And what would you say?" He pressed her front forward against the wall of some room off to the side of the hall, the gilt edge of something assuredly expensive pressing into her palm as the warmth of him pressed against her back. She moved her hands to either side of what seemed to be a painting.

"I—I—" her voice hitched as he did something with the edges of his thumbs, pressing them up under her bodice. "I simply would thank him." The oil would surely melt beneath her heated exhalations. Melt the posed expression on the portrait, turning it into something wild and unknown.

"For what? A tawdry book?"

"His lovely words."

"Words aren't lovely." His lips pressed against her throat. "Actions are."

Her head tilted back. "His actions then too."

"You will forget all about him."

She gasped as his palms curled around the front of her dress and cupped her breasts.

"Did you hear me, Miranda?"

His fingers moved, setting off a thousand sensations. "We were just speaking."

"That wasn't your author."

His fingers drew up her skirt, bunching the material as they drew higher. As they curled around her through the layers. She might as well have been bare beneath his hands. Clay waiting to be molded beneath skilled fingers.

"How do you know?"

"C—" His voice abruptly cut off, and his lips clamped around the vein in her neck, sucking hard enough to leave a mark. His fingers pulled against the core of her, a long press of exquisite force that lit everything in her as they circled, dipped in, and pulled again. She crushed her palms against the wall and arched back.

"The boy barely knows how to use his overabundance of libido yet."

His other arm reached around her waist and played with the edge of her low bodice, the delicate, scalloped edges giving easy way to the questing fingers dipping beneath.

She could feel him behind her, pressed against her. Ready. Ready at any moment to toss up her skirts and mark her as his.

He abruptly turned her and pulled her against him. His head buried into her throat. To the crook between her neck and shoulder, his breathing heavy. He gripped her hips and turned her, swinging her toward the settee. Depositing her on the plush cushion with urgency.

"You acquiesced earlier, but I'll ask again. Will you let me have you, Miranda?"

He crouched on the floor between her knees, her legs spread to the sides, one edge of her gown bunched up around her thigh. Like the pages of a book, opened and splayed. Waiting to be read or written upon. Branded with ink and purpose.

He pushed a hand slowly beneath the covered layer, up her other leg, and around her thigh.

"I-yes," she whispered.

He leaned forward and upward, his lips curling around the soft flesh behind the lobe of her ear. "I won't let you regret it," he whispered. His fingers gripped her thighs, the balls of his feet pushing him toward her. Each fraction of space his hands moved increased her heart rate.

She shivered at the feel of him, so close, nearly nestled against her. Opening her farther. She leaned her head against the back cushion of the settee, exposing her neck to his meticulous onslaught, feeling his shiver beneath her frank acceptance.

She touched his cheek, softly pulling him back to meet her eyes. "Nor I you."

One corner of his mouth tugged. "Never." His lips

hovered above hers, even crouched on the floor as he was, and the lovely feminine power washed over her that he was finally matching her emotion, breathing as if he'd run to Marathon. "I'd apologize for where we are, but I've been waiting to taste you for so long that I have forgotten the taste of honey and the sweet nectar of the finest wine. Neither of which tastes half as good as you do."

He took a long sip. Heat stole over every fiber of her being.

"Lady Banning was incorrect," she said when she could speak once more, gripping the unraveled edge of the cravat at his throat. "You have a honeyed tongue. Not one of silver."

"That I can speak at all is a miracle." His hand stroked up her leg, over her stockings and to the ties. "By rights I should be stumbling with a tongue tied worse than my neckcloth at present."

"You seek to amuse." The man had the whole of London's female population at his feet.

He slipped a tie free, and her heart picked up another beat, in time with the faster reel playing through the wall.

"Amusement is what I have sought in the past. Alas that now I can't claim its arms. It is far easier on the heart."

Another tie pulled, the silk manacles slipping free. He rolled the stockings under his fingertips, curling them over and back, rubbing silk against silk, the sound of it barely evident with the cello rumbling beyond, but there, heard in the acute sensitivity of her heightened senses. Instead of dulling them, the onslaught had just brightened everything to white-hot.

There was a courage, a power in not looking away.

In meeting his eyes, watching as he undressed her piece by piece.

"I had planned to wait until we returned to the house, but—"

She touched his lips, warm and still so near to hers. The heat was running just beneath her skin, treading impatiently at the promise of a final release. "I don't want to wait. This is perfect. Serenaded by violins?" The soft strains of the orchestra sifted through the adjoining wall. "I never expected to hear the actual music of the angels." The lights from the patio filtered through the shadows of the half-pulled draperies. "Besides, this is far more private."

His brows pulled together. "We are in the middle of a ball, and I can scarcely keep myself from pawing your dress like a schoolboy on his first outing." He deftly freed her of her undergarments, marking his claim false.

Of course he wouldn't even think of the servants in his own house. They were like the furniture to him. Always there, even more accommodating than a leather ottoman as he didn't need to step around them, they simply melted to the side as he passed. She opened her mouth to say so, but he finished slipping her undergarments down and placed an openmouthed kiss on the inside of her knee, and the words escaped without sound.

She could feel him smile against her skin, confirmed when he glanced up, the fringe of his hair falling across his brow.

"I've been waiting to taste you in many ways."

She couldn't credit that her heart could beat any more quickly, but it gamely gave a try.

"Did you read the illumination, Miranda?" His

thumb touched her, rubbing lightly, just a slip of his smooth pad against the warmest part of her. "Or better yet, did you look at the pictures and imagine the words describing the acts for yourself?"

"Yes."

"So honest. It's intoxicating." He placed another kiss, one inch higher. "Almost as intoxicating as the pure taste of you. As the way you live in the moment yet dream of the future."

Another kiss, a gentle pressure on her other thigh spreading her farther, his thumb gliding over her once more.

"Do you know what I'm going to do to you, Miranda?"

Her tongue darted out, tasting him on her lips. "Yes. Page seven."

He smiled. It was a full, real smile, masculine and lovely. "Lovely page seven. Do tell me if you will mark it as a winner afterward, will you?"

He placed a kiss on the inside of her inner thigh. So close to his thumb, which was stroking a soft rhythm to the harmony's line.

"I promise to critique it fairly, my lord," she breathed, as the kisses grew ever closer, ever deeper. As his hands lifted the fallen edges of her bunched dress and shift, drawing them back, pushing, his fingers lighting her bare skin to fire.

"Oh, I'm hoping that you will be less than objective."

His mouth finally reached her, and she forgot how to breathe. His hands pulled along her belly, then around her hips and under her. Lifting her, the back of her head hitting the padding behind, the shadows of the gilded ceiling swimming above her view.

Lifting her, teasing her, tasting her. Making anything in any illicit tome pale in comparison to the way her body responded—movement, not static pictures on a page—to grip with her fingers, to breathe in quick gasps of sound, to squirm closer.

And then he devoured her. The intensity of it made her grasp the first thing with which she came into contact that her fingers could wrap around, writhing beneath him, arching back, a litany of sounds falling from her lips.

Her knees fell apart like downed reeds, the shadows swam above her, dark and light, like the man at her feet. Life and chance twining together. Here they weren't a lord and a shopgirl. For the lord crouched at the feet of a shopgirl was a ludicrous thought. She was a woman on the verge of freedom, and he was the key in her lock.

The orchestra hit a run of notes, an increase to a crescendo. She gripped his hair, feeling open and wanton and alive. On the crest of a crashing wave.

And then he was above her, and her head rested on a pillow, her back on the cushions. "I feel far too selfish at the moment to let you continue alone. I've been waiting too long to watch your face. To see the color bloom in your cheeks as you experience passion for the first time."

She thought maybe it was a bit late for that.

He smiled slowly. "Oh, merely prologues, I assure you." He leaned down and gripped the lobe of her ear between his lips. "I will chain you to your bed later. Feast on you all night." His lips moved to her throat and down the bared flesh of her chest. "But I can't wait any longer to be inside you."

His lips hit her breast, and she arched up into him.

Somehow, he had freed himself from his clothing, and her flesh met his. Warm and strong. Slipping together like two halves searching to be whole.

"Do you know what we are going to do now, Miranda?"

"Page . . ." Her breath hitched as he captured her nipple in his mouth. She couldn't even remember her own name even though he'd just uttered it.

"I'm going to bathe in your beauty. Claim your vibrancy. Make you mine."

He slid inside her, and she clutched him. Every inch of it caused her to tremble. He continued forward until the entire length of him claimed her.

He pressed forward, rocking his hips just the slightest bit, her body strained automatically, sensing that there was at least one millimeter of ecstasy further she could travel. "Are you going to make me yours too?" he whispered, his hand cupping the base of her rear.

Her body answered automatically by arching up, closing the last gap, pushing past it, making lights explode. His lips clamped around her throat, uttering something against her skin, the blood flowing hotly through her veins.

She panted beneath him and watched as he pulled back, his eyes glittering. She madly wondered what he could or would say. His lips curved, his eyes hot and black. Sucking her into their ink, splaying her open on the page.

The feelings that he engendered coiled together in a knot of wild longing and desire. Her body clamped around his, instinctively clasping him to her. His eyes half closed for a moment, then his fingers wound into her hair, and he kissed her hard.

He pulled back and looked down into her eyes. "I

always knew you would." Then he thrust up into her, hard and smooth, fierce and sure, causing the lights to explode again. Something escaped from her lips. Some sort of groan or fervent prayer. But she had no time to determine which as he rocked into her again. As she reached for the gold glittering in the shadows. As she met his eyes and movements, mesmerized and more than a little love-struck.

As the world exploded around her in shards of crystal and violin strings. Lights and sound and heat. And still he moved within her, stirring the explosions, making her feel like she could touch the skies. The heavens. Him.

She stared up at him, shuddering breaths still wracking her as he slowed, as the fullness of it all grew. Feelings she couldn't identify clogging her throat.

"Ch—" He cleared his roughly. "I won't let you regret it, Miranda."

Her breath caught. Had he been about to call her Charlotte? Were the rumors true? But the beginning of the syllable had been all wrong. Unless maybe he was more formal with ton ladies and had been about to say Chatsworth, dropping the Miss.

Her heart stopped as another thought occurred. A thought that connected with a thousand little dropped hints that had been scattered like bread crumbs. Connected and formed into a solid, tangible notion.

Maybe . . . maybe he had been about to say *Chase*.

Chapter 15

Someone attempting to be me? Do not be fooled. I would not deign to reveal myself to the masses.

Eleutherios to Miranda Chase

Miranda drummed her fingers on the counter, face freshly scrubbed of the lingering paint from her costume and the viscount's lovely warm lips, and tried to figure out how to go about her inquisition.

She'd needed to rid herself of all traces of him in order to think straight. Even so, he'd touched her cheek as she'd slipped from her room in his house, after the ball, leaving an invisible trail of scent marking her as she'd left his house and ridden back to hers, clad once more in her everyday wear.

Her uncle had been awake, figures in front of him upon her return. He'd seemed unsurprised to see her arriving so late, but then again he was trying to reconcile all of the books in order to get everything ready for the creditors coming in the following week. And it would be a strange thought to anyone in their circle—other than Georgette now—that quiet Miranda Chase might be having a wild time. Her uncle probably thought she had fallen asleep in the retiring room, hiding from the guests at the Mortons'.

"You told Lord Downing that I would catalog his library."

Her uncle nodded absently, hunched over his ledger. "Yes."

"When?"

He waved a distracted hand. "When he asked."

"When exactly did he ask?" she pressed.

"He first mentioned it a month ago? Said it was a possibility. Why does it matter?" He looked up over the top rim of his glasses. "He came back a week later and said the project could go for as long as it took. He would continue to pay. And quite well, I can tell you. Might just be keeping us afloat."

"A month ago?" Her mind churned. He hadn't entered the shop a month ago. Were her mad thoughts true?

"Think it was a Wednesday?" Her uncle tapped his lip with his messy quill, ink spotting the surface. "Yes, you had just stepped out for your weekly book-club meeting. Must have just missed you."

A strange buzzing began in her mind.

"Left precipitously right before you returned. Yes, just missed you."

Or had known exactly when she'd be gone. But no, that was silly. All of these thoughts were silly. She was simply asking the questions in order to eliminate the strange suspicion from her mind.

"Was going to introduce you too." He waved his quill, head down. "He said he wanted the best worker I had. Didn't care that you were female."

Didn't care that she was female. That sounded awfully familiar. But, no, surely not. These were all mad thoughts.

"Oh? Did he say so before or after you told him I was available to help?"

Her uncle looked up and tapped his quill against his lip again. "Before? What difference does it make? Quite good of him, I thought. Never had cause to think less of your work for being a female, myself. Better than anyone else I've seen."

Amidst the churning confusion, a warm rush of fondness for her uncle flowed through her. "Thank you, uncle. But I do not find that sentiment often, especially in the wealthy, so I must admit to surprise."

"Seems a decent sort. Likes books. Nothing wrong with that."

"No." She spread her hands. "But did he say anything specific?"

"Said he wanted someone who knew Shakespeare and sonnets. Knew then that the best choice was you. And it didn't take any convincing. He accepted immediately. Decent sort, he is."

The buzzing became an ocean wave breaking upon a cliff face.

She excused herself and ran to her room, upending her lap desk onto the bed. She shuffled through her papers, pushing them in all directions until she found the clipped articles from the *Daily Mill* that she had saved. She thumbed through them until she got to the first one—the one that had caused her to respond.

I can't understand the absolute hysteria over this blatant piece of trash. What could have the whole of London so excited over drivel intended to commonly seduce members of the opposite sex? Does anyone have anything of merit to say besides the sexual fawning over this tawdry piece?

It just goes to prove that everyone is so sex-starved

that they find a novel about sex more interesting than the sonnets of old.

Why hadn't she thought of it before? Their first meeting . . . his reference to Shakespeare and thus the *great sonnets of old*. His talk of the tawdry book. It was as if he had been hoping she'd know it was he.

She shuffled through more of the papers. From the initial, sarcastic ones, to the more intense.

Dear M. Chase,

You sound like a veritable ray of blooming sunshine.

Dear <u>Miss</u> Chase,

I was absolutely <u>prostrate</u> in wait for your reply.

Dear Miss Chase,

Do you really think such thoughts of the wretched piece? And how would you define a classic?

Dear Chase,

I must admit you were an amusing distraction at first. Now I find you most intriguing in full.

She had developed such a preconception about Mr. Pitts that she hadn't entertained the thought that he might walk through her door in disguise. And be a *viscount,* no less.

No, that wasn't correct. Mr. Pitts was the disguise.

She shifted, uncomfortable with that thought. Mr. Pitts was real. But so too was Lord Downing.

She had never thought the two men could be one and the same, until it had struck her dead in the chest in the dark, sweat-drenched room at the Hannings. For all her talk of looking beneath, she hadn't bothered to do aught but skim the surface.

Could she blame herself though? For not thinking that a viscount would write scathing pieces to the paper, then write to *her* in answer to her own piece, then subsequently strike up a lively personal correspondence. For not thinking that a man who looked like that would be on the other side of the pen.

Would chase and strike up a *romance* with someone like her.

She found it suddenly hard to catch her breath.

She hadn't been wrong when she'd said to Georgette that it felt as if he'd engineered her work in his library. But for *how long* had he done so?

The man on the page, the one she had confessed *everything* to, was the same man . . . the same man she was confessing *about.*

Oh.

Oh.

Oh, he was going to pay.

And at the same time . . . he was her confidant. The secret friend with whom she could share everything. *The same man she had been consorting with for the past two weeks.*

The strange feminine power that had been blooming within her suddenly exploded. He had tracked her down. He had started this seduction, this romance with her. Already knowing who she was.

She flexed her fingers. The insecurities that had been

plaguing her seeped out, like ink finally unblocked from the nib of a pen. As Georgette was wont to say . . . why *not* her? Why not her if he was the same man. The ink-stained mate of her soul.

But why approach her this way? What had he to gain?

Why the elaborate charade? The Shakespearean farce?

The reason eluded her, but other things slotted into place. Gaps in the viscount's demeanor that she could suddenly understand and read. Sloping invisible script between the written and spoken lines that suddenly formed a more complete picture with the two men combined.

But why had he approached her in that way?

To be an anonymous persona without the handsome face and expectations of seduction clouding the conversation? Perhaps to share himself without repercussion? It was something that had always appealed to her about her own letters. The freedom of them.

Her breath caught. Written confessions he had actively responded to. Ones she had sent from her very soul. To him. About him. *About him, though she hadn't known it.* Her throat closed, dry and heavy.

The utter bastard.

The lovely beast.

She narrowed her eyes and took a deep breath.

The question now became—what was she going to do with her information?

She shuffled through her papers, determined to piece together a draconian plan that would have him wrapped in chains until she was ready to release him. Other pieces of correspondence slipped from the box. Letters from Eleutherios. Lovely, lyrical lines.

She had always thought it seemed as if Mr. Pitts knew him personally. But why would the viscount hate Eleutherios so?

She paused, her hand upon an original handwritten sonnet splayed upon crisp parchment. Because he practiced his own brand of seduction? Did he see the author as a threat? What made it personal?

The threads of overheard conversation filtered through.

Why not go back to your correspondence and literary pursuits? Sell your melancholy memoirs?

He wouldn't be caught holding a book of sonnets he hadn't written himself. The words permeated the heavy haze.

His brother Colin had lighter hair. Brown with a bit of a wave. If he styled it correctly and affected a less dour attitude . . . he could have been the man in the hall.

But sober Colin who supported order and rules? He was a man she would hardly credit with writing a tome on *seduction*. Then again, it appeared that same sober man was perhaps fighting a fierce flirtation with her maid at the house.

Could Eleutherios be the viscount's brother? It would give the viscount a personal push against her interaction with him.

She thought hard on the man from last night. Not Colin. Similar, but not the same. But . . . but there was a younger brother. The youngest. A hellion. He had been in the papers before, going on his Grand Tour. His name started with a C too. Georgette would know it.

Pretending to be his middle brother?

She thought about the interaction between the viscount and the fake author with that information in mind. She tapped the sonnet militantly. Yes. She'd bet her monthly stipend that the viscount's youngest brother was the man at the Hannings'.

The viscount had been irritated. Extremely irritated, yes. But that seemed true for his family in general. For he hadn't seemed to hate Colin at Lady Banning's. He had been defensive and fed up.

He had been more irritated that Miranda might be taken with the idea she had met the author, and her response again to the author's writings. Jealous even.

She looked down at her correspondence—the pages from Mr. Pitts interspersed with those from Eleutherios—and traced the letters absently. Everyone seemed to like sonnets these days, she thought just as absently.

Then stopped. Her fingernail creasing a small dent in the sheet.

What was to stop the viscount from also . . . but no, that would be silly.

She looked at the sheets splayed around her. At the vitriol against Eleutherios. Surely someone wouldn't write that against oneself? She gripped the page, creasing the words.

Muttonheaded, rattle-pate, twit . . .

And yet, when she went over the papers with a critical eye, and clenched fingers, there were similarities in sentiment, in voice. Though one voice was full of darkness, and the other light. Only that small dark current under Eleutherios's words was a link.

She put a hand to her forehead, to the cold sweat gathering there.

The marquess . . . the brother . . . even the mother stepping in to help her husband play whatever trick had been concocted that night. The marquess had been looking for the fake Eleutherios before he had entered. Had said of his own admission that he had thought to *play him himself*.

She wiped her palm on a cloth, searching for something that would put the mad thoughts to rest. The handwriting . . . it was completely different. Written by two different hands.

She gave a relieved, if slightly hysterical, laugh. Perhaps she would be accusing Galina of being Eleutherios next.

Her laugh cut off, and she promptly felt the need to put the cloth directly to her head. The viscount had a hundred servants. And his valet would know all of his secrets. And he traveled with him everywhere. Could put everything to the page that Eleutherios wrote.

Or everything that Mr. Pitts wrote.

The viscount had declared Eleutherios to be a fake right off. Perhaps simply because he knew that the man was his brother. But it could also be a simple statement of normal fact.

Was he truly both men? Sent to bedevil her?

She examined the notes. Never had she been so affected by a man, and in the space of half a year she had been affected by three in succession. But perhaps not three men, at all. Instead, three thirds of a man. Incomplete.

She swallowed. All of the feelings that she had for each of the three swirling around and striking against one another. Looking for places to absorb. To connect.

Why?

Who was Viscount Downing? Which one of these incarnations was the real man himself, if any?

Sent to bedevil *her*. A shiver of warmth followed a sudden heaviness in her throat. Hope and unease mixed in a strange cordial. Why had she been the one he had singled out?

And what was she going to do with the knowledge . . .

Chapter 16

Secret #6: Find the secret. What ~~she~~ *he keeps hidden from others. That is the key to* ~~her~~ *his embrace.*

The Seven Secrets of Seduction

(annotated by Miranda Chase)

"**G**ood morning." His voice was a purr in her ear. It sent the hair on her arms straight up and the heat of her body climbing, but she concentrated on her hand atop the shelf. She tapped the book there, militantly, casually, with purpose. *Il Principe.*

She turned and ran a finger under his chin. "Good morning," she purred back.

His smile froze for a fraction of a second, then grew. He lifted her hand and brought it to his lips, the touch of his mouth searing her palm beneath the silk.

"New gloves?"

"Oh? Yes. I thought it was time for a new pair."

That morning, she had dipped into her savings to purchase a pair that was better than most of the gloves she owned. *All* of the gloves she owned, for she didn't feel she owned any of the ones he had given her to wear. The new gloves were worth every penny. The price of a shield never to be underestimated in battle.

And gloves such as these were something she had wanted but always denied herself. Her practicality quashing extravagant pleasure.

"Do you like them?" She pressed her hands against the waist of her gown and pulled them down, defining her hips through the material, letting go only when they reached her thighs.

He paused, eyes following the motion, then glanced up. A lazy regard was the only thing in evidence. The moment of unease quickly buried. She would never have even noted it had she not deliberately inspired it. He was too good really.

The man needed to be taught a lesson.

She stepped nimbly off the ladder, and his arms automatically went out to steady her. "Oh," she said, breathlessly, stealing Georgette's best material ruthlessly, and with a single-mindedness even her friend couldn't claim. She knew her delivery was flawless because her determination wouldn't allow for anything less. "Thank you."

His arms tightened fractionally, but then he twirled her. "Of course, sweet Miranda."

She let her hands drift down his chest and wrap around his waist, hugging him. "I had such a lovely evening." She let her body rub lightly against his, and as soon as his arms tightened to secure her, she whisked herself away. "I have this section nearly complete. Isn't it wonderful?"

She didn't turn around to see his expression though she desperately wished to. The hook wouldn't work if she tipped her hand too soon.

Let him feel the topsy-turvy emotion for a while before she ground him to dust.

"A whole section done?"

"Yes. I decided that I was being silly with the way we were organizing by author." She smiled at him. "Much better to organize chronologically."

"Chronologically?" he echoed.

"Yes. It's brilliant, isn't it? That way you have to simply want to find a Baroque author or a Renaissance one, go to the section, and *voilà*! A whole bevy awaiting perusal." She brushed by him, allowing her skirts to curl around the edges of his trousers as she spun to point at the titles. "Think of the Enlightenment section."

"Indeed." He looked as if he could dearly use some enlightenment at the moment. Her smile spread.

She turned, her chest brushing his elbow. "And you are brilliant, of course, so it should be easy to find and increase the breadth of categorizing." She leaned in just a bit, then retreated before he could grab her.

She couldn't tell which was confounding him more, the thought of what she had suddenly done to his library or the way she was teasing him, breaking from her passive role.

She smoothed her hands down the bodice of her dress as if there were a crease there in need of pressing. "I have a silly status report from my uncle though. It needs a statement from you that work is progressing apace. Oh, and a signature." One finger curled a lock of hair against her ear, her nail rubbing down the strands, a calming well-used tactic, then waved out in a careless fashion toward the library desk.

She sauntered over, bent slightly—unnecessarily—and picked up the paper she had laid there. A small inkpot stood at attention. She was hoping it wasn't the only thing doing so in the room. She turned slowly, bending back up, stretching the material taut over her front. If only a lower-necked gown had been at all appropriate, she would have been dipping forward, allowing it to gape instead.

His eyes caressed her. Her traitorous body reacted, not averse to a seduction taking its toll upon the perpetrator as well.

"A status report?"

"He just wants to make sure you are satisfied."

"Oh, that is one emotion I feel quite strongly." His hot eyes engulfed her, turning her body into flames wherever they lit as he walked toward her.

"Very good," she said more huskily than intended. She stretched into him under the pretext of handing him the quill. "I do so hope it continues."

He lifted the quill from her fingers with his left hand and started to put it to the page, his eyes still upon her. Then he paused and casually, too casually, switched the quill to his right fingers, looking down. Awkward lines scratched the surface. A sentence, then a scripted signature.

She'd bet the entire rich sum he was paying that he was left-handed. That he didn't write that chicken scrawl with his left and instead produced the beautiful sloping and cutting lines she loved to trace.

He pushed the paper toward her. "Acceptable?"

She took the paper and smiled brilliantly in return. "That was perfect. Just what was needed." She ducked from his arms and folded the paper into the sleeve she had brought with her. She would compare it later. There were only so many ways one could change one's handwriting before certain elements connected.

His eyes traveled over the shelf behind her. His brows creased. "What is this?"

"Oh. Your travel books are wonderful. So many lovely tomes." And she truly meant it. She had been hard-pressed not to lose herself in their midst. But she had needed to get them on the shelves, and so she'd put them up in a most interesting fashion.

"Are they arranged . . ." He paused, the barest hint of concern sifting in to the tone. "By the length of the title?"

She laughed lightly. "Don't be silly." She waved a hand, and sauntered away, determined to get his eyes off them. "You have delightful engineering books as well. Travel and engineering are interesting subjects."

And she had intermixed them in a way that even she would be hard-pressed to explain.

She turned in front of a waist-high pedestal, hiding the vase she had placed there thirty minutes prior. Perhaps they'd need to rename the Red Room the Bone Room now. The skull she had placed in the room below was lovely in its own way—if one enjoyed the macabre. Personally, someone who treasured Shakespeare should be pleased.

She ran a finger along her lips, entreating his eyes to follow, moving them away from things better left for a later surprise. "I saw a grand phaeton on the way here and have been engrossed in locating your books on transportation. It must be wonderful to travel with the wind upon one's cheeks in such a vehicle."

His eyes sought the stacks once more, a touch of consternation mixing with the heat still present.

"We must satisfy your curiosity," he said, lifting a hand as if to escort her away. "I have been meaning to have another look at the Serpentine since you defied me to give it a second glance."

She could almost hear the underlying thought that perhaps he should get her out of the library until sanity returned.

"Oh?" Turned away from him as she was, her real emotion was allowed free rein. She smiled slowly and smoothed her hands together, the silk gliding, then creating friction in the opposite direction. She altered her expression into one of innocence and turned. "That sounds lovely."

"And you can show me what beauty I can possibly concentrate on with you so near."

"'*Sweet lord, you play me false,*'" she said lightly, quoting her namesake.

"'*I would not for the world.*'"

Oh, yes, a lesson awaiting teaching, indeed.

He snapped two fingers, and immediately a servant appeared, as if he had been waiting behind the doorframe. "Tell Fredericks to ready the phaeton."

She could decide when they left the room as to whether she wanted him to see the new position of the Vermeer or not.

The servant cleared his throat. "There is a light chance of rain, my lord." He had obviously been listening to their conversation and was loath to impart the news.

"Oh." Miranda spared a look at her hands, a secret smile curving her lips before she wiped it away. "I don't want to ruin my new gloves—"

"Then we will go tomor—"

She met his eyes once more. "—but I would like nothing better than to visit the waters with you on a misty day."

The viscount's eyes suddenly narrowed the slightest bit as he regarded her.

She silently repeated a mantra of innocence. "To see the mist's shadowy fingers curl over the surface." She smiled artlessly.

He watched her for another few seconds of held breath, then said over his shoulder, "Ready the closed carriage then." There was some odd hint of relief in his eyes that she couldn't pin down. "You don't mind if we don't take an open-air vehicle?"

"Actually, I quite enjoy the interior of the closed carriage these days. Perhaps I might impose on your good humor to try the open-air another day?"

"I insist."

But there it was again, that small hesitation.

It struck her suddenly. The masks, the closed spaces, the empty theaters, the games. Was he trying to help her, to guard her reputation? Or was he ashamed of her? Her heart sought the former, but her mind clasped around the latter.

She put her hand on the volume of Shakespeare's sonnets that he claimed to have stolen from his brother. "Thank you for lending the book to me. It has been quite enlightening."

"You are finished with it?" He looked at the cover, the edge of a finger touching the paper innocently sticking out.

"Not yet. I'm just getting started, really."

She turned so he couldn't see her face. So that he could satisfy his curiosity, peek under the cover, just as she wanted him to.

She hummed and picked up a book on a stack as if she were returning to her task during the wait for the carriage to be ready. "I heard from Eleutherios this morning. I was composing my response."

The letter had been a lovely thing, full of vibrant words and glittering phrases. It had made her sigh and clasp the paper to her chest. It had nearly changed her mind about the course she had planned.

She could hear the soft crinkle of paper behind her.

"Did you tell him what a disappointment he was?" The words were dark. But there was a thread of emotion beneath. A rash longing.

"No. Why would he be a disappointment?" She kept looking straight ahead, away from him, for surely she would give herself away in that moment. "I don't think he could ever be a disappointment," she said quietly. There were limits to revenge. Making his world topsy-turvy was excellent, deliberately hurting him was unacceptable.

"I am sure that is not true."

"Well, I wasn't the least disappointed in his letter nor in meeting him." She waved a hand over her shoulder. Shocked when she realized she had met him long ago, yes. Disappointed, no. "I was quite surprised at his appearance, I must say. But I am intrigued enough by his words to want to see underneath the mask."

She could *see* him reading the unfinished note she had left in the book, even though her back was still turned. "Now that he has shown himself, I think we can meet face-to-face. He seemed quite the charmer, if young."

"You wish to meet with him?" The words were dark.

"Why would I not? He wrote me an exquisite sonnet." She shivered in real remembrance. The words had wrapped around her and squeezed. All the more so because she knew exactly who was on the other side of the pen. That he had written it in the dead of night after their activities. "He writes the most beautiful words. Full of emotion. I can feel the longing and desire. I just want to—"

"You want to what?" He spun her around, forcefully pulling her against him, leaving her breathless.

"Clasp him to me." She clutched him against her. "The way he writes emotion," she said, nearly panting. "Veritably Shakespearean."

"Never." He crushed his lips against hers.

She responded, wrapping herself around him gladly. For her plan included plenty of opportunity for seduction. Tipping his world as he had tipped hers.

"Your lor—"

The servant's words abruptly cut off, melting away to leave, but Miranda untangled herself from the viscount anyway, breathing hard. The viscount's eyes were dark and intense. He barked over his shoulder without taking his eyes from her.

"What?"

The underbutler stood at the door with his eyes averted. "Whenever you are ready, the carriage is out front."

There was no apology. For to apologize would call attention to the fact that something had been interrupted. It again made her wonder how many women had been brought here in the past. Giving way to the unsettling thought of what type of guest it truly made her.

They made it into the carriage before a light drizzle started, pattering upon the roof. She burrowed into the plush carriage blanket. Her knee brushed his, her shin loosely touching his ankle.

Here in the carriage, armed with her new knowledge, able to act with an abandon she otherwise wouldn't employ. Another game, a masked maneuvering that allowed her to be free.

"We can head home, or wait it out." His eyes were hot, enticing, watching her. They had been since they'd been interrupted in the library.

A thrill coursed through her—a thrill stemming purely from the way he made her feel, her gambit almost forgotten beneath the heat he generated within her. The layers that restlessly awaited discovery. She moved toward him across the space, allowing her new resolve to carry her forward to what she truly wanted to do. To turn his world around. To turn her own in the process, under *her* control for once.

She let a soft bump move her hands to his knees to steady herself.

Her hands slipped up his thighs, almost of their own volition. She heard his intake of breath and smiled. Whatever else, he affected some deep feminine wile and want inside of her. Made her feel both powerful and powerless at turns. She gripped the power and pulled her silk-encased fingers down his strong thighs and back up. Letting the motion of the carriage guide her actions, pulling her forward between his legs. His dark eyes turned fierce, and his hand slipped into the hair at her nape, caressing the soft skin there.

"Miranda, what are you doing?"

"Enjoying the thunderstorm."

She slipped her fingers around the fasteners at the top of his trousers and flicked them free, her new gloves doing nothing to hinder the motion, their quality, clutching and hugging each furrow and tip, giving her unparalleled dexterity. The image from the pages of the scandalous illumination rose in her mind. The devilry depicted of a woman chaining a man to her bidding. Putting forth a siren call, but without sound, through the touch of fingers to skin, mouth to limb.

He reached for her, as if to bring her back to the seat, to take control of their movements. She flicked his hand away and pushed his chest so that he was leaning back against the cushion.

His eyes were black. Anticipation, lust, and uncertainty in their depths. Just as she wanted.

She took him in her hand, pulling the new silk along hot skin. "Page six intrigued me just as much as page seven. You will let me satisfy my curiosity, will you not?"

If it was possible for black to go a darker shade, his eyes did. He breathed in a long stretch of air, his head tipping back as she explored.

A wild drumbeat thumped in her, under her, over her. Her heart beating as quickly and loudly as she could ever recall. He thrust in her grip, giving her a wild sense of power.

She touched her lips to him, much as she'd seen in the picture, and within half a beat, she was pulled up and on top of him, the rocking of the carriage immediately thrusting them together in an intimate dance, her lips crushed to his. She wrapped her arms around his neck and gripped on for dear life as he clutched her to him. His hands ran along and under her, lifting and spearing her. Sounds were lost to the rain and thunder, the beat of the stones beneath them.

"My beautiful Miranda."

She rocked against him, in time with him, buried deliciously deep within her, each thrust touching something white-hot.

Thunder crackled, and the carriage swayed more wildly. A wheel caught the edge of the stones and lurched dangerously as he thrust inside of her more intensely. She hung on, drugged and delirious with the urge to move closer, to connect that extra bit, to merge, the almost violent sensations coursing through her, burning her skin, her blood, urging her forward.

The carriage could rip apart, her biggest fear realized, and still she'd likely clutch him all the more to her breast, between her thighs. His mouth hot against her skin, whispering words lost in the thunder. His lips pledging a thousand words that even the finest sonnet couldn't capture.

She came apart above him as he grabbed her hips and made her world explode. Clutching him as the shudders wracked them both. As the rain pelted the windows.

But, no matter what game she would continue to play, there was something that told her he would always have the upper hand. For she was willing to risk everything in the game, and he had no need to do so.

He rested on the carriage blanket, the thickness of it unable to keep away the damp grass that clung to the edges of the fabric when their actions moved it. Here in the afterglow of the light rain, they were alone. She rested against him, absently pulling a piece of wet grass between her fingers. Everything was still. The silver of the sky reflecting against the glass of the water. Two ducks coasted across the surface, a light triangle of movement in their wake.

He toyed with a lock of her hair. He had been sent reeling in the carriage. He had been reeling all morning actually. He didn't know what he had set into motion with his actions last night at the masquerade, but she had been liquid fire all day. It tempted and unnerved him.

He had been driven to a craze when he'd seen her speaking to . . . His mouth tightened. Nothing his father or family did should surprise him. Like taking the identity he had carelessly cultivated and using it against him. Forcing him into a corner.

The identity he had created in an attempt to mock London's masses. To mock his parents and their conquests. To mock himself.

Worse for the way the public had responded. Had gone mad. He'd been driven to write a note against himself. What were people thinking to find Eleutherios a man to admire? Writing tactics to seduce and enslave.

An identity that he'd locked away with mockery, until he'd seen the letter to the editor from an M. Chase. Only a person half-hidden in the clouds of her own guilelessness could have been responsible for writing such a note. And yet there was something in the note that had spoken to him. Some deep desire within to be the man that M. Chase thought he was.

And so he'd done the only thing he could. He had written a scathing note directly to M. Chase in the same manner that he'd written the scathing invective against his own work. Determined to bury it. Destroy it.

When an equally compelling rejoinder crossed his desk, he had responded even more harshly, but with new inklings of the type of person he might be responding to. That maybe M. Chase was *real*. Note after note was exchanged, leaving him with the increasing determination to find out who the person was on the other side of the pen. He'd sat in his carriage outside the bookseller's shop for two hours before she'd exited. And he had known who she was immediately.

No need for her to confirm that she was a woman. He'd known as soon as he'd seen her that she was M. Chase. Would have known her anywhere, quite possibly. The faraway look in her eyes, the practical bent her step. She stood out from everyone else on the street. She shone like a lighthouse beacon. He couldn't credit why the men passing her on the street didn't stop and stare in wonder. But it was as if they had blinders on, looking in every other direction.

It had taken him two days to figure out a proper response. A way to develop a more personal, informal exchange. To lure her to admit she was female. To start a flirtation, a devious, hidden one. A plan within a plan.

And still there had been that desire to destroy it all. For it would all be destroyed sooner or later. Why prolong the inevitable and make it remotely painful? Especially when she continued to support Eleutherios. Damn author. Damn writings. He had urged her to write to the man. Determined to crush her illusions of him. To respond in the manner that he always mocked.

And yet . . . when she had written, he had been unable to do it. He'd gripped his pen and tried to write each crushing word. To slaughter the illusion.

But he'd been unable to do it. Had thrown the inkpot against the wall.

And then had promptly written her back, all of the sappy, stupid emotions that he repressed finding their ways onto the page.

Another inkpot destroyed, he had directed Jeffries to obtain a copy of the Gothic he knew she would enjoy. Had sent it with the shortest note of which he was capable.

Had destroyed a third inkpot afterward, then had gone straight to his club to drown the thoughts of his intentions.

He looked down at her uncovered hair. At the way the filtered light caught the shine, unable to dim it even in the clinging darkness after the storm.

For all of the strangeness of the morning—for what had come over her in the library organization?—he had to acknowledge that this newly freed facet just added to the intoxication. She would make the absolutely perfect mistress. She just proved it over and again. Made him further determined to secure her to him.

He wondered if one could chain one's wife to the country house and stay with one's mistress all the day and night.

He thought of the draft betrothal document sitting upon his desk, awaiting his revisions and additions. Distasteful business securing a wife. His mother would know. But he would not make the mistake his mother had.

He wouldn't fall in love with his wife. He wouldn't marry for love.

Chapter 17

*Element #2: When you find the perfect specimen
to enchant, you must make sure to guard
yourself in return. For enchantment, like seduction,
can quickly be turned upon the enchanter.*

The Eight Elements of Enchantment

(work in progress)

She stared at him, her hand upon a stack of books once more. "Go with you where?"

"To Windsor. There is a small estate I have to visit. And some business I must attend to."

"You actually do something constructive during the day?"

"Amusing."

She had only been half joking.

"For the day?"

"The weekend."

She blinked. "I can't go with you for the weekend."

"Why not?"

"It's . . . it's unseemly."

"Is it?" He looked amused. "Unseemly *now*?"

She ignored the question. "For all of his blissful ignorance to my behavior these past weeks, I'm sure my uncle will notice my absence for a whole weekend."

"I'm sure your uncle won't mind." He tossed a book on the table. She could see the letters on the binding. *The Bengal Returns*. A short sequel that was even more rare than the original.

She touched the cover, not looking at him. "You are too used to getting your way," she whispered.

"It is better that way. Besides, tell him the library could use a scrub."

"A scrub?" She'd give it a scrub. She tapped her fingers on the leather, then looked up. She smiled widely, innocently. "I will take care of it as soon as we arrive. When do we leave?"

Max watched her across the swaying carriage. He thought about using the interior in the same manner they had previously but found himself absorbing the way her features changed when she took in the new sights, when she talked of things especially dear to her.

"The Louvre." She sighed. "Someday."

"You say that often."

She smiled faintly. "I do." A delicate crease appeared upon her brow. "And I can't simply carry on as is, or nothing will change." It was almost as if she were speaking of something else. "But it is so hard to change, to take a forward step when one's current situation is not terrible. Is in fact pleasant."

"But the rewards aren't as great."

She gazed at him, something in her eyes making him want to shift on his seat. They were speaking of her, not him. And he hadn't felt tendrils of unease over his own actions in a very long time. Why did he always feel them around her?

"True." She looked away again, and the constriction in his chest eased a fraction. "But then why wouldn't one grab those rewards? Fear is a powerful motivation. One can't realize one's true potential if one clings to fear. Or hate."

"Hate?"

"Sometimes hatred of the self is the reason." She said it lightly, gazing out at the countryside. He felt it like a brick to the head.

"Do you hate yourself?"

"No." She looked from the window to him again. There was a strange calmness to her gaze. "Do you?"

"Hard to hate perfection."

She shook her head and looked back through the pane. But her expression was pensive. Not the amusement or irritation the words should have caused.

He tapped a finger against his leg militantly. "A strange response. Hatred of the self? Where did you come up with such nonsense?"

She didn't say anything for a long moment, then she shrugged. "It matters not."

"I must know."

"Simply a sentiment that I've encountered lately in a . . . friend."

He didn't like that answer at all. He wanted to pursue the inquiry, but something held him back. He wouldn't like where it led. Somehow he knew that.

"And fear? What do you fear?"

She tilted her head, watching him. "Stepping outside of that which is immediately comfortable. But I've been working on my trepidation," she said a bit wryly. "And some of the fear is spawned from guilt. I survived, they did not."

She had told him of the carriage accident that had claimed the lives of her parents and brother.

"Yes," he said, simply. Then coughed into his hand, realizing too late that she had only told him the story on paper. That she had never told *Viscount Downing* the tale. He coughed again. "Yes, that would do it. What happened?"

She looked down. Her hands knotted in the carriage blanket. He wished he could see her eyes. "Oh, I feel I've repeated the story too often as of late, and I don't want to be a bore. Suffice it to say there was a carriage accident, and my family did not survive."

"The scar on your thigh." It was something he had wished to ask her before.

She looked up, her eyes brimming with unshed tears. "The least of my wounds."

He reached across the space and tipped up her chin, wiping away one escaped droplet. "Yes."

They'd been on their way to the seaside. To take a boat to Calais. To go on the Grand Tour.

"Tell me of them."

Her emotion always spilled onto the page. And while he abhorred the weakness of it in himself, he found himself craving it from her. Wanting to share her feelings and vitality.

"My father and brother were both full of life. Mischievous. Always trying to make my mother smile." She smiled fondly under her misted eyes. "However unwillingly."

Her mother, the schoolmistress.

"My mother was a strict disciplinarian. But she loved us. She just held us to her standards. I would present quite the disappointment at the moment," she said lightly.

"I don't know. If she had your happiness at heart, wouldn't she have wanted what made you happy?"

She tilted her head, regarding him. "With my happiness at stake? Perhaps." She fingered the blanket absently. "I'd like to believe so."

"And you? Where did you reside in the mayhem?"

"Caught in the middle, I suppose. As a girl, a woman, I was held to standards that my brother didn't have to observe. He was able to be freer with his thoughts and actions."

"You don't seem to possess a block against your own freethinking."

She looked at him through her lashes. "I am paralyzed at times. Torn. But I wish for joy. For a happy life."

It was one of the things that had pulled him to her immediately. Her optimism. Her realism tempered with good humor. None of the crushed idealism that had turned him cynical and sour.

"What about you? Your family?" she asked, watching him as if she were asking after the secrets of the universe.

"Catherine, Colin, Conrad, and Corinne—in that order—have their endless amusements or causes. You would enjoy Corinne and Conrad."

Unbeknownst to her, she had already enjoyed Conrad. Damn puppy and their damn father for cooking up the Eleutherios scene at the Hannings'. "They have your flair for happiness in the face of trouble. And Catherine is the model of a lady, though it gets passed over in the face of the rest of us. Colin is a priggish cuss. Stubborn. Though we seem of a similar bent, as you've already observed." He grimaced.

She smiled. "How did you end up being a Maximilian?"

"Ah, a black joke of Mother's, though Catherine Philippa was already innocently named before the joke took hold with Colin. All of their middle names start with a P as well. C for cuckold. P for philanderer. Alas that she couldn't find one for M." He smiled without humor. "And if only she'd named Catherine Lydia or Lisette . . . an L would have given her far more to play with. Libertine, libido, lecher, lothario . . . lover. She was quite unhappy with my father, then it became something of grim irony."

He watched her lips part and her eyes widen. The sudden silence lasted two beats too long. She shook her head and opened her mouth, assuredly to change the subject or speak of his siblings. She'd not push him for further revelations—he knew that. But his own lips moved, words tumbling out as if they'd been held behind a dam far too long.

"Mother began her quest to be the most notorious woman in England after Colin's birth, even though people question all of our existences and parentages as well in retrospect."

She laid a hand upon his knee. In other circumstances, in a different conversation, he might have taken the action and turned it into a more physical dialogue that would have her arching beneath him, her eyes focused on nothing but how much further he could push her tolerance for pleasure.

"I'm sorry," she murmured.

But there was something in him, between them in this space, that demanded a different outlet.

He touched her gloved fingers against his trousers, playing with the tips. "I care not what people think.

It amuses me usually. And they have no conception of what is truly behind their gossip."

He had been four and at his mother's side when they'd walked in on his father tupping two maids in his parents' bedchamber. He'd never asked her later if that was the first time she had found her husband with another woman.

"Mother is a flitting, alive thing when she is involved in a mad scheme. A butterfly who shouldn't be caught, lest she be crushed in your palm."

He'd also been there with his mother when the eighteen-year-old niece of their neighbor had been splayed out under his father in the rolling meadow behind Bervue. And when the most notorious widow of their county had been moaning and riding his father in the stable house, both bare as the days they were born.

Miranda tilted her head.

"Mother was in love with Father." He shrugged, not feeling the sentiment. "He is constantly in love. With many things. All of them real. For a time. It took her a long time to realize it."

And there had been many times he had observed his father without his mother present. His libidinous father, for all his marital faults, always had time for his children. Always took Max on trips to the estates, to Parliament, to social appointments. Inevitably seduced yet another woman at the end of a meal or in the hall or in a back cottage, all while his son was at his side. Oh, he didn't take them there on the floor or table or whatever surface was readily available while Max was present. But he'd work his wiles. Make appointments for later.

And doors occasionally got left ajar. Loud sounds permeated even the heaviest oak. Women would stumble out, ravished and glowing. Would give him sly glances and sometimes touch his young cheeks telling him that they'd be back for him someday.

"Oh. Poor woman," she whispered.

"She is fine," he said, unable to stifle the bitterness that always lingered when thoughts of his parents' marriage surfaced. Unable to stifle it when speaking to the woman in front of him, at least. For she called within him a need to be clean, to fly free. "Now."

Yes, fine. If one could call what his mother did in order to hide *fine*.

He remembered his father's reaction the first time he found his mother with another man in London. Max had been ten. His father had watched for a moment, given a laugh, booted the man out of his home, then ravished his own wife. Luckily, Max's tutor had pushed him down the hall and into his room before he had witnessed anything that would scar him further. His mother had had a smile on her face all that next morning. Max had been giddy, her happiness infectious. Thinking that perhaps his parents would be happy together finally. For he loved them both.

And then he and his mother walked in on his father rutting with a maid in the sitting room a week later. The woman's eyes had been glassy and unfocused. Little ohs on her lips. Just like the ones that had been on his mother's.

Her happiness had dissolved. His youngest sister had been born nine long months later.

Max had never quite forgiven his father for the light that had seeped from his mother's eyes though he loved him still.

"It is silly to marry for love." He stroked the underside of Miranda's first finger.

Her brows knit. "There is nothing wrong with marrying for love."

"To see the same longing face in the mirror every morning? To be emotionally constrained to that other person for the rest of one's days? Better to marry some cold, expensive fish who can entertain and do her duty and not expect a thing."

"That's horrible." She looked appalled.

"It's smart business," he said intently, trying to make her understand.

"How can you say that? You who wri—" She took a deep breath. "You who rides the line of seduction."

"I'm not against marriage, nor love." He had to make her understand. He stroked her finger. "I'm just against love *in* marriage."

She stayed silent for a moment. "I feel sadness for your mother. And even your father. But I think emotions are lovely," she said softly. "Even if they fall to the negative for a time. The sun will rise again another day. The sadness perhaps never forgotten, but a new day enjoyed in another way. A way that could not have been but for the sadness's existence."

"That seems to be Father's view on life. That there is always a new day. A new *friend*."

"I don't mean something that changes. I mean something that evolves because of changes. Something to be enjoyed."

A feeling, a mad want opened in him. "It makes one weak."

She tilted her head, leaning toward him, the play of her freed fingers bearing down just a touch on his knee. "Does it make me weak then that I love sentiment?"

He tugged her silk-covered digit between his forefinger and thumb. He was still surprised to see the new gloves on her hands. The girl he had "met" in the bookshop would not have purchased such no matter how much she wanted them. Too practical and cautious. "It is a feminine prerogative to do so."

"Shakespeare wrote wonderful sonnets. Only a man with a keen eye toward sentiment could have done so. Even if one simply seeks to mock."

The words hit too close to home. His fingers slipped from beneath hers and drummed against the seat. "And look where that landed him. Disillusioned in marriage. Grand sentiment directed elsewhere."

"His written work is lovely, whatever his rumored problems in spoken life."

Like your Mr. Pitts, your Eleutherios? he wanted to ask, to demand. He tapped his fingers a little viciously. Idiotic of him to hold her to some lofty standard that he had manufactured. And yet, he couldn't help the emotion. The weakness of it.

"Those things that you cannot fully have make the impressions last. They keep relationships interesting." Untethered and free. Able to breathe and live. Something that would keep him alive, and that he too could not crush.

She lifted her hand and leaned back against the seat, the weight of her palm missing from his knee. "So if you fully embrace something, you feel it will disappear? Slip between your fingers?"

"Yes." His eyes tightened, something inside of him upset, no, not upset, *irritated,* by the conversational turn. He tapped the seat more furiously.

"I disagree. I think that it allows you to more fully explore. To become more within that embrace."

"You who will barely even step a foot outside of

your bookstore, much less England." He narrowed his eyes on her.

She raised her chin. "Yes."

"So I seek to ignore and take, and you seek to dream and withhold."

"Perhaps that is why I'm consistently drawn to you," she said lightly, strangely, her face once more turned to the window. "But as I said, I am evolving. Slowly."

He narrowed his eyes further, something inside him reacting violently. "I don't think I like the sound of that."

"I can't seem to help the *weakness*."

Every muscle in his body tightened unpleasantly. He didn't like it when she claimed her emotion for him as weakness.

Not one bit.

And yet he couldn't very well argue, or else he would be arguing against himself.

Tangled in his own web.

He looked out the other window, the countryside blurring in his unfocused view. The problem was that it hadn't been thought that had prodded him into this situation. It had been the dreaded emotion. His vulnerability.

And the cure?

Having her didn't seem to be sating anything inside him. He just wanted her more, every time he saw her, spoke with her, buried himself inside her.

The carriage swayed to the side as they turned. The vehicle moved up the drive, the trees forming a tunnel of beautiful shade and dotted, hovering sunlight.

They drew up to the charming stone manor that stood nestled at the end of the drive, surrounded by the forest. No formal gardens or maze. Simply a retreat. A gem nestled in the glade. Far enough away from the castle and town to create a different world.

Somewhere where he could let the masks fall.

"It doesn't look as I imagined it." Her voice was soft, the meaning of her words twofold. He hadn't disabused her of the notion that they would be visiting a sprawling, ridiculously grandiose property. Something so grotesque in its magnificence that she would be put off by it.

"My father uses the property sometimes, but it is more often abandoned."

Just the way Max liked it.

"Oh, but it is lovely."

"Too far from town for the others." Thank God.

She stared at him. They were hardly even outside the city.

He smiled wryly. "Even for Colin. They can't leave their pursuits. And this house is hardly big enough for a party. They go to Bervue or Ratching Place if they want to entertain."

"And you?"

"Oh, I require my pursuits as well."

He couldn't read her eyes, but she stared at him for a long moment before turning back to the window. He badly desired to know what she was thinking in that moment.

"At one time I might have wondered about your pursuits," she said. "What you did with your time. But now I know."

His chest tightened. "Oh?"

"You seduce starry-eyed young women, of course, and then take them on ridiculously expensive and outrageous outings in order to make them your slaves."

The knot loosened, and he smiled, relieved to be back on firmer ground. Flirtation and light barbs. Anything deeper hidden once again, even as it strained against the bonds. Wanting to be freed now that it had tasted a measure of sunlight. "You are my test subject, and I have to admit the pursuit is without equal."

"Men are all about the pursuit. Even Eleutherios says so in his work."

That hadn't been what he meant. In the conversation, that is, not the book.

Damn.

He was going to develop true madness at this rate.

He had *verbally* meant the term "pursuit" in its original meaning in the conversation—as an activity. And even though usually he would have been quite happy to have the knowledge of his affections hidden within the chase, something about it bothered him now.

Bothered him along with her allusion to the author in that respectful tone of voice. His fingers curled into the fabric of the seat as if he could claw it in two. God, he was a piece of work. He wondered if her talk of self-hatred did indeed have roots.

He pulled her to him, quickly, roughly, as the carriage drew to a stop, and kissed her with all the confusion, rage, and hope that were mixed together in him. She startled, then returned the kiss, her lips equally crushing his in some sort of answer.

He pulled away just as fast as he heard Benjamin on the other side of the door, preparing to open it. The boy would knock first, of course. But even so, Max needed to get his bearings. To replace at least one mask.

To remove the naked look that was assuredly in his eyes, as he stared into the slightly incoherent, slightly wise eyes across from his.

* * *

Miranda smoothed her hands down her dress once again. Surely she looked a mess, though no one had given her a glance askance. Didn't seem surprised to see her at all. Of course, news traveled fast. And between households assuredly everyone was kept abreast of things that concerned their master.

That a bookish nobody was having a torrid affair with the viscount was probably a pretty poorly kept secret.

The waiting staff welcomed them inside.

"Welcome back, your lordship." The housekeeper fussed over him. "Been nearly a month." The woman made a sound between her lips and put her hands on her hips.

Miranda watched as he allowed the woman to fuss over him in a motherly fashion. Not too far out of town for the viscount, obviously. And just what sort of pursuits did the man follow here? His writing? Surely he wouldn't bring her someplace that close. Risk her figuring it out. But then again, he was a gambler. The gossip pages always had some outrageous quest of his embedded in the ink.

Though after listening to him speak of his parents, the gossip pages took on a different hue. The personal reasons known only to the people involved, lost in the translation to the inky lines. Unable to be shared in the space of a gossip column.

She watched him smile at the housekeeper. Watched the way his shoulders eased, the stiffness of the conversation on marriage and his parents sliding from him.

He motioned to Miranda, and she stepped forward to be introduced. The staff watched as well, trying to deduce just where in the viscount's long-term hierarchy she might fall.

Miranda wondered that too.

They stepped inside the house, and she was given a quick tour, the housekeeper pulling the viscount up to date on recent changes and events. There was a small but lovely library on the ground floor.

"You don't need me to do a thing to it." She ran her hand along the dark wood paneling of the hideaway retreat. "Everything is in perfect order." Hard for her to justify mixing up every title. She'd find some other way to wreak havoc. "Not quite as grand as yours." Most libraries weren't. "But quite beautiful."

"It's adequate." But she heard the fondness in his tone. "But you haven't seen Bervue. The estate doesn't have a library—it has a separate manor dedicated to literature. My father is rather rabid about books." He ran a hand along the paneling. "You'd likely be found buried beneath the spines there. Forgetting to eat or drink and withering away amidst the tombey tomes."

"I enjoy eating far too much."

"Mmm. I enjoy that as well." He nipped her shoulder and ran a hand down the curve of her waist and over her hip, swirling around her body and lifting her hand to his lips.

Her body responded, but something in the conversation kept her from giving in. Curiosity peaked. A remembered tidbit from the Hannings'. "Your father likes literature?"

"He fairly salivates over it like he would a debutante in a white dress." The viscount might as well have been discussing the weather. "Would like nothing better than to write the next tome of seduction. Unfortunately, he can't keep his trousers up long enough to put pen to paper. He hates your Eleutherios as much as the rest of us do." He smiled unkindly.

The statement and the sentiment behind it made her suddenly sad. She had a feeling that his father had only recently discovered that his son was the author. Was proud of his accomplishment but didn't know how to tell him so. The way he had talked of Eleutherios, the way he had looked at Max at the Hannings', made her sure of it.

That neither the father nor the son could fully expose himself to the other because of past events—though both of them wished to—squeezed her heart.

She touched his shoulder. Then reached up on her toes and touched her lips softly to his.

He kissed her back, then looked down at her. "I appreciate the lovely kiss, but what prompted it?"

She smoothed a hand down his front. "I wished to do so, so I did."

His lips curved. "Finally listening to me?"

She tilted her head. "More so than you know," she said softly.

His eyes narrowed, and she pressed another kiss to his lips before he could think on her statement further.

A softly cleared throat echoed in the room.

The viscount held on to the kiss for another second before pulling back and staring at her. Miranda held her breath at the look. She wished she could write to him right now and receive the response on what he was thinking at the moment. There was a naked look, bared for her to read, if she dared.

He turned to the housekeeper in the doorway.

The housekeeper bowed. "You said to inform you when the refreshments were ready."

"Thank you."

"That was fast," Miranda said. Though the servants

had probably been more than ready for their master to arrive.

He tilted his head at Miranda, a smile touching his lips. "There is refreshment to be had in multiple places on this estate."

Two hours later she stretched in the water of the natural spring located in a wooded glade just far enough from the house to be private. Cool and refreshing. Just a hint of ice to manage the heat from the man near her.

"Old men trying to make decisions for everyone," he said.

She tilted her head, thinking of the jabs Mr. Pitts had made about Parliament. "You dislike Parliament."

"On the days it is most frustrating, I veritably loathe it. And it is hard to blow off steam to one's peers . . . *about* one's peers. I have to choose . . . different confidantes."

So he had blown off steam to her. In his letters. Her throat felt unaccountably tight at the thought.

"Why do you return?"

"Oh, it isn't always dreadful. Sometimes it is downright invigorating. I have a seat in the Commons. I originally used it to control the Werston vote when Father was . . . unable to concentrate on the matters at hand. To tell him which way to cast." He lazily drew his hand over her foot, bringing it to just beneath the surface of the water. The cool air was just in reach of the top of her skin, misting over the warmth in a delicious way. "He does his duty, but his passions obviously lie elsewhere."

She shivered as his fingers curled around her heel.

"I was young and at loose ends in life." He shrugged. "It turned out brilliantly. The men in the Commons are highly motivated individuals. Some are younger sons or those in line. Others are just brilliant commoners."

"We fodder can be smart for all our humble beginnings."

He smiled and gave the underside of her foot a slow caress. "So I've found."

"Perhaps you should spend more time mucking about with us. Renounce your ways. Start a lending library."

"My siblings would be aghast."

She withheld a wicked smile at the direction of the conversation. She had been waiting for the introduction of the topic. The carriage conversation had been too honest, and far too serious for her to inject any topsy-turvydom. But now? Here in the cool water? "You said your brother is a writer."

He tilted his head. "Did I?"

"Yes, at Lady Banning's."

"Ah. Yes."

"He enjoys writing?"

"Enjoys . . ." He ran a finger up the inside of her leg, causing her to catch her breath. His body followed the path, allowing him better access to all of her. "His passion for written communication is nearly ridiculous, and he spends far too much time rallying the servants."

Or perhaps just one servant. Miranda would have to test the theory at the promised social gathering.

"There is nothing wrong with correspondence," she said. His palm brushed over her. Warmth pooled below the touch causing her breath to catch. "I quite enjoy it."

His lip curved along with his fingertips as he grew closer in the pool. "I'm very happy to hear your enjoyment." She couldn't stop the sudden intake of breath as he worked his magic.

"It is good to have a passion in one's life," she said a little breathlessly.

"Mmmm, I'm starting to understand just how much."

She twisted and arched under his ministrations. "You don't have a passion already?"

"Nothing on a par with my want of you."

His words shivered over her skin, but his continued evasion fueled her words.

"Your brother. There was a look about him."

"Why are you speaking of my brother?" He nipped her ear, and his fingers twisted. She gasped.

"Perhaps your brother is Eleutherios." She could hardly form a thought as his actions overpowered her reason. She gripped on to the edges of her plan, to the words, trying to withstand the onslaught. "In disguise."

He stilled. "What?" There was a dangerous undercurrent to the viscount's undertone.

"Your brother. Yes, of course." She wanted to move, to touch him and never stop. "There *was* a look about him. It could be him."

The viscount pulled back, his eyes obsidian. "Ridiculous."

"Why? It could be." She stretched, wanting, but unwilling, to beg him to continue. Wanting to push him beyond. "Imagine it. Your brother with all of that passion and wit. Hiding behind his stubborn mockery."

"What are you on about?"

"I can't decide if it is more dashing or completely unsavory, him hiding like that."

"*What?*"

"Dashing to be a masked man." She ran a finger down his chest in a manner that was meant to seem absent, but was decidedly planned. "But I'd feel quite betrayed to discover that Eleutherios was someone I had already met. *Imagine* the betrayal. I might never speak to him again."

She allowed her hand to drop farther down, beneath the surface. Any reluctance to do such things had long since disappeared in her discovery of his many masks, all of them swirling around her.

The viscount stared at her. A man in lesser control might have been gaping a bit at the jaw.

She resisted the urge to raise a fist in triumph.

She squeezed, then released him, the long length of him begging her to continue, to make *him* beg. But she kept her arms and hands behind her, propping her up on the bottom of the pool. "Or I would start a torrid affair with him."

"A what?" The words were clipped.

"A torrid affair. The man writes so beautifully." She shrugged, half-amused at her gall and half-determined to give him a dose of his own medicine. "Of course, I am in a torrid affair with you instead. And quite enjoying it. But—"

His hand slipped into her nape and tilted her head back. "You are not starting a torrid affair with anyone but me." His eyes were fierce.

She couldn't help the satisfied smile that curved her lips. Like her own unwillingness to connect that he was all three men, it was only his unwillingness to realize that she would still want him in all of his incarnations, to admit to someone that he *was* all of those men, with all of those feelings, that made him refuse to see that she already knew.

"You are the only one I want to be torrid with." She couldn't stop the sincerity from leaking in, the words from forming even though she wanted to poke further. To make him jealous of himself, perhaps.

"Am I?" His lips whispered over her neck and down her chest. "I will make sure you always believe that."

And then he was doing mad things to her. Things that there were no pages for. For such feelings couldn't be captured in a rote manual. It was quite a bit later, wrapped together on the shore, that she thought continuing to make him wroth with her over this farce held more than a bit of puckish charm.

Miranda lounged in the library the next morning, devouring a lovely tome on Paris that she hadn't encountered before. The viscount lay on the settee, his feet propped up on the arm, his sleeves rolled up and shirt partially unbuttoned. He looked perfectly rumpled and delicious, and she occasionally found herself staring at him over the top of the book.

A whisper of sound preceded a cleared throat. "I'm sorry to disturb you, your lordship, but there are guests demanding to see you," the housekeeper said from the doorway. She cast a quick glance at Miranda before looking back to the viscount. "I've put them on the garden terrace. Your valet is waiting with garments."

Miranda looked curiously at the viscount, still splayed across the furniture, but the muscles of his arms were suddenly taut. He tilted his head as he pushed himself out of his relaxed pose, and the servant bowed and disappeared back through the door.

The viscount leaned over and planted a quick,

strong kiss on her lips. "Don't move. I'll be back in an hour."

She stretched as he strode out, then lazily rose and walked around the room. Should she set the room to chaos? Or simply wait for something else to present itself for retribution? The side of her mouth quirked. She touched some newspapers on a stand, then ran her fingers over a globe. Movement outside attracted her attention to the window, and she peered through as the viscount emerged from the house, formally dressed once more. He firmly walked toward two men in the garden enclosure.

An older man, wealthy from his dress, shook the viscount's hand and introduced a younger man wearing spectacles. The younger man bowed slightly in deference, but it was apparent from his demeanor that he was excited about something. He looked like an eager new businessman. Like the fresh ones down on the row, with their shiny new satchels and starry-eyed determination. Fresh from school or an apprenticeship. The barristers, accountants, stewards, publishers.

Publishers?

She leaned forward for a closer look. Their lips were moving, but she couldn't hear a thing through the glass. The older man did look like the head of the *Times* though, whom she had seen barreling through a crowd, yelling orders and expecting them to be completed by the men who were hurrying to keep up, taking notes, and clearing a path.

Brilliant. Harsh. Wealthy. Ambitious. Though there was an edge to the man. As if he had something great to lose but was trying to appear as if the opposite were true. Eleutherios's new book?

The viscount motioned to chairs situated in the shade around a comfortable table. She cocked her head, then looked back to the room she was in. Everything was more comfortable and plush here in this house, not ornate, yet not severe like in London. Someone else's decorating sense? Was it the starkness that defined him or the sensuality threaded beneath?

She shivered as the viscount jabbed a finger on the arm of his chair, and the other two nodded along, almost unwillingly. In complete command, his siren call just under the surface, straining to be free, pulling to him all those in his path.

The man was like a walking addiction.

The younger man's head bobbed more quickly, and he pulled out a sheaf of papers. He pointed to something on the page and looked over his spectacles. The viscount's eyes narrowed.

She tried to make out anything on their lips. Something about the book, maybe? Or deadline? An admission of his authorship?

She couldn't make out a thing, and the glass was too thick.

But they were just near enough the house . . . she touched the window and looked around. She tried to act casual, not furtive. The window inched up beneath her eavesdropping fingertips.

A bit of a breeze would be nice. Just a bit. She was sure that any servant entering the room would feel the same way.

The window casing creaked. She twisted, back splayed against the wall, the drapes pulling against her elbows. She waited a moment, then peeked around the corner. The men continued to talk. She strained to hear, hunching down and peering through the opening she had made.

"Downing, about time you came to the table."

The viscount tilted his head. "Are you sure? You seem beyond eager to see the papers signed, even following me here." There was a dangerous thread beneath the words.

"There are arrangements to hammer out. You will be free to do as you please as long as the main points of the contract are followed."

"Like a tethered goat. With the way you are speaking of personal conduct we might as well be making funeral arrangements instead of a contract."

"Hardly." The older man gave him a look. "If you are determined to scrub your name, it is but a formality. And I've seen your determination to do so. It is the only reason we are at the table."

Scrub his name? Was he going to publish under a new pseudonym? Perhaps he really would realize the book of sonnets she had been encouraging in her letters. A smile lifted her lips.

The viscount's mouth twisted in a parody of the same. "Is it? Not the money, then?"

The older man's eyes tightened. "Everyone benefits from the arrangement."

Assuredly. The publisher must be making a pretty penny off him already. A book of his sonnets would be a strong seller. She knew it. All of the ladies who swooned already would need a double dose of smelling salts.

The older man continued. "Boone is here to make sure that everyone's needs are met." He waved a hand at the younger man. "And that assurances are written and contracted."

The viscount's brow lifted cynically. "Assurances?"

"Considering your past, I'll require a few."

Was he usually late to deadline?

"And that of your family."

His family?

"Charlotte is a gem. Together you can overcome whatever the rumors bring."

The viscount laughed unpleasantly. "And if we can't, you will reap additional settlements to pay your debts, hmmm?"

Charlotte? Charlotte Chatsworth? The woman who was rumored to be linked to the viscount?

Oh. *Oh.*

She slid down the wall, the breeze from the open window stroking her hair.

It was true then, what they said. No good ever came of eavesdropping.

Max walked back into the house, conflicting feelings running through him. Satisfaction, determination. Anger. At his father? At Chatsworth? At himself?

Chatsworth hadn't needed him to give up a mistress. Chatsworth had scoffed at the notion. Of course, with his long-standing mistress, Chatsworth would be a hypocrite otherwise. Mistresses—normal mistresses—were completely in keeping with the way things worked. Keeping his mistress within her bounds and out of Charlotte's way was, of course, necessary. No keeping Miranda in the house with him and exiling Charlotte to the country.

His father hadn't been able to do that with his mother either. A daughter of a duke couldn't be hidden away.

As long as his mistress was kept within her "bounds,"

then it wouldn't matter. The problem with his mother and father was that they had never adhered to any bounds. If they'd just kept to the normal channels, they'd have been unremarkable in the social whirl.

But, no, his father loved the younger ladies. And not the younger ladies of the demimonde, where he could have dabbled freely. He liked the younger ladies of the ton. The unmarried or newly married ones. Any woman who presented a challenge. A conquest. A seduction. The call of Juliet to Romeo in some repeated doomed tale of "true love." And his mother had decided within her broken heart to affect the same on the young men.

No, he wouldn't make Charlotte Chatsworth watch him with a thousand other women. Nor would he seduce her. Nor make her love him as his father had done to his mother. He'd make it very plain that he had a mistress. Very plain that their marriage was only a business transaction. That she would be free to have her own quiet affairs once the legitimacy of children was established.

A sad thing that she would be required to wait and not he, but such was nature. Once she was pregnant, she would be able to have an affair again. Only the few months around the actual conception would require her abstinence. Some men were mad for pregnant women.

It was all . . . cold. Quite cold. But Charlotte Chatsworth had never struck him as a particularly romantic girl. It was one of the reasons he had spoken to her of marriage. She was business-minded like her father. Smart. Focused. Strong. She wished to run an empire and would make a fabulous Marchioness of Werston someday. She would make the name shine.

He thought they would get on quite fine, in an

analytical way. But there had never been any thought to something romantic between them. Marriage and love did not go together. In any way, shape, or form. It should be a pure business transaction.

He could love Miranda though.

He walked to the library to find her, but found the room empty.

A paper slipped from a side table. He leaned down to pick it up and a breeze from the cracked open window ruffled his hair. He absently leaned over to close the pane, then stopped still, looking at the view.

How could he have been so stupid?

He strode upstairs to find her room empty as well. His housekeeper greeted him at the foot of the stairs as he hurried down.

"Where is Miss Chase?"

She shook her head. "I'm sorry, my lord. She left."

Chapter 18

*Element #2 continued: If something should
go wrong with the initial plan, step back and
reformulate. Never undertake a new tack precipitously. This is a sign the cards have turned
against you and are in your opponent's favor.*

The Eight Elements of Enchantment

(work in progress)

"**G**et the carriage ready. I'll be leaving for London,"
he said over his shoulder to his valet as he
quickly strode through his sitting room. He could hardly
think clearly. He just had to find her.

"So soon?"

He froze, his fingers upon the tops of his trousers.
"I was told you had left."

She came into view, lovely flowing hair and simple
lilac dress, her brow knit. "Yes. I went to the stream.
To think."

She was near enough that he could touch her. Had
been afraid that he'd never get the chance to again.
He couldn't resist the powerful urge and stroked her
cheek, feeling the softness, the strength.

He thought quite possibly she was the most beautiful woman he'd ever seen. He didn't care who wanted to debate it. "I thought you had left."

"Why?"

Because I saw the open window. Because you heard. Because I'm an ass who cannot offer you everything you deserve.

"Because . . ." he said a little lamely.

She touched the back of his hand at her cheek, her eyes far too knowing. "Are we to leave then?"

"Do you wish to leave?" Every muscle in his body strained in wait for her response.

Five beats of his heart passed before she answered. "No."

The response was quiet, but firm.

Relief, swift and sure, rocked through him. Followed by a bit of unease. Had she not heard them?

Her head tilted. "Yes, I heard."

He stared at her. She smiled, a pull of curved lips. "For once I have made you speechless. Swapped our roles. It is quite satisfying to know what you are thinking for once."

"Then you know—"

"That you are to be betrothed? That you have started thinking that perhaps becoming respectable will be a better alternative to merely covering up the sins of your parents with your own?"

He stared at her. "You are a dangerous woman."

"Then we are even, for I have long thought you a dangerous man."

He looked away, then back to her. "So, you don't care?"

"Care?" She said it lightly, but her eyes were serious,

watchful. "I'm not sure that is the correct question. What did you expect my reaction to be?"

"I wasn't sure."

She pulled his hand down, twining it with her own. "I admit to surprise. But then—" Her head dipped, hiding her face. "But then, it is not such a surprise."

"You will stay with me then?" There were a thousand different meanings in that one question.

"Stay with you? I think I am far too entangled to find an end to the snare should I wish to flee."

She lifted her head. "But I must admit to ignorance and seek your guidance," she said calmly, softly. "We are going back to London, to your house, at the end of this trip. What is the next move one makes?"

He stared at her.

"I suppose one attends the opera. Dresses well and submits to the scrutiny?" She spread her hands along her dress. "I doubt I will make a very stunning companion, but *Don Giovanni* is playing, and I have always wished to see it."

He'd been steadily chipping away, working toward this moment, and she was just offering? Giving in to being his mistress?

He brushed her cheek, the soft skin smooth beneath his knuckles. Then walked to the window, staring through the pane. Out into the yard where he'd been sitting such a short time ago.

He had thought that this would be the crowning achievement. That once she declared herself his mistress, everything in his world would slot into place. That it would confirm that no one was above temptation. That this was the normal sway of things and couldn't be helped. For if innocent, optimistic Miranda Chase was able to be corrupted, then no one could resist. Everything in his world would be a fait accompli.

Why, then, did he feel as if everything were turned on end instead? That her acceptance of it meant only that she cared more for him than for some outward rule of respectability, more for him than for society's strictures, more for him than for simple pride.

But why would she care for him in such a way? She didn't know who he really was. That he haunted her in every guise. Needing to be near her. Some crazed stalker in the shadows. That he wanted her to love everything about him.

"Maxim," she said softly.

He froze, then turned. It was the first time she had used his name without prompting.

Her soft eyes watched him. "Speak to me."

He walked back to her, lured there despite any misgiving. Wanting to be near her. Always.

She watched him as he drew nearer. She wished she knew what he was thinking.

He touched her right hand, smoothing his fingers over her glove. "You are wearing your armor."

She tried to tug her hand away, but he kept it captured in his. "Silk can hardly be a good shield," she said.

"No? It is a barrier. I can hardly touch you through them."

"You have touched me in far more intimate places."

"Mmmm. Intimate for most people, but mayhap not your most intimate place." He ran his finger down the material.

She tried to remove her hands again, more casually. "I hardly think hands are an intimate place."

He held fast. "But the definition invokes your most private feeling, your deepest nature."

"My mother used to say that a proper lady was never without her gloves." The dual nature of the comment was not lost on her.

"Even the most straitlaced of ladies sometimes goes without." His fingers pulled along hers, from the crevices to the tips. He gripped the edge of one and pulled, the material stretching on her fingertip the barest bit. He touched the next one and pulled, that one stretching as well. Her heart picked up speed as she watched his motions, felt the pull.

"Don't you have business to attend to?"

Betrothal documents to sign? Wedding plans to make?

He lifted her chin, making her meet his eyes. "I am attending to the most important business."

Another finger stretched. Three pulls of fabric gripping with relentless need to the tips, the gloves molded to her in the best of shields. Expensive, fine.

"I want to lay you completely bare, Miranda."

"Have you not already?" Her voice nearly shook. The whisper of it vibrating her throat.

He cocked his head but said nothing. His eyes tightened before his expression smoothed, hiding his true response to the question. He pulled the silk over her smallest finger, his warm, strong fingers sure around the slim digit. No hesitation in the motion. Stripping her bare indeed.

He pulled the fabric slowly toward him, revealing more with each inch. The soft skin above her elbow. The sensitive areas under her wrist. The snow of the glove hesitated at the heel of her palm, and she drew in a breath. Let him find what he would. She tried to look away as the fabric continued its descent, but she couldn't.

Morbid fascination froze her. What might he do when he saw them in dry, full light? Not in the water of a pool, nor the darkness of a chamber. Examining the roughened edges of her heel, the chap that began up the side of her thumb and continued into the broken nail beds, the ink stains. Clean hands, but irreparably blemished. Nothing like the beautiful skin Georgette maintained.

She closed her eyes, unwilling to see his expression as he turned her hands in his strong, warm palms.

"I would bathe them in milk, if you wanted. If you wished to heal them. Or simply clasp them to me as they are, because they are part of you."

Her eyes shot open and her throat closed. It was hard to swallow over the sudden rush of emotion. "Oh?"

If only she could be wittier, come up with something snappy and wise. But she was just Miranda. And Miranda Chase said things like "Oh?" in the face of comments that puddled her into a soppy mess.

He brought her forefinger to his mouth. "Yes." His lips closed over the tip, pulling it in, the point of his tongue swirling around her flesh.

His mouth slowly released the tip, and his fingers wrapped around the nape of her neck, pulling her closer. "Yes," he whispered against her lips.

"Your lips are the most delicious treat I've ever tasted. And I would still love them were they chapped and dry. Still drink from them like the finest crystal because they would give me the essence of you."

She had always assumed that she would experience the thrill of passionate love through a written text. Internally and with great joy. Perhaps a softer kind

of love with a husband. The kind of love her parents
had enjoyed—soft words and respect—her mother's
strict decorum keeping them respectfully apart in the
physical sense, at least in any way outside of a closed
door.

He lowered her to his bed, watching her, his eyes
dark and promising. Branding her with some bit of
leftover fervency from when he'd thought her gone.

Here was a man who challenged her in all ways.
Who thrilled her intellectually on paper, who captivated
her with his words, who physically flooded her senses.
Who was every man that she had desired on any level
she could comprehend.

His fingers, smooth and strong, hooked beneath
her knee and drew a slow path to her center, circling
the indentation there.

She was laid bare. Not just in the physical sense
as he slowly stripped each piece of clothing from her,
smoothing his hands along her skin, kissing each curve,
but naked in truth. Belonging to him, even if he didn't
know it fully yet.

Her eyes lit upon the ceiling, the moldings, simpler
here than in the London house but still expensive,
tasteful, cupids leaping and frolicking, shooting the
unwary. The gilded edge apparent on every surface
of his life.

His mouth moved over her, and her lips parted on
a breath, back straining in an arch.

A sweep of his mouth, his tongue. She could hardly
think. Could hardly breathe. The breath left in her
lungs panting out between her lips.

It was her move. To stay with him. To be his mistress.
A step up for a woman like her. Georgette would be

over the moon for her. He'd shower her with gifts. *Gifts she didn't need.* And take her to places she had always dreamed of visiting. *With the ones she loved.*

Fingers on her thighs, gripping her backside. Setting claim to her skin.

But being a mistress didn't preclude her from loving him. It didn't preclude *him* from loving *her*, though she had no notion if he felt such strong feelings for her. But he felt something. She'd never be in this position if she didn't know that much.

Lips kissing her stomach, the undersides of her breasts. Her fingers automatically threading through his hair. Strong thighs clasped between her knees.

She wanted him. At the moment she'd take him however she could have him, and she'd think of the future later.

She touched his arm, strong, long, and beautiful. His fingers capable of such beauty of words and such dismissive coldness.

She pushed him to his side, wanting to touch him in the same way. Wanting to pull every reaction from him. Groans and passion-hooded eyes. To make it so that he could only think of her in this moment, this scene. Here, he was hers.

She could kiss inside his elbows and stroke along his ribs. She could nip his throat and wrap around his warmth. Long, slow strokes, then shorter ones at the tip. Listening to him breathe like she had. Make sounds like she did. Give in to everything she was.

And then she was on her back again, cupids hazy in her view, dark, chiseled, lovely features inches from hers. And he was within her, completing her. The dark sword of Mr. Pitts, the soft feathers of Eleutherios, the powerful stride of the viscount, the seductive pleasure of Maxim.

Truly, she simply loved everything about him.

The rush of emotion filled her. And she uttered three little words. Words that she couldn't take back, even should she choose to do so. Words from her heart. Lost and bare, given to him to crush, to keep safe.

A vow.

His eyes pinned her—disbelieving, desiring, hungry— and long, deep strokes pushed her over the edge, arching into him, and repeating the vow over and over again.

She put her cheek upon the palm of her bare hand, her knees bent, toes in the air, the silken sheets curving around and under her. The air was full of languid entreaty and relaxing embraces. The invitation in the sheets to roll about in the silken embrace. To while away the hours of the day.

His fingers traced imaginary lines on her back. The fingers of his left hand. She didn't think he realized it in the laziness of the moment.

"I could write all over you. Mark you with ink that claims you as mine."

She pulled her hand along the valleys of the silk folds, toes kissing in the air, embracing together. "And then I'd be nearly unrecognizable, stained and Stygian."

His finger drew something in the center of her back. "I'd recognize you. *Always*."

And she could almost imagine as she looked over her shoulder and into the reflection of the glass that it had been a heart there in the center of the design.

Chapter 19

Dear Mr. Pitts,

I have always found it to be careful what I wish for. For sometimes it is not the true desire of my heart, but rather the way I have been taught to think.

From the desk of Miranda Chase

The carriage rocked slowly as they made their way to the opera house. Max wondered at the change that had taken place in a few short weeks. Her fingers no longer gripped the seat cushion. The lines around her eyes no longer grew pinched and creased. She didn't keep her weight distributed, body spread to dive from the carriage or cover her head in case some disaster befell her.

She seemed to be able to overcome whatever she wanted to as soon as she put her mind to it. He envied the ability, even as getting her to take those first tentative steps was what had prompted many of his plans in the first place.

That and the insatiable need to be near her, to speak with her, to have her smile at him.

She smiled at him now. A steady, determined smile. *She loved him.*

Thinking it made everything inside him clench. He couldn't even chastise himself for the weakness of it, like the emotion brimming from the sonnets he loved, for the feeling was too all-encompassing. It tore and bit and ached.

They entered the opera house, and the whispers of the crowd turned in their direction. He had used the machine of whispered lips too many times not to pay partial attention to what was being said.

The princess unmasked. Not Russian, then the talk after the Hannings' was true. English. Who is she?

Normally he would turn it in his favor. But tonight, tonight was different. The gossip touched him in an uncomfortable way. The stage not set by his design, nor in a reaction to his parents. For once, he was in the thrall and pull of someone else. Pulled along by Miranda, befuddled by her acceptance. Stumbling along, feigning confidence by escorting her here.

Attending the opera had been somewhere in his initial grand plan. Having her as an active part of his life, should all the things he hoped to have with her bear true. And they had borne more fruit than he could have ever wished.

She loved him.

Now that he was here, though, he didn't like the way the men were watching her. Weighing her as they walked past. Taking bets on when he would tire of her. Of when they could lay their own claim. Men who wouldn't have taken notice of her on the street. Who had no care of the beauty and depth inside of her. Her light, her intelligence, her warmth. Who were simply seeing her as his conquest, something new and interesting, another player to be debauched.

And why wouldn't they? That is all he'd ever given to this stage. Never seeking anything more.

More whispers followed them as they ascended the stairs to his box.

Look at the way Downing touches her.

Has he finally taken a mistress?

Who is she?

Did you see her necklace?

Miranda looked beautiful. Delicious. Far superior to the necklace he had given her. The one she had stared at for a long time in the mirror after he'd clasped it around her neck.

She had sat so still, he had thought for a moment she had turned to stone. But something had loosened in her again now. Sitting gracefully and leaning forward in her seat, gazing down at the stage to the preentertainment taking place. Forgetting her discomfort at being stared at. Or maybe just accepting it.

She loved him. She'd said it.

And wasn't this life a good one, the one he would give her? Freedom and independence. The ability to move on should he prove less than ideal. He looked at the women in the boxes around them. Some laughing gaily, some boldly showing their skills. A few loftily gazing, looking for new protection. Many more avidly searching for the same.

A coiled knot formed in his gut as one woman's eyes surreptitiously searched the faces around her, a feigned laugh upon her lips. The look was repeated on the carefully constructed features of the others as well. The knot tightened, cutting.

There was a sort of tension to the scene that he'd never paid attention to before, never cared to see previously. Even the women who appeared to be having a grand time had a look about them. Trying to please and entice their partners. Both predator and prey. As if it were . . . paid work, and they simply doing their job, trying to retain their positions.

And wasn't that truly the case?

Mistresses, with their freedom and passion, were also constrained by the same. Their security and protection dependent on their benefactors. Independent and dependent within the same space.

A sliver of the knot shredded and splintered, stuck in his midsection. But Miranda would never need to worry about that. For he never intended to let her go.

The splinter grew, heedless of any rational thoughts.

He could keep her at his country estate. In his town house. Protect her from the looks. Protect himself from his violent reaction to them. Protect her from any needless insecurities.

She would probably acquiesce to staying in the background—*she loved him.*

The knotted rope, now burning, twisted inside him.

Words freely given. The same declarations that shredded his stomach to ribbons and ripped through his shields—great holes of leaking emotion.

Miranda was so easily able to love and give of herself. She had struck up friendships with his servants, even the crusty, grumpy ones. She didn't hold on to bitterness and triumphed over fear. She was the type of person who would always find a new friend or engender a confidence.

All in all, he was fairly certain that his need of her likely exceeded her need of him.

The thought made him still.

She was a vibrant woman. Bursting with passion beneath a gentle, understated exterior. It had been part of the initial draw. Wanting to release that passion, to see what she'd do with it. To see what he could teach her and learn—*take*—from her in return. To have her look at him in the manner that she spoke of, and to, his paper personas.

His eyes latched onto movement at the door as Chatsworth entered the box. Fury replaced the stark terror that had suddenly gripped him. He should have told the hall staff that they did not want to be disturbed.

Messerden clumsily stumbled in after. The notorious gossip, always wanting to discover any and all information first. Max had used him well over the years to turn the gossip how he wanted. Undoubtedly, he was here in hopes of receiving a priceless tale.

Chatsworth made himself comfortable, and Messerden spread himself into a chair, nearly missing the seat as he was so busy staring at the back of Miranda's head. Obviously trying to determine who she was, as he had every time he'd crossed her path. Trying to fit her into a slot of the gossip he was formulating.

Miranda. Sweet Miranda.

Chatsworth followed Max's eyes, then turned to him. "Settling down in truth, Downing?" he said knowingly. A constant mistress to have alongside a constant wife. Chatsworth had had one for years.

"Chatsworth." He nodded coolly.

He saw Miranda stiffen, her eyes continuing to watch the festivities below.

"Gads, man, you could have let me know earlier." Messerden turned to Max as well. "Means I've lost eighty pounds on you."

"I'm sure your pockets can afford it." He had taken Messerden for a hundred times that amount over all the years they'd known each other.

"Still wish you had told me earlier though." Messerden eyed Miranda over his red nose. "Could have made a pretty penny. Thought this one would be your usual fare—seduced and dumped."

Max had never liked the man less.

Chatsworth smirked. "Downing is turning over a new leaf."

Messerden's eyes narrowed, then he smiled slyly. "And how is your lovely daughter, Chatsworth?"

"She is well. The perfect girl. Had to leave the Peckhurst rout earlier due to a slight headache, but she should be right as sunshine come the morning. Ready to sparkle, as usual."

Messerden turned back to regard Miranda, his gaze crafty and fixed. Max didn't like it in the least. Even in his cups, Messerden could be counted upon to be perceptive at awkward times. Max had needed to funnel the man's interest more times than he could count.

And right now he looked like he was beginning all sorts of new bets. How long Miranda would last. When she might meet Charlotte. What the first awkward meeting might entail.

The bets would be on the books as soon as Messerden reached White's. Max barely restrained his itching fingers from wrapping around the man's neck. It would be a relief to the roiling emotions within him. Tossing the man over the balcony. Maybe with Chatsworth along for the ride to the orchestra below.

Or he could simply hide Miranda. Save her from the speculation and gossip.

Tuck her away after he'd rejoiced in seeing her bloom.
Something inside of him died at the thought.

He'd make sure they never met—Charlotte and
Miranda. He'd make sure Miranda wouldn't wilt
beneath a torrent of petty gossip.

And he'd find a way to make sure she needed him
as fiercely as he needed her.

He turned to start weaving a spell around Messerden.
He'd not let those bets reach the books.

Perhaps then he could loosen the unbreakable knots
within.

Miranda tried not to listen to what the men were
saying. The preperformances on the stage were almost
at a close, and she cast about for something else to
focus upon. She glanced at the boxes around them,
blushing a bit as she spied a man and woman engaged
in something that should have been a little more, well,
private.

She turned her eyes to look at the boxes across from
them instead. At least from this distance she could
pretend that someone had dropped something to the
floor and was merely taking a long time in picking
it up.

A flash of blue had her looking back to a figure
sitting alone in a box. In the shadows, a heavy cloak
was pulled up and over the figure's head. A woman
with a regal set to her shoulders. Even the way she
hugged the shadows couldn't hide her poise.

The woman's eyes met hers across the space. Her
head tilted.

Miranda's world drew to a momentary stop. The
last person that Miranda expected to see at a night
when the innocent were occupied elsewhere and the

naughty were making their rounds was sitting in the shadows across from her, hood pulled over her hair, mask in place. Unrecognizable unless one accepted the possibility that anyone might attend. Unless one had been thinking of the person mere moments before the glance.

Charlotte Chatsworth was not so ill after all. Nor did she seem to follow blindly along as her father had implied.

Miranda stared at her, and Charlotte stared back. The main entertainment began, a woman singing of doomed love and dastardly deeds. The viscount, Messerden, and Chatsworth began speaking in low voices so as not to upset anyone around them—though many in the crowd and surrounding boxes were socializing as well.

During the entire first act Miranda barely took her eyes away from the figure across from her. The woman's eyes seemed to be connected to hers as well. Every so often Miranda would look at the viscount. At Max. Would shakily try to return his smile—his smile more intense than it had been before—and not shiver beneath his fingertips. His reassuring hands.

The curtain finally drew closed, indicating a break before the second act. The woman across from her tilted her head in question, then rose and walked to the door behind her. Her hand touched the curtain, and she looked over her shoulder to Miranda before ducking through.

Miranda excused herself as well. The viscount, still in conversation with Chatsworth and Messerden, cast a questioning look her way. He would stop conversing and accompany her, should she wish it. She could see it in his eyes. That he would leave his future father-in-law and come with her.

Her throat tightened.

But he would not leave the path they were destined to travel.

She forced a smile and shook her head at him, then slipped through their door, heading for the retiring area.

There were a number of women chatting inside, some masked and some not, but Miranda's eyes sought only one. The woman sat with her back to the door, a padded chair next to her for someone wishing to sit and relax for a moment.

Miranda slipped into the chair and stared straight ahead, into the curved mirror, into the shadowed eyes of the woman next to her.

She was beautiful, in both visible features and poise. She veritably screamed wealth and accomplishment. Her elegant royal blue hood put the outrageous costumes of the others to shame. As if she didn't need to dress or hide herself at all. She was Charlotte Chatsworth, darling of society, diamond of the first water.

But the deep hood still served to hide her well. For even she could not get away unblemished if she were found here.

"Good evening," Charlotte said eventually, her tone low and somewhat musical.

"Good evening," Miranda returned the greeting, the abyss of the unknown opening around them.

Miranda felt like a pale bit of paste pretending to be a jewel. She looked down at her gown. The glorious satin. No. She lifted her head. Even the most expensively dressed women wore paste. Paste could be lovely. And touchable. Something that could be enjoyed with more freedom than the heavy choker of sapphires and diamonds that sat upon Charlotte

Chatsworth's neck, visible just above the throat of her cloak.

Or the outrageously expensive piece that graced Miranda's own. She, a piece of paste wearing a diamond.

Charlotte must not have returned home after the Peckhurst rout. She must have come here instead, choker still heavy about her throat.

She looked up from Charlotte's neck to see the girl watching her.

"Your necklace is beautiful," Miranda said softly.

The girl tilted her head. "Thank you. I find it to be quite heavy though at times. Not unlike your own, probably."

Miranda touched the necklace at her own throat. Could still feel the viscount's fingers against her skin, clasping it there.

Laughter rang behind them. A few of the women making bawdy jokes.

"You shouldn't be here," Miranda said quietly.

Charlotte tipped her head. "No. But I had to know. Had to see. Before."

Miranda swallowed and looked away. "I'm sorry."

"Why should you be?"

"I shouldn't be here either." But for different reasons entirely. Miranda looked down at her gloved hands, as if she could see the work-roughened fingers through the silk. She smiled without amusement. "I can't seem to help myself though."

Charlotte watched her, weighing her. "You love him."

Miranda said nothing.

"You don't have to say a word. I can see it. In the way you look at him." She looked at her own reflection in the mirror. "My governess was nearly a mistress. Secretly. In her youth. She always looked sad and wistful." Her eyes dropped for a moment, hidden, then she turned back to her. "You know we are to marry, yes?"

Miranda responded simply, "Yes."

Charlotte nodded. "It is the way of things. My father has had a mistress for years. My mother . . . she pretends she doesn't care."

There was a resigned, strong look on her face. Like she knew this was her lot in life.

"Even should I want to, I wouldn't be able to part you from him. I've seen the way he looks at you. I wanted to meet with you, especially after the Hannings'. I saw you there. Knew that my father had plans." She dipped her head to hide her features as a woman brushed by them. "I know that Downing will do the 'respectable' thing and keep us apart. For all of his wild ways, he has only ever been like his parents in reaction to them."

"You know him well."

Charlotte tilted her chin back up. "No, not at all really. He keeps his cards close. But his face is easier to read when he looks at you."

Miranda said nothing, for what was there to say?

"I just wanted to meet you." The girl's eyes were even, calm. "It seems like it might make things easier that way, don't you think?"

"I don't think it easy at all."

"No." Charlotte smiled a little stiffly. "But then I don't love him. I know him not. And I do not presume to think that he will try to love me even a little. It seems that men save those feelings for those on the other side." She looked away. "I envy you your freedom."

So strange to hear her own thoughts on the lips of another, in reference to her instead.

"Sometimes the specter of freedom presents more of a chain." Love, the greatest chain of all.

"Ah. I do see how that could be so." Charlotte crossed her hands, pulling at a heavy ring on her finger. "Yet, I have no experience of it myself. And I may never have. So perhaps I crave that chain, just a little." She rose and pulled her hood down lower. "Forgive me for my curiosity, in any event. A good evening to you, madam."

"Good evening," Miranda echoed, as Charlotte disappeared in the crowd of women, through the door. She expected not to see her upon her return to the theater, and she was correct. The box across from theirs stood empty.

The viscount looked at her, eyes searching, still intense. "Are you well?"

She smiled, a decidedly sad attempt at brightness. "I'm well. And looking forward to Act Two."

She just hoped it didn't end in tragedy.

Chapter 20

From hence through eternity,
You are my muse, my salvation.
My eternal damnation.
Maximilian Downing to Miranda Chase
(note never sent)

Miranda rose from the bed, untangling herself from warm sleeping man and crumpled sheets. There was something odd and coiled within her. Waiting for the pin to drop. For the kettle to come crashing down, spraying scalding water everywhere. The opera had been tense and wild. Strange and exciting in one way, terrifying and draining in another.

She gazed down at the sleeping form on the bed. Did she want that life? If it was the only one she could have with him?

She thought of Charlotte Chatsworth. Sitting in the shadows. Not judging, simply watching. Coming to the opera on a debauched night, hidden and viewing. To see her. To see what her own future held in store.

Miranda picked up the night rail that had been placed on the curling bench at the foot of the bed. She had seen it before. In "her" wardrobe in "her" room. A lovely, diaphanous material. Not like her father's robe. Something instead made for a man's pleasure.

She knotted the ties around her waist. *Her room.* But not for long. She'd not be able to stay here. Would have to have her own household. Get her own staff.

Her throat tightened. She tried to relax under the thoughts. She had accepted this path. Goodness, the other woman about to grace her lover's life had given her some sort of resigned blessing.

She put a hand to her forehead. She felt a little faint, truth be told. She shook her head and felt around for a lamp and the means to light it. Her hand touched the handle of a door in the dark. Ah, a sitting room. Perfect. She fumbled the handle, then walked into the adjoining room, realizing too late that the viscount's valet was probably on the other side.

But there was no one there. He must have excused the man when they'd come in.

She lit the small lamp she had found and sunk into a chair. She'd just wait here for a bit. Until the spell passed. She didn't want to wake the viscount. Her thoughts were already in a muddle, and she needed to clear them before he touched her and made every rational thought disappear from her head. Again.

The soft light of the lamp lit the room, casting golden light onto the comfortable space, obviously the viscount's personal area. The thought that perhaps she shouldn't be here sifted into her mind, but then the light caught a series of shelves, and her feet unwillingly carried her to them.

The bookshelves here were the opposite of the Red Room below. Everything here was. There was a lived-in, touched feeling. The side of the viscount that she read in his correspondence, that she glimpsed in the country, and that sometimes she even saw on his face when he was sincere. When he looked at her and melted her insides.

She touched the books dotting the shelves. Lovely first editions. Rare works. Personal pieces. Her hip knocked against something at the edge of the desk, and she had to extend a hand quickly to catch the book there.

Lovely sloping handwriting dotted a page that slipped from between the covers.

She touched the paper and lifted the lamp over it. *The Eight Elements of Enchantment* was scribbled across the crown.

This was where he worked. Something strange thrummed through her.

She hadn't needed confirmation; but if she had, it lay in front of her. Feeling like a wayward youth—she really shouldn't be pawing through his private papers—her curiosity overcame her good sense, and she opened the cover, unearthing the other pages within. Draft pages. There were only two "elements" listed, as if the other six hadn't yet been created. Scribbles dotted the pages, long, sloping letters. Questions in the margin.

Will she agree if you approach her with a challenge?
She gamely accepted the bet.

Need to see the look in her eyes that says you have won.

Uncover her hands.

Her eyes creased. What was this? She had expected to find new material, and instead the lines littering the margins had all the keys to her seduction. Everything about her. Crisscrossing lines thrusting back and forth on the sheets. The pen and ink his tools to create the dance. Branding her name here just as he had branded his own upon her flesh an hour past.

"Miranda?"

Her fingers curled around the page. She felt him come up behind her, heard his bare feet padding across the rug.

"What are—" He stepped to her side, then stopped dead when he saw what she was holding. "I can explain," he said quickly.

She looked back at the papers. "I don't think you need to." Was it strange that she felt so cold? So calm and removed?

He took the page from her, her fingers relinquishing the paper as he pulled. He put it on top of the others and pushed the papers together. "These are old."

"They don't look old to me." Was that cold, removed voice hers?

"I—"

"Why?" There was a calm stillness to her. Ice settling into her bones. A cold relief seeping into her that they would finally have this out. That they could be through with the secrets and lies.

"Because I had to," he said, a note of desperation behind his usually controlled expression, the shadows of the lamplight shifting over his face.

"You had to make a cake of me? To make me confused eight ways to Sunday and back again? To make me doubt my own judgment?" She lifted a brow. "I see. I was expecting a slightly more florid and charming response from the venerable Eleutherios, I must say. Or at least something suitably scathing and self-assured, like Mr. Pitts."

His face reflected a combination of emotions—too many to name. But shock stood out sharply. "It was not to make a cake of you. I wanted to make you trust yourself more. And to . . . to be myself without having to hide behind the layers."

The words chipped at the ice. She put her bare hand to his cheek, the roughened pads touching his roughened chin, then let it drop.

"You used me. I just didn't know how severely that use was."

"I can explain."

"You don't need to. I'm just foolish enough to have thought it amusing for a few deluded days." She tugged the night rail more firmly, then walked through the door, back into the bedroom proper.

"I *do* need to explain, I . . . wait. You knew." He spun her around, his eyes narrowed, the pages still gripped in his left hand. "You *knew*."

"Knew that you were making a cake of me, yes. I've known that since the Hannings' ball. That you were doing so in order to get new material, no."

"My library," he said, as if something suddenly made sense, slotting into place.

"Yes, your precious library." And other things not yet discovered—things she didn't feel a desire to name now. "It will survive, I assure you. I only shuffled up a few sections. Nothing that you can't fix. Especially since you are the one who created the disorder in the first place."

He flinched. "I needed you to have something to do."

She nodded. "You couldn't have your research walk away from you."

"I decided not to write a sequel." His eyes bored into hers, willing her to understand. "After that first week."

"Why? You should." She shrugged a hand toward the pages in his tight grasp. "It is all there. I'm sure you will make a pretty penny from it." She turned and gathered up her clothing in a bunch. "I will likely even buy a copy, fool that I am."

"What are you doing?"

Now that hot emotion wasn't clouding her judgment, now that the warm desire to be with him however she could wasn't forefront in her mind, the clear view of their future path spread before her in cold, crystalline glory. And cool anger made the first step away from that path easier.

"I'm leaving." She looked to the window, clothing strewn across her arms, bunched in her fists, just like his papers were in his. "Good evening, your lordship."

"Leaving?"

"Yes. Good luck with your marriage." She began to take a step around him.

He stepped into her path, gripping the pages, the edges crumpling beneath his fingers. "You are leaving? Giving up?"

She looked to the window for a long moment. "I'm not giving up. I'm going forward. Perhaps to Paris." She looked back at him. "Just as you've always told me I should."

"I thought you loved me," he said, a thread of bitterness and disillusionment. As if he had just been waiting for her to leave him, and now she had finally decided to make the break.

Miranda watched him. A blanket of calm settled over her, soothing the edge of her fury. "I do love you. In all the forms you've presented to me. As a complete picture of a man fractured and broken."

He said nothing. His lips forming a hard line.

"And that's why I am leaving. If I stay here, like this, I will only ever be a balm for you. For me." She gripped the clothes. "Not a cure. Not a panacea. You will always wait for me to leave you. I will always wait for you to tire of me."

She turned to go. She found herself suddenly spun around. The clothes fell from her hands, intermingling with his papers that now littered the space. Firm lips pressed to hers, and she responded, angry and confused, but with the strange calmness threading through.

He pressed her onto the crumpled sheets of paper that had fallen to the bed. "Marriage wouldn't change that."

"No." She arched into him as his hands wound around her rear. "Not as it stands now. Not as we stand now."

"I'm not going to change," he said into her ear. *I can't change.* His lips pulled at the soft skin at the side of her throat. She'd have marks there in the morning.

She tilted her head, allowing them to be made. A last reminder. "I know. That is why the choice needs to be made."

His hands suddenly framed her face, his thumbs stroking her cheeks. "You can't be happy with what I am? The most I am capable of offering? What I've *never* offered to anyone else?" The echo of *happy with me* filtered through the air.

"Your mother never got past it."

His eyes turned dark. "My mother's situation was different."

"Different, yes, but was it any worse?"

"I'm not my father."

She touched his hand at her cheek, reassuring him for a moment. "No."

"You are all I can think of."

"But it's not enough, is it?" She flipped on top of him, fingers digging into his shoulders.

He arched up into her, pulling her hips down to connect them, making her skin, *the very core of her,* light on fire, the mad yearning never darker or more fierce. "It can be enough."

She rolled off him, her back to him as she perched on the edge of the bed, trying to calm her breathing.

"Stay with me." His voice was quiet.

She looked at her hands. Her stained, chapped hands. "I've met Charlotte Chatsworth. I think you can be happy with her." It hurt to say it.

"Stay with me."

"You will be married. Duties to your wife. Your children," she whispered, closing her eyes, unable to look back at him. While marriage to the viscount, so out of her realm, had never been a thought, marriage to Mr. Pitts, her confidant on the other side of her pen . . . marriage to Eleutherios, who wrote such lovely, thoughtful lines to her . . . those tugged at the core of her, whispering what-ifs.

Watching his children gambol around while she stayed in the background with a pleasant smile, avoiding his wife, his wife avoiding her. Perfectly acceptable to the masses. Perfectly unacceptable suddenly to her.

She stepped away from the bed, from him. "No, I can't." She looked back at him kneeling in the middle of the mussed sheets and parchment, the sight of his face almost enough to make her recant. "I'm sorry," she whispered. "I can't."

"And if I tell you . . . if I tell you I love you?"

The pain of it ripped into her. "I . . ." The thoughts swirled around, making her mad with the desire to grab what she could. To have him however she could. She pushed backward on her feet, stumbling away from him, turning. "I—I must go."

"Miranda."

She stopped at the door, hearing the pain in his voice. She could believe he did love her, in that moment. That she could have that whispered to her every night. Could have children of her own, locked away in some manor, only gossiped about when they made their way into society. Maybe even made respectable—with bright futures and opportunities. Holding her own court across from Charlotte Chatsworth, no *Lady Downing*, a strange sort of tug always pulling at the viscount, away from Miranda.

"I do love you, you know," she said without looking at him. "In all your guises, with all of your strengths and faults. There has never been anything I've been so sure of."

"Miranda." She couldn't look. Couldn't bear to see his face. She closed her eyes against the pain and put her hand upon the handle of the door, pushing down and cracking it open.

"And I also know that I must go. Perhaps to Paris. For a time. See what I've been hiding from. Perhaps, perhaps I will see you upon my return." It was a question. A sorrow. A wish. A broken bone, unevenly set.

She drew her fingers over the juncture of the door, where the wood protruded, separating the spaces into two—the halls for the servants, the rooms for the masters. "Farewell, Maxim," she whispered.

And she walked through the portal and into the hall.

Chapter 21

The morning light shone through the windows. Too early for most Parisians to visit. She had discovered that going right after the museum opened was the best time. The light was soft and divine, the benches free, the mood calm and serene.

She had been in Paris for a month. A strange month. At first filled with introspection and regrets, then steadily filled with resolve, with a new thought to where she would carve her future.

A thrice-weekly reading club was already in the works. To be held in the back of her uncle's London bookshop—which was undergoing renovations, expanding into the shop next door. A backer had been lined up to help find and fund staff to teach the classes. For free. To anyone who might want to attend. Miranda knew that Galina, at least, already planned to do so.

She caressed the sturdy parchment on her lap. The

echo of bergamot lifting from it. Unsurprisingly, it had been easy to find someone interested in backing the project.

She touched the rest of the notes at her side, written by one hand, not three. Combining all of the men she loved into one, making it so hard to stay away, and at the same time reminding her of the tentative bridge between them. Of a relationship built on truth and trust. Honesty and friendship. Intimacy and humor. And of course, passion. Tentative, sensual notes that had turned into seductions of their own.

Questions answered, and others that she had been too afraid to pose.

Her pen had never flown over—and her eyes had never devoured—as many notes as she had exchanged in the past few weeks.

Notes full of recrimination had arrived first.

I can't apologize for all of it. For tasting you or having you. Holding you in anyway I could. But for the half-truths and misdirection, for my willingness to expose and have you in the only way I thought might last, I would lie before the butcher should you desire my split heart.

Then more chatty ones, less emotional, but equally personal.

Spoke to the marquess this eve. He confessed that he has known about the authorship for months and was delighted. We shared a bottle of port and even Mother joined in when she saw it was I in his study. They have decided to take a trip across the sea. To stop in each port and see what

*they discover. The marquess seemed to think you
might find the news amusing. As to why he would
think such, I have no idea, but his thoughts do
sometimes run to madness . . .*

And finally to a renewed sense of kinship and seduction. One where they were finally equals on the
field.

My love. My salvation.

She looked up from the note she had been caressing.
She had to keep her wits together. Couldn't fall apart
after everything. Not after the most recent news had
hit her desk.

She was as aware of the events in London as someone
could be so many miles away. Georgette had written
her immediately upon her arrival. Kept her up to date
on what was happening in town. Encouraged her to
go forward, her stalwart supporter.

Her uncle had tasked her with speaking to their
contacts. Finding new books. And she had written
him, first posing, then beginning to implement plans
for the new additions to the shop. He had responded
with absent tidbits that she wouldn't have been able
to glean from other sources.

The ladies in her book club and friends around town
had also written and imparted interesting information, though they were still mystified by her sudden
departure.

And then . . . then she had seen the news. A clipped
piece from the *Daily Mill* that Georgette had sent and
others had echoed. Followed by the note in her hand.

Arriving on her doorstep—the contents giving her little time to grasp the words, no matter that she had had four weeks at large to do so.

She heard the strong footsteps upon the marble in the hall. The echoed scent of bergamot and parchment. Of jasmine and lilies. A strange sort of calm descended upon her, over the fast thump of her heart. The picture in front of her blurred and brightened.

The news had shaken her world again.

Miranda stared ahead of her, barely seeing the paintings. Feeling the caress of movement at her back. The taste of all things delicious. The desire that arched under her skin.

"So what do you think of the museum? Of Paris?" The voice curled from behind her. Husky. Not as if the owner had been playing naughtily all night but as if he had traveled without sleep. Needing to be somewhere.

"I think that I shouldn't have waited so long," she said quietly.

He stepped to the side of her, dark clothing with the hint of white, black hair, and chiseled features. The most gorgeous thing she had seen all day, week, month. "I was thinking the same thing," he said. "Though my desperation to leap at what I wanted most only led to the near destruction of what I held most dear. And so waiting became my penance."

She turned back to the wall, swallowing. "Have you seen this one?" She pointed blindly at the painting she had been absorbing before he'd entered.

"When I was on my Grand Tour I must have gazed upon that one a thousand times."

"You must be tired of it then."

"No." He touched her crown. "No, each time is a new lure. One I never want to be without."

She looked down for a second, then back up. Asking the question that had been on her mind since she'd seen the speculation in the gossip sheet, forwarded to her from Georgette.

"Your wedding?"

He sat next to her, and she turned toward him as he touched her cheek. "I'm not going to marry Charlotte Chatsworth."

"No?" Her heart picked up speed. The rumors were true then. She had been too scared to ask him on paper. And then his most recent note . . .

"I'm cold enough for two. I need something warm to wake to every morning." He lazily twirled a finger around a curl touching her temple.

"Separate beds are a time-honored tradition."

"I've always hated the notion of separate beds."

"Oh? Whatever will you do then?"

"I suppose I will just have to make sure that I marry someone I look forward to curling around every morning. Whom I can't be without before breakfast. Or in the noon. Whom I need to race home to see after each appointment. Determined to lock her in my rooms, not because I need to hide anything but because I'd just as soon have her all to myself. To look upon her beloved face and hear her lips whisper in my ear."

"That sounds . . . divine," she whispered. The resonance of his words echoed the print in her hand.

"Then I must be speaking of you." His lips touched hers. Soft, beautiful. She could almost have wept from the emotion that exploded inside of her. "You can't imagine what this last month has been like."

"Oh," she said lightly. "I lived it too."

He touched her chin. "Had you decided to stay silent, not to answer my letters, I don't know what I would have done."

"I never had ill intentions toward you." She swallowed. "I left because I had to. Because I needed to. And you needed me to as well."

"I know. I know." His eyes closed. "I can't tell you what it was like, the wait between my first letter to you and your reply."

"You sent your own courier." She raised a brow. "He lurked around the corners, you know, waiting to see if I'd post mail. Offered to take whatever I had, free of charge."

"I—I can't apologize for it."

She touched his thigh. "I told him right off that I was going to reply. I must say that he amused me, kept my mind off what I had done, waking in a brand-new city, having everything in front of me and not knowing where to start. He was a touch of home."

"I will make sure to increase his wages." His lips curved, but his voice was sincere.

"I'm happy you are here."

He stroked her cheek. "And I as well. Have you answered my most recent letter?"

She touched his cheek in return. Words nearly clogged her throat—relief and hope and happiness that she had read it right. The question that she had thought he would never ask. "I received it only an hour past."

"That was forever ago." His hand slipped down her side. "I watched the clock tick each tock."

"You posted it from Paris."

"Yes." He lifted her hand. "I wrote it on the way over. I had to know. Couldn't wait one moment longer. I love you, Miranda."

"And I love you, Maxim." She smiled, then touched a hand to the papers surrounding them. Lifting a page that had her answer on it. An answer that would always be yes. "Take me to the Cirque Diamant, then take me home?"

He didn't even look at the sheet. He simply smiled. "With pleasure, and always."

Unforgettable, enthralling love stories,
sparkling with passion and adventure
from Romance's bestselling authors

*At Avon Books, we know your passion
for romance—once you finish one of our
novels, you find yourself wanting more.*

May we tempt you with . . .

- **Excerpts** from our upcoming releases.

- Entertaining **extras,** including authors'
  personal photo albums and book lists.

- Behind-the-scenes **scoop** on your favorite
  characters and series.

- **Sweepstakes** for the chance to win free books,
  romantic getaways, and other fun prizes.

- Writing **tips** from our authors and editors.

- **Blog** with our authors and find out why they
  love to write romance.

- **Exclusive content** that's not contained
  within the pages of our novels.

Join us at
www.avonbooks.com

AVON   *An Imprint of* HarperCollins*Publishers*
www.avonromance.com

Available wherever books are sold or please call 1-800-331-3761 to order.

FTH 0708